Mended Hearts

LINDA SHERTZER

JOVE BOOKS, NEW YORK

A QUILTING ROMANCE is a trademark of Penguin Putnam Inc.

MENDED HEARTS

A Jove Book / published by arrangement with
the author

PRINTING HISTORY
Jove edition / October 1999

The Penguin Putnam Inc. World Wide Web site address is
http://www.penguinputnam.com

ISBN: 0-515-12611-X

A JOVE BOOK®
Jove Books are published by The Berkley Publishing Group,
a division of Penguin Putnam Inc.,
375 Hudson Street, New York, New York 10014.
JOVE and the "J" design
are trademarks belonging to Penguin Putnam Inc.

PRINTED IN THE UNITED STATES OF AMERICA

10 9 8 7 6 5 4 3 2 1

1

"IF THAT NICE FRED Ingram and my own dear Louise weren't a match made in heaven, no couple was!" Mrs. Kingston declared, clasping her hands to her bosom and lifting her gaze.

"No doubt the cause of her unspeakable joy," Jessica Griffith leaned forward and whispered in the ear of her older sister, Maude.

"Hush," Maude muttered.

Maude's admonition, as usual, went ignored. "Although I can't recollect any other occasion when Mrs. Kingston's been rendered incapable of speech."

"Hush! If you're going to gossip, at least try to be more subtle about it." Maude tried not to laugh at Jessica as she bent her head to her stitching. No sense encouraging her sister, but she, too, always believed Mrs. Kingston was far too given to displays of melodrama.

Maude, of course, was too sensible to make such a spectacle of herself. Even though she often thought the same things Jessica said out loud, at least she had the good manners not to speak them. After all, she had to set a good example for her younger siblings, although sometimes she believed, with Jessica, it was a hopeless cause.

Mrs. Kingston had invited the ladies of Apple Grove to her home to view the quilts her daughter and her friends had made, and to admire the wedding gifts arranged on the long table set against a wall in the parlor. The wedding was tomorrow, and Maude still had a lot of work to do.

While the ladies chatted and circulated around her, Maude sat in the lady's chair by the fireplace. The bridal quilt Louise's friends had made for her rested on her lap, complete except for the finishing touch to the center block—that final, special stitching everyone in town knew only Maude could do.

Even Jessica, who usually spent her time wandering about town in search of trouble, had deigned to attend this strictly feminine gathering. Maude could hear her standing behind her chair, shuffling impatiently from one foot to the other. Jessica never had been able to remain still for any length of time.

"Such *wunderbar* . . . no, no! Someday the English better I will learn. Such *wonderful* presents," Mrs. Ingram corrected herself.

"Indeed." Mrs. Hardesty ran her fingertip around the edge of a bread tray, with a beehive and the motto "Be Industrious" pressed into the pale green glass, that Maude and her family had given Louise and Fred. Then she made her way down the table, touching all the other gifts as well.

"Does she think by pawing everything she can know what each one costs?" Jessica grumbled.

"Hush!" Maude scolded. Jessica never could remain silent for long, either.

Mrs. Hardesty lifted a blue and white china pickle dish and turned it over to inspect it. Out of the corner of her eye Maude watched the lady's upper lip curl with disdain. "My, what a charming *little* gift from the Kellermans."

"Yes, indeed. Such nice presents," Mrs. Lester said as she followed her friend. Her daughter, Florence, trailed behind.

"Almost as nice as the ones my Katy received."

"How clever of Nell to display them this way." Mrs. Lester gestured down the table. "I hear this is what those society matrons do in New York, Boston, San Francisco. Even in Chicago. Probably even in St. Louis."

The three stopped at the end of the table, beside Maude. She kept her head lowered as she stitched and pretended she wasn't paying a bit of attention to a thing they said.

"My goodness, Thelma. What a pity you didn't think to do this with all those lovely wedding gifts Katy got," Mrs. Lester said.

Mrs. Hardesty whispered, "That's because I lack the pretensions Nell Kingston aspires to."

Mrs. Lester gave a little laugh, ill-disguised by a cough, behind her hand.

"Taking on airs just because Louise is marrying the man whose father owns the general store," Mrs. Hardesty muttered. "As if marrying a farmer, like my Katy did, wouldn't be good enough for her daughter."

"Well, he does stand to inherit the business."

"But, I mean, it's not as if he'll own a railroad or a stage line—something *big*." Mrs. Hardesty gave a disdainful sniff and moved down the table, continuing to inspect the rest of the gifts. She shook her head and clucked her tongue. "So pretentious."

Mrs. Lester mumbled something that might be taken for agreement.

"You don't suppose there'd be room in our parlor to do this when I get married, do you, Mama?" Florence asked eagerly.

Mrs. Hardesty coughed.

"Well, I'm not sure, dear," Mrs. Lester responded.

"Our dining room is a little larger, so maybe we ought to use that instead," Florence persisted.

"I suppose. But it really depends on your father—"

"I'm sure Papa won't object to eating in the kitchen for just a little while. I mean, not when it would be for a very worthwhile cause," Florence pleaded.

Maude could just picture the officious banker torn between doing something so common as to eat in his kitchen, and doing something so acceptably ostentatious to please his only daughter and to elevate his wife's standing in Apple Grove society.

Mrs. Hardesty grunted even more harshly to indicate her opinion of the whole affair.

"Well, Thelma, I suppose asking you to lend me that really long table of yours would be completely out of the question, then," Mrs. Lester ventured.

Mrs. Hardesty made no reply.

"To have Louise as my daughter-in-the-law, happy I will be,"

Mrs. Ingram said. "Such a pretty girl, she is, and sweet, too."

"Sensible, too, although a body'd hardly notice," Mrs. Hardesty said. "She's so shy and quiet—almost *too* quiet for her own good."

"To be loud and *talk-ish* a need she has not."

Mrs. Hardesty shrugged. "Well, then, if the girl's determined to be shy, what more can one do?"

"Never was much anybody could do about Mrs. Hardesty, either," Jessica muttered.

"Hush!"

Maude shot a quick glance at her unjustly maligned friend. Louise, as the guest of honor, sat quietly on the sofa. Looking like some sort of honor guard, Wilma Dietrich sat to one side, and Katy, the new Mrs. Willard Konigsberg, sat to the other. Maude smiled at Louise, who merely smiled back helplessly.

"Fred's certainly friendly enough for them both, and I believe he encourages Louise to talk more," Maude said in defense of her shy friend. "They're very good for each other and will get along very well. That's what really matters, isn't it?"

She quickly turned her attention back to her stitching, but not before she caught a glimpse of Mrs. Hardesty heading her way.

I should have just kept my peace, Maude thought with a sigh of regret as she feigned concentration on embroidering the second upstroke of the *M* in her initials. *Maybe I can pretend I don't notice her.*

But Mrs. Hardesty, standing directly in front of her, her steely blue eyes staring out from under her thick brows, was impossible to ignore. Especially when Mrs. Lester joined her, and Miss Randolph and Mrs. Dalton came to stand behind her chair. Maude could sense them peering over her shoulder at her work.

Well, let them look, she decided with a bold lift of her chin. She felt her shoulders rise and her spine straighten with confidence as she began to stitch the second downstroke of the *M*. She knew her work could withstand their criticism—even Mrs. Hardesty's—any day. This time she felt more confident than ever. This one was undoubtedly her best work yet.

Miss Adelaide Randolph gave her customary cough. Never having heard that the schoolteacher suffered from consumption, Maude had always assumed it was a habit she'd developed from many years of teaching, to get everyone's attention before saying something she considered worth noting. "Of all the ones you've done, Maude, I've never seen a finer block than this.''

"Thank you.'' Maude felt she ought to offer some sort of self-effacing protest (although it would be noticeably weak at best) or at least blush modestly at her former teacher's high praise, but she couldn't be that hypocritical. Her work was good, and she knew it.

"Maude's even outdone *herself* this time,'' Mrs. Kingston agreed, then quickly added, "I'm not saying that just because this one is for my daughter.'' She turned to Louise. "You and Fred are destined for happiness.''

"Who is this Fred fellow?'' a man's voice demanded from the doorway, so loudly that Maude started and almost stuck her finger. "How in the ever-lovin', blue-eyed, rosebud-smellin' world does he think he'll be able to make Louise happy?''

Maude held her breath and, from the reverberating silence surrounding her, she figured every other woman in the room did the same.

"Jack!'' Louise exclaimed, springing up from the sofa and dashing toward him.

Maude stared as her normally shy friend flung her arms around the man's neck and kissed him resoundingly on the cheek. He caught her around the waist and spun her about. Her skirts swung out in a wide blue arc, and several hairpins went flying to the corners of the room.

"Jack! I never imagined you'd be able to come!''

I never would have imagined he'd be able to come either, Maude thought wryly as she resumed her stitching. *The last I heard, he was still in jail.*

Jack laughed. Rich, deep. Disturbing.

In spite of herself, Maude looked up.

"Nothing could keep me away from my favorite cousin's wedding,'' he managed to gasp between Louise's fierce hugs.

Louise pulled back and glared at him playfully. "I'm your *only* cousin.''

"If I had a thousand cousins and they were all getting married on the same day, *yours* would be the wedding I'd attend.''

Louise laughed and released her hold of Jack. Maude watched her friend fairly dancing on tiptoe around him.

"My, my.'' Shaking his head, he stepped back. Maude couldn't help noticing the merry twinkle in his green eyes as he studied Louise. "How my little cousin has grown in four years! How very beautiful you've turned out!"

Louise giggled and blushed.

"Jack, it's so good to have you home again!" Mrs. Kingston exclaimed. "We've missed you so much."

Maude figured Mrs. Kingston, approaching Jack, was dancing as much on tiptoe as the plump lady could manage.

"Aunt Nell!" He bent over to place a kiss on her rounded cheek. "You look so beautiful. Who exactly is the bride here?"

"My dear boy, you always were such an incorrigible, silver-tongued devil!"

Maude seemed to recall her father referring to him more appropriately as a damned lying scoundrel, destined only for the gallows.

She watched with one skeptically raised eyebrow as Wilma joined Louise and gawked at Jack with cautious fascination. Florence, who was betrothed to Edgar Baumgartner, and Katy, a happily married woman, had joined them to stare at him, too.

Maude's gaze narrowed. My goodness, for that little trollop Clarice Dalton to get any closer to him, she'd have to be standing on top of his feet.

Jessica edged her way over to him, too, practically pushing Clarice out of the way. Maude winced as she watched her sister eye him with awed curiosity. That girl had never had the good sense to avoid trouble whenever she saw it.

The other ladies—even Mrs. Hardesty—were so crowded around the returned prodigal that Maude could scarcely see him, except that he stood at least half a head taller than the lot of them.

What was there—what had there always been?—about Jack that gave him this influence over women? Maude wondered. Whatever it was, she was determined not to be as easily impressed. She was the sensible Griffith sister—and she intended to live up to her hard-earned, well-deserved reputation.

Let them all rush over to him like a bunch of silly hens flocking around the only rooster—no, make that the only *worm*—in the chicken yard. She wasn't about to go making a fool of herself over *any* man, especially not over the black sheep of that family—"Suicide" Jack Kingston.

She remained seated, studying him. He was as tall as she remembered, but his shoulders seemed broader under his threadbare coat, and his neck seemed more muscular. He carried himself with an even more arrogant swagger than he had before he'd left town four years ago. She wasn't about to reinforce that arrogance one wit by paying him any more attention than he was due. She tried to return to her stitching.

"I was so afraid you wouldn't get my letter in time to come to my wedding," Louise said.

"The United States mail always comes through," Jack declared.

"How odd," Mrs. Hardesty remarked. "I'd have thought you didn't set much store in the Federal Government—"

"I wish you'd told us you were coming—given us a bit of warning," Mrs. Kingston interrupted quickly, and continued to rattle on. "I'd have repapered your room, or at least repainted. Bought new draperies—"

"No, no. I really don't figure to be staying very long. Even if I were, there's no need to go to so much trouble. You know any old thing is good enough for me."

"I wish I'd have at least had time to air your room, fix your favorite dinner—I'd have even made your favorite dessert—to welcome you home. . . ." Her voice trailed off, as if she were incapable of expressing the lengths of self-sacrifice to which she'd go to accommodate her nephew.

He reached up and ruffled his black hair. "Yes, I do apologize, Aunt Nell. I guess I should've written but . . . well, I'm afraid it's a little hard to write when I'm on the move most of the time."

"I don't suppose you were moving around much down in Dry Creek," Mrs. Hardesty commented slyly.

It was certainly no secret. Everyone in town had read the newspaper reports when Maude's father, with a smug "I-told-you-so" expression on his face, had printed the tales of the local boy who was arrested and convicted for bank robbery in Dry Creek, Kansas, and spent time in prison. But at least Maude had enough consideration for the feelings of Louise and her family never to mention it.

She thought she heard Louise gasp and Mrs. Lester snicker, and would have bet any amount of money that Mrs. Kingston was now plotting how she could best slip arsenic undetected into Mrs. Hardesty's glass of punch at the wedding tomorrow in retaliation for bringing up the sensitive family scandal.

But Jack just chuckled and shrugged off the insult. "Not too much to write about there. One day's pretty much like every other, and I've never been one to want to bore the ladies."

Too late, Maude thought. Listening to these women drooling honey all over him, and Mrs. Hardesty dripping her usual venom, was boring her to distraction. She could be putting her time to much better use. When she completed Louise's quilt, she still had to go home and hem her sister's gown and her own, not to mention pressing her father's and her younger brother's best shirts to wear to the wedding. She couldn't trust Jessica with the task, unless her father and Georgie thought it was fashionable to sport big brown scorch marks.

Yet, when she looked down at her lap and saw her hand poised in midair with her fingers frozen around the needle, Maude realized that she'd been staring at Jack all along and hadn't added a single stitch.

This was preposterous! She couldn't afford to waste her precious time watching him. She tried to resume her stitching, but she couldn't bring her unaccountably uncooperative fingers to make the needle stick in the correct place. She wasn't about to have to go to the trouble and annoyance, not to mention the embarrassment, of ripping out stitches in front of all these ladies—especially not if Jack was the cause of her errors!

Jack confronted Louise. "Now, what's all this balderdash I hear about you being deliriously happy with some fellow named Fred?"

2

LOUISE BLUSHED, GIGGLED, AND at last murmured, "Oh, you remember Frederick Ingram."

"Yes, he was that chubby little tow-headed fellow who was always munching on that terrific strudel his mother made."

"He's all grown up now and very handsome," Louise protested. "He's changed so much you'd barely recognize him."

"I suppose I'll be able to spot him tomorrow." Jack nodded knowingly. "He'll be the one with the terrified, doomed look in his eyes, the one your pa's gagged, hog-tied, and propped up beside you at the altar."

"Jack, you're horrible!" Louise protested with a laugh. The ladies giggled.

"I just hope his mother hasn't stopped making her wonderful strudel," Jack said, casting a playful wink at Mrs. Ingram.

"Oh, no. *Nein!*" Mrs. Ingram protested emphatically. "Just for *you,* some I will make when home I go."

Maude feared Mrs. Ingram would simply melt into the carpet. How foolish could a grown woman be? What an incurable flirt Jack was!

"Nice enough fellow, then. I suppose I'll give my consent. But how can anyone know their destiny?" Jack demanded with a devilish grin. "How can anyone predict a lifelong marriage will always be happy?"

"But they will be!" Mrs. Kingston staunchly maintained.

"Yes, indeed," Louise asserted. "Maude has it all figured out."

"Maude, huh?"

At the sound of her name on his lips, Maude completely gave up any pretense of trying to stitch. She looked toward him. The ladies standing around him parted like the Red Sea at Moses' bidding, leaving an aisle between them that stood open invitingly.

Jack slowly sauntered down the vacant aisle until he stood directly in front of her. She clutched at the quilt in her lap, as if it were a shield constructed by her friends and herself to protect her from this man. Yet all the while she felt the soft, padded fabric beneath her fingers, some devilish little voice in the back of her brain reminded her that quilts weren't made simply to cover people and shelter them from the cold, but for people to cuddle under, to sleep under and . . . *No, don't think about it!*

"No, it can't be," Jack said. He shook his head as he scrutinized her, the same way he'd looked at Louise.

Maude felt a little shiver travel up and down her back, and was forced to correct herself. He'd never looked at Louise that way. Why in the world was he looking that way at *her?*

Because the man is a cad, she answered herself. Hadn't he even had the gall to wink at Mrs. Ingram? No doubt he'd looked at Wilma, Florence, even Katy, and especially Clarice the very same way. Merciful heavens, she didn't want to imagine all the horrendous possibilities if he should wink at her foolish sister!

"This can't possibly be Maude Griffith!" Jack exclaimed. "Not little Maude, who was always so darn disgustingly smart in school. Who was always cleaning or straightening something. Who wouldn't even get her *old* shoes dirty when we all went out to play."

Open your mouth and say something, you fool! she silently commanded herself. *Something scathingly witty. Don't let him think you're as dumbstruck by his presence as all these other silly females.*

"Yes." Why did her voice sound like a whisper? Why did her answer sound like a question—as if his very presence made her unsure of her own identity? For heaven's sake, it was only

Louise's cousin. They'd grown up next door to each other. James Madison Kingston—in spite of the imposing name, he'd never impressed her that much before. Why should he affect her so now?

"My goodness," he said. "I never would've recognized you if we'd passed on the street, Miss Maude."

"Of course not. I—" *don't usually frequent the parts of town where they have gambling halls and houses of ill repute,* she was tempted to retort, but stopped short and closed her mouth.

Jack had blown into Apple Grove like a summer wind, and he'd be gone again just as quickly. For the short while he'd be here, she could manage to be civil to him, for Louise's sake. She didn't want anything to mar the joy of her best friend's wedding.

"But seeing you sitting behind a quilt with a needle in your hand—why, I'd recognize you that way anywhere," he continued. "As I recollect, you were always sewing something."

"When I wasn't cleaning or straightening," she reminded him. She forced a sweet smile. She was surprised. She would have supposed he didn't remember her at all.

Jack laughed again, his deep voice reverberating in her ears and echoing within her breast. "How is it that you're the one who holds Louise's fate in her hands?"

"Not mine," Maude protested. She held up both hands, demonstrating her innocence. Her left hand spread palm out, but her right tugged at the thread running from the quilt to the needle pinched between her forefinger and thumb. Her fingers—the middle capped with her pewter thimble—pointed upward.

He gave her a sly wink. "So it's in your thimble instead? Just a thimbleful?"

The ladies giggled. Maude felt her lips twitch into a smile, but swore she wouldn't laugh with him. She wouldn't allow Jack to think she found him the least bit waggish.

"No, it's in the quilt," she corrected, lowering both hands.

"Really?" Jack reached down and lifted the edge of the quilt.

Maude felt she must surely be going insane. How else could she explain the sensation that some ethereal emanation from Jack traveled along the threads of the colorful cotton right into her own fingertips?

"Well, not the whole quilt," she corrected. "Everyone had a part in making that. It's just this center block that's my work— and mine alone."

She didn't bother trying to keep the pride from her voice. If he could walk around with that arrogant swagger for no reason at all, she could certainly allow herself to show a little pride in her artistry.

She should have heeded the sage warning that pride went before disaster. She should have kept him at his distance. She never should have drawn to his attention the part of the quilt closest to her body.

He moved his hand until it hovered over the center block where she was working. She feared he might decide to touch the quilt again, and she'd feel that same powerful sensation still emanating from him. Or that his fingers might come so close they'd brush against the back of her hand. Then the worst thing possible happened. He actually touched the block resting in her lap.

"Tell me," he drawled slowly, while his fingers just as slowly and firmly caressed the layers of fabric.

She could feel the pressure of his fingertips on her thigh. Her heart pounded in her breast. An unaccustomed stirring in the pit of her stomach stretched and uncurled like a cat aroused from sleep, gentle and purring, with concealed claws that hid danger—and excitement.

"What exactly is so special about this?"

She swallowed hard to dampen this rising feeling. She had to keep it suppressed, or at least under control.

"Not . . . just this block. I've made many of them with . . . I make a special design, individual and . . . distinct for everyone." Why should it be so difficult to explain to Jack what she'd been doing so easily for several years? "I intertwine the couple's initials and the wedding date with the stems and leaves of flowers and ferns, and some ribbons. I embroider some and I quilt a pattern through it and all around it like a frame. All I need to do to finish this one is add my initials, hidden among the flowers."

Resting his hand on the back of the chair, he leaned forward, obviously to see better. It was bad enough having his hand so close to her, but she couldn't bear to have his entire body so near. There were no arms to the lady's chair—could she possibly slip away to the side? Not without dropping Louise's precious quilt. She pressed into the back of the chair, but was all too aware of his hand so close to her cheek. Was there no escaping this man?

"Right here," she said, quickly pointing out to him the small green *M* and the bare spot where she still needed to embroider the *G* where it would disappear into the overall design.

She didn't ordinarily show people exactly where all the initials were. She preferred to have everything blend in with the rest of the design and have them discover it, if ever, as a pleasant revelation. But, she figured, the quicker Jack found it and moved away from her, the better.

But he remained there, peering down at her.

As if he knows so much about quilting he can stand to pass judgement on my work! she thought peevishly.

She berated herself for suddenly not having the steadiness of nerve to continue stitching while he watched her. She could only sit there, noticing how his dark hair curled across the top of his head and around his ears, and how his threadbare jacket stretched over his broad shoulders; inhaling the scent of bay rum and the faintly blended aromas of tobacco and whiskey—just the scents she'd imagine she'd find about a man like Jack!

"It's sort of a tradition in town," Louise explained. "If Maude can make a beautiful design out of the couple's initials, the marriage will be a happy one."

"Do people really believe this superstition?" Jack demanded. "That their prospects for lifelong happiness rest in someone else's arrangement of colored threads?"

He didn't even bother to hide his laugh. This time Maude found it less disturbing and more downright irritating.

"If that's true, I've got some land out in Dakota Territory I'd like to sell them."

Before Maude could say a word, Louise scolded him, "Don't make fun of Maude! She's truly uncanny about this."

"The quilt she made for my Katy is absolutely beautiful!" Mrs. Hardesty asserted. The other ladies murmured their agreement. Mrs. Hardesty turned and demanded of her daughter, "Isn't it?"

"Yes, Mama," Katy answered dutifully.

"She and Mr. Konigsberg are *very* happy. Aren't you?"

"Yes, Mama."

"How long have you two been married?" Jack asked.

"Two months last week," Katy answered with a shy grin.

"Ah, then you're still on your honeymoon. Just wait until you've been married a year or two." Stroking his chin and nodding ominously, he warned her, "Just you wait."

"Katy's *very* happy," Mrs. Hardesty insisted. "She'll continue to be so."

"Yes, I am," Katy echoed meekly. "I will!"

"Do you think the prospects for all marriages are so bleak?" Maude demanded.

Jack gave his lips a wry twist. "I haven't seen too much evidence to the contrary."

Maude gave a disdainful sniff. "Perhaps you ought to associate with a different class of people."

"I've been trying to tell him that for years!" Mrs. Kingston lamented. "But he's never paid me any more mind than that sister of yours does you."

"I suppose you've seen so much evidence in this town to support your theory," Jack retorted. Before she could reply, he demanded, "Just how many of these designs have you done? How many marriages have been completely happy?" He looked down at her, one eyebrow raised skeptically, awaiting her response.

Maude gave a derisive laugh. "I don't have to present you with my credentials. But I'll tell you I've done plenty."

"There's Fred and myself, Katy and Willard, Prunella and Charlie . . ." Louise offered in Maude's defense.

"Daisy and Gilbert," Wilma offered when Louise ran out of names. "They're all *very* happy."

"Is there anyone you've done this for who isn't happy?"

"Not that I know of."

"Of course, they wouldn't tell you they weren't, would they?"

"I . . . no, it's probably not something they'd discuss, but . . ." She faltered, then asserted more confidently, "Yes! Yes, indeed, they're all happy." She'd always considered her friends were. What did he think he was doing, coming back here, trying to start trouble? "Surely even *you* realize how quickly gossip travels in a small town. Take my word for it, I—*we* would all know if something was wrong."

"Well, then, if you're sure. . . ."

Maude allowed herself to breathe a bit more easily. She expected that to be the end of it. He'd take himself off in search of someone else to pester—maybe spend a little time with Clarice, who was watching him like a cat who hadn't eaten in days watched a plump mouse.

"So, tell me, Maude. How does it feel to be a sacred oracle?"

She should have figured that, like a riled badger, he wouldn't let go. She opened her mouth to reply, but wasn't exactly sure what to say. If she admitted to actually being some sort of prophetess, she'd only give Jack fuel to fire any further mockery he might try to make of her. If she told him she had no uncanny gift, she'd only be giving him further opportunity to ridicule her beautiful work and her friends' belief in her.

Thank goodness she didn't have to make that choice.

"Maude won't be predicting anything if we don't allow her to finish," Mrs. Kingston complained. She took Jack by the elbow and led him toward the parlor doorway.

"I'd wager every one of us has so much yet to do to get ready for the wedding," Miss Randolph said, following her hostess into the vestibule.

Maude had always admired the teacher's intelligence, wit, and powers of observation. No one had ever had to drop a hint twice to her, and no student had ever gotten away with much for very long—not even Jack.

"I must fetch my new bonnet from Miss Hawkins's millinery before she closes for the evening. I'm sure when you all see it tomorrow, you'll think it's quite attractive." The schoolteacher swept up her small handbag from the table in the center of the vestibule and headed for the door. "Thank you so much for entertaining us this afternoon, Nell." She gave a little wave with her fingertips and left.

The other ladies, following her example, gathered up their shawls, their handbags, and their daughters, and bade their hostess farewell.

Maude looked about for Jessica, but couldn't spot her anywhere. No doubt she'd slipped out a long time ago, heading for more interesting activities. At least Maude ought to be glad her sister didn't find that rascal Jack warranted any more of her attention. So many times her father had sworn to kill Jack—or volunteer to hold the coat of anyone else who did—for pranks he'd pulled as a youth. She didn't think her respectable father would countenance any daughter of his becoming involved with Suicide Jack the man, either.

Maude merely shrugged at the futility of trying to keep an eye on her hoydenish sister, and turned her attention back to her needlework.

"You sit there and finish, Maude," Mrs. Kingston told her, "while I get Jack settled into his room."

"I'll let myself out when I'm done." Maude threw Mrs. Kingston a bright smile. She was sure the lady would assume it was her usual pleasant expression. How could Mrs. Kingston know it was Maude's way of silently thanking her for removing that annoying Jack from her presence so she could work in peace?

She watched Jack snatch up the heavy-looking, well-worn carpetbag he'd left lying by the doorway and follow Mrs. Kingston before she resumed her stitching. Even though he was out of sight, she could hardly keep him out of mind when she could hear the rhythm of his boot heels as he trod the floor overhead. It was almost as if he knew exactly where she was sitting, and was deliberately stomping over the spot just to disturb her even when he wasn't right there with her.

She carefully folded the finished quilt and laid it on the seat of the chair, then gathered up her sewing basket and made her way across the expanse of lawn between the Kingston house and the Griffith home. The leaves of the sycamore standing between the two houses were budding. The air was damp and smelled of newly turned earth. The big lilac bush in the Kingstons' backyard sent over its fragrance on the passing breeze.

Maude headed up the back stairs for her bedroom, where she could hem her gown in peace.

The rose-beige taffeta felt crisp in her arms as she took it down from its peg behind the door. She headed for the chair by the side window, where she got the best light for her stitching. She opened her little sewing box on the half-round table under the window and pulled out a needle already threaded with cotton. After stitching a few inches, she glanced out the window to rest her eyes. What she saw made her catch her breath.

Through the bare branches of the giant sycamore she could clearly see that annoying, arrogant Jack, leaning out his bedroom window. No doubt he could see her. Even in four years, how could she have forgotten that Jack's bedroom window faced directly out to hers?

He was leaning his arms on the windowsill. Suddenly he stood up straight and waved in her direction. It wasn't a cheery "Hello-how-are-you" sort of wave. It was more of a languid "I-can-see-what-you're-doing-in-your-bedroom" wave—the kind that brought sharply back to her recollection how it felt to have his hand caress the quilt that had covered her.

Botheration! He mustn't think she was staring at him. He mustn't believe for one minute she was even remotely interested in him. She shook herself, nodded politely—that was all the acknowledgement the reprobate deserved!—and bent her head to her stitching.

There were plenty of other girls in town, she thought angrily as she stabbed at the material, all the while being acutely aware that he was still watching her. Why couldn't he flirt with *them?* Why couldn't his window look into *their* rooms instead? Why couldn't his window look out the other side of the Kingstons' house into that shameless hussy Clarice's window? *She'd* enjoy putting on a show for him, the little trollop! Why couldn't he leave *her* alone?

For the first time in months, Maude was suddenly not at all looking forward to her best friend's wedding tomorrow.

3

THE REVEREND LEONARD HOFFMANN'S wife struggled to coax a lilting air out of the creaky pump organ located to the right of the altar. The tune washed over the respectfully hushed and waiting congregation, and poured out into the vestibule where Maude waited with Wilma, Louise, and Mr. Kingston.

"You look so handsome in your new suit of clothing, Papa," Louise whispered.

"Not to mention mighty uncomfortable," Mr. Kingston replied, alternately tugging at his collar and the back of his trousers. "I don't know why I let your mother talk me into buying this dang thing. There wasn't nothing a needle and thread couldn't have fixed with the one I had."

"Mama wasn't about to let you wear that after you split the seat of the pants at Mr. Tyler's funeral."

"I—well, none of us—ever expected Pudge to be so darned heavy letting down. How was I to know I'd have to go and overexert myself, and that dang cheap suit I bought off that bandit Chalky Pike wouldn't hold up to the strain?"

"You've got to stop fidgeting with your collar. You've mussed your tie again." Reaching up to straighten it, Louise fumbled with and almost dropped her small bouquet of lilacs.

"Do you need some help?" Maude offered.

"No, I'm fine." Louise clenched her flowers more tightly to her bodice.

"Louise, your hands are shaking." Wilma indicated the bobbing blossoms and dancing, dangling white ribbons.

"I think I have every right to be nervous." Louise's voice was shaking almost as badly as her hands.

"*Your* hands are shaking, too, Wilma," Maude pointed out.

"Are you the only one here who's *not* nervous?" Wilma demanded testily.

"How can you be so calm all the time?" Louise wailed. "Doesn't *anything* make you nervous?"

Maude reached out to lay a steady, comforting hand on her friend's arm. "There's nothing to be nervous about. Everything is going just as you and your mother planned."

"I can't make my feet work right in these new slippers," Louise complained as they lined up to make their entrance in the proper order. "I'm sure I'll trip and fall and make a complete fool of myself."

"Nonsense. You'll be fine if you remain calm," Maude counseled.

"Or I'll faint," Louise suggested in increasingly panicked tones. Her father extended his arm toward her. She linked her hand through the crook in his elbow, as if she needed his support to keep from keeling over. "I believe I let Mama lace my corset too tight this morning."

Maude glanced back over her shoulder. "Take a few deep breaths."

"I can't! My corset is too tight." Louise tugged at the sides of her blue satin bodice. "Is it too late to go home and loosen it?"

"Yes," Mr. Kingston answered flatly.

"Your bodice won't fit correctly across your bosom if you loosen it too much," Wilma warned in a whisper. "You *have* put on a little weight, you know."

"Oh, no! Can you notice it that much?" She yanked at her bodice so hard, Maude was afraid she'd rip the stitching.

"Hush and be still. What could possibly go wrong?" Maude gently pulled Louise's hand away from her bodice—for safety's and modesty's sake. "Your bride's quilt is all finished, and the design is perfect. You look absolutely lovely in that gown. You love Fred, and he loves you. All your family and friends are here to celebrate with you. Wilma and I will be right by your side."

"To catch me when I faint?"

"You will *not* faint!" Maude insisted, and hoped God was listening and would take the hint as quickly as Miss Randolph always did. "There's nothing to be the least bit apprehensive about."

Louise smiled a little more brightly, but Maude noticed her hands hadn't stopped shaking one bit.

They faced front. Maude surreptitiously fingered the small vial of smelling salts she'd hidden under her own bunch of lilacs, for just such an emergency.

Oh, Lord, she silently prayed, *I hope I won't have to use this.*

"I think I have to use the necessary again!" Louise lamented.

"No, you don't," her father stated. "Anyway, it's too late now." He placed his right hand over hers, as if to keep her from bolting out of the church and dashing around back to the outhouse.

Mrs. Hoffmann began playing an appropriately dignified, if somewhat wheezy, processional march. The bright sunlight of the Sunday afternoon poured through the windows, making the guests seated in the pews, decked out in their best attire, all the more brilliant. The scents of lilacs, beeswax, and wood varnish filled the air. Maude looked down the patterned red-and-green-carpeted aisle toward the benignly beaming Reverend Hoffmann, open prayer book in hand, standing before the altar. His abundant silver hair caught the light of the candles behind him and gleamed like a halo.

Frederick Ingram stood up there, too, waiting with his friends Matthew Conway and Isaac Jamison. He was smiling and looked so red in the face that Maude was afraid his new collar was choking him. She hoped he and Louise wouldn't both faint. She'd only brought one vial of smelling salts.

Wilma, in her pale lavender taffeta gown, began her trek down the aisle. Maude looked down the familiar aisle, the same one she and her family walked down every Sunday on the way to the traditional family pew. Odd, she speculated, this aisle never seemed this long all the other times.

If it wouldn't be too much trouble, Lord, Maude quickly added, *I'd ask that I don't have to use the salts for myself, either.*

Wilma was halfway down the aisle: Maude's cue to begin. If Wilma could make it without tripping or dropping her flowers,

Maude figured she could, too. She took a deep breath and stepped out in faith.

Fine, fine, everything is going just fine, she repeated to herself in time to the music. Each careful step brought her closer to her destination. Wilma had already reached the security of the altar rail. Pretty soon she, herself, would be halfway down the aisle.

The loud cough from the pew directly to her left tore through the hush, causing Maude to startle and almost drop her flowers—not so much that everyone else would notice and take it for an ill omen (certainly not as unlucky as holding the wedding on a Saturday would have been considered), but just enough for her to notice and berate herself for her clumsiness. She glanced quickly to her side to see who was to blame for distracting her.

There he sat, grinning up at her. She might have known the cause of all her misery would be that damned Jack Kingston.

Oh, no! Cursing in church! Just look what that unregenerate sinner made me do, she lamented to herself.

Well, she wouldn't let him drag her down to hell with him! She jerked her head high, focused straight ahead, and continued down the aisle. She'd felt so calm and in control. Now, knowing Jack was there, watching her, made the rest of her journey seem even longer and the formerly benign church aisle fraught with unseen snares.

She was sure she'd stumble over a piece of lint, or a loose knot in the new carpet, or a huge splinter that had suddenly decided to poke up out of the usually smooth wooden floor. Or her knees would give out, and she'd collapse facedown in a rose-colored heap, with her crinoline flipped up behind her, so that everyone—even Jack—could see her underpinnings. She'd be sprawled out in the middle of the aisle, so that Louise and Mr. Kingston would have to climb over her to get to the altar. During the service, would someone just quietly push her out of the way? Or would they leave her there and let the wedding party and all the guests climb over her to get out?

She would *not* fall! She clasped her lilacs more tightly, as if that were some measure of her determination, and did her best to proceed down the aisle.

Make me mess up my best friend's wedding! she thought with righteous indignation. If she ever had cause to hate Suicide Jack in the past, she surely did now.

She'd ignore him, she decided, for the rest of the day, for the entire rest of the time he'd be in town. If he choked on wedding cake, she wouldn't thump him on the back. If he caught on fire from one of the candles, she wouldn't waste punch putting him out.

Mrs. Hoffmann turned the page, pulled out all the porcelain stops, and pumped harder for more volume. The rest of the congregation turned to the back to watch Louise make her grand entrance. Just as Maude turned, she caught a glimpse of Jack out of the corner of her eye. He wasn't watching Louise. He was still looking directly at her.

He winked at her. Such reprehensible behavior in church!

Ignore the scoundrel, she repeated sternly to herself. She had the best intentions of watching Louise. Truly she did! Then why did her gaze keep straying back to Jack?

He winked again and raised one eyebrow speculatively.

What on earth could he possibly be speculating about her? Maude almost choked on her own imaginings. How awful to go into a coughing spasm just as the service was about to begin! *No, no, concentrate on Louise!*

He grinned and wiggled his eyebrows at her—the very thing he used to do when they were children in school. Even though he was three years older than she, he was a year behind her in schoolwork, and Miss Randolph had seated him directly in front of her, where she could keep a watchful eye on the unruly rapscallion. At least he hadn't sat behind her, where he could dip her pigtails in the inkwell, as he'd once done to Jessica, who had promptly turned around and punched him in the nose. But he had managed to turn around each time Miss Randolph's back was turned, and make faces at Maude. He'd also somehow always managed to face front again and appear to be engrossed in his times tables, just as she stuck her tongue out at him—just in time for Miss Randolph to catch *her* misbehaving! It was the only time she'd ever been punished in school. "You're the smart one, the mature one; you should be able to ignore his antics," Miss Randolph had told her. It was the only time a student had *not* been able to convince Miss Randolph that everything was Jack's fault. Oh, she had so many reasons to hate Suicide Jack!

Maude was sorely tempted to stick her tongue out at him now. No, it wouldn't look right at Louise's wedding, and she was determined not to let this sinner spoil the sanctity of the service or the celebration of the happy day. She clamped her lips together and forced herself to concentrate on Louise and her father, marching down the aisle.

Suddenly she realized what a horrible face she must be making! The kind her mother had always warned her not to make or it would freeze that way. What an awful impression she must be making to everyone here! They probably assumed she didn't approve. She wouldn't want anyone to think she had no faith in a match her very own quilting had pronounced good. Once again, it was all that darned Jack's fault.

Maude straightened her posture and spread a pleasant, if cramped, smile across her face. She shouldn't be paying any attention to him anyway. If she should be looking for anyone besides Louise, it ought to be Caleb Johnson.

Yes, concentrate on Caleb, she urged herself. Her gaze swept the congregation until she found him seated with his four older brothers in the pew right under the window of Jesus in the Garden of Gethsemane.

Handsome, hard-working, ambitious, law-abiding Caleb. *He'd* never spent time in jail. *He* didn't traffic with Demon Rum or smoke the Noxious Weed. He and his brothers struggled to work the farm their father had left them. But Caleb had dreams for a future that extended far beyond that little plot of land. Yes, indeed, Caleb was a man who was destined to make his fortune, and she was just the woman to share that destiny.

Hadn't she already secretly figured it out the best way she knew how? Didn't their initials make a wonderful design? *MG* and *CJ* with pink rosebuds, lilies of the valley, ferns, and lavender ribbons surrounded by the most intricate quilting she'd ever designed. She had it all worked out on paper. She'd even been so bold as to begin to embroider the design. She used unbleached muslin, so the pure white lilies would show up better. When she finally convinced Caleb he was the man for her, she'd be ready.

Although only her two bosom friends, Louise and Katy, knew she'd set her cap for Caleb, *no one*—not even her own sister— knew about her block. Although she wasn't usually superstitious, just so she wouldn't risk tempting Fate, she'd wisely omitted the as-yet-unknown date of the wedding. It looked perfect!

Well, *almost* perfect, she silently had to admit, especially since she was in church and really shouldn't lie, not even to herself. There was just something not quite right about the arrangement.

But she'd work on it. After all, Caleb wasn't going anywhere yet—and she still had obligations.

She'd never fulfill the promise she'd made to herself when her mother died if she couldn't concentrate on her goals. Why, even now, she couldn't keep her attention fixed on Louise or Caleb. Even with her back turned to him, trying to listen to the Reverend Hoffmann, she couldn't stop her thoughts from continually returning to that aggravating, annoying, irritating Suicide Jack.

∽

MAUDE STOOD WITH SOME of the ladies, watching Caleb with silent admiration. His blue eyes shone with excitement, and the shock of fair hair falling across his broad forehead bobbed back and forth with the force of his conviction.

"There are still fortunes to be made in California, or Montana, or even up north along the Cariboo," Caleb declared to the small group gathered around him in the Kingstons' noisy, crowded barn. "Plenty waiting in Colorado, too. Mark my words. It's all out West! That's where the future lies, and that's where I'll be."

Ruthie Brickham rapturously clasped her hands together under her chin. "What woman wouldn't be impressed by so impassioned a man?"

It certainly came as no surprise to Maude that anyone else would be interested in Caleb. She just wished Ruthie would stand in *silent* awe so she could hear what else he had to say. After all, his plans would affect her—someday.

"Such an ambitious young man," Mrs. Dalton commented. "Hard-working, too."

"An admirable trait, I suppose," Mrs. Hardesty grudgingly agreed.

"Caleb will make such a good husband," Ruthie said.

Mrs. Dalton nodded. "A very good provider."

"Probably," Maude replied.

She'd much rather have devoted all her attention to Caleb, but she knew the other ladies wouldn't be satisfied unless she joined in the conversation. But she didn't want to sound *too* interested— at least not until Caleb had made his own vague intentions a bit clearer to *her*. She wouldn't want anyone in town to accuse her of doing anything so improper as chasing after a man.

"Tell us more about your plans, Caleb," Edgar Baumgartner urged. The other men agreed.

"I'll bet none of them would have the nerve to follow him," Ruthie muttered scornfully.

"Probably not." Maude herself wasn't too enthusiastic about this part of his plan, but she'd keep her opinions to herself—for now.

"New claims are fewer each year, I'll grant you, and the new veins are harder to mine without a lot of labor and expensive equipment, but it's still there. That's why a man has to seize every opportunity."

Caleb clenched a fist out in front of him to emphasize his point. Maude heard some of the ladies sigh, and the men mumble agreement. She had to admit he cut quite an imposing figure!

"He's not only ambitious. He's intelligent, too," Mrs. Dalton said.

"No, young man. I must take issue with you." Mr. Lester tucked his thumbs into his waistcoat pockets and rocked on his heels. "Now, you can correct me if I'm wrong, and I don't think I am, but I *am* the president of the Apple Grove Farmers and Merchants Savings and Loan Association, and I think not a few other bankers and businessmen in this country will bear me out if you'd care to ask them. Many have gone west and made their fortunes, 'tis true, and far more have come home empty-handed. The future is in investing in good, solid, established business, my boy. Always has been, always will be."

"Begging your pardon, sir, and it's not that I'm not grateful for your advice, but I'd just as soon be heading west."

Mr. Lester frowned. "Where do you think you'll get the initial capital?"

"I have a little put by—*and* part interest in that farm."

Mr. Lester snorted. "A mere one-fifth."

"Still, that ought to be worth some sort of a stake."

"What do your brothers have to say about your plan to mortgage the family farm?"

"They have faith in me. Even if they don't intend to go with me, they'll want to invest their shares. Probably."

"What of *my* shareholders at the savings and loan, who have placed their trust in me?" Mr. Lester demanded.

"That's not my concern," Caleb asserted. "My business is to

get the money I need from the bank and turn it into more. Where the bank gets it from is your concern.''

"I can't go advancing capital for just a share in a plot of land—and not a very big share, either, I might add.''

"But—''

"Especially not for something so ephemeral as making a hole in the ground in search of buried treasure. Why, you might as well go out and try to find the Lost Continent of Atlantis or the fabled city of Troy!'' He chuckled loudly at his own wit. "Maybe a few years ago I could have advanced you the money, but times have changed. You realize that.''

For once, Caleb had no reply.

"Didn't think of that, did you, son?'' The rotund banker jabbed a pudgy finger in Caleb's direction and smiled with evident self-confidence that there couldn't possibly be any further opposition to his argument.

"Not really,'' Caleb admitted sheepishly.

One would suppose he'd been defeated. But when Maude looked at Caleb, with his lean face flushed and his blue eyes still gleaming with sparks from his thwarted ambitions, she knew that next time Caleb would have an answer for Mr. Lester.

"Oh, dear,'' Mrs. Dalton lamented. "There are times when Caleb's plans turn out to be a bit ill-conceived.''

"They aren't quite the sort of plans for the future a responsible married man with a wife and family to provide for would make, are they?'' Mrs. Hardesty asked.

"I suppose not,'' Maude reluctantly replied, although she knew very well the lady didn't expect an answer at all.

My, they could all change direction more quickly than a weather vane in a tornado, she noted. But, as much as she hated to admit it, they did have a good point—one that she herself had frequently pondered with concern.

"On the other hand, I suppose a sensible wife could help him improve his more acceptable plans and discourage him from the completely foolish schemes,'' Maude offered.

"Perhaps,'' Mrs. Dalton answered.

"She'd have to be *mighty* sensible,'' Mrs. Hardesty said with a derisive sniff.

Well, I am *sensible,* Maude figured. In the past nine years since her mother had passed away, hadn't she proved she could manage the household? She washed and sewed, cooked and baked, did the marketing, and even set aside a nest egg for a rainy day. Not to mention helping her busy father raise boisterous Jessica and shy Georgie.

Yes, indeed. She was just the one to make Caleb see the reasonableness in carefully thinking out a plan before jumping in feetfirst and being surprised by the results.

Suddenly Albert Wilson interrupted them all with a frantic waving of his arms over his head and a loud exclamation. "Over here! Over here!"

4

MAUDE HAD NEVER HEARD that Albert suffered from fits. What could be causing him to make such an outburst now?

"If it ain't Suicide Jack!" Albert exclaimed. "Come on over here and catch up on old times, you ol' horse thief!"

Jack grinned as he strolled toward them, stopping briefly to greet various people in the crowd, who were shaking his hand and patting him on the back. He wore a brand-new suit of clothing, dark brown finely woven wool, in the latest style. How could he afford such a suit? Maude wondered.

She caught a glimpse of Georgie weaving through the crowd, trying to stay close to Jack. When her shy brother was younger, he'd worshipped that reprobate Jack and, much to Maude's dismay, he seemed all too eager to renew the friendship now.

Why couldn't Jack just approach them straight on like a normal, honest person? Maude thought grumpily. Why did the man have to circle the group like a vulture seeking carrion? Why, when everyone was jockeying for position to get him to stand next to them, did he finally decide to wedge his way into the circle directly beside her? She'd just as soon have turned and left, but everyone crowded in around Jack. Georgie had managed to stand behind her. Now she was stuck there and she certainly couldn't be rude and push her way out.

"You ol' snake oil salesman!" Hiram Culligan awkwardly balanced a glass of whiskey in one hammy hand and clapped Jack on the shoulder with the other. "I thought I saw your ugly head pokin' up above all those good folks sittin' in church who don't quite have the altitude on you."

"You wouldn't have noticed me even then," Jack replied with a laugh, "if you weren't trying to hide in the back pew so the preacher wouldn't spot you and point you out to God-fearing folks as a bad example."

"Oh, how could anyone not admire so quick-witted a man!" Ruthie said breathlessly.

Maude shot her a frigid glare. "I thought you liked them *impassioned,*" she remarked with a wry twist to her lips. Why would any woman in her right mind want to become involved with a scoundrel like Suicide Jack? Why should she even bother to comment on it if that silly twit Ruthie wanted to ruin her life?

"Oh, yes!" Clarice agreed.

Maude started. When had *she* joined this group? Even though her mother had been here with them all along, the last time Maude had noticed Clarice, she was over by the edge of the dance floor, chattering away to Rafe Baxter while he was paying more attention to tuning his guitar. Somehow, wherever men congregated, Clarice eventually found her way there.

"Impassioned men are so . . . so passionate," Clarice agreed. "Quick-witted men are so . . . so—"

"Witty?" Maude supplied. She could have suggested many more adjectives that might better apply to Jack, and a few, unmentionable in polite company, that definitely applied to Clarice.

The group had been composed mostly of men listening to Caleb and Mr. Lester argue. But now that Jack had joined them, more and more ladies were drawn in.

Poor Louise. Maude silently lamented for her friend. The girl should have had better sense than to invite her notorious cousin to her wedding. With Jack around, not even as the bride would Louise be the center of attention.

"Jack, I thought you were dead!" Sam Ferguson exclaimed.

"Lots of folks have thought that," Jack replied with a laugh, "and I've proved them wrong every time."

"I still would've thought somebody would've killed you by now."

"As I seem to recall," Mr. Lester said with a chuckle, "ever

since you came to live here when you were six years old, someone's been wanting to kill you.''

"Thought ol' Doc Fogle'd take yer head off with one o' them
wicked instruments o' his the very first day.'' Walt Sawyer
slapped his lanky thigh and guffawed. "Whatever possessed yer
aunt to take a perfectly healthy young'un to a dentist, I'll never
know.''

"How'd you like it if somebody stuck their big, dirty finger
in *your* mouth, Walt?''

"When you nigh to bit off his finger, I'll bet it gave 'em
second thoughts 'bout havin' took you in when yer ma and pa
died. Pulled a stunt like that on me, and I'd have sure sent yer
ass packin' off out to them wild Indians where you'd feel more
at home than with us civilized white folks.''

Clarice and Ruthie were giggling madly at Jack's escapade.
Maude failed to see the humor they and Walt seemed to derive
from this incident.

"Maybe,'' Maude stated firmly, casting Walt an icy glare,
"Mr. and Mrs. Kingston were wise enough to realize it wasn't
so much that he was bad, but that he was just a frightened little
boy who'd been sent all alone to live in a strange town with
relatives he barely knew.''

Walt snickered. "Well, now, Miss Maude, as I recollect, you
was just a li'l bitty thing at the time, so I don't see how you'd
rightly be rememberin' none of it, much less pronouncin' judgement on it.''

"Come on, Walt,'' Jack said. "I'll bet everybody in town has
heard this one so much, they could tell it to you backwards. It's
a good thing I came back, to give you all some new tales to
tell.''

Walt tried to laugh again, but Maude didn't think it was anywhere near as hearty as before. She ought to be grateful to Jack
for coming to her defense. On the other hand, she wouldn't want
him to mistakenly believe she, like giggling, empty-headed
Ruthie and Clarice, found him in any way the least bit appealing.

Jack's green-eyed gaze studied her again, but not with the
same sweeping, speculative expression he'd had before. This
time there was almost a look of gratitude in his eyes. Did he
think she would actually belatedly come to the defense of the
scared little boy he might once have been?

"Of course," she hurriedly added, "I'm in no way condoning such misbehavior."

"I never imagined you would," Jack agreed.

"Naw," Bob Townsend maintained. "Ever since we were in third grade together for a couple o' years, I've been countin' on Miss Randolph to do him in. The old girl always did have it out for you, Jack, ever since you kicked her in the shins."

"But she made me sit on a stool in the corner and wear that dang-fool-looking dunce cap!" Jack protested.

"Yeah, you, me, and just about everybody else—except maybe little goody-two-shoes Maude," Bob admitted. "But none of us ever had the guts to actually kick her!"

"No, no, everybody listen!" Albert solemnly held up both hands to get their attention.

A hush fell over the expectant crowd. Maude figured they were waiting to hear something else wicked about Jack—and she was sure that, out of his mysterious, checkered past, he'd be able to supply it.

"We've got to admit it," Albert continued gravely. "No matter who else we might like to blame, we—and I do mean *we all*—always had our money on good ol' Jack himself"—he gestured grandly toward Jack—"to do himself in with one o' those crazy stunts he was always pullin'."

The crowd started to protest.

"No, come on. Confess," Albert staunchly maintained. "There's not a man among us who don't remember—and admire him for—the time (just to name one incident out o' many) that he liked to got blowed up tryin' to climb up the church steeple durin' that electrical storm just so's he could slide down that rope to the house next door and sneak a peek into Molly Fischer's bedroom window up on the second floor."

Most of them began to laugh, although a few still held out in weak protest.

"You know I'm right," Albert persisted. "Even though Molly—bless her!—did tend to leave her window shades up as sort of an open invitation to the fellows in town, seein' as how she was on the second floor, and how her pa was the double-barrel-shotgun-totin' sheriff at the time, well, now, if that ain't the actions of a man hellbent on suicide, I don't know what is. How else would we have come to call him Suicide Jack?"

"You have us there, Albert," Edgar at last conceded, along with the remainder of the cheering crowd.

"Tell us, Jack," Mr. Lester asked as the laughter died down, "do you have any plans for seeking your fortune out West like Caleb?"

"Shucks, no. I've already seen the elephant." Jack chuckled, but Maude noted his laughter seemed to lack any genuine humor, as if he'd just as soon have left the metaphorical, and highly overrated, elephant alone.

The discordant strumming, sawing, tootling sounds that came from Rafe Baxter's guitar, Herb Grayson's fiddle, and Micky Carmichael's fife as they warmed up suddenly met in the surprisingly harmonious music of a recognizable tune. Ruthie and Clarice gazed expectantly at Jack. Jack, on the other hand, seemed to be gazing with longing at the exit. He had said he would be leaving town right after Louise's wedding. Maude wondered if he'd decided now was the time to run away once again. Why should she feel so disappointed if he'd decided it was?

Mr. Lester gave a loud harrumph. "As president of the Apple Grove Farmers and Merchants Savings and Loan Association—"

"Oh, fa-la-la, let's not start that again!" Mrs. Lester piped up, trying to distract them with a high-pitched, lilting voice and an airy wave of her hand. "Must you men always be so tedious, insisting upon talking such horribly complicated and hopelessly confusing business matters in front of us ladies?"

Undaunted, Mr. Lester continued, "I feel it behooves me—"

"Come now, gentlemen. This is a *wedding party!*" Mrs. Lester insisted. "The musicians are tuned up, and I, for one, don't intend to miss a single dance while there's a man among you left standing to escort me."

"Oh, no!" Ruthie and Clarice chorused, and looked hopefully toward Jack.

Oblivious, Mr. Lester still expounded, "—to warn you against any ill-conceived ventures promoted by scoundrels, mountebanks, and charlatans—"

Maude almost laughed aloud. If anyone here could be accused of being a charlatan, a mountebank, and a scoundrel, it would most likely be Jack.

Mrs. Lester gave a little laugh as she leaned closer to her husband. The other people might think it was simply a gesture of marital affection, but Maude noticed the fabric of Mr. Lester's sleeve wrinkle tautly as Mrs. Lester tightened her grip.

Maude figured no one in the crowd but she heard Mrs. Lester whisper ferociously in her husband's ear, "As the Almighty is my witness, Jeremiah, if you pursue this line of discussion right now, or any more for the rest of the day, you'll sleep in the barn for a month. If you think eating in the kitchen is going to be bad—"

Mr. Lester coughed and made a show of straightening his tie. Maude figured that was the best way he reckoned he could release himself from his wife's death grip and restore circulation to his arm.

"My dear wife, you look positively enchanting this afternoon," he said, making an awkward bow. "Would you grant me the honor of this dance?"

When he again extended his bruised arm to her, Maude had to give him credit. Mr. Lester was a brave man.

With a pleasant smile, Mrs. Lester linked her arm with his. Together they moved toward the large space in the center of the Kingstons' barn that had been swept clean and cleared of bales of hay, horse tack, and farming equipment.

As the crowd readjusted its arrangement, Jack leaned over and whispered in Maude's ear, "Mr. Lester's a wise man." Maude started with surprise and shivered at the nearness of him.

Perhaps it was the pleasant excitement of the joyous day and her own nervousness from his proximity that made her laugh at his remark. It had to be. He certainly wasn't *that* witty.

"Hey, Jack, if you ain't going back out West, you got a job in town yet?" Albert asked.

"No."

"Guess your uncle could put you to work in his hardware store."

Jack shrugged. "Maybe."

Maude couldn't picture the impulsive youth, who at the age of sixteen had run away from home to fight in the war, donning apron and sleeve garters so he could stand behind a shop counter all day, doling out saws, hammers, and ten-penny nails.

"Maybe Mr. Foster could use you at the barbershop," Albert suggested.

"I don't think so."

Neither could Maude. Who in their right mind would trust Jack with a sharp razor to his throat?

"Maybe Mr. Griffith could get you a job at the *Gazette,* setting type or something."

Not the newspaper office! Maude couldn't bear to have him underfoot constantly at her father's newspaper office.

"Naw, you got to be able to read to work at a newspaper!" Walt protested.

"Is that why you work at the livery, Walt?" Albert asked, laughing.

"Do you have any plans *at all,* Jack?" Mrs. Dalton demanded.

"Yes, ma'am," Jack answered. "I've got . . . prospects, but . . . well, I don't like to talk about them so I don't jinx myself. It's just a little superstition of mine. You know, like you folks seem to believe in Maude's quilts."

If he couldn't be a believer, Maude thought, the least he could do was leave her and her quilts alone.

"But what do you intend to do while you're here, Jack?" Mrs. Hardesty asked.

"Just visit my family. Then I'll be moving on."

"Horrors! Whatever will we do when you leave?" Clarice and Ruthie chorused.

"You know me." Jack ruffled his fingers through his dark hair and slowly replied, "Always on the move."

"When you can be." When Jack made no reply, Mrs. Hardesty continued, "I really would've supposed you'd stay around here now. I mean, what sort of a job do you figure a man who's been in prison can get, if not with a relation?"

"Just about anything I set my mind to, ma'am," Jack answered with very evidently strained politeness.

Maude could see a wariness in his eyes. As he stood beside her, she believed she could feel a tension, like a taut bowstring, throughout his entire body. It was pretty obvious he didn't like the direction this conversation had taken. Maude didn't, either, but what could she do about it?

Hiram joined in the attack. "Don't suppose Mr. Lester'll be too eager to hire you to work at the bank."

"Don't suppose you have too much luck with banks, do you, Jack?" Walt continued the offensive. "The reports in the newspaper were sort o' confusin', so why don't you clear it up for us? Were you actually once the sheriff in that little town? What made you turn bad and be in league with those bank robbers? Was it the money? Politics? Huh?''

Without another word, Jack stepped out in front of Maude, taking her completely by surprise. With a grandiose gesture, he extended his right arm for her to take his hand.

''Miss Maude, would you grant me the favor of this dance?''

Walt, Hiram, and Mrs. Hardesty glared at Jack.

''Please?''

Clarice and Ruthie glared at Maude. She knew if she refused him, they'd jump at the chance, and Jack wouldn't ask her again. She knew if she accepted, they'd envy her with a passionate jealousy for at least the rest of the day—that alone was inducement enough. If she accepted, it also meant that she'd have helped Jack escape his tormentors' verbal attacks. While she had no qualms about seeing Jack squirm, she certainly couldn't allow anyone to spoil Louise's wedding.

But Maude didn't have the least desire to dance with Jack. She didn't want to have to make tedious small talk with him about the weather, Apple Grove's inhabitants, or life in prison as they glided across the floor. She didn't want to think about touching him, not even just his hand or the shoulder of his jacket, and risk feeling once again the powerful current that ran between them. She didn't want to think about his hands touching her, or his arms encircling her as they swayed about the dance floor in time to the sensuous rhythm of a waltz.

But he had said please. It was so unlike Jack to say please, especially to her. It would be rude to refuse him, and she'd never deliberately been rude to anyone in her life—well, except Jack when they were children, but he'd deserved it then. Did he deserve it now, when he seemed so desperate to escape the prying questions of Mrs. Hardesty, that old harpy, and Walt Sawyer, who was always just itching for a fight anyway, and Hiram Culligan, who seemed to harbor an old hatred of Jack from the day he'd run away to join the war? At least Gordon Potter hadn't shown up. He was the worst of all!

There was something else, too. Something in Jack's eyes.

He watched her in what seemed an eternity of waiting while she made her decision. His eyes were the same vivid green she remembered, yet there was something very different about them. That sly, boyish mischief still twinkled there, but somehow it seemed merely superficial now. He kept something hidden deep inside him. It was a look she couldn't fathom, and didn't want to; but she couldn't help it. She was being drawn into the deep whirlpool of his gaze.

"I'd be delighted."

She felt as if someone were working her like a marionette, making her say and do foolish things. Smiling pleasantly, she reached out to him, being careful to allow only the tips of her fingers to rest lightly on his upturned palm.

It was her imagination, of course, as her hand touched his. Yet she felt as bound to him as if they were opposite poles of two magnets—attracted, connected, inseparable.

Maude didn't need to see them. She could almost *feel* the envious green daggers of jealousy Ruthie and Clarice hurled in her direction sinking deeply into her back as Jack led her to the dance floor.

He tucked her fingers gently into the crook of his left elbow. Once again, she could smell the bay rum and the pungent, earthy scent of clean tobacco. She drew in another breath. She missed the smell of whiskey. Maybe she'd been mistaken yesterday. Maybe he wasn't as bad as she'd feared. Maybe a little time in jail had taught him a bit of prudence and put some sense into his head after all.

She'd never intended to get this close to him. How had she managed to link not just her hand, but her entire arm with his? Had she, like Louise, laced her corset too tight this morning and was she suffering from lack of circulation to the brain? She leaned a little closer to him for support. In spite of her brain telling her he was bad, her body insisted on telling her he felt good.

His forearm was strong and muscular. The fabric of his new jacket was soft. His side against her arm was warm and lean— and hard and bumpy. What in heaven's name was that?

She wouldn't want him to believe she was anything like that shameless Clarice, but she had to know—and there was only one way to find out. Under the pretense of avoiding another couple heading for the dance floor, she leaned against him just a bit more.

There was no mistaking it now.

Maude stiffened and tried not to jerk away so quickly that Jack might suspect she knew. But there was no doubt about it.

There was no mistaking the steel-and-leather bulge of the shoulder holster under his jacket.

What in the world was Jack doing wearing a gun to his cousin's wedding?

5

THERE WAS DANGER HERE with Jack, Maude knew. She wanted to run away before it reached out and engulfed her—and she wanted to stay. She could hardly bear the sensuous way he slowly, deliberately placed his hand on her waist and turned her around to face him.

She'd known Jack was a wild, unpredictable, uncontrollable child. He'd run away to war, breaking his aunt's heart. Then he'd taken a job as a sheriff in a small town and briefly redeemed himself in the eyes of his uncle. But he'd taken to consorting with outlaws, robbed a bank or two, and ended up in jail, leaving his family mortified before the entire town.

Jack had always been trouble, but right now he was worse than trouble. He was dangerous. What she couldn't figure out was—dangerous to whom? Why here? Why now? Who was he waiting to shoot? Or who was he expecting to shoot him?

As she looked into his eyes, she could hear the pounding of her own heart in her ears.

Suddenly, behind her, she heard Willard's voice urging, "Come, Katy, my tweetlebird."

"Tweetlebird?" Jack whispered to Maude.

She could feel the warmth of his breath on her cheek. "Hush."

"Not now, Willie-poo," Katy protested.

"Willie-poo?" Jack whispered.

"Hush!" In spite of herself and her good intentions, she couldn't help but quietly giggle.

"Do they always call each other those things?"

"Yes."

"How nauseating."

"You haven't had to listen to them for the past six months."

Willard was trying his best to urge Katy past them onto the dance floor. She, on the other hand, kept pulling her hand out of his grasp and seemed to be doing everything but clutching at a nearby support beam and digging her heels into the floorboards in order to avoid it.

"But, my dearest dumpling, I thought you loved to dance."

"No, I do not, Willie-poo," she told him petulantly.

"Why such a grumpy-wumpy puss? What's wrong with my little sparrow today?" Willard crooned.

"Nothing!" Katy snapped.

"She's angry because he didn't call her tweetlebird again," Jack whispered even closer to Maude's ear.

Maude glared at him and punched his shoulder hard so he'd hush—and she could hear clearly what was going on.

"What's the matter?" Willard asked. "Did the pickled eggs and vanilla custard not agree with you, my fuzzy bunnikins? You did eat a lot of them."

"I'm fine. They were delicious. The pickled pigs' feet Mrs. Ingram brought look mighty tasty, too. I just don't feel like dancing," Katy answered. Her stout insistence was rapidly degenerating into a pathetic whine.

"I'm sure you'll feel better once you start dancing."

"No, I will not! Now leave me alone!" Katy snapped again. She snatched her hand away from him and turned back toward the heavily laden refreshment table.

"Tweetlebird, wait for me," Willard called as he hurried after her.

"Go fetch me a lemonade!" she commanded.

Jack chuckled. "What do you think Willie-poo's chances are of getting her to dance today?"

Maude pursed her lips and didn't answer. Katy was one of her best friends. She wasn't about to be disloyal to her friend—not with Jack, of all people!

"What do you think his chances are of coming up with even

more ridiculous pet names for his tweetlebird? Clearly the man suffers from an overabundance of poetic imagery. Why can't she think up something else to call him besides Willie-poo?"

"You really don't like that nickname, do you?"

"You must admit it's a darn sight worse than Suicide Jack."

Maude couldn't worry about that now. She was more puzzled by why Katy should be arguing with her precious Willie-poo in the first place. She'd never heard them argue before. She'd never heard Katy even obliquely mention any disagreements.

"Say, aren't they one of the couples you made a quilt for?" Jack asked.

She knew exactly what he was aiming at. Well, he might have drawn a bead on her, but she didn't intend to allow him to keep her in his sights for one moment.

"Just one block," she corrected. "You know, I'm becoming heartily weary of you and your unnatural fixation with my prophetic needlework."

"Well, aren't they?"

"Yes. You know they are."

"They don't look completely happy to me."

"Do you want me to tell you your prediction was right and mine was wrong?"

"Would you?"

"Don't be silly. Of course not. I'm *not* wrong." She cast him a knowing look. "They might be having a slight disagreement now, but—"

"Slight?"

"*But,* she still calls him her Willie-poo, doesn't she? She's still his little tweetlebird, isn't she?"

"God help them, yes."

"When they stop calling each other that, *then* they've got a problem."

Jack laughed. "You've made your point. Well, even if you *are* infallible, we shouldn't be wasting our precious time contemplating the woes of the world when there's dancing to be done."

Throwing his earlier propriety aside, he pulled her closer to him and swept her out onto the dance floor with all the other couples. His gentle touch on her waist urged her body to comply with his lead. She felt there was some sort of invisible cord binding them together as they moved about the barn.

At Katy's wedding, she'd danced with Willard—then a *happy*

groom. She'd danced with pompous Mr. Lester, jolly Mr. Kingston, and even with Ol' Man Grunder, who wheezed and drooled a thin, brown trickle of chewing tobacco out of one corner of his mouth. She'd even reluctantly danced with Hiram, who had the nasty habit of letting his hand slide just a little lower than was proper but never enough so that a lady could just haul off and slap him for his impertinence.

Of course, she'd danced several dances with Caleb, who was a very good dancer. They'd had a lovely conversation, although at the moment she couldn't recall what it had been about. She'd felt content to be in his arms. But she'd never felt this whirl of excitement coursing through her as she did now in Jack's embrace. She'd never felt as if the very spirit of her being longed to surge toward him and entwine herself around him—no, not even with Caleb, the man she intended to marry someday.

What in the world was wrong with her? Without even realizing it, was she actually as wanton as that silly Clarice? She couldn't wait until Jack left so she could go back to her normal, ordinary way of life and stop feeling this way. How would she feel once she no longer felt the way she did right now?

She looked up at Jack and realized he wasn't paying one bit of attention to where they were going. He was looking intently at her.

Why did I cut the bodice of this gown so low? she lamented.

"Stop staring at me," she whispered. "It's rude."

"Sorry. I thought it was rude not to look at one's partner."

"Staring is rude no matter what," she told him flatly.

"I guess I didn't learn very good manners in prison."

"Don't try to blame your life of crime for your bad manners, you shameless reprobate." In spite of herself, she grinned. "You never had any when you were living with your aunt and uncle, either, no matter how hard they tried to teach you."

"If it makes you feel better, I'll just pretend you're not here. Will that be polite enough for you?"

Without giving her time to answer or the opportunity to resist, he pulled her even closer to him. She risked feeling his warm breath on her cheek. She risked getting much too close a look at his green eyes, his firm jaw, his strong but ultimately pliant lips. *Don't think about it!*

She started to pull back, but that would only give him a better vantage of the accentuated cleavage revealed by her gown. She couldn't win, no matter what!

He lifted his head and looked out over the crowd. He *seemed* to be paying strict attention to where he was going, and never once glanced back down at her—but she'd learned early on a body never could trust Jack completely.

"There, see? I'm not staring at you."

"Thank you."

Very slowly and purposefully he let his gaze sweep over the crowd. "I swear, I've been gone so long, there are so many people I don't remember anymore."

"They all certainly recognize you."

"I'm flattered."

"You must remember Edgar Baumgartner." She nodded to where he was dancing with Florence, even though she was sure—she thought she was, she *hoped* she was—that Jack wasn't watching her anymore. He'd told her he wasn't, but she wouldn't trust him any farther than she could toss a cannonball.

"By golly, he was finally able to grow a mustache, I see—dancing with . . . goodness, that looks like Florence Lester, only . . . My goodness, it seems as if Mother Nature's been quite generous with her endowments since—"

"Don't talk about such things!"

"Sorry. I suppose that's rude, too."

"Of course it is."

"More rude than staring?"

"Only when you talk about it." She grunted and twitched her lips in an effort not to laugh. "Why am I not surprised you'd notice that sort of thing?"

"Things," he corrected with a wicked grin. "Be reasonable, Maude. I just got out of prison. A poor, deprived fellow such as I needs to feast his starving eyes on some feminine beauty." His gaze grew more serious as he turned back to her. Just as intently as he'd avoided her before, he studied her now. Very quietly he asked, "Why do you think I was staring at you?"

She missed a beat as he swept her around the floor.

"Yes, well, you're not deprived, you're depraved. Florence is betrothed to Edgar. They're planning to be married in September."

"What does your quilt oracle have to say about them?"

She gave a little laugh and hoped it didn't sound as nervous as she felt. "They have so much in common, they don't need my quilting to predict anything."

"Do you mean to say you place no faith in your own creations?"

"No. I mean we're not all superstitious heathens out here, living for the next augury of chicken entrails." She wasn't about to admit to him that this was one of the few blocks she was having the dickens of a time with. Worse than with hers and Caleb's!

"Look out! Make way!"

Maude groaned as some careless dancers slammed into her, propelling her against Jack's chest. He was warm and very comfortable. Too comfortable!

Quickly she pulled away and turned around to give the offenders a piece of her mind. Instead, she could only give a sigh of resignation.

"I might've expected as much," she muttered as she watched Jessica bounce away, tugging along a reluctant-looking Matthew.

"If that careening object had wheels, it might've been a runaway stagecoach, but since it didn't, it might be your sister."

"No one but."

"Did she learn her dancing techniques from the Mongol Horde?"

"Yes."

"I don't recognize the poor unfortunate she's dragging around the floor."

"That's Matthew Conway."

"He doesn't seem to be able to dance very well."

"He might be very good if Jessica didn't continually step on his toes."

"He keeps pulling her off balance. That's why she steps on his toes."

"She steps on his toes, knocking him off balance."

"I'll concede the argument, not because you're right, but because I'd prefer to dance—not argue—in circles. So, who is he?"

"He moved here from Philadelphia about three years ago and opened a bookstore. Opens at nine, closes at six, six days a week, regular as clockwork. Every Friday afternoon he picks up his weekly order of groceries from Ingrams' store. Every Thursday, Widow Ross cleans house for him, and on Sunday he goes to church. He sings tenor in the choir. He was just elected recording secretary of the Savings and Loan—the youngest man ever to hold that office, according to Mr. Lester. He subscribes to my father's paper and occasionally writes a letter to the editor. He's a quiet, sensible fellow, careful with his money, almost, some might say, to the point of being miserly. But then, you know how some people in town like to talk.''

"Indeed, I do.''

"He's a temperance man. He's kind to animals—just the sort to make a good husband and father.''

"You seem to know an awful lot about him. So, I take it you've set your cap for him?''

"Matthew? Gracious, no! But—'' She watched as he and Jessica swirled between the other dancing couples.

"But you think he's just the sort of husband your sister needs.''

"Frankly, yes. Logically, a quiet man like Matthew would be just the sort to curb Jessica's spendthrift ways, make her stay home and tend to her housewifely duties.''

"So you're not just predicting happy marriages with your quilts. You're actually in the business of setting them up?''

"Don't be silly. This is America. A person is free to make his or her own choices.''

"You just sort of strongly suggest—''

Maude laughed aloud. "If you knew Jessica better, you'd know that whatever anyone suggests to her, she does the exact opposite.''

"I remember,'' he replied, rubbing his nose.

Suddenly Jessica and Matthew came careening by them again. "Papa's dancing with Miss Randolph,'' Jessica announced. "Again!''

6

"*AGAIN?*" MAUDE REPEATED. SHE frowned and searched the crowd. She blinked with surprise when she saw her father—Benjamin Franklin Griffith, the esteemed editor of the Apple Grove *Gazette*—escorting Adelaide Randolph around the dance floor.

Jessica continued to bounce in place in front of her as if her perpetual motion was the only thing that kept the planet revolving. "This is the third time he's danced with her, and we've only been here an hour."

"It's only a dance." Maude dismissed it all. "It doesn't mean anything."

"Maybe. Maybe not." Jessica bounded away, dragging Matthew along with her.

"Honestly, that girl has the most annoying habit of taking off without warning," Maude muttered.

But her sister was correct. Maude had been so busy listening to Caleb and watching out for Jack that she hadn't been paying the least bit of attention to her other responsibilities. A single dance didn't signify anything, she told herself again. Neither did two or three. What if they did? Wouldn't this be part of what she was hoping for? Part of the obligation she'd promised to fulfill?

"Looks as if your father's dancing with Miss Randolph again," Wilma said as she glided by in Peter Fitzroy's arms.

"Yes, indeed." Maude wondered if she stood in one place long enough, would the entire population of the town stroll by to tell her the momentous news?

"This is the second time he's danced with her this afternoon." Wilma laughed, but there was a certain snide pleasure Maude didn't think she was hiding very well.

"No, the third," Maude corrected on the strength of Jessica's information—if that could be deemed reliable. If it couldn't, so what? At least she'd had the satisfaction of appearing as if she knew more than Wilma.

"And you approve?" Wilma demanded.

"The choice really isn't mine to make, is it?" Maude countered.

"Well, I mean, he *is* your father!"

"Miss Randolph is a very nice lady."

Maude fairly pushed Jack over in her effort to direct his steps away from Wilma and Peter. She breathed a sigh of relief as she lost them again in the crowd.

Why should it surprise her so much to see her father escorting her former schoolteacher around the dance floor? The two had frequently met to discuss Georgie's recent, uncharacteristically poor achievements, and it was the polite thing to do, to dance with a lady he knew. He'd been a widower for many years. Miss Randolph had never married at all. It wasn't as if Maude didn't like her.

Suddenly she gave herself a little mental shake. Where in the world was she allowing her thoughts to take her? A single dance didn't *actually* signify anything important. After all, here she was, dancing with Suicide Jack, and that didn't mean anything at all—no, not at all!

Rafe, Herb, and Micky ended their song.

"Thank you for this dance, Maude," Jack said as he led her back to the sidelines.

Maude reasoned she ought to feel relieved as Jack released her. She didn't. For some reason she couldn't account for, as he released her hand, even in this crowd of people, she felt incredibly alone.

"I guess I'm just not much of a dancer, Miss Jessica," Matthew seemed to whine as he escorted Jessica to Maude's side.

"That's all right," Jessica replied lightly.

Maude was glad to see her sister being so pleasant to him.

"I'm really sorry about stepping on your feet, Miss Jessica," Matthew continued. "I really don't think your toe is broken."

"It's *all right,*" Jessica replied a little more forcefully.

"I hope you'll do me the honor of dancing with me again sometime," he ventured.

"Why, Mr. Conway, I'd be plumb tickled to dance with you again anytime," Jessica replied, flashing him her sweetest smile and casting him a look from under her long, dark eyelashes.

The little vixen! Maude thought. Poor Matthew had turned almost as red as the pickled beets Mrs. Crowley always brought to the Independence Day celebrations, and he was grinning from ear to ear as he sidled away. He'd be back, Maude felt sure.

To her side, Maude heard Jack give a little groan. She noted a bevy of girls watching him. She also noted Walt and Hiram descending upon him from the other side of the barn.

"Excuse me, Maude," Jack said with an exaggerated bow. "As a gracious guest, I have certain obligations to my hostess, and I'm afraid duty calls."

Maude watched him sidestep the onrushing couples as he crossed the barn toward the waiting damsels, and effectively cut off Hiram and Walt's pursuit. With moves like that, she was surprised he hadn't been able to elude the marshal and his posse when he'd robbed that bank.

"Do you still have those smelling salts you carried for the wedding?" Jessica asked.

"Not with me."

Jessica laughed. "Too bad. You know whichever one he picks is going to faint dead away from sheer ecstacy, and the rest are going to pass out from disappointment."

Maude gave a little cough. "Let them all collapse into a huge heap of dismayed femininity. I've had one dance with Jack—a highly overrated affair—and one was quite enough, thank you."

She was determined not to pay Jack any more attention, anyway. She was looking for Caleb.

"My goodness!" Jessica exclaimed. "He's picked Patsy Plain!"

"You're joking." Maude looked up in surprise.

Sure enough, there was Jack, escorting thin, quiet Ann Engles—who some of her less charitable sisters in town referred to as Patsy Plain—out onto the floor. Pathetic little Ann, who never could get that mouse-brown hair of hers to curl, not even with a curling iron, not even with spit and her fingers. Ann, whose large, pale blue eyes peered out owlishly from behind her spectacles. Ann, whose elderly, widowed mother wouldn't permit her to wear any color but gray or brown.

"Why on earth did he pick *her?*" Jessica demanded testily.

"Would you rather he'd picked you?" Maude asked slowly—almost, she reluctantly noted, as if she didn't want to hear the inevitable answer.

"Of course. I'm not completely senseless, you know. But . . . why, that girl wouldn't say 'boo' to a goose."

"Not everyone was blessed with a personality as dynamic as yours."

"Well, there she is." Jessica flung her hand out in a gesture of complete and overwhelming surprise. "Floating about the dance floor, the envy of every single girl in this place."

"Including you?"

"Yes."

Jessica was noted for her bluntness, Maude acknowledged. "But not me," she stated proudly.

"I swear, a body's got to give Jack his due. The man certainly knows how to create a furor."

"Indeed, he does," Maude admitted, keeping to herself her belief that the biggest furor he'd created yet today was the one within her own breast.

"Well, I'm not standing around here like the rest of the girls he didn't pick, gawking at the single men like a desperate old maid," Jessica declared. Turning around, she seized the hand of Bob, who had the misfortune of being closest to her, batted her long eyelashes at him, mesmerized him into putting down his mug of applejack, and hauled her willing victim out onto the dance floor.

Maude stood alone and watched the couples dancing in the center of the barn. Her father and Miss Randolph were still out there together. Willard had not yet managed to coax Katy away from the refreshments and out onto the dance floor. Blushing, beaming Ann was out there with Jack. Here she was, standing on the sidelines alone, like a desperate old maid.

She looked about for Caleb. He'd dance with her. He really ought to if they were going to be married someday. At last she spied him in the far corner, arguing with Mr. Lester again, with Edgar Baumgartner listening in. If she'd had to place a wager on the whole thing, she'd have said he didn't harbor a single thought about her—or any other lady at this gathering—at all.

Oh, well, she consoled herself as she turned as a last resort to the enticing offerings on the refreshment table, when a woman chooses to align herself with a man of destiny, she ought to become accustomed to spending a good deal of time alone.

Yes, indeed, she told herself as she drew nearer the table. Katy was correct. Those vanilla custards did look tasty. Standing in front of the refreshment table did look slightly better than standing completely alone on the sidelines.

She reached for another custard.

"If you eat too many of those, do you turn into a tweetle-bird?" Jack's voice flowed, warm and deep, over her ear.

Maude started and almost dropped her custard.

"I-I thought . . ." She fumbled with the custard dripping over and through her outspread fingers and reached for a napkin just out of her grasp. "I thought you were dancing with Ann."

Jack handed her a red-and-white-checkered napkin. "Is that her name?"

"Didn't you ask her?"

"Yes, but she didn't seem capable of speech at the time."

"You seem to have that effect on some women."

"I seem to recall a few times you were unable to answer me."

Maude mopped the custard off her fingers. "I wasn't unable to answer you. I simply deemed it more prudent at the time *not* to say what I was thinking."

Jack nodded. "Someday, will you tell me what you were thinking?"

"What happened to your dance with Ann?" Maude countered instead.

"I was very rudely interrupted by some fellow I didn't recognize, but apparently she knew, who was seized by the sudden, uncontrollable urge to dance with her. Who would've imagined she'd turn out to be so popular?"

"Only you, Jack."

"When I found myself again without a partner, however, I was seized by the sudden, uncontrollable urge to dance with you." He held his hand out to her.

Maude watched him in a frozen state. "But . . . there are so many others you haven't danced with yet, waiting—"

"They'll still be here when we get back."

She would have added, "So many others more willing," if he'd let her. She had no idea what he was trying to prove. Unlike Ann, she certainly didn't need his charity. It couldn't be because he truly enjoyed dancing with her when she thought she'd made it pretty clear she didn't like him, and refused to fawn all over him like the other girls did. Nevertheless, there he was, asking her again for a dance.

One dance didn't mean anything, she repeated to herself. Not even two. She took his hand.

∞

JACK SAT ON THE edge of his bed, fully dressed and waiting in the dark. Dang, he hated this secondhand jacket! It reeked of whiskey, no matter how many times he had it cleaned.

It was too soon. They wouldn't communicate with him yet. He'd only just arrived and hadn't had time to scout the place, and they should know it. He'd had no time to find out if things were still kept in the same places they were when he'd left Apple Grove four years ago. The town had grown a lot since then.

Neither had he had the time to talk to folks he knew, find out who could forgive and forget, and who still harbored old animosities—although just from the wedding this afternoon, he had a good idea. He'd had no time to find out who the new people were and where they'd come from; find out who he might be able to use in his plan or if he was on his own with this one, too.

Walt and Hiram were bound to prove troublesome. Those two were always trying to stir something up. As he recalled, skinny Walt, who looked like a stiff breeze could blow him over, would start the argument in the saloon, and burly Hiram would be only too quick and too glad to offer to take it outside and finish it.

He didn't know the new sheriff, Orville Tucker, either. Louise had written him a few years back that old Sheriff Fischer had taken a bullet to the leg from a rowdy drunk and died of lead poisoning not long afterward. And Molly—Jack grinned at the recollection—had met a man who had struck it rich in the silver mines of Nevada and was traveling homeward. She'd married him, set up an ostentatious marble monument for her father—a body riding into or out of town couldn't miss the danged, angel-laden monstrosity—and moved to New York City.

Jack lit the lamp on the small round table beside his bed and checked his gun and his ammunition one more time. He hefted his gun, a Remington-Rider five-shot .31-calibre in blue plate with an ivory grip. He hadn't liked the look of the mother-of-pearl handle, and didn't like the way the gutta-percha felt. He liked the way the ivory felt in his hand, warm and smooth, and tried not to think of the huge beast that had lost its life so he could take the lives of human beings.

He didn't think he'd need to use his gun tonight, but he had to be prepared. A good gun, a tough pony—those were about the only two things a man in his position could rely on.

What a stroke of luck he'd been able to combine his cousin's wedding with this job! Who'd have thought they'd be planning on hitting the savings and loan in his own hometown?

Somehow he'd figured he'd just come here, pay a long-awaited visit to his family, and get the job done. Then, just as easily, he'd be on his way again. No complications. No entanglements. Just another job.

He'd never figured that seeing Maude again would have this effect on him. Except to tease her, he'd never given her a moment's thought in his young life. He hadn't given her a second thought when the war started, either. He'd been sixteen, and she was only thirteen. Even though she'd been fun to torment in school, she wasn't exactly interesting then, and the prospect of fighting had seemed so much more so.

Jack gave a disgruntled snort. Lots of things never turned out to be how they seemed.

When he'd returned home after the war, it wasn't hard to leave again. Half the people in town hated him because they could never be sure which side he'd fought on, and he could never tell them. Maude had been seventeen then. A little prettier, and a whole lot more grown-up since her mother had died. But he'd been twenty, in his prime, and anxious to get out and make his fortune, like that foolish Caleb. Boy, he'd sure like to set that jackass straight on a few matters concerning the reality of life in a mining camp.

Things were a lot different now. He was twenty-six. He was tired of traveling, tired of risking his life, tired of taking lives. Maybe he was even entertaining dangerous thoughts of settling down, buying a farm, finding a wife, raising a family. Maude was twenty-three and still playing little mother to that heedless, helpless family of hers. It was about time she got set straight on a few matters concerning what real life was like, too. It worried him a bit that he'd actually be the first to volunteer for the job.

When he'd come back this time, he'd never counted on finding Maude looking so beautiful, so rounded and desirable. No, he told himself, it wasn't only because he'd recently been released from prison, either. None of the other women in town looked as good to him as Maude.

This time, there was just something appealing about the way she bustled busily about, trying desperately to keep everything under control when she couldn't even control what was going on in her own life. Something about the lavender scent of her thick, dark hair twisted back into a prim bun. Something about her sparkling blue eyes that challenged him to misbehave just once, and she'd box his ears. Something about that smug, self-confident grin on her full, rosy lips that just begged to be softened by his kisses.

Keep your mind on your work, boy, he told himself gruffly.

He ran his fingers through his hair and stood up. He tucked his gun back into the holster he'd slung on his hip for quicker access on tonight's foray. He blew out the lamp.

∽

"YOU'D THINK I'D DROP right off to sleep just as soon as my head touched the pillow, wouldn't you?" Maude questioned thin air as she lay under her quilt, staring up at the ceiling of her bedroom. "You'd think after dancing the night away, I'd hardly make it up the stairs. But no."

She gave the uncooperative pillow a thump on the chance that its misalignment might be all that stood between her and a good night's rest. She sighed and flipped over to one side. The wall her bed was set against was dark and blank—perfectly boring— just the sort of thing to make her fall asleep. But it didn't.

She flipped over to the other side.

The Kingstons' house raised a dark silhouette against the starry sky. The pale upper branches of the sycamore cast a tracery of white over the house, like a spider's web. She'd already tried counting sheep, and that hadn't worked. Maybe she ought to try counting stars. She'd start at one end of the Kingstons' roof and work her way over to the other.

"I hope Louise and Fred will be happy in their new house," she said as she gazed out her window. "I hope they're sleeping better than I am—oh! No, don't think about *that!*"

Restless at the mere suggestion of what her friend and her new husband might be doing, Maude was just about to flip over again when she noticed a flickering light coming from the house next door. She sat bolt upright in bed.

"A fire?"

She rushed to the window, but by the time she got there, the light had gone out. Suddenly she caught a glimpse of a dark shadow in the bare branches of the sycamore.

"What in tarnation is that?"

She hadn't heard of any mountain lions venturing into Iowa lately. She hadn't read any reports coming into her father's newspaper office regarding any lions escaping from any traveling circuses. She didn't think any tigers that might have escaped from the Lincoln Zoo in Chicago could wander all the way into Iowa without being spotted. But she wasn't about to take any chances.

If it had managed to climb that far up into the tree, what was to stop it from making the short leap into her home—or the Kingstons'—and devouring them all? She should warn them!

Then she noticed the shadow was moving down the tree, not up it. The moon was at the waxing quarter, so she couldn't see very well. But as the dark object moved against the pale branches, she could clearly see it was human—and there was only one human being she knew who'd be crazy enough to pull a stunt like this.

"Bless my soul! It's Suicide Jack."

7

"WHAT DOES HE THINK he's doing?" Maude demanded, speaking more loudly than she'd dared before.

After all, she didn't have to worry that some raging mountain lion would hear her, mistakenly think she was extending him an invitation to dinner, leap into her room, and devour her. It was only Jack. What if Jack should leap into her room? No, she refused to speculate on it. Why would he even want to come to her, anyway—except to annoy her? For goodness' sake, he was still outside and he was doing that!

"Just look at him! He probably still thinks he's as limber as a ten-year-old."

But how could she be scornful of his physical condition when she hadn't been able to ignore his broad shoulders and the strong muscles of his chest when Jessica had pushed her against him? Still, she worried, big muscles don't necessarily constitute agility.

"That oaf is going to fall, land on his head, and break his thick skull. Papa'll be only too happy to hold the undertaker's jacket while he fits him into his coffin. Albert will rejoice in his complete vindication when Mr. Volz actually carves 'Suicide Jack' on the headstone. Come to think of it, there'd probably be a few people who'd try to bribe Doc Ketcham to pronounce Jack dead even if he wasn't." Her eyes narrowed. "Then watch that horrible Mrs. Hardesty, and Walt and Hiram, and all those others, gather 'round his coffin just to gloat.''

Which will you be? the little voice inside her head slyly inquired of her. *A gloater? Or a mourner?*

''What if he only breaks a leg or two?'' she murmured, trying to distract herself from the troubling question, and the even more troublesome answer.

Then, instead of leaving town immediately after the wedding, he'd be convalescing in his aunt's home, and she'd be stuck with having him right next door all summer.

It looked as if he'd changed into completely dark clothes. If the tree had been covered with leaves, she'd never have noticed him, but his somber silhouette contrasted too sharply with the pale branches.

''What's he doing climbing down the tree, anyway?''

Jack never had been one to refuse a dare, no matter how ridiculous or dangerous. But she didn't see a drunken, cheering crowd standing around below, waiting to find out who won the bet.

Even if he was answering the call of nature, Mr. and Mrs. Kingston wouldn't be annoyed if he just walked through the house and used the back door, like ordinary people did. If he was too lazy or too drunk to get up, there was always the chamber pot under the bed.

Why wasn't he carrying some sort of lantern? Admittedly, it would be difficult to carry one while climbing a tree, but that brought Maude right back around to her original question—what was Jack doing sneaking out of the house in the middle of the night?

There could be only one reason for all this dark, midnight madness. He didn't want anyone to know he was leaving.

Jack dropped safely to the ground and quickly sought the shadows at the side of the Kingstons' house. He disappeared, but she still watched. She knew better than to trust Jack.

Sure enough, he reappeared, heading across the frontyard into town.

''Why? All the good townspeople—and even the ones with more dubious reputations—are asleep in their beds. Except Jack and me.''

How she hated to place herself in the same category as that reprobate!

"There's only one way to find out what he's up to."

She pulled her dark blue skirt over her nightgown. She slipped into her shoes. The insides felt cold and rough to her bare feet, but she didn't have time to bother with stockings and garters—not if she wanted to keep pace with Jack. She grabbed her black woolen shawl—the good one she always wore to funerals—not the old white one, which would be far too noticeable. She pulled the shawl up to cover her head. If Jack could play this silly game of camouflage, she could, too.

"This is so unlike me!"

But she just *had* to do it!

Noiselessly she closed the bedroom door behind her. If she *had* to go sneaking out after Jack, at least she could try to keep it a secret, even from her family.

"No more talking to yourself, either."

Maude made her way down the front stairs. What if the hinges squeaked and Jack heard them? Then he'd know someone was following.

The door swung open silently. Maude breathed a sigh of relief and allowed herself just enough space to slip through. She waited on the porch until she spotted Jack again, down by the turn in the road where Elm Street met Main Street. Now, she figured. It was safe to follow him now.

∽

SOMEONE WAS FOLLOWING HIM. He could feel it in his bones, in the tingling of his scalp, the prickling of his ears—just the sort of sixth sense that had seen him through dangerous situations in the past. But who? His family, neighbors, or friends would call out to him.

So would Runt—Jack chuckled as he recalled the nickname he'd given him. Georgie had grown from the worshipful little boy who had shadowed him around when he returned from the war into a tall, sturdy, but shy youth. He'd changed in other ways, too. Now he seemed more concerned with being late for school than he seemed to be eager to go on adventures with Jack.

Maude seemed to think he was a complete waste of humanity, and wouldn't trust him an inch. She'd noticed his gun. That might give her reason to keep an eye on him. On the other hand, she was too sensible to be traipsing around in the middle of the night—especially not after him.

"Jessica," Jack muttered and shook his head. No one could ever accuse her of being shy or sensible. This was just the sort of thing she'd do. What might she tell the townspeople of this adventure?

Should he postpone his reconnaissance? But the moon was waxing, and each passing night made it increasingly difficult to slip around undetected. He didn't know how much longer he had to get the necessary information, either. The last thing he needed was for something to happen and him not to be prepared for it. In his line of work, that was how men got killed.

He kept walking into town.

As he crossed Mill Street, the darkened houses gave way to neat shops. Suddenly he stopped, pretending he'd found something mighty fascinating in Chalky Pike's clothing store window. Jessica would have to pull up awful quick if she didn't want to run into him.

Out of the corner of his eye he noticed her stop and flatten herself against the wall of the store on the corner. Did she believe that shawl she'd thrown over her head provided camouflage? She might as well have stuck twigs in her hair and tried to pretend she was a bush that happened to be growing in the middle of the sidewalk.

Wait a minute!

Jack frowned and examined the figure more closely out of the corner of his eye. He'd studied those appealing curves very carefully during the wedding service and while she'd been dancing with him. That wasn't Jessica. It was Maude! What in the world was *Maude* doing following him?

His frown deepened. For the first time in his life, he'd sorely misjudged a person. He shouldn't be slipping like this. In his line of work, one mistake, one misinterpretation of whom he could trust—even a seemingly harmless old maid keeping house for her widowed father—could mean his life. What was he going to do? Could he trust Maude to keep her mouth shut? Should he confront her? Or should he just get on with his job?

He headed past the Masonic Lodge with its two gleaming, white-painted wooden columns on either side of the single entrance, and moved on to his destination—the red brick building next door that housed the savings and loan.

The iron-banded front door was securely locked. Iron bars, firmly cemented into the bricks, crossed the single front window.

Before venturing down the alley, he pushed back the front of his jacket to allow easier access to his gun, should he need it. Would Maude be foolish enough to continue to follow him? There wasn't much he could do to stop her if he wasn't supposed to know she was there. He wasn't expecting trouble this soon, but if there was any, he hoped she'd have enough sense to stay out of his way.

Neither the brick wall on one side, nor the clapboard wall on the other side of the alley had windows. The single window at the rear of the bank was just as securely barred as the front. The back door didn't look as heavily metaled as the front, but that could be deceiving.

Cautiously he returned through the alley, looking in both directions before stepping out into the street. All he had left to do was check the building on the other side of the bank—the Fitzroys' Regal Hotel.

He chuckled. Imagine them taking on such airs, just because Mr. Fitzroy's family maintained the old tale that they were descended from some English king's bastard way back when! But the hotel had two stories and a railed balcony running across the front with several windows looking out over it. It was a place where strangers were always coming and going. That could mean big trouble for him.

He looked up and down the street for Maude, but he couldn't find her. She'd probably gone home, feeling certain, from what she'd seen, that all her original condemnations of him were justified. She probably wouldn't be bothering him much anymore while he was here. Just as well, he thought with a shrug. Keep her out of danger.

8

"SO I LAID MY gun on the table, pulled the ace out of his sleeve, and said, 'Gentlemen, I think this pot's mine.' " Jack finished his tale just as Maude and Georgie entered Ingrams' store.

The crowd of men grouped around the pot-bellied stove laughed uproariously. No matter what the rest of the story might have been, Maude didn't think the joke could have been all that funny. She wasn't surprised to see Hiram and Walt there—those two always managed to weasel their way out of doing an honest day's work. She was surprised to see Willard Konigsberg sitting there when he was usually working his farm.

"Oh, swell! Jack's still here!" Georgie exclaimed. "He was still sleeping when I left for school this morning."

Maude wasn't surprised. "Going to school is more important."

"Shucks, no. School's always here, but Jack's never here long enough."

"Georgie, wait!"

But it was too late. Her brother was already making a beeline for the crowd. Then he hung back and perched himself atop one of the big barrels, as if he were too shy to allow himself to become a part of the group.

In spite of their mother's chronic illness and the hard time she'd had giving birth to him, Georgie had been a robust, happy baby. After all the attention the adorable, tearful five-year-old had received at his mother's funeral, Maude would have thought her brother would have grown up to be more outgoing. Instead, he'd curled up inside himself with his toys and then his books. Not that reading was bad, but she wished he had more friends.

When he did take his baseball and bat outside, he was always by himself; he'd just toss the ball into the air and try to hit it on the way down. Maybe if their mother had lived a little longer, she'd have helped Georgie make friends more easily. Maybe if their father hadn't tried to bury himself in his work and paid a little more attention to what his family was doing, Georgie wouldn't be so shy. Maude had tried, but she guessed she hadn't done enough—and Jessica was no help at all!

Maybe if Jack hadn't been away when Mama died, Maude thought. Georgie adored Jack, and had never learned the devilishly charming man couldn't be trusted. He'd always looked up to Jack as a beloved older brother—until he'd run away to war without a word of good-bye. Georgie had forgiven him too easily when Jack had returned, and been betrayed again when Jack left a second time, just as abruptly, to go who-knew-where.

Now Jack was back, and Georgie was ready to forgive again. What could she do to protect her brother if he insisted on leaving himself vulnerable to callous people like Jack?

Maude tactfully skirted the group and, with the deliberate intention of completely ignoring Jack and his outlandish tales, she inspected the contents of the glass cases and the colorful labels of boxes and bottles lined up on crowded shelves.

Mrs. Ingram emerged from the back room, dusting her hands off on the front of her crisp, white apron. "So, Maude, to help you today, what can I do?"

"A set of those tortoiseshell combs, please." Maude indicated the least expensive pair displayed under the counter.

"To buy expensive ones there is no sense if Jessica will bounce them away with the dancing."

"She can't *walk* without losing something." Maude twisted her lips.

"Never worry. Mr. Kingston's horse the combs will find— and then, so pretty he will look!" She patted her own steel-gray hair in imitation.

Maude chuckled. Mrs. Ingram was a dear to try to cheer her up, but why was she feeling so gloomy in the first place? Watching Jack inspecting the bank meant nothing to her—not unless he actually robbed the place. Even then, what did Jack mean to her?

"Anything else?"

Maude hated to request this. "A bottle of Clark Stanley's Snake Oil Liniment."

"*Ach,* too much the papa has been dancing," Mrs. Ingram commented with a laugh as she placed the bottle on the counter.

Maude didn't mind buying her father the liniment. A man his age needed relief from his rheumatism. She didn't mind him keeping company with Miss Randolph, either. It was just, somehow it didn't seem proper to her that he should be needing liniment *because* of Miss Randolph!

The crowd around Jack laughed again.

"All day the funny tales Jack has been telling."

"I hope whatever he's telling them is suitable for the ears of a fourteen-year-old boy. Perhaps I should listen, just in case—"

Mrs. Ingram waved her index finger back and forth in front of Maude. "For a boy of fourteen years, perhaps. For you, no."

"But, I have a responsibility—"

"A son I have raised who did not turn out half so bad, I think. Leave Georgie alone." Mrs. Ingram must have thought Maude still looked doubtful. "If the tales best left to the barroom Jack starts telling, one of the other men the good sense will have to up shut Jack—or off chase Georgie—or the boy something new will learn."

Maude could hardly be rude and tell Mrs. Ingram she didn't know what she was talking about, or correct her English. The best thing to do under the circumstances would be to finish shopping and take Georgie home.

"I also need a spool of thread."

"Of course, now that the quilt for Louise you have finished, the quilt for Florence you must start."

"Yes, I must." Maude couldn't bring herself to confide, even to discreet, sympathetic Mrs. Ingram, that she'd already started working on it, and it wasn't turning out well at all.

"To see it, I cannot wait," Mrs. Ingram said as she wrapped everything in crisp brown paper. "As lovely as all the others it will be. As happy as all the others, Florence and Mr. Baumgartner will be.''

"Thank you for your confidence in me and my work, Mrs. Ingram." Maude only wished she herself still felt as confident of her skills.

She turned to find Georgie still hanging at the edge of the crowd. *Oh, Lord,* she thought, *please don't let me have any trouble dragging this poor child away from the temptations described so enticingly by Suicide Jack.*

"Georgie."

He was leaning forward, chin in hands, elbows on knees, listening to every word Jack uttered. She got no answer.

"Georgie!" She tapped him on the shoulder.

He started. "What? Oh, no! Not you!" His outburst was half whine, half protest.

"That's a fine greeting for your loving sister."

He grimaced. "What do you want?"

"It's time to go home."

"I want to listen to Jack some more." His blue eyes gleamed. "He's got some really exciting tales—"

"Oh, he's full of tales," Maude agreed sarcastically.

"Don't be so stuffy, Maude. He's really swell! You'd laugh yourself silly listening to him. I never would've imagined going out West could be so much fun!"

"That's because, in truth, it probably isn't. You're a very sensible young man and should've figured that out already."

"But that man Molly Fischer married struck it rich," Georgie protested. "Caleb's bound to strike it rich, too."

She could hardly deny that, but still, she ought to warn him about Jack. "Don't allow yourself to be swayed by any fabrications a drifter like Jack has to tell."

"He's *not* a drifter," Georgie protested. "He lives next door. He just has to travel a lot because of his job."

Maude pursed her lips. "We don't even know what his job is—*if* he actually has one. Come along, now. It's time to begin dinner. We have to go home."

"What do you mean 'we'? *I* don't have to start dinner."

"You have chores to do before you settle down to your studies," she reminded him firmly.

"But I don't have to keep hanging around you everywhere you go, like some sort of baby—"

"Babies don't have chores or studies. Now, come along."

Before Georgie could slide down from atop the barrel, the shop door flew open. The two little brass bells hanging at the top of the door jingled madly.

Gordon Potter stood poised in the doorway—one thumb tucked into the top of his gray pinstripe trousers, the other hand holding a long, brown cigar with a smoking, glowing red tip— as if he were waiting for everyone to admire him.

Maude didn't care if smug, self-important Gordon Potter did own the only shipping line into town or that it supplied her father's newspaper with ink and newsprint. All that would change whenever the railroad finally ran a spur into town. She didn't care if he was planning on running for mayor in the next election, and everyone said he was sure to win. If she could vote, she certainly wouldn't vote for him. She didn't care that he admitted to having his sights set on the governorship or beyond. She didn't like him, and when she finally married Caleb Johnson she was *not* going to invite Gordon Potter to the wedding.

She sniffed. Already she could feel her eyes beginning to water and her nose to run. Mr. Potter hadn't been inside two minutes, and already his cigar was smoking up the entire store.

Maude found herself pondering why Mr. Potter's cigar reeked, yet there was a pleasant, earthy smell of tobacco about Jack. It certainly couldn't be because she liked Jack better than she did Mr. Potter. Well, she didn't like either one of them—especially not after what she'd witnessed last night.

"Well, well," Mr. Potter drawled slowly. Even though they parted before him, he still seemed to find it necessary to shoulder a few men out of his way as he sauntered through the crowd toward Jack. "If it isn't James Kingston, returned once again to favor our fair town with his glorious presence."

"Yeah, that's me." Jack leaned back in his chair, stretched his long legs out in front of him, and laced his fingers together behind his head. In his ill-fitting, coarse wool jacket and worn boots, he looked as supremely self-confident as Mr. Potter in his tailored jacket and custom-made shoes.

Mr. Potter slapped him heartily on the back. Jack just gave the man a wary grin.

"Golly, Maude," Georgie whispered. "Mr. Potter looks like he wants to beat Jack senseless by way of greeting."

Maude shrugged. "Well, why not?" This might be just the

opportunity her father'd been waiting for. She wondered if she ought to run next door and get him so he could hold Mr. Potter's coat.

"Sam Ferguson told me you were back, and I almost fired him on the spot, because I'm not particularly fond of liars," Mr. Potter said smoothly. "I said to myself, that damned Suicide Jack wouldn't be stupid enough to come back here now, not after all these years, not after everything that's happened."

Jack continued to give him an icy stare. "I might be stupid, but I'm not so cold-hearted I'd miss my only cousin's wedding."

Mr. Potter had hated Jack ever since he'd come back from the war and his son, Clarence, hadn't. Mr. Potter wasn't the only person in Apple Grove who had lost a loved one in the fighting, and Jack wasn't the only man from Apple Grove who had survived. Mr. Potter wasn't the only one who perpetuated a loved one's memory, either—although Maude was surprised Mr. Potter hadn't yet erected a monument to his son to rival Sheriff Fischer's. He certainly had enough money. But for some reason, Mr. Potter was the only one who had singled out Jack personally to blame for his son's death.

"You know, some of the boys brought back little reminders with them. You know, souvenirs. What did you bring back, Jack?"

With his index finger, Jack drew a line along his left side. "I got a nasty scar right about here." He traced the line on his other side, too. "Or is it here? Yeah, I brought it back with me. But I'm not all that fond of it, and I'd just as soon not have it, so I try not to pay too much attention to it. But I figure, as I'm stuck with this thing, I don't really need or want anything else to remind me of war anymore."

"Some of our boys wore their old uniforms," Mr. Potter persisted, as if everything Jack had just said meant no more than if he'd whistled in a wind storm. "Belt buckle. Knapsack. What did you bring back?"

With a wary chuckle, Jack replied, "I never did see much use in keeping old, worn-out things that I hope to God I'll never need again."

"Robbin' banks'd get ya enough money to buy a new suit," Walt interjected with a laugh.

"Not if you get caught," Jack reminded him.

"I heard when ya leave prison they give you a new suit o'

clothes,'' Hiram said, chuckling at his own and his friend's wit.

"*And* a five-dollar bill,'' Jack added without missing a breath.

"When you first came home, I noted that while your jacket was the truest shade of blue ever to grace a Northern boy, you had a strange-looking pair of boots and the oddest color trousers.''

"I'm flattered you noticed so much about me.''

"Your belt buckle didn't seem to match any of the ones issued to Federal troops. So I'm asking you now why it should be that you'd be wearing parts of a uniform from one side and parts from another.''

Jack averted his gaze from the curious men surrounding him. Could it be, Maude wondered, that some people in town were right? That Jack did have something to hide?

He looked directly at her. Why would he do that? she asked herself. It wasn't as if she knew the answer to the question and he didn't, and he was trying to coax her into telling him, as he had during all their examinations in school. It wasn't as if she could help him out of this fix by dancing with him.

Jack drew in a deep breath and let out a forlorn sigh. "I know I should be ashamed to admit it. . . .''

The men leaned forward. In spite of herself, and her own determination to remain disinterested in Jack and anything that had to do with him, Maude found herself listening intently. This just might be the answer they'd all been waiting nearly ten years for, the answer to the question they'd all been too cautious—or too afraid—to ask.

Exactly which side *had* Jack fought on?

9

"I'LL ADMIT," JACK SAID slowly, dragging his hand across his lean face as if trying to wipe away bad memories, "during the hardest days of the war, when we had nothing to eat but hardtack and weevils, and a man would sell his soul for a sip of water; during the coldest nights of winter, when snow lay knee-deep, when every breath a man took to keep body and soul together seared down through his windpipe, froze his lungs, and threatened to suffocate him to death instead..."

Goodness gracious, Maude thought. Jack ought to go onto the stage. He certainly knew how to keep this crowd of shrewd merchants, tough farmers, and coarse wagoneers hanging on his every word.

"...I wasn't above scavenging the belongings of a fallen comrade." Jack hung his head. Then, in a voice barely above a whisper, yet carried to every corner of the store, he continued, "I pray the Lord, and that poor man, and all his loved ones, will forgive me my shameful thievery."

He lifted his head and looked at his audience with a bold challenge in his gaze.

"But when I was soaking wet and fairly freezing, when I couldn't even feel my fingers and toes anymore, I felt certain that this fine fellow, who'd shuffled off this mortal coil to leave this veil of tears, wouldn't begrudge me a few paltry items he no longer had need of here on earth when he'd claimed his treasure laid up in heaven.''

Goodness, Maude decided, if he didn't go onto the stage, he could certainly make a living from the pulpit or, if he could find a good choir, even take a traveling camp meeting on the road.

Some of the men seemed to find his actions reprehensible— but they'd have found fault with Jack no matter what. There might even be one or two people, such as herself, who saw through his tales to the fantastical constructions they undoubtedly were, and didn't believe him for an instant.

If one really considered, Jack hadn't said precisely what he'd taken from that soldier, or which sides they'd been fighting for. Knowing Jack, more than likely he'd actually got whatever it was by duping some gullible innocent in a crooked game of chance.

Georgie leaned over and whispered, ''I'm glad he found someone whose things fit him.''

Maude sighed. There would always be some naive soul—like Georgie—who was forever ready to excuse and forgive, and be hurt once again.

''I'm just curious, Jack, you know,'' Mr. Potter continued, ''because my boy Clarence wrote me saying he'd seen you the night before, at the Federal encampment at Vicksburg—''

''I recall writing home to Aunt Nell about that very same encounter, and how much I enjoyed seeing a familiar face.''

Jack's eyes were brighter and more alert now, Maude thought as she studied his face, almost as if he were on the lookout for trouble. He'd certainly come to the right place for that, she figured. Even if he hadn't, trouble always seemed to have a way of finding Jack.

''In the last letter he ever wrote to his ma and me,'' Mr. Potter continued, ''Clarence told us how you'd sat there the night before battle, with him and the other fellows with Lawler's Brigade.''

''It was good to sit in front of a homey fire, with a fairly drinkable cup of coffee, and catch up on—''

''He said you also speculated on the positioning and disposition of the troops for the coming battle.''

''Just about the same thing every man in every battle has done since war began.''

"Our Iowa boys took the devil of a beating capturing that Railroad Redoubt—almost as if them damn Rebs knew exactly where to shoot."

"It doesn't take too many brains to figure out to shoot at the folks who are coming at you firing guns."

"And then, it was all for nothing. They had to surrender the damn thing again to the Rebs. I hate to think my boy died for nothing."

"He didn't—" Jack's voice was insistent, but Mr. Potter cut him off again.

"I hate to think he's lying now in his cold, lonely grave in some far-off cemetery in Rebel territory."

"It's all Union now, Mr. Potter," Jack reminded him.

"When you came back after the war ended, I didn't know some of the things I know now. The more I got to thinking about it, the more I got to wondering how it was that you hadn't signed up with the Twenty-first like Clarence did, like Bob and Albert, and Melvin Crowley, who didn't come back, either. So I called in a few favors with friends—political friends—in the War Department. They looked up a few things, and they tell me they can't find any record of any James Kingston, James Madison Kingston, or Jack Kingston with the other Iowa boys in Lieutenant Byers' Company E, Fifth Infantry, either."

"Yeah, what about that, Jack?" Hiram demanded, firing up the crowd.

"If I were you," Jack said, "I wouldn't have bothered."

The men leaned forward again. Maude held her breath. Would Jack now confess to what so many people in town already suspected—that he'd actually joined a Confederate brigade? That he'd actually fought *against* his own fellow Iowans?

"Don't tell me you never did any fighting at all!"

Mr. Potter's voice was rising. His face was growing redder with every angry word. The crowd was silent, waiting. Out of the corner of her eye, Maude saw Mrs. Ingram reaching for her stout broom handle, just in case she needed to keep the peace.

"My boy saw you. Are you calling my boy a liar?"

Very slowly and calmly, Jack glanced around, staring them all down with a frigid, green glare. "If you'll settle down, you'll be able to think more clearly, and recall correctly, Mr. Potter—and every last one of you—that when the war started and the recruiters came around to Apple Grove, they told me I was too young to sign up. So, as you'll also recall, I ran away from home. I not only had to lie about my age and where I'd come from in order to enlist, I gave them a false name, as well.''

"Ah, yes," Mr. Potter remarked as if it was no miraculous revelation to him, "I'd forgotten lying was a particular talent of yours.''

Maude gritted her teeth. Why didn't Jack call Mr. Potter out into the street for a duel after an insult like that? Even more astonishing—why was she suddenly taking Jack's side?

Jack threw Mr. Potter a mocking grin. "I'm afraid I'm not as good—or as bad—as you give me credit for, Mr. Potter. In one matter, I did tell the truth. I *am* an orphan.''

Jack rose from his chair. Mr. Potter stood his ground, but a few of the men scooted back the chairs and empty crates they sat on, or backed up a pace or two. Maude didn't blame them. After all, who knew what a man like Jack could do when he was riled?

These men probably didn't know about the gun he carried. Maude felt sure he was still wearing it today, hidden beneath his coat. If trouble started, could she hustle Georgie out the back door of the store without getting wounded or killed?

"Tell you what, Mr. Potter," Jack said, tapping the air in front of the man's chest with his index finger without ever touching him. "Next time you have your influential friends at the War Department do some checking for you, why don't you have them see if they can find a John Smith? That *might* be me. Now, if you'll excuse me, gentlemen.''

Once again, Maude had to give Jack credit. He hadn't even given the man a hint about which state's rosters to check.

"Wait a minute, Kingston!" Mr. Potter roared. "This isn't over yet!''

"Yes, it is," Jack replied with amazing calm in the face of Mr. Potter's storm of anger. "You see, I have a lovely lady and a young gentleman here—neighbors of mine—in need of my assistance.''

Jack gestured toward Maude and Georgie. Why did he have to drag her and her brother into this?

"It would be rude to ignore them. I may be a dirty, lying skunk, Mr. Potter, but I'm not rude.''

Leaving Mr. Potter with his cigar hanging limp from his fingers, Jack strolled through the dividing crowd, and headed directly toward Georgie.

"So what'll it be today, Runt?"

"Peppermint!" Georgie replied and slid down from atop the barrel.

"Georgie, you'll spoil your dinner," Maude cautioned.

"Oh, Maude, don't be such a wet blanket." Georgie laughed as he and Jack headed for the jars of candy Mrs. Ingram kept on top of the counter. "You remembered, Jack."

"Of course, Runt. How could I forget when every day I asked you the same question, and you made it your solemn duty to come up with a different answer, and Mrs. Ingram made it her solemn duty to provide us with a different selection of candy?"

Mrs. Ingram lifted the lid off the jar. Georgie eagerly pulled out a stick.

Jack laughed again. "The last time I was here, I had to grab you under both arms and hoist you up so you could see over the top of the counter. You shot up like a weed in wet weather. I reckon I can't rightly call you Runt anymore now, can I?"

"Not hardly."

Maude had gotten used to her little brother slowly growing year by year until, at last, he was taller than she was. She could just imagine what a surprise it must be to Jack, who hadn't seen "Runt" in four years, to see almost eye to eye with him and see his shoulders almost as broad as his own. She had to laugh as she watched Georgie straighten his back and lift his chin, trying to pull himself up even taller.

"See, I'm almost as tall as you."

Jack placed his hand on top of Georgie's head and lightly pushed down. "You're not quite fully grown—only mostly grown."

Then Jack turned to her. "What will you have, Miss Maude? Peppermint? Lemon drops?"

"Nothing, thank you."

Jack dug into his pocket and pulled out a small coin purse that jingled and sagged with the weight of its contents. A few silver dollars, perhaps, Maude speculated. Lots of copper cents.

"Candy isn't an inappropriate gift for a lady to receive from a gentleman—or even from me," he cajoled, giving her a wink. "One little piece isn't going to ruin your appetite—or your reputation."

"Thank you, no," Maude repeated a little more forcefully. She didn't know where his money had come from—she didn't want to know. But she wasn't about to have him spend any of his ill-gotten gains on her.

Jack dumped a small part of the contents of the purse into his hand, thumbed several shiny coins onto the counter, then slid the remainder back into the bag.

Maude blinked with surprise. Where on earth had he gotten *that much* money? Had he actually robbed the bank last night after all? Surely Mr. Lester or one of the clerks would have noticed the loss by now and raised the hue and cry.

Could she tell them anything? *Should* she tell them anything? After all, what was there to tell—that Jack had a gun? So did everyone else, except maybe the Reverend Hoffmann. That she'd seen Jack prowling around town in the middle of the night? Half the town would be ready to string Jack up as a common thief. The other half worshipped him and would string her up as a dirty snitch. How would she explain how she'd come to see him? Better to keep her mouth shut, she figured—for now.

"Miss Maude," Jack said, offering her his elbow, "if I can't persuade you to have some candy, may I at least escort you and Runt home?"

"Ha! You can't call me Runt anymore!" Georgie declared. He stuck the peppermint stick into his shirt pocket and bolted for the door. "I'll race you home!"

With Georgie making his hasty exit a challenge to Jack, Maude supposed she didn't have any choice. Now she *had* to walk home with Jack.

What in the world could she and Jack possibly discuss on the way home? she worried as they headed out the door. His prison cell? The number of cockroaches in prison food? To get all that money, who did he have to rob or kill?

10

MAUDE BREATHED A SIGH of relief when she spotted Georgie waiting out on the sidewalk. *He* could always find something to talk to Jack about, and now she didn't have to.

Georgie leaned against the rail, crossed his arms over his chest, and grinned at Jack. "I was going to race you home, and then I thought maybe I ought to have mercy and give a decrepit old man like you a chance for a head start."

That was even better, she decided. A race would get them both out of her way, and she could walk home in peace.

Jack rubbed the small of his back and chuckled. "I'm afraid even a head start wouldn't help a decrepit old man like me today, Runt."

"Too much celebrating yesterday for you to handle?" Georgie teased.

More than likely he'd thrown his back out climbing down that tree after all, Maude decided.

"You know, Runt, it's a beautiful day. Why don't we just take a leisurely stroll?"

Just what she needed, Maude silently lamented. Not only did she have to walk home with Jack, but now he was intent on prolonging her misery.

"So, what are you studying in school nowadays, Runt?"

"Not much."

"You can't tell me you've studied all the Plato, Shakespeare, Pythagoras, and Michelangelo a man can handle."

"About all *I* can handle," he complained.

"You can't tell me you can recite the Declaration of Independence, the Preamble to the Constitution, and the Bill of Rights."

"Nope. But I know where they're written down whenever I do need them. That's what books are for."

"Wiseacre!" Jack leaned over to Maude and whispered, "The boy's sharper than I gave him credit for."

She'd sworn never again to feel that same thrill at Jack's nearness. The memory of the heartbreak she'd felt as she'd watched him studying the layout of the bank should have left her feeling nothing but cold toward him. Why should she allow anything Jack did to break her heart? Even now, she fought the breathtaking urge to draw closer to him.

"You know, Runt, the world is changing all the time," Jack continued. "Smart folks are inventing things. Bold folks are exploring new places. There's got to be something else worth studying."

"I don't want to study it," Georgie protested. "I want to go out and *do* it—like you did!"

"But I was sixteen. There's a world of growing up in the two years between fourteen and sixteen," Jack reminded him. When Georgie didn't seem comforted, he patted him reassuringly on the shoulder. "You will, Runt. But first, you have to know what you're getting into."

"Did you know what you were getting into?" he countered.

"No, I didn't," Jack answered bluntly. "But that doesn't mean I can't advise you against making the same stupid mistakes."

"But I'm the oldest kid in the whole gol-durn school!" Georgie finally let loose a flood of increasingly vehement complaints. "I'm taller than all the other kids. Shucks, I'm even taller than the teacher. I can't fit my legs under those consarn little desks. My coat drags on the floor when I hang it on the pegs in the cloakroom. My lunch is bigger than some of the first graders. All the other boys my age have quit school and are working on their fathers' farms, or are driving for Mr. Potter, or—"

"In the first place, I think you're exaggerating just a bit,"

Maude told him as calmly as she could, so as not to rile him any further.

"All right, maybe my lunch *isn't* as big as the first graders," Georgie admitted.

"In the second place, do you really want to work for Mr. Potter?"

Georgie shook his head.

"In the third place, Papa's told you before you can work for his newspaper—"

"But I don't want to just set the type and print the headlines. I don't want to just edit them or even report them. I want to *make* them—just like Jack."

Just like Jack. Maude swore if she heard her brother repeat that phrase one more time, she'd scream.

"First Papa wants to send you to college. You know what great store he sets by an education."

"Some folks set a great store by experience, too," Georgie muttered. The belligerence seemed to have gone out of him, but he still kept kicking the stones, real and imaginary, that got in his way.

"Don't mistake education—or experience, for that matter—for wisdom, Runt."

"What's that supposed to mean?"

"Haven't you ever heard of the educated fool?"

Georgie shook his head.

"The man who's read so much and knows so darn much and hasn't got a lick of common sense in his head to do anything with that education."

"That's what I'll be turning into if I stay in school much longer," Georgie said glumly. "That's why I've *got* to leave!"

"Then there's the fellow who's been everywhere and done everything, and still hasn't learned a thing from it all. Still makes the same dang-fool mistakes every time."

Georgie grunted. "Golly, Jack, I didn't think you'd come back this time to take the Reverend Hoffmann's job."

"I'm just sharing a bit of my experience with my friend, even if he is a hard-headed runt!"

Jack broke off from them, heading toward the Kingston house while Maude and Georgie headed across the lawn for their own back door. He turned and pointed a finger at Georgie. "Be in school tomorrow," he commanded.

"Are you going to come looking for me there?" Georgie challenged.

"I just might."

Tarnation! Maude silently cursed. That only meant Jack would be staying yet one more day in Apple Grove. Wasn't it about time he headed west?

Maude had no sooner entered the kitchen than Jessica came bounding up to her.

"Did you get my combs?"

Maude set her basket on the kitchen table. She reached inside and pulled them out.

"Thanks." Jessica snatched them from her hand.

"Did you peel the potatoes and open up the jar of green beans?" Maude asked.

"No. Should I have?"

Maude grimaced as she put her basket onto the top shelf in the pantry. "Only if you want to eat something besides bread and water for dinner tonight."

"Oh."

"Where were you today?"

Jessica gathered up her skirts and tucked her feet beneath her as she settled down into the chair. "Miss Hawkins's cat had kittens this morning—"

"Can I have one?" Georgie asked.

"I thought you were going to run away tomorrow, in which case you won't have time for a pet," Maude countered as she tied her apron around her waist.

"Five of the cutest little things, all gray and white," Jessica rattled on. "Then I went to see Widow Ross and we discussed what she ought to put in her kitchen garden besides broad beans, carrots, cucumbers, and—Oh!"

Maude dropped several potatoes into Jessica's lap. "Work *and* talk."

"But I'll cut myself," Jessica protested, her lower lip protruding ever so slightly.

Maude shook a paring knife in her direction. "If you don't, I will. That pretty little pout might have all the menfolks trailing at your feet, but I'm immune. Now, peel!"

She was feeling cantankerous enough, what with worrying about Georgie's complaints about school and Jack's midnight forays into town. She wasn't ordinarily a violent woman, but when it came to listening to her sister babble about her pointless perambulations about town today while she'd been working her fingers to the bone—well, she'd just plumb run out of patience.

"Matthew got in a new shipment of books," Jessica continued as she dumped the potatoes into a pile on the kitchen table and went in search of another paring knife.

Maude had to admire her sister as the girl rattled things around in the drawer. Jessica had a great talent for looking as if she were working her fool head off all day and, in the end, still not getting a blessed thing done.

"I helped him put them on the shelves, but there wasn't anything there that really interested me. Then I went to the Johnson farm to see the litter of piglets—my, how they've grown!"

"No, Georgie," Maude interjected. "If you can't have a kitten, you sure as shooting can't have a pig."

Georgie muttered something unintelligible and, since he'd been listening to Jack tell stories this afternoon, Maude figured, it was just as well for the sake of their feminine sensibilities.

"Nothing for me tonight, Maude," Mr. Griffith announced as he hurried into the kitchen.

Maude blinked in surprise and almost dropped the jar of green beans. Georgie stopped muttering and stared. Even Jessica stopped rattling through the drawer in order to stare at her father.

"Papa," Maude managed to say at last. "Why are you wearing your Sunday suit on Monday evening?"

"Is my tie straight?" Mr. Griffith asked, pulling and pushing at the knot in the length of black cloth.

"Yes. You look very handsome. Why—?"

"Because I'm just an incredibly handsome man, that's why," he replied with a grin that flipped the edges of his white mustache higher up his flushed cheeks. "My father was, as was his father before him. I hold out great expectations that my only son and heir will grow to be an incredibly handsome man, too. He's already off to a good start."

Mr. Griffith fiddled with his gold and garnet stickpin until he at last threw up his hands in despair. "Help me with this blasted thing, Maude."

Maude set down the jar and wiped her hands on her apron. "I take it you won't be wanting the liniment right now."

"I wouldn't mind a bit on my leg, but I'd greatly prefer not to go out smelling like I'd been dipped in kerosene, camphor, and turpentine.''

He shifted from one foot to the other and pulled at the cuffs of his shirt sticking out from the sleeves of his jacket. Maude couldn't remember ever having seen her father so agitated.

"If you don't stop moving around, I'm afraid I'll stick you. Now I know where Jessica gets it from." In his first motionless moment, Maude deftly stuck the pin into his tie. "You haven't worn this since . . . goodness, since the reception they held when the Reverend Parker retired."

"Well, there's never been another such occasion."

"Why are you wearing your Sunday suit on Monday?" Maude repeated.

"Because a gentleman customarily wears his best attire when . . . when . . ." Her normally glib father seemed to be faltering, searching for the appropriate excuse. "Well, when he has to call upon . . . his son's teacher to . . . to discuss his scholastic achievements."

"I see," Maude replied.

"Swell!" Georgie cried with glee. "Does that mean I'll have a commencement this June and won't have to go to that darned school anymore?"

"No, of course not," Mr. Griffith replied. "You're destined for Yale, my boy. Or Harvard. Or at least a university here in Iowa."

"But—"

"I always wanted to go to a university, but my parents were too poor to send me. I became so occupied with making enough money to finance my education that I ended up making a living and never going to a college at all."

Georgie started fidgeting, listening to the same story they'd all heard time and again.

"Yes, indeed, I'm largely self-taught, and while there's a certain satisfaction to be had from saying that, it'll get you nowhere in today's world. A man needs an education. I made a vow when you were born to send you to college."

"Doomed at birth!" Georgie kicked at dust balls on the floor and sauntered off. She could hear his shoes pounding up the stairs, down the hall, and into his room.

"What about Georgie's . . . scholastic achievements?" Maude asked.

"Miss Randolph and I have . . . certain matters to discuss,"
Mr. Griffith continued. "I'll be conferring with her regarding
these matters at the elegant and eminently respectable dining
room of the Fitzroys' Regal Hotel. The selection is limited, but
the fare is edible—"

"Oh, Papa, you must have some particularly important 'scholastic' matters to discuss!" Jessica teased.

Mr. Griffith harrumphed. "I beg your pardon. It's a completely appropriate, public place for a respectable maiden lady
such as Miss Randolph and a widowed gentleman such as myself
to share a fine meal and hold a polite conversation without arous-
ing undue attention or inciting unwarranted gossip."

"That never stopped anyone before," Maude warned him.

"I'll be there this evening, if you need me. Of course, my dear
offspring," he added, looking pointedly from Maude to Jessica
and back, "I trust I'll *not* be needed. As tomorrow is a work
day, I'll be home by ten. Don't wait up."

Maude stared after her father as the door closed behind him.

"Why do I have the feeling you should get out your pencils
and sketch pad and start making up another one of those darned
quilted designs you're so famous for?" Jessica asked.

"Because *you* are an idiot." Maude dumped the green beans
into a cookpot and set it on the stove.

Jessica just laughed off the insult. "How about blue forget-
me-nots for constancy and red roses for *passion?*"

"How about blue for the sky I can see through your empty
head and red for your blood dripping onto the floor?" Maude
grumbled.

"Yes, indeed," Jessica continued, undaunted. "You might
even want to start stitching up the design this very evening."

"I'll do no such thing. I'll wait until Miss Randolph asks me—
if she ever asks me at all."

Jessica gave a knowing chuckle. "You're just afraid to make
one for Papa and Miss Randolph because you're afraid it *will*
turn out."

"That's the most ridiculous thing you've ever said."

"If I were you, I'd be prepared," she warned.

Now it was Maude's turn to laugh, but her laughter sounded
bitter, even to her. "You're a fine one to tell me to be prepared.
I've got a hope chest full of lovely things and you haven't got
a pillow slip to your name. You can't wash clothes without

shrinking them, or press things without scorching them. You don't even know how to peel a potato without cutting yourself, much less know how to cook an entire meal. Now, before the roast dries out, would you please finish peeling the potatoes—and try not to bleed on them.''

"Don't be so cantankerous. You know, ever since Mama died, we've been hoping Papa would find some nice lady so he wouldn't be so lonely."

"Well, *after* an appropriate period of mourning."

"That's you, Maude. Always appropriate. I think nine years is *more* than appropriate." She grimaced. Then, just as abruptly as she did everything else, Jessica laughed. "Imagine! After all this time, who would've thought he'd set his sights on the schoolteacher, who'd been there all along?"

"Imagine," Maude muttered.

Wasn't this what she'd wanted? Maude asked herself as she stirred the boiling green beans. Why wasn't a broad smile of satisfaction spreading across her lips instead of this worried frown she felt creasing her forehead? Why was she feeling so horrible when everything seemed to be working out even better than she might have planned?

Miss Randolph as a stepmother might be just the influence Georgie needed to give him the confidence to make more friends, and to get this fool notion of running away out of his head.

Jessica had even helped Matthew at the bookstore. Not only would she be a helpmate in his home, but she'd be an asset to his business, too.

Once Jessica was married to Matthew, her father and Miss Randolph were happy, and Miss Randolph became a caring stepmother to Georgie, Maude would finally feel she'd fulfilled the promise she'd made to herself when her mother passed away. Then she'd feel free to impress upon Caleb her suitability as his wife.

Then why, when it seemed as if everything was beginning to turn out just as it should, did she feel as if her entire world was suddenly falling apart?

11

"THIS CINNAMON CAKE IS delicious, Maude," Louise said, placing another slice on her plate. She strolled about, peeking over her friends' shoulders as they stitched on Florence's red and yellow calico nine-patch quilt stretched across the large frame set up in the Griffith parlor. "I especially like the way you've sliced the preserved peaches very thin and laid them on top."

"Thank you," Maude answered, without glancing up from the last line of quilting she was doing on the muslin square.

"Do you think it'd work with brandied peaches, too? I have to find something new and unusual to make," Louise complained. "It figures it'd be just my luck to marry a man whose mother's the best cook in town."

"Oh, *every* man thinks his own dear mother's the best blasted cook in the whole blasted world," Katy grumbled.

"Look on the bright side, Louise," Clarice suggested with a laugh. "If you burn dinner, you can always pay a surprise visit to the in-laws."

"Yes," Katy muttered again. "He never wants to pay a visit to his in-laws, but you're supposed to just love paying visits to yours."

"When the weather improves, Fred and I are traveling to visit his aunt and uncle in Minnesota as my bridal trip." Louise helped herself to more cake.

"I declare, are you having *another* piece of cake, Louise?" Wilma asked, shaking her head in despair. "Even after I warned you you'd put on weight? If you keep this up, you won't be able to fit into any of your clothes for that bridal trip."

Louise swallowed her bite and laughed. "I'm an old married woman now."

"Yes, three whole days," Katy mumbled. "Wait until you've been married for months and months, and it seems like years."

Maude looked up from her quilting and frowned at Katy's remark. What a strange thing for her usually cheerful friend to say! Especially after the unusual conversation she and Jack had overheard at Louise's wedding. She wanted to ask Katy what was wrong, but what could she say?

Cautiously Maude watched her and waited for her to say something else that might shed some light on her odd remark. She glanced around the quilt frame. The rest of her friends weren't quilting, either. They were watching Katy just as curiously as she was.

Louise, on the other hand, appeared to completely ignore her friend's complaint. "I don't have to worry about catching a man anymore. Now I can eat what I like, and as much as I like."

"I pity poor Miss Randolph," Florence said. "Imagine, having to watch what she eats her whole life just on the chance some man might finally take a fancy to her."

Maude winced as she stuck herself through the quilt. She must be very tired or very upset. She hadn't stuck herself in a long time. *Please don't bleed on Florence's quilt,* she prayed as she jammed her aching finger into her mouth. *We're almost done.*

"I pity poor Miss Hawkins even more," Louise said. "At least Miss Randolph still has all her original teeth."

"You'd think that after a woman got to be a certain age she'd just sort of give up," Wilma said. "Like Lucille Grunder."

"Is that what you've done?" Florence asked.

"Of course not," Wilma declared. "I have every confidence that Peter Fitzroy will be courting me. I'm very favorable to it, and so are my parents."

"Ha! *His* parents are favorable to shipping him out of town in order to get him away from you," Florence said.

"Mrs. Fitzroy likes me," Wilma insisted.

"Mrs. Fitzroy is pleasant to everyone in town—even Mr. Potter," Florence said. "But do you really think Mr. Fitzroy, with his fancy hotel and farfetched claims of descent from some king, is going to let his son marry the daughter of the man who makes the bread and rolls for his restaurant?"

Wilma pressed her lips tightly together. "My father's baking is very good. You've got no reason to talk. You think you've got Edgar all roped and hobbled."

At last Maude could bear it no longer. She punched her needle straight down into the center of her block and sprang to her feet. "Goodness gracious, just shut up! All of you!"

Louise put down her fork to listen attentively. Florence and Wilma stared at her with guilt-stricken faces.

She felt horrible! How could she scold her friends like that? She was usually so calm and detached when settling little disputes.

"I've seen a flock of magpies get along better than we do," Maude continued a bit more gently. "What's wrong with us today?"

Only Katy kept stitching; she muttered, "Ha! You all don't even know what arguing is."

"Maude's right," Wilma admitted. "I'm sorry. I just feel so overwrought lately."

"Me, too," said Florence.

Maude had to admit she'd felt equally unnerved. How odd, since she'd felt very pleasant . . . until Jack had come to town. She had to find something else to blame for all her problems besides Jack. In the short time since his return, he was becoming far too important in her life—and she didn't like that notion one bit.

"Spring fever," Clarice diagnosed. She stretched her arms over her head. "I feel the same way. It must have infected us all."

"Yes. I'm sorry, too," Florence apologized. "I suppose we all need a good strong dose of sulfur and molasses."

"Or Lydia Pinkham's Vegetable Compound."

"Or Pe-ru-na, that patent medicine."

Maude silently wished their problems could all be diagnosed— and treated—that easily.

She sat down and picked up her needle again. She began the slow, steady rocking of the needle that created the long, even lines of tiny stitches that held the fabric together. The motion was soothing, and she stitched quietly and peacefully for a while.

"I'm almost done with this section," she announced.

"But you work faster than any of us," Florence protested. She pulled her thread through until she reached a corner of the red square in the center of the nine-patch. "I never can get my stitches so tiny."

"My mother taught me," Maude said. "She said, 'Maude, I'm not always going to be around to do this for you, so you better watch carefully, and learn, and remember.' "

"Too bad she couldn't teach Jessica anything," Florence said.

Maude sighed. Even after nine years, she still missed her mother. There were so many things—besides quilting—that she could really use her advice about. "She was too sick to do a lot of quilting with Jessica."

"Not to mention the fact that Jessica'd never sit still long enough even to thread the needle," Louise added with a laugh.

"Let me know when you're ready to roll it up," Maude said, leaning back to rest in her chair. "One more row of blocks to quilt, then we can take it off the frame and put the binding on."

The others sitting around the quilting frame nodded, then bent all the more diligently to their stitching.

"This one, plus my light and dark Log Cabin, the red and white Carpenter's Wheel, and the LeMoyne Star, makes four," Florence happily announced. "Thank you all so much for your help."

"You worked on ours, so we'll work on yours," Louise said. "We're all doing this together, and it's so much fun."

"Quilts or not, we just have fun chatting together," Clarice said.

Maude had to admit when men weren't around, Clarice was so much more bearable to be with. Men—not money—were the root of all evil.

"It beats staying home," Katy muttered.

"If we can keep quilting at this rate every Wednesday afternoon, I'm sure we'll have all your tops quilted in time for your wedding in September," Louise said encouragingly.

"We'll have plenty of time to work on my special quilt." Florence giggled with excitement. "I can't wait to see what sort of design Maude's come up with for me and Edgar."

"Maude's so talented, I'm sure it'll be wonderful," Louise said.

"Louise, you say that for *every* quilt Maude makes," Wilma said.

"I just wish she didn't insist on keeping them all a secret until they were done," Florence lamented.

Maude just smiled. She really hoped Florence could wait. She'd started the custom of keeping the block a secret as a surprise for her cousin Prunella's bride's quilt, and the secrecy had sort of become just another part of the superstitions about every block. For once, she was really glad for it. She was also glad there were still four more tops to quilt before they'd have to start on Florence's special bride's quilt. Maybe by then she'd have worked out all the problems.

She'd tried to fix the uncooperative design on paper. She'd changed the flowers—substituted pansies for lavender and lilies for marigolds. She'd rerouted the way the ribbons wove through the leaves, and the way the quilting design framed the flowers, and it looked worse than ever. She hadn't even begun stitching the design on the muslin block yet.

The main thing that bothered her was she had a dire premonition she knew what was really wrong with the whole thing, and it had nothing to do with the flowers or the quilting. The problem was with the initials. No matter how many stems and ferns she added or erased, *FL* looked very nice in the design, but not with *EB*. *EB* looked fine, but not next to *FL*. How could she explain that to her friend?

Florence already had three quilts completed and a stack of hemmed dish towels and pillow slips in the fancy dower chest her godmother had sent her when she turned thirteen. Grandmother Lester had sent her a set of china, service for eight, *with* serving dishes—even a celery dish—all the way from Boston. Mrs. Lester had paid for the Brussels lace, and Miss Hawkins was already working on the bridal veil. Mrs. Baumgartner had even offered to let Florence wear her mother's good blue crystal beads that she'd brought all the way from Frankfurt, in Germany. How could Maude tell Florence she thought her quilt was telling her it wasn't such a good idea for her to marry Edgar after all?

"Yes, every blasted quilt Maude has designed has been just wonderful!" Katy grumbled. "Just blasted wonderful!"

"What are you talking about, Katy?" Clarice turned to her

and demanded. "What's wrong with you today?"

"Nothing!" Katy snapped. "There's absolutely nothing wrong with *me!*"

She stuck her needle into the quilt, tore off her thimble, and slammed it down so hard that it skittered across the taut fabric, bounced off the edge of the quilt frame, clattered to the floor, and slid under the bookcase.

"Oh, we're going to have to wait for fall cleaning to find that," Wilma cautioned.

"It's all Willard's fault!" Katy cried. She covered her face with her hands and began to weep. "I swear, I can bear it no longer! I can't live with that horrible man another day!"

Wilma sat with her needle poised motionless above the quilt, staring in surprise. Louise's fork dropped to her plate with a clink as she rushed to Katy's side.

"Who would've thought we'd have such a scandal in our little town!" Florence declared.

"Merciful heavens, Katy!" Clarice threw her arms about her friend. "What's that monster done to you?"

"He . . . he . . ." Katy tried to speak between sobs.

Maude held her breath. All her friends leaned toward Katy to hear her horrendous tale.

"It's all right, Katy," Maude assured her. "We're your friends. You can confide in us. We'll do what we can to help you."

"He . . . *snores!*" Katy wailed.

Clarice leaned back and stared at Katy.

"He snores?" Maude repeated, just to make sure she'd heard her friend right.

"Yes, he snores."

"That's not all that horrible," Maude said, hoping to reassure her distraught friend.

"You might not think so now, but night after night, month after month. I haven't had a good night's sleep in so long!" she whined.

"It's just because you're newly wed. You're not used to . . . sharing a bed. Surely you'll get used to it in time," Louise said.

"I can't get used to it," Katy protested. "It keeps changing. One minute he'll sound like the steam engine chugging into Des Moines, and just when I think I've gotten used to the rhythm of that and might be able to doze off, he'll change and sound like the tornado that came through here last spring. Just when I think it can't get any worse, he'll snort like a pig! Two or three times, and then go on to sound like a busy day at Harold Springer's sawmill.'' She burst into sobs again.

Seeing how truly upset Katy was, Maude was trying very hard not to laugh.

''Not only that, his feet stink! The first time he took his shoes off, the cat bolted from the room. Being a little more polite, I quickly found something else that needed immediate attention in the kitchen. I've been contemplating putting one of his socks in the wardrobe to kill moths, and the other in the pantry to keep away mice, but then I don't know how we'd be able to eat the food. I know it's not warm yet at night, but I insist on opening the window just so I can breathe.''

''Why don't you make him a special new pair of socks?'' Maude suggested. ''Maybe a new pair every week, and tell him the dog chewed up the old ones?''

''Why didn't I notice all these horrible things *before* I married him?''

''I hardly think you could know about smelly feet, and especially the snoring!'' Louise exclaimed.

''Why can't men wear signs in clear view around their necks stating all their faults?''

''Then we'd *never* marry them!'' Clarice declared.

''Why can't there be some sort of central directory where a girl could research these things beforehand? Maude, you were supposed to be looking out for me,'' she accused angrily.

''Me?''

''Your design for my quilt was perfect. Why isn't my marriage?''

''It is,'' Maude tried to assure her. ''I think it's . . . normal to go through a brief period of adjustment. Isn't it?'' she asked Louise, glancing toward her for corroboration.

Louise shrugged, eyes wide with puzzlement.

Maude turned back to Katy and patted her hand. ''Try to remember how wonderful you felt when you first fell in love. Remember how much you loved him on the day you two were wed.''

''The night before was the last time I've had a good night's sleep!'' she wailed.

''I'm sure everything will be fine in a very little while.''

"Really?" Katy began to blot at her tears with her handkerchief.

"Oh, yes." Maude wished she felt as confident of her advice as she sounded. She knew her design had been perfectly good. But what if Jack had been right? What if it really was merely a silly superstition? If he hadn't said anything to Katy when he'd first arrived, she'd never be having these silly doubts. Katy's misery was all that darned Jack's fault!

"If you don't believe me, ask the Reverend Hoffmann or Mrs. Hoffmann, or your mother."

"You know," Florence said very slowly, "sometimes I wonder if our mothers would actually tell us the truth."

"What?"

12

"I MEAN, THEY WANT us to get married and have children because . . . well, if we didn't, what else would we do?" Florence looked around at her friends for some sort of answer. No one seemed to have one. "Become schoolteachers like Miss Randolph? Run a hat shop like Miss Hawkins? Take care of a cantankerous, aging parent like Lucille Grunder? Live with a married brother, taking orders like a servant from a condescending sister-in-law, and doting on spoiled, ungrateful nieces and nephews without ever being allowed to truly feel a part of the family, like poor Angelina Whitehouse has to do?"

"I don't know," Maude admitted.

If she didn't marry Caleb, what would she do? Live in her father's house, watch Miss Randolph take over her household responsibilities, and spend the rest of her lonely life doing charitable work? Maybe she and Miss Randolph could just switch places, and Maude would be the new old-maid schoolteacher. No, she was worrying needlessly. Of course she'd marry Caleb! What in the world was putting these silly thoughts in her head?

Maude noted all her friends were very quiet for a moment, too, probably pondering their own prospective fates.

Florence broke the silence. "I suppose we don't really have

much of a choice. But, still . . . sometimes . . . I don't think I want to marry Edgar after all.''

"Why not?''

"He . . . doesn't like my mother.''

Maude wasn't surprised by this announcement.

"He hasn't told you that, has he?'' Louise demanded incredulously.

"Well, not in so many words, but I can tell. And he . . . keeps stirring his coffee.''

"What's wrong with that?'' Louise asked.

"He just keeps stirring and stirring. . . .'' Florence's index finger made little circles, round and round. "Even after the milk is mixed in and the sugar is dissolved, he keeps stirring and stirring—''

"We get the idea,'' Maude said, reaching out to stop her. It *was* an irritating habit, she had to admit.

"No, no.'' Once Florence got started, she wasn't about to stop. "Every time he stirs, he keeps hitting the side of the cup with the bowl of the spoon, making this annoying tinkle.'' Suddenly she stopped and seized Maude's hand. "Please tell me my special quilt is just perfect. Please tell me all this is just anxiety before the wedding, just normal little doubts and fears every bride experiences. Please.''

"What else could it be?'' Maude replied, trying very hard to smile confidently.

"Hello, everyone!'' Jessica exclaimed as she burst into the parlor.

Maude would have loved to spring up, grab her sister by both arms, and shake her until her head rattled—which probably wouldn't take too long, she figured. If Jessica did that to her, no one would pay her any mind. But *she* was the sensible Griffith sister, she thought bitterly. *She* was always supposed to be in control. *She'd* never be able to do something so outrageous in public and get away with it as Jessica always seemed to do.

So she merely forced a smile and demanded, "Where have you been all day, Jessica? You were supposed to help me this morning with baking the cake, and with moving the parlor chairs out of the way and the kitchen chairs in here for—''

"I forgot it was Wednesday,'' Jessica said with a laugh.

"Darn, that happens every week,'' Maude commented sarcastically.

"What have I missed? What's all this about horrible habits? Oh, I smell cinnamon."

"Nothing." Katy rose to help herself to a piece of cake.

Did she think she could hide those tear-reddened eyes behind a plate and the tines of a fork? Maude wondered.

"You shouldn't ask about other people's horrible habits," Maude said. "You have enough of your own."

"Oh, pooh!" Jessica waved her hand in dismissal and headed for a piece of cake.

"Speaking of bad habits," Clarice crooned under her breath, gazing with appreciation toward the doorway. "That's one I'd like to acquire."

Maude turned, then realized she hadn't really needed to turn around. She should have guessed who'd arrived, just from Clarice's customary reaction to any man—well, except maybe Ol' Man Grunder.

Jack stood in the doorway. He was leaning against the doorjamb, one of his long legs crossed over the other at the ankles, and his arms folded across his muscular chest. It just wasn't fair that a man that darned ornery should look that darned good!

Please, Maude prayed, *let them just happen to have arrived here at the same time. Don't let Jessica have been out running around with him all day. Don't let my foolish sister fall prey to the wiles of Suicide Jack.*

"Good afternoon, ladies. My, my," Jack said with a wicked grin and a gleam in his eye, "the last time I saw this many beautiful ladies all under one quilt together . . . well, it just plain wasn't legal!"

The ladies tittered and blushed. Maude refused to laugh, and did her utmost not to blush. She really wanted to return to her quilting, but with Jack here, she'd stick herself again for sure.

"I took Jack out to the Johnson farm," Jessica said.

"Nice place those fellows have there," Jack said. "They've done a lot with it since their father passed away. I hadn't realized a tornado had taken down that big old cottonwood. Josh said it barely missed the house when it fell. Took them two days to clear it all away."

"I showed him the new corn crib Caleb built, too," Jessica said, "and the litter of piglets."

"Yes, I was *really* impressed with them."

"Come on. They're adorable!"

"I don't know. They reminded me a little too much of Pudge Tyler for me to really warm to them. I think I might've been happier seeing the kittens Jessica kept talking about."

"What did you think of the *farm?*" Maude asked.

"As I recall, old Mr. Johnson wasn't too much for new-fangled ideas, and I'm sorry to see Josh, Phineas, and Tobias apparently seem to want to stick to the old man's ways. But Caleb and Reuben seem to have some interesting plans for new things."

"Oh, yes," Jessica said with a laugh. "That Caleb's got lots of plans—too many plans—for almost everything."

"Some people like to make plans and stick to them, Jessica," Maude said. "Plans sort of help things turn out the way you want them to, like a good recipe or a pretty quilt."

"And sometimes they don't," Jessica said, "in spite of all a person's plans."

Maude frowned. Could Jessica possibly have been sneaking into her room and snooping through her sewing things? She wouldn't put it past her. Could she have found Florence's design, that didn't look quite right? Horrors! What if her sister had found the secret block she'd made for herself and Caleb—that she couldn't make turn out no matter how she tried?

Jack pushed himself off from the door frame and started to stroll across the room. "I must admit, sometimes life has a way of taking a body's plans and twisting them around until you get something entirely unexpected—but that doesn't necessarily make it bad."

Jack paused behind Clarice. He leaned over slightly, the better to see what she was doing. She continued to quilt, but Maude could see, even from this distance, that she wasn't concentrating very hard on the length of the stitches and wasn't being too particular about where they were going. Years from now, on a chill autumn night, Florence was going to look at that rough spot in her beautiful quilt and be able to blame the big, loopy, meandering line of stitches on Clarice's inability to think about men and anything else at the same time.

"How interesting," Jack commented, and moved along to the empty space Katy had left, to study her section of the quilting.

Then he moved on and stopped directly behind Maude. He bent down over her shoulder. She could hear the pewter buttons of his jacket tapping on the wooden slats of her chair. She could feel the fabric of the front of his jacket resting on her shoulder. If he'd bent this close to Clarice, she probably would've appreciated it, the flirtatious little minx. Maude cringed. Why did he have to get so close to *her?*

Then, as he continued to lean over, he placed his hand on the back of her chair. She could feel his knuckles pressing against her shoulder blade. How dare he be so familiar? Only Jack would do this, she figured. Only Jack would be able to get away with this by appearing to be totally oblivious to what he'd done. But Maude knew she could never be completely oblivious to what Jack was doing to her.

She was nowhere near as silly as Clarice. She could continue to stitch with the same even rhythm because she was a sensible creature, a lady of breeding and refinement. She had higher ideals, loftier goals, and nobler aspirations. She refused to allow foolish thoughts of mere physical attractions to interfere with her duties. Years from now, when Florence looked at this section of her quilt, Maude thought with smug self-assurance, she'd never be able to tell at precisely which spot Jack had been able to make her heart begin to pound, her knees begin to shake, and her hands begin to tremble.

"It's never failed to amaze me how such lovely, delicate creatures as you ladies can work so hard to produce such lovely, delicate things that bear up so well for so long."

"I suppose, like quilts, we're a bit tougher than you'd at first imagine."

"Yes, even the pretty ones."

Jack reached his arm out and touched the red and yellow squares lined in neat rows. She was glad this quilt wasn't resting on her lap, so she couldn't feel his fingers pressing firmly against her thighs again, causing her legs to quiver, her knees to go numb, and her stomach to twirl with excitement.

"So now, as I understand it," he continued, "you sew together all these little squares."

"Sometimes squares, sometimes triangles or other shapes."

"I see. Then you layer it up and stitch all three layers together. Is that right?"

He moved his finger along the line of quilting she'd just finished. His arm moved in front of her, drawing his body closer to hers. The man was a consarn nuisance!

"Jack Kingston, you know perfectly well how to put a quilt

together," she told him. "Even if you've never made one your-self, you watched your aunt and my mother, and the other ladies, do it often enough when we were children."

"I wasn't paying a lick of attention."

"Yes, you were. I sat there with you under the big frames when we were very young, finding lost needles, helping poke needles through thick spots, and fetching dropped thimbles."

"I only did that because Aunt Nell made me," Jack protested. "I wasn't really paying attention to any of it—sort of like I used to do in school."

"I can believe that."

"Yes," Louise interrupted with a laugh, "until the time he handed Mrs. Hopkins a frog instead of her dropped thimble."

"Aunt Nell never made me sit there again," Jack concluded with a self-satisfied grin.

"No wonder Mrs. Hopkins died not too long afterward," Maude said.

"It was the middle of winter, she was ninety-four years old, and had pneumonia!" he protested. "You *can't* blame that on me."

"I'm surprised you're so interested in quilting now."

"Well, when a fellow gets a little older, a little wiser, he gets to thinking it never hurts to know something. Does it?"

Jack might get older, but never wiser, Maude thought, and turned to tell him so.

The irritating man was standing there with his nose practically stuck in her face! And he was grinning! He was even closer to her now than when they'd been dancing at Louise's wedding. She saw very clearly the little flecks of gold in his green eyes, and noticed how the color got a little darker around the edge of the iris. She smelled the bay rum and tobacco again. She didn't notice the odor of whiskey, but she did note he wasn't wearing that one particular jacket, either. Maybe it had something to do with that.

She felt his warmth radiating out to her, making the spring day unseasonably hot. If only she could loosen her corset! Maybe then it wouldn't be so hot in here. Maybe then she'd be able to breathe better. If only he'd move away!

She saw a fine dusting of dark stubble on his jawline and upper lip. She'd never before studied so closely the way a man's beard grew—how the dark line dipped to either side of his mouth, left a clear space beneath his lower lip, then raised to a single point in the middle. Then again, she'd never been this close to any man before—not even Caleb.

She saw how very enticing his lips looked. She felt his warm breath on her lips, making them all the more sensitive. She could almost feel his lips pressing on her own, lingering on her cheek, trailing down her throat.

If, by some miraculous intervention, everyone else in the room should somehow disappear, and just the two of them should be left here alone—

She pulled back. *Don't do that, it only makes your chin look fat!* She tried to scoot her chair along the floor, but it only dragged on the rug, threatening to tip over, spilling her across the carpet. Was there no way to escape him without looking completely stupid?

"So, you put these three layers together. Is that it?"

"Yes, that's how we make our quilts," she replied quickly. She hoped she didn't sound too breathless. She hoped her face wasn't as red as the warmth she was feeling right now would seem to indicate. "You . . . must be hungry after going all the way out to the Johnson farm. Why . . . don't you have some cinnamon cake? It's over there. Over there," she repeated, and pointed insistently toward the cake on the table on the other side of the parlor.

She wished she'd set it up in some other room, or in someone else's house, or all the way over in the next county!

"It has peaches in it," she added by way of incentive. If that didn't get this annoying man away from her, she'd have to stick him with her needle just to make him move!

Jack straightened up. "Is that the kind your mother used to make?"

"Yes. Help yourself." She hoped he did, or Jessica and Clarice might knock each other out trying to serve him.

"I don't think I can resist." He strolled away. Sure enough, Clarice sprang to her feet. Too late! Jessica was already there.

The entire atmosphere around her seemed to thin and lighten. Maude could breathe so much better now. She thought little damp tendrils of hair were probably sticking to her neck but she was afraid to move. She didn't want to admit he had that kind of power over her. She didn't want to destroy the lingering effects of the warm and languid way his closeness made her feel.

She never felt this way when she was around Caleb—warm and soothed, yet at the same time as if every nerve in her body were exposed. She always felt proper, safe, and in control with Caleb—exactly the way she felt with just about everybody else she knew. He might have big plans for the future, but when it really came down to the truth, Caleb was as predictable as a sunrise.

Damn Jack! What was he trying to prove, doing this to her? Why could he make her feel this way when no one else could?

Should she reconsider her choice? No! She hadn't chosen Caleb on some silly, spur-of-the-moment, emotional, physically stimulating whim. She'd been very logical, very sensible in choosing the man who would make the best husband for her. These lustful emotions had nothing to do with a successful marriage. Just look at the sort of problems all their silly, irrational emotions were creating for her friends.

She might be able—and very willing—to blame Jack for so many of the woes of the world. But she wasn't about to allow him to have any part in any problems of hers.

∞

WHILE JACK ATE SEVERAL slices of cinnamon cake pressed upon him by each of the ladies, the rest had finished Florence's fourth quilt. They folded the quilt and dismantled the frame. The ladies—all except Maude—had fawned over Jack and his big, strong muscles when he'd moved the sofa so they could tuck the quilt frame away on the floor behind it.

"Let us help you clean up the dishes," Louise offered.

"No, thank you," Maude said. She figured if they all left, would Jack's departure be far behind? If she could have physically pushed them toward the door to get them out sooner, she would have. "Jessica can help me."

She knew her sister wasn't one darn bit of help, but she threw her a threatening glare anyway, daring her to set one foot out of the house again until after supper.

"What are you doing for dinner this evening, Jack?" Clarice asked.

"Aunt Nell is cooking something special for me," he replied. "All she's talked about since I got home are all the delicious things she wants to make."

"We'd all like to make you something special."

Jack patted his flat stomach. "Even after all the pieces of Maude's cake you ladies have made me eat, Aunt Nell will throttle me if I don't manage to eat every last bite of dinner tonight."

"I'm sure Mama plans to invite you—and your entire family, of course—to dinner before you leave, Jack," Clarice said.

"That's very nice, but she really shouldn't go to all the trouble. I really doubt I'll be around here much longer." When the ladies moaned, he added, "You know me, always on the move."

"You can't leave Apple Grove without a good meal!" Clarice protested.

Jack just grinned. "Miss Clarice, I learned a long time ago that I never could know which meal was going to be my last, so I try to make every meal a good one." He nodded to the awestruck ladies, then slipped out the back door just as quickly and easily as he'd entered.

The ladies, clearly having nothing to keep them here now that Jack had left, Maude noted, departed through the front door.

"Bring the chairs back into the kitchen, please," Maude told Jessica, "while I put the last of the cake in the pantry."

Maude was wrapping a clean cotton towel over the cake as Jessica dragged the first chair in.

"I think I heard a knock," Jessica said. She left the chair in the middle of the floor and made for the front door.

"Oh, no, you don't just go leaving that there!" Maude scolded. "I didn't hear a knock, so neither did you."

Jessica grimaced and hauled the chair back to the table. She stopped and stood still. "No, there it is again," she insisted. "I *did* hear a knock."

"I didn't."

"Oh, pooh! Maybe Jack's come back."

Maude grimaced. "Jack would just come bursting in through the kitchen door."

"Like that one winter when it snowed so hard, and he barged in on you while you were warming your bottom by the stove." Jessica began to guffaw. "Standing there with your skirt flipped up over your back and your bloomers—"

Jessica was laughing too hard to continue. She bounced off to answer the door.

"I hope you trip and fall," Maude muttered. Why did she have to bring up *that* embarrassing incident?

"Ha! I told you!" Jessica stuck her head in the doorway and gloated. "It's Miss Randolph."

"Oh, my."

Maude quickly wiped her hands on the towel and hurried into the parlor to greet her visitor. What could she want here? In some bizarre twist of social convention, was Miss Randolph calling to ask Maude's permission for her father's hand in marriage? Ridiculous! Maude would laugh if she didn't have a nagging suspicion Miss Randolph wasn't here on a purely social call.

"Good afternoon, Miss Randolph," she said with a broad smile as she entered the parlor. "To what do we owe this pleasure?"

Miss Randolph perched on the edge of the sofa. Her thin, pale hands were firmly clasped together, resting on her knees. Her straw bonnet sat precisely on top of her head with architectural precision. Her gray eyes peered out through her thin, steel-framed glasses from under furrowed brows.

"I'm not certain it's so much of a pleasure, Maude. I've come to enquire as to the health of your brother. I hope it's nothing serious."

"Georgie? Serious?"

"Little Fulton Purdy told me Georgie was ill and couldn't come to school today. Have you called Doc Ketcham in to see him, or did you just give him a dose of Hochstetters Celebrated Stomach Bitters and hoped it would pass?"

"Neither."

"Excuse me for saying so, but I don't believe that's a wise course—"

"I'm sorry, Miss Randolph," Maude interrupted, shaking her head in an effort to clear her thoughts. "I sent Georgie to school this morning perfectly healthy. He had his books strapped together, and he carried his lunchpail."

"He never arrived at school. I thought it was rather odd that Fulton would give me the message, seeing as how he's only six and doesn't usually play with Georgie—what with the age and size difference and all. He was awfully difficult to understand, until I made him take that dreadful peppermint stick out of his mouth before it rotted his teeth and repeat what he'd said. After all, good diction is essential to proper communication. Even then, the tot isn't ordinarily extremely reliable, but . . ."

Maude frowned. She had a bad feeling she knew exactly what

had happened. No, she refused to believe it. Her brother couldn't possibly be that stupid!

"Excuse me, Miss Randolph. I need to check on something for just a moment."

Maude tried to walk very calmly out into the vestibule and up the front stairs. She wouldn't want to alarm Miss Randolph—and who knew what her sister would do? She wished Papa were home. She'd grown very tired of dealing with Jessica's problems alone. She hated to think her usually obedient brother had suddenly decided to start causing trouble, too.

There were so many possibilities. Georgie may have skipped school and gone out to play, just as hundreds of normal boys had done hundreds of times. He may have managed to slip back home, up the stairs, and into his room, unnoticed while she was busy with her Wednesday quilting bee.

Slowly she walked up the stairs, but as soon as she reached the top of the stairs, she rushed down the hallway to her brother's bedroom.

The door was closed. She knocked. No answer. No sense wasting time bothering to knock again. She turned the knob and pushed the door open.

His room was empty. She stood there breathing heavily for just a moment, trying to think. He might be out playing. No, the bat was there, propped up in the corner. Well, perhaps he'd gone for a walk.

Then she noticed his schoolbooks, lying at the foot of his bed, still wrapped in the worn leather strap. He'd taken them with him when he left this morning. Somehow he'd managed to sneak back into the house while she was busy and sneak back out again.

She yanked open his wardrobe. His sturdiest boots were gone. His jacket and the haversack Jack had given him when he came back from the war were gone, too. She pulled open his top dresser drawer. Yes, indeed, he'd taken his wooden cigar box with his savings in it, too.

Georgie had run away, headed out West for sure! Once again, it was all that damn Jack's fault! This time the man had gone too far. He'd affected her family directly. She'd get even with him now, if it was the last thing she did!

13

MAUDE HEARD THE FRONT door close. It was Georgie! Oh, Lord, she prayed, please let it be her brother coming home from some harmless outing.

"Papa!" Jessica shouted.

"Benjamin!" Miss Randolph cried.

"Adelaide! What are you doing here?" her father exclaimed. "Not that I'm not glad to see you, but—"

Her heart sank. It wasn't her brother, but at least now that her father was home, she need not bear the responsibility alone.

She ran down the front stairs. Her father was hanging his hat on the hall stand.

She drew in a deep breath to try to calm her rapidly beating heart. "Georgie is gone," she announced.

"What do you mean?" her father demanded.

"Georgie is not here," she repeated more emphatically. "Nobody knows where he is."

"He probably went to see the kittens or the piglets," Jessica said.

"His haversack, some of his clothing, and his savings are gone," Maude said. "Those aren't the sorts of things a person takes with him for a brief visit around town. This is serious."

"You're making way too much fuss over this, Maude," Jessica told her.

"You're not the only one in this family who's allowed to do stupid things," Maude snapped. "Although you do seem to be the only one who manages to avoid the consequences." Then she turned to her father—the only member of her family she figured was sensible enough to do something useful right now. "Papa, I'm afraid Georgie's run away."

"Balderdash! He'd never do anything so—"

"But he has," Maude insisted.

"He must have," Miss Randolph agreed, wringing her hands in front of her. "I was so afraid something like this would happen."

"So was I," Maude muttered. She should have known the temptations recounted by Jack were too potent to resist. She also knew better than to mention that to her father. On the other hand, her father wasn't stupid. He'd probably figure out Jack and his influence over Georgie was to blame for this, too, just as he was for so many other things.

"I kept hoping I was wrong," Miss Randolph continued. "I didn't want to say anything until I was certain, not wanting to alarm you unnecessarily. It seems I was wrong in waiting."

"There, there, Adelaide. Who could have foreseen?" Mr. Griffith said comfortingly.

"He's seemed so unhappy, so restless lately," Miss Randolph lamented. "I attributed his change in disposition to a case of spring fever, particularly virulent in fourteen-year-old boys."

"I shouldn't confine the epidemic to fourteen-year-olds. I believe it has the power to affect us all."

"I must confess I have felt slightly restless of late. While I've never had children of my own, I flatter myself that, in my many years of teaching, I've dealt with enough children of various ages to understand some of a young person's thoughts and feelings."

Miss Randolph headed for the sofa and collapsed onto the blue damask cushions. Her head was bent and her shoulders stooped as she studied her fingers, fluttering restlessly in her lap.

"I should have seen the indications of unrest and malcontent in the boy, I tried my best to keep his lessons interesting and challenging. I should have known something was amiss as soon as Fulton gave me that unusual message." She lifted her head and looked pleadingly at Mr. Griffith. "I should have alerted you immediately. Oh, Benjamin, it's all my fault!"

"My dear Adelaide, it is *not* your fault," Mr. Griffith insisted. He sat down beside her on the sofa and took her small, chalk-whitened hand in his large, ink-stained one. "If anyone is to blame, it is I. I never should have badgered the boy about going to college."

"You mustn't blame yourself," Miss Randolph told him. "You were only doing your fatherly duty."

"If I had been, Georgie wouldn't have felt the need to run away in search of perilous adventures."

Miss Randolph sighed. "I thought they were uplifting classics of English literature. How could I have known reading *Ivanhoe, The Last of the Mohicans,* and *Robinson Crusoe* would influence the boy in an adverse manner? I should have taken those worthless novels away from him the very first day I spotted him reading one behind his grammar book. Why, if this sort of thing were allowed to continue unchecked, he might take to reading the sensationalist press, or those horrid, scintillating dime novels."

"Excuse me," Maude interrupted loudly. "Don't you two think we ought to stop trying to figure out who's to blame and try to find him before it gets too dark? He's already got several hours' head start on us."

"Yes, indeed!" Mr. Griffith sprang to his feet and headed for the front door.

Miss Randolph rose and followed him. "We should find Fulton and ask him where he last saw Georgie, and in which direction he was heading. Perhaps we could ask other people around town if they've seen him, too."

"That's an excellent idea." Mr. Griffith turned to Maude and Jessica and ordered, "You two remain here, in case he returns."

He grabbed his hat from the stand and escorted Miss Randolph out into the bright afternoon.

No sooner had the door slammed shut than Jessica turned to Maude and announced, "I'm going to see Miss Hawkins, and then probably to the Johnson farm."

"I thought you said he wasn't missing," Maude reminded her.

"Well, yes," Jessica said slowly. Then, with more spirit, she asserted, "But that doesn't mean I won't help look for him. I just won't go wasting my time like Papa and Miss Randolph, talking to that witless little Purdy brat. They're both wrong, anyway. He probably doesn't know any more than what Georgie told him to say—and even then, he probably got it all wrong. I'll bet Georgie went visiting, lost track of the time, and doesn't even realize he's thrown us all into this uproar.''

''What makes you think you're so superior to Papa and the schoolteacher?''

''Georgie doesn't have the courage to run away,'' Jessica told her as she headed toward the kitchen. ''He's sort of like you for that, Maude.''

Jessica's remark angered her, but she had too much to worry about now to get into an argument—and, although she hated to think her sister was right, in a way, she was.

''But Papa said to stay here,'' Maude said.

Jessica gave a derisive laugh and grabbed her shawl from the peg by the door. ''*You* can. You're more the kind to sit home waiting for him than I am. Don't worry. It won't take me long to find him.'' She bounced out the door.

Maude stood in the empty kitchen, listening to the creaking sounds of the empty house. The last time the house had been this silent was the day after Mama's funeral. How she hated the sound of an empty house! All the while she listened and worried, she grew increasingly angry.

So, Jessica thought she was the kind to just sit home while everyone else did all the exciting things—even if they were the wrong things. Everyone else had gone off on a wild-goose chase. They ought to be able to figure out exactly who had prompted him to run off like this—certainly not sensational literature; and who would best be able to bring him back—certainly not Fulton Purdy.

Her father had blamed Jack for everything from lightning hitting their chimney because Jack had taken their lightning rod to try to make a telegraph with it, to having to repaper the dining room when Jack tried to play Michelangelo and paint the ceiling with the only things he could find—lamp black, whitewash, and red barn paint.

But this was far more serious. Jack was responsible for her brother running away, and only Jack could bring her brother back.

Maude closed the kitchen door firmly behind her and headed across the lawn. She was growing angrier and more upset—with Georgie, with Jessica, with Jack—as each step brought her closer to him. If she got any angrier, she figured she would probably leave singed footprints in the grass.

She knocked on the back door of the Kingston house.

Mrs. Kingston, in a flour-dusted apron, greeted her, smiling broadly. "Hello, Maude. What can I do for you?"

Maude tried to look calm and pleasant for her neighbor's sake. There was no sense in alarming Mrs. Kingston when, no matter how much she might care what happened to Georgie, there wasn't a thing she could do to help fetch him back. Maude didn't need to waste time trying to calm her neighbor's fits of hysteria when she could be doing something truly useful.

"Hello, Mrs. Kingston. Is Jack around?"

"Yes." Mrs. Kingston looked clearly puzzled.

"Thank you." Maude didn't have time to explain. She strode past her, around the large table in the center of the kitchen, and toward the hallway that led to the parlor.

"He's upstairs, taking a nap before dinner."

Maude abruptly changed direction and headed up the back stairs. She could hear Mrs. Kingston's worried, high-pitched voice yodeling after her as she mounted the stairs.

"Maude, do you really think it's such a good idea to go calling on a gentleman in his bedroom in the middle of the afternoon?"

As a child, Maude had spent many happy times playing and chatting with Louise in her best friend's bedroom, and just about as many irritating moments ignoring Jack, teasing and tormenting them from his room across the hall. She knew exactly how to get to his bedroom.

Ordinarily she wouldn't be so bold to do this, but her little brother was heading across the prairie alone, on foot, without a horse, without a gun, without a guide. He'd probably even forgotten to take any food along with him. He was heading right for Indian territory, full of marauding Indians on the warpath. Or outlaws who'd kill a man for the boots on his feet. Or renegades who still refused to believe the war was over, at least until they'd personally settled a few old scores.

If she allowed him to keep going, she might never see him again. She'd lost her mother long before her time. She wasn't about to lose her brother, too. She *had* to bring him back.

She pounded on the bedroom door with her fist. Mrs. Kingston had said Jack was taking a nap. He might be lying there, naked as the day he was born, but she didn't have time to wait for him to answer. She needed him *now!* She pushed open the door.

She came face-to-face with the barrel of a gun.

"God in heaven!" Jack pointed the gun upward, then spun sideways. "Maude!"

She heard him uncock the gun, but was so stunned and confused, she couldn't say for certain if she'd seen him put it away. All she knew was, the gun had disappeared.

"Maude! What the—What are you doing here?" Jack demanded in a harsh whisper, adjusting his jacket over his shoulders. "Criminy! I could've shot you. Don't you have better sense than to burst into a man's room when he's sleeping?"

"Don't you have better sense than to pull a gun—?"

"How was I supposed to know it was you?"

"Who else were you expecting—Aunt Nell? Uncle Tad?— that you needed to greet them with a gun?"

"Look, never mind about that now."

His voice sounded more relaxed—in fact, rather jovial, Maude thought, as if confronting someone entering his room with a gun was a normal occurrence, and she was silly for being alarmed by it. In fact, she figured, he was working far too hard at making it sound so. What had scared him? How could anyone scare Suicide Jack?

He took her by the arm and firmly escorted her out into the hallway. "What are you doing here, anyway?"

"Georgie's run away."

"What?" At first he sounded shocked, but then he laughed. "No. He's probably just gone out to play and lost track of the time, or went out to see the kittens or the pigs Jessica was talking about."

"No," she insisted. Why did it take so long to make them believe her? "He's taken the haversack you gave him, his savings—"

"He's probably trying to buy one of the kittens, and he'd certainly need something to carry a piglet home in. Runt's sensible, like you, Maude."

"Sure. Sensible boys always carry pigs around in their haversacks."

Jack laughed, irritating her further.

"He's also taken his jacket—"

"The weather's unpredictable this time of year, and he's prepared for it."

"No! He's gone—and it's all your fault."

Jack slammed his fist against the doorjamb and glared at her. "How do you always keep figuring everything is my fault? I'm surprised you're not blaming me for the Black Death and the fall of the Roman Empire."

"You're the one who filled Georgie's head with all those wild tales of adventure out West. You're the one who presented such a sterling example to him by, not once but twice, running off in search of those adventures."

She jabbed her finger into his chest with each accusation. She didn't care if it wasn't ladylike to touch a man's body, or polite to hit him with as much force as she could summon into one fingertip. At this very moment her brother might be in danger, and it was all this man's fault.

Jack never winced as she hit him twice, three times, punctuating her complaints. Drat! The rat deserved to feel more than a little pain for his sins against her family.

Suddenly he grabbed her, his fist enveloping her entire hand, except for her index finger, which was still aimed directly at him. She struggled to pull her hand away, but he held her there. Her attack had turned into her own entrapment. She should have expected as much from Jack.

But even though he'd stubbornly refused to admit to any pain, and even though, realistically, she had to admit her single finger couldn't possibly cause him any unbearable discomfort, at least she had the satisfaction of knowing she'd bothered him enough that he'd needed to make her stop. She hadn't won, but for the first time in their lives, she'd made Jack flinch.

He glared at her, and, with renewed confidence, she boldly glared back. She felt his grip on her hand tighten. She'd never escape him now. Although she wanted to pull away, she didn't want to leave him.

The hardness in his eyes seemed to soften. Did he pull her toward him, or had he taken a step closer that she, in the confusion generated by the nearness of him, had failed to notice? She needed his help, but she didn't need to feel this unaccountable longing to draw even nearer to him.

She stepped back and averted her gaze. He released her. This time he'd made her back down, and she silently berated herself.

"You know how Georgie's always looked up to you."

She changed the tone of her voice from an angry scold to a

shameful reprimand. She figured a little guilt could go a long
way with any ordinary man—except Jack could hardly be considered an ordinary man.

"Well, now at last he's decided to emulate you. A poor choice,
if you ask me—a man who betrayed the law he swore he'd
uphold, spent time in jail..." Her voice trailed off as she
thought the unthinkable. Had Jack even betrayed his own country? Not that he'd look at it that way. "Goodness, if he wanted
to follow a bad example, he could just as well have picked John
Wilkes Booth."

"Thank you very much for that flattering comparison."

"Do you expect me to thank you for leading my little brother
down the same road that led to your ruination?"

"I guess not." Apparently some of the guilt she was trying to
impose on him was finally beginning to sink through his thick
skull.

"But I do expect you to find him."

"What?"

"Can I help you two with anything up there?" Mrs. Kingston's high-pitched voice called up the stairs. "You know, I have
a lovely sofa in the parlor that would be just delightful for you
two to sit on and chat."

"We're coming right down, Mrs. Kingston," Maude called
reassuringly. Then she turned back to Jack. She looked down at
his bare feet and ordered, "Get your boots on."

Jack turned back into his bedroom. "I'll be right out," he said
as he moved to close the door.

Maude's hand caught the door. "I'm waiting here."

"Do you have some sort of prurient interest in watching men
put their boots on?" He grinned and raised a provocative eyebrow. "Most women would find it more interesting watching
them take them off."

"No!" She swore she wouldn't blush—not this time. She
swore again, a little differently, as she felt her face growing hot
in spite of her firm resolution. "But I'm not about to let you go
locking the door so you can dodge your responsibility again."

"What do you think I'll do? Climb out the window and down
the tree to escape you?"

"No!" Her answer was far too abrupt. Her voice was much
too hoarse with guilt. She *knew* he knew she'd followed him.
She'd been so careful. *How* could he know?

She stood there in silence while Jack sat on the edge of his rumpled bed and pulled on his boots. Somehow she'd never imagined that the man she'd be watching dress on the edge of a bed still rumpled and warm from sleep would be Jack.

She *had* to concentrate on making sure he didn't slip away from her. She *had* to concentrate on finding Georgie. She shouldn't be letting her thoughts lead her, even in her imagination, toward Jack, toward the edge of the bed. . . .

He rose and headed for the door. Before she had time to move out of the way, he'd slipped past her—so close that she could feel his jacket brushing against her bodice, so slowly that she thought she'd faint before he allowed her to breathe again.

"So," he asked as he turned his back on her and descended the stairs, "where do you think Runt's taken off to?"

"You know very well where he's gone." She hurried after him.

At the bottom of the stairs, Jack stopped and turned. Stuck one step up, Maude stood eye to eye with him. He frowned at her.

"Just what do you mean by that?" he demanded. He'd once been so close to her she could see the small flecks of gold in his green eyes. Now those eyes blazed a fire of molten anger. Had she blamed him one time too many for her troubles? Of course not—no more than he deserved!

"He's been listening to you and all your blasted tales of adventure out West," she accused. "That's where he's gone."

"How can you be so sure?"

"Are you that stupid? Weren't you listening to a word that boy said when he was talking to you? He adores you. He thinks you can do no wrong."

"Unlike yourself. You seem to think I can't do anything right."

Maude paused.

"Don't deny it."

"I won't."

"But you won't tell me so to my face until I bring Runt back, will you?"

"I'm not about to get involved in a silly argument with you when I have more important things to think about. The fact of the matter is, you went out West. That's all Georgie could talk about—leaving school and running away for adventures, 'like

Jack.' That's where he's gone because of you—and you owe it to us, to my father and to Georgie, to bring him back safe.''

"All right," Jack said. He stomped through the kitchen, all the while muttering, "Wild-goose chase. Dang-fool woman. Dang-fool kid."

Maude cast an apologetic glance to a very puzzled-looking Mrs. Kingston, then hurried after him as he headed across the lawn for the Kingstons' barn.

"I'll saddle my horse and head out—"

"I'm coming with you."

14

"NO, YOU'RE NOT," JACK told her as he pulled his saddle off the rack and began to tack up his horse. "You'll only slow me down."

"I am coming with you," she stated in very clear, measured tones so that Jack could never claim he hadn't heard or understood her. "Don't tell me you don't understand English anymore."

He stopped abruptly. "What on earth do you want to come for? You don't ride that well—"

"I don't have to. You know, not everybody travels as much as you do."

"I'm sure a lady as fine as you at least goes to church—every Sunday, I'll bet." He turned and grinned at her.

"I can walk everywhere I need to go in Apple Grove and, until this moment, I've never needed to be anyplace else." Then she lifted her chin and shot him a challenging glare. "But I can stay on that horse."

"What do you know about tracking?"

He had her there. "Nothing, but—"

"I'll bet the last thing you tracked down was a good bargain at Chalky Pike's. Before that, you were tracking down hidden Easter eggs."

She shot him a deflating look. "I'm coming with you because . . . well, because . . ."

How could she tell him she trusted him to find her brother, but not to bother to come back? If she wanted his help, how could she tell him she wanted to make sure he didn't just say the devil take them all, and take off across the prairie, leaving them worrying and wondering once again? As long as he brought Georgie back, why would she even care if Jack came back or not? She didn't know—but she did.

"Because he's my little brother, and I need to find him."

Jack studied her quietly for a moment. What was he thinking? Maude couldn't guess. His face was completely devoid of expression. Even in his eyes she couldn't detect a thing—not the boyish playfulness that usually confronted her, or even the strange look of hurt she'd once seen flicker there briefly.

At last he said, "Yes, I guess you do. Come on. But no whining!"

"*I* never whine," she told him haughtily. Then she smiled sheepishly and tried to sound sweet and apologetic, almost helpless. Goodness! how she hated to do it. It made her sound like Clarice or Ruthie. But there really was no other way. "I do need your help saddling the horse."

"Somehow I thought you would."

She was relieved to see his usual playfulness light his eyes again. Leading his own horse, he headed for her father's barn.

∽

"WE'VE BEEN RIDING FOR two hours now." Maude shifted in her saddle.

Jack figured, since she wasn't used to doing much riding, her pretty little behind must be getting mighty sore by now. If he were really pressed into service, he just might be persuaded to rub a little of Clark Stanley's Snake Oil Liniment on her—very reluctantly, of course, he thought with a sarcastic grin.

"We should've spotted him by now."

Jack shrugged. "Not necessarily."

"But he's on foot. We're on horseback. We're traveling faster than he is."

"Not the way you're riding."

"If we haven't seen him by now, how can you be sure we

went the right way? How do you know he took this road? He could've headed—''

"Because . . . I do,'' Jack muttered.

"He could've headed down to Kansas,'' Maude suggested. "There are lots of forts along the trails heading west. Plenty of opportunities for these silly adventures he thinks he's going to have.''

Plenty of opportunities for a lot of trouble, he thought gloomily. He didn't care to elaborate, for Maude's peace of mind, but he figured she'd already heard enough tales of his misadventures in Dry Creek, Kansas. The trouble was, he'd only told Runt his tales of fun and adventure, never the sordid side of saloons and bank robberies. Jack just hoped he could catch Runt and bring him back before he had to pay the consequences that he himself had been lucky enough to escape.

"He could've headed toward Sioux Falls in Dakota Territory, then toward the Black Hills.''

"Nope.'' Jack just had a gut feeling the boy had headed directly toward Cedar Rapids, the biggest staging town in Iowa for parties headed west, a good place for a boy running away to lose himself.

He never knew how he knew—when people were watching him or following him; which card the dealer would draw next and who would draw his gun first; which way to go when he wanted to follow someone. He just knew. He was glad he knew. It had saved his life—and the lives of his companions—on several occasions. He hoped he was right about Georgie now. If he couldn't find him, knowing Maude, his life wouldn't be worth a plugged dollar.

"How can you be so sure?'' she demanded.

He had to come up with a better explanation. "I saw a few boot prints in the dust at the side of the road, heading out of town, that looked about Georgie's size.''

"That's all?''

"I spotted a freshly discarded apple core a ways back.''

"You're tracking my brother on the strength of an apple core?''

"That's not the sort of evidence a passing rabbit usually leaves.''

"No, but just about any human who passed this way could do the same.''

"Do you want me to tell you I can tell his bite from everyone else's?"

"Don't be ridiculous." She gave a derisive chuckle. "No one can do that. The next thing I know, you'll be telling me you found a few strands of hair that look like his, clinging to—"

"I thought we'd agreed—no whining."

"I'm not whining. I'm complaining."

"Look, you want me to find him, don't you?"

"Of course."

"Then stop complaining. I have to use everything I can, no matter how silly it sounds to you. I've tracked men on slimmer evidence than this—and found them, too. We're heading in the right direction," he stated. "You can just thank your lucky stars there's no railroad out of Apple Grove yet. If he's still on foot, we'll catch up to him. If he's boarded a train, we might never find him."

"Don't say that!"

She was right, he thought guiltily. That really was the wrong thing to tell her.

"I'll . . . *we'll* find him." He tried to sound confident and re-assuring, but he had a bad feeling she didn't believe him for a moment. Why should she?

They rode in silence through the late afternoon, facing the orange glare of the setting sun, until it was almost dark.

"I thought you said you'd be able to find him," Maude said.

She sounded so weary, and not just from riding most of the afternoon. At least she'd proven true to her word and stopped complaining. He knew worry was taking a toll on her emotions.

"I will."

"Do you think it might be anytime soon?" She raised her hand to shade her eyes.

He wished she wouldn't do that. She was having a hard enough time staying on the horse holding on with both hands. If he wasn't so busy looking for Runt, he'd grab her around the waist and haul her onto his horse to sit in front of him, with his arms wrapped around her, and her back leaning all soft and warm against his chest.

He shifted in his saddle. Better concentrate on finding Runt and stop thinking about Maude, or he'd be more uncomfortable riding than she ever could be. It wouldn't be anything he'd want to use liniment to fix, either.

"Do you want to turn back?" he countered with deliberate sarcasm to help him think more clearly.

"Of course not! But you could hurry—"

"I warned you before we set out, I'd travel faster alone. But, no—you had to insist on coming. You're the one who's slowing me down."

"Now who's whining?"

"I don't whine or complain. I state facts. If you can't keep up, the least you can do is be quiet and be patient. It takes time to track down someone."

"But it's getting dark."

"Are you worried that being out here alone with me in the dark is going to ruin your reputation?"

"Don't be silly," she answered icily. "The darker it gets, the more difficult it's going to be to find Georgie."

"I told you before, I work alone. If you can't handle this, you can always head back."

"I will not." She lifted her chin. In the golden gleam of the setting sun, she looked like some sort of bronze goddess mounted on a horse, riding off for untold adventure. He smiled. No, not Maude.

"Just hang onto the horse the best you can, and stay straight on this trail." He turned in the saddle and pointed back down the long, dusty road. "The horse will probably be able to take you back by himself. But I'm going on. I've got to find Runt."

"Why are you so determined now?"

"I've *always* been determined to find him."

"You took an awful lot of convincing earlier."

"I did not. I'm just not real tickled with being rudely jarred out of my nap, dragged out of a nice, cozy bed, and being blamed for the woes of the world. Whether I'm truly responsible for putting those fool notions to run away into Runt's head, as you seem to think I am, or not—well, dang it! It's just that he's the next closest thing I've got to a little brother."

Damn it! Some things were best left unsaid, best left forgotten. The damn, irritating woman had forced it out of him.

"There! Now I've said it. I've completely ruined my reputation as a cold-hearted son of a bitch. Are you happy?"

"There's no need for profanity."

"Sorry." He'd never be able to explain to her how much she

got him riled. "But I can't just let him disappear out on the prairie."

Maude was silent again. She kept riding along, every once in a while shooting him a sidelong glance, but in the increasing darkness, he couldn't see her expression to try to figure out what in the world was running through her pretty head. One thing he could be sure of, though. Boy, he'd said the wrong thing once again.

"There he is!" Maude exclaimed. She pointed toward the stooped, dusty figure, wearily toting his haversack, trudging along the road.

She spurred her horse forward, teetering in the saddle as she went. Jack urged his horse on to keep pace with her, but whether it was to catch up to Georgie or to catch Maude when she fell, he wasn't sure.

"Georgie!" Maude exclaimed. "I've—we've been so worried about you!"

For a minute, Jack was afraid she'd leap—no, having watched Maude ride, more than likely she'd tumble—from her horse and gather Georgie into her arms in just the sort of melodramatic action his aunt Nell might take. But Maude remained on her horse—just the sensible sort of thing he'd expect of her. Georgie briefly glanced up at her, but just kept plodding along the rough, dirt road.

"Shucks! How'd you find me?" Georgie grumbled. He shot disgruntled glances at Maude and back at Jack. "It was that half-wit, snot-nosed Fulton Purdy told on me, wasn't it? I should've known better than to trust him. Probably didn't even get the story I told him right, did he? Wasted a good peppermint stick on him. Miserable little bugger."

Maude tugged awkwardly at the reins of her horse so she could keep pace beside her brother. "No, it wasn't. It doesn't matter now, anyway. I'm just so glad we found you. Let's go home, Georgie."

Georgie kept walking along. Jack trailed along a slight distance behind them. No matter how he felt about Runt, this really was a moment for the family alone, he reckoned—one that, no matter how a body added it up, he never really would figure into.

"Papa and Jessica don't know we've found you safe. They're still worried about you."

"Yeah, I'll bet Jessica's just prostrate with anxiety." Georgie grimaced.

"She's probably still running around town, looking for you, asking people where they saw you last and what direction you were heading in."

"Except for the part about asking people about me, Jessica's always running around town anyway. Nothing special there."

"Papa and even Miss Randolph are looking for you, too."

"Together?"

"Yes."

"That's really swell!" Georgie kicked at a rock that got in his way, and kept on walking. "I'll bet you think it's just fine that they're keeping company."

"Don't you like Miss Randolph?"

"Yeah, sure. She's a good teacher. On the other hand, seeing as how I've never had a different one, how would I know?"

"But, as a person . . . ?"

"As a stepmother?" Georgie asked bluntly.

"Well, yes, if it comes to that," she answered reluctantly.

"Look, I've really got nothing *against* her and Pa, but— Do you have any idea how those kids in school will tease me about being teacher's pet when they find out about them? Do you see now why I have to go away?"

"But we don't know where you're going. Why would you do something like this to worry us so?" Maude demanded. "Couldn't you at least have left a note?"

Georgie just grunted.

"Come on. Let's go home."

"I can't," Georgie answered, and kept on walking.

Maude sat atop her horse, watching her brother still heading westward in spite of all her attempts to talk him out of it. She had the most horrible, desperate, puzzled look on her face—as if, for the first time in her adult life, she'd completely lost control of her family. She might not know what else to do, but Jack had already figured out what he could do for her.

He didn't care if Runt was almost as tall as he was. He didn't care if the boy did think he was the biggest, smartest kid in the whole school. What the thoughtless lout needed now was a good clout up alongside his thick head!

He spurred his horse on, then reined him to a halt directly in Georgie's path, forcing him to an abrupt stop.

"What in hell do you think you're doing!" Jack demanded. He didn't usually use profanity—at least, not in mixed company, or with someone so young—and Maude would be sure to scorch his ears about it afterward. But he figured it was a sure way to get the hardheaded boy's attention *and* to impress Runt with exactly how angry with him he truly was.

Of course, what he really wanted to do was jump down off his horse, grab the rotten kid, and hug him—he was so glad to see Runt safe. But he figured, for what he needed to do now, the scolding was probably going to be more effective.

"I *was* walking down the road, until some stupid oaf put this big horse in my way," Georgie replied with a grimace.

"Why the devil would you be doing a fool thing like this?"

"I have to walk. I can't rightly take Pa's only horse. If I'd asked anybody to use theirs, I'd have had to tell them why, and then they'd have told Pa on me, and he'd have stopped me. Taking anyone else's without permission would be thieving, and they'd string me up."

"That's mighty thoughtful of you. Too damn bad you weren't as considerate of your family's feelings when you took this fool notion into your head to run away—no matter how you did it."

"*You* didn't think about your family when you ran away, did you?" Georgie countered.

"No, I didn't. I disappointed my uncle, who took me in when my parents died, and I repaid him unkindly with my ingratitude. I broke my aunt's heart, when she'd only always tried to do me good. I know now I was wrong, and I also know now it's too late to change anything. I told you before I didn't want you making the same stupid mistakes I did. But did you listen to me? Hell, no!"

Georgie opened his mouth and looked about to give some sort of lame excuse. But then he just shut his mouth firmly.

"I've a good mind to reach out and swat you up alongside your hard head. What's the matter with you, Runt? Why would you want to go hurting your father and your sisters this way when they've only tried to do you good?"

Georgie stood there, looking everywhere but at Maude and him. But at least he'd stopped walking. It was just a short move from stopping his walk westward to getting the boy to turn around and head back home where he belonged.

"I know you probably figure I'm still sounding like the Reverend Hoffmann, don't you?"

Georgie nodded.

"I don't mean to sermonize you, Runt. But I figure you and I are friends enough that I can speak plainly to you."

Jack extended his hand down to Georgie.

"Come on, Runt. Get on the back. Let's get you home."

"You know I'll just try this some other time," Georgie warned.

Jack had been threatened by a lot of men—and a few women, too. He'd learned enough to figure out a bluff, and this sure sounded like one of them. But he wasn't about to call Georgie out on it—not now. He'd also learned not to force the hand of a desperate man.

"Yeah, I know, Runt. I hope the next time I find you heading out of Apple Grove you'll be a couple years older, a lot wiser, have a horse of your own, a decent carpetbag full of decent clothes, a bit more money saved up, and be traveling in the opposite direction, to a university back East."

"Now you sound like my father."

"At least you're not accusing me of sounding like the Reverend Hoffmann anymore," Jack said as he helped Georgie climb up onto the horse behind his saddle.

He saw Maude still watching him. She had to be purely flabbergasted, listening to him scold Georgie. She'd have been more flabbergasted if he'd hugged the boy. It probably came as a shock to her that he'd think of anybody but himself. It probably came as an even bigger surprise to her to hear him admit he was sorry he'd broken his aunt's heart.

Boy, he sure hoped he hadn't completely ruined his reputation.

⎯⎯

"WELL, YOUNG MAN."

Maude watched her father trying to stand up tall and threatening over Georgie. She figured he must be having the dickens of a time, seeing as how Georgie, even with his head hanging low on his breast in an obvious effort to look abjectly repentant, was already as tall as he was. Her father crossed his arms over his barrel chest and glared at Georgie from beneath his furrowed brow.

"What do you have to say for yourself?"

For all his height, Georgie cowered under that familiar, intimidating glare. "I told you I wanted to quit school."

"Does that mean you wish to quit this family, as well?"

"No, sir. But I couldn't rightly figure any other way out of it."

Georgie threw Jack a hopeful glance. Was he looking for support from him? Maude wondered. She noticed her father threw a glance at Jack, too. The only hopefulness in that glance would be her father's fervent wish to see Jack keeping Judas Iscariot company in the lowest concentric circle of hell.

Goodness, she wondered, in the face of all this turmoil, why was Jack still staying around? His usual style was to take off by now.

Georgie peeked out at his father from under his worried brow. "I'll warn you, Pa, like I warned Jack, you know I'll just try this again someday."

"Yes, I know." Mr. Griffith was silent for a moment, obviously in deep concentration. "While I have no patience with cowards who flee an unpleasant situation instead of facing up to their duties like a man and overcoming them, or at least using their intellect to find a mutually agreeable solution, I'll grant you this is somewhat different, and I must—albeit grudgingly—admire you for your persistence."

"You're not going to switch me, are you, Pa?"

Mr. Griffith pursed his lips, causing the tips of his white mustache to pull down, like a drawn bow. "I ought to," he answered at length. "I suppose any ordinary father with any ordinary son who did something so completely inconsiderate, selfish, and foolhardy, probably would. I, however, shall not."

Maude could see Georgie's troubled brow ease with immediate relief.

"Do you know why not?" Mr. Griffith asked.

Then, knowing his father as well as they all did, Georgie frowned again.

"Because I'm supposing that my only son possesses intelligence and powers of comprehension above the average individual. Correct me if I'm mistaken."

"No, sir. I'm not. I mean, you're not—mistaken, that is. I am—intelligent, that is."

"I'm also of the firm belief that sufficiently intelligent persons may be reasoned with by the strength of words and intellect alone, while those of lower mental capacity, those nearer to the beasts, need to be taught by the only way they're capable of understanding, in more . . . physically applied terms, if you take my meaning.''

Georgie stuttered a bit and at last uttered, ''I do, sir.''

''Therefore, I needn't switch you—at the moment. I assume I need only talk to you, to express my abject disappointment in your ill-considered actions, and my sincere hope that you will never again repeat this folly. If I find I'm wrong in my suppositions, and that you *aren't* of sufficient intelligence, then . . . well, then I'll not be responsible for the deserved punishment you have, of your own accord and volition, called down upon yourself. Am I mistaken?''

''No, sir.''

''Then I do make myself clear on this matter?''

''Yes, sir. Abundantly clear.''

''I'm so glad to see that, in spite of the evidence posed by this afternoon's ill-fated adventure, my son is as intelligent as I had supposed him to be.'' Mr. Griffith clapped his hand on his son's shoulder. ''Go to bed, boy.''

Georgie heaved a deep sigh of resignation as he stumbled for the stairs. ''Yeah, I've got school tomorrow.''

''Well, perhaps, taking into consideration that you *are* a person of superior intelligence, and so am I,'' he quickly added, ''perhaps we can come to some sort of compromise.''

Georgie slowly started trudging up the steep flight of stairs. Then, in the middle, suddenly the realization of what his father had just said apparently hit him. His long legs pumping, he took the steps two at a time to the top.

Mr. Griffith returned to the parlor, rubbing his chin in contemplation. ''Jack, I do appreciate your efforts in returning my son.''

''Glad I could help, sir.''

''I don't, however, appreciate your interference with the personal affairs of this family in the first place. I don't appreciate your filling my son's head with foolish notions that result in foolish actions.''

''I only meant to entertain him. I never realized he'd take my tales seriously.''

''Georgie's only fourteen, and, for some reason I've never

been able to comprehend, he *trusts* you—why, he actually *likes* you.''

Jack pursed his lips and frowned, as if thinking. Either that, Maude thought, or he was doing a darn good job of pretending to appear repentant. Knowing Jack, she figured it was probably the latter.

''I never meant to cause any trouble.''

Mr. Griffith glared at Jack. ''Ever since your aunt and uncle took you in, you've been nothing but trouble, fabricating tales and elaborate schemes that got you into one scrape after another, and fabricating even more fantastic ones to get yourself out of them. I never did expect you to amount to much. I always warned them you'd turn out to be a ne'er-do-well at best. It's a darn shame I turned out to be so right.''

''I'm real regretful you feel that way, sir.''

''Oh, Benjamin,'' Miss Randolph said gently. ''Over the years, people change, mature, gain experience, knowledge, and perhaps even a bit of wisdom. You oughtn't be so condemning of the young man just because of a misspent youth.''

Maude clenched her jaw. Was even sensible, intelligent Miss Randolph not immune to Jack's charms?

''After all, Georgie's not a baby anymore,'' Miss Randolph continued. ''He's almost an adult. He's very bright, a good scholar. He's slightly older and significantly larger than his schoolmates. He's quite bored with playing their juvenile games. It only stands to reason he'd want to experience the sort of adventures he's read about, or that his friend Jack has told him about.''

Maude blinked with surprise. Only a few hours ago, wasn't Miss Randolph berating herself for allowing Georgie to read adventure stories? Now she'd found a new scapegoat, and she couldn't even bring herself to fully condemn him.

''After all, Jack doesn't seem to be any the worse for having had these adventures. While I'm sure his experiences during the war weren't pleasant, they taught him many worthwhile lessons in loyalty to his friends and duty to his country.''

Maude's eyes narrowed as she watched him. She could almost swear the man was trying not to laugh. If Louise had been here, Maude would have had more consideration of her friend's feelings and would never have brought this up. But some fiendish impulse made her add, "I'm sure he's also learned valuable lessons while he was in jail, too."

"Honesty, courtesy, patience, temperance," Jack recited with equal sincerity.

For her own part, she almost laughed aloud at the mention of temperance. She'd smelled that old jacket.

"He did serve as sheriff in that little town, however briefly," Miss Randolph continued. "I'm quite certain he'll never again consort with ruffians, thieves, and bandits. Will you, Jack?"

"No, Miss Randolph. Never, ever," Jack told her, shaking his head vigorously.

Maude thought he looked the same as he had during their school days, swearing never to misbehave again if it would help him escape his deserved punishment, all the while never intending to keep his word.

"Adelaide," Mr. Griffith said, frowning deeply, "I don't mean to be rude and tell you you don't know what you're talking about, but . . . well, you don't. You don't know the fellow as well as I do."

"Fiddlesticks, Benjamin! He sat in my schoolhouse all day, every day, for many years. Many were the times I had to keep the little rapscallion after class, too. So I suppose I know him at least as well as you do."

Mr. Griffith stuck his hands in his trouser pockets, paced the parlor floor, and grumbled. "But, Adelaide, you didn't read the newspaper reports about—"

"I read everything you printed."

"But you didn't read what I *didn't* print."

15

THERE WAS A CAUTIOUS look in Jack's eyes and a tension to his stance that told Maude he was waiting and ready for whatever trouble might befall. Ordinarily, she figured, Jack would have just taken off again. But she figured he, too, was consumed with a need to know what her father meant by his cryptic remark—even more so because it pertained directly to him.

Maude could feel her own eyes widening with surprise, and her heart sinking with despair. She didn't know which revelation disturbed her the most.

Her father was a staunch supporter of the First Amendment—and everything else in the Constitution of the United States of America. What could have been so unbelievably horrible about Jack in the reports her father had received that, for the first time ever, he'd done, to his way of thinking, the unthinkable? What was there about Jack that her father had decided *not* to print?

Miss Randolph's pale gray eyes searched Mr. Griffith's face. Her expression wasn't one of complete confusion, as Maude felt her own must be. Rather, Maude believed, the schoolteacher was absorbing everything, carefully evaluating what was happening, and calculating her next move. "Benjamin, whatever are you talking about? I don't understand."

"Yes, I suppose this situation does warrant some sort of explanation."

Mr. Griffith strode to the center of the parlor and held his hand out in front of him, as if to command their complete attention. It wasn't as if he didn't already have it, Maude thought.

"Before I go any further, I know you all realize that I have a certain reputation in this town for honesty and integrity, both personally and professionally. I'd like to maintain it, and I hope you'll help me to do so. I trust that this information will go no further than this room."

"Of course, Benjamin!"

"Of course, Papa."

"Not that you'd believe me, sir," Jack replied, "but for what it's worth, I do give you my assurance on the matter."

Mr. Griffith just grunted his grudging acceptance. "I suppose you would, since all this ultimately pertains to you."

Maude figured her father and Jack both could thank their lucky stars her sister hadn't yet returned. It wasn't that Jessica would deliberately spread an evil rumor, but once she started talking, there simply was no way to close the floodgate between her brain and her mouth.

"But I still don't understand what it is you feel you've done," Miss Randolph said. "Or that Jack has done."

"How do you think the business of publishing a small-town newspaper works, Adelaide?"

"Well, I never really gave it much thought," she admitted with obvious reluctance.

"Surely you never supposed that I just invented those stories—"

"Well, certainly not the ones about the war and President Lincoln!"

"That I mixed them in with the advertisements and my editorials, as well as Matthew Conway's occasional letter to the editor, did you?"

"Truly, I never gave it much thought."

"Some of the news stories are reprinted directly from other towns' or big cities' newspapers. Some of the more important stories, about the nation or other countries, are sent to me from larger reporting bureaus. Most editors looking to supply news and fill space just print it all and, most times, I do, too. But . . . well—"

"But not in Jack's case," Miss Randolph supplied.

He nodded.

"But surely, Benjamin, the boy couldn't have done anything so horrendous as to warrant your violating your own ethics in order to hide it."

"I had reasons for my actions that I can't . . . *won't* go into— not here, not now," Mr. Griffith said. "It's . . . not fit for ladies' ears."

"Oh, blast your notions of our feminine sensibilities, Benjamin," Miss Randolph scolded him. "It's good to have integrity, but let's not carry it too far. If other editors in other towns printed it in their newspapers, it can't have been all that horrifying to the general populace. Apparently it's only horrible to the people of Apple Grove. Well, let me tell you, I've known this boy for twenty years, and if he's done something so dastardly that it should prompt me to warn him never to darken my doorway again, then, by Jove, I want to know exactly what it is."

"I can't tell you, Adelaide."

"How can you not trust me to keep a secret? How can you trust me with your secret, but not with Jack's? Am I to assume from this action that you believe men are more trustworthy than women? I assure you, I've held the confidences of many a student and parent in my years of teaching."

"I *do* trust you, Adelaide," he protested, "but—"

"Then how can I believe you? You know me well enough by now, Benjamin, to know that unsubstantiated speculations and groundless accusations hold no sway over my mind."

"The man's a scoundrel, a cad, an out-and-out bounder. You must trust me on this, Adelaide."

He stuck his thumbs into his vest pockets and reared back, trying to look imposing and authoritative. Maude feared he'd made a fatal error in this argument.

"I've much more experience with the world than you, and a woman ought to submit to the authority of—"

"Poppycock! You claim you want my assistance with your son. You claim you admire me for my wit and logic, my education and intellect. Then you must regard me as an equal in *all* matters."

"But there are some matters from which women are best left excluded."

"How can you say you must continue to exclude *women* when we've just fought a war to include all *men?*"

"Adelaide!"

"Benjamin!"

"It's just in this matter . . . you'd never understand. Oh, it's useless to try to reason with an emotional woman!" He slapped his arms at his sides and paced back and forth across the parlor floor.

Miss Randolph stood her ground, lifted her chin, and scowled, obviously affronted by Mr. Griffith's philosophy. "You claim I'm emotional. Indeed, I freely and gladly admit it. Then I tell you, I—and all women—are doubly blessed with emotions *and* reason. You claim this conversation is futile. I both feel and know enough to agree with you on that point, and on that point alone. Therefore, I tell you I'm relieved your son has been safely returned to you. Then I must bid you all good evening."

Miss Randolph spun on her heel and headed toward the front door.

Maude watched, wide-eyed. Would her father not stop his silly pacing and run after her? Or, at his age, at least walk? Or, if only for the sake of common courtesy, at least see her to the door? But her father just stood there until it was far too late, and Miss Randolph had closed the door between them.

Mr. Griffith turned to Jack. He wasn't frowning as he had at Georgie. His face wasn't red as it had been when he'd argued with Miss Randolph. He appeared very calm and in control—showing no emotion whatsoever. Was his hatred of Jack so strong that he dared not allow it to show at all?

"I'll wager you didn't know I'd censored your stories, did you?" her father demanded. "I'll wager you thought I despised you so much that I'd grab hold of every bit of scandal I could get my hands on about you and print it on big broadsides, plastered all over every barn and building in town, just to discredit you and sell more newspapers."

"No, sir," Jack told him calmly. "I know what you printed about me."

"Yes, I suppose your aunt would've sent you old copies of the *Gazette,* so you could keep up with what was happening here."

"I know what you didn't print, too," Jack stated boldly. "How I shot the sheriff in the back while serving as his deputy—

and that's how I got his job. How I took up with a group of outlaws. How I shot some of my own men while we were trying to escape the Federal marshals and the posse, they say so I could keep more of the loot for myself.''

Maude gasped. She hated to do that. She'd always thought the action seemed so false and exaggerated. But this time, she couldn't help herself. That her father might have censored what he published came as less of a shock when she considered he'd undoubtedly done it to spare the Kingstons' feelings. But that Jack had deliberately killed not one, but several men, disturbed her more than she could bear.

Jack glanced over to her. Could he see in her face the distress she felt in her heart? How she hated to let him think she cared anything about him in the first place!

Somehow, no matter how much she disliked him, she'd always thought Jack wasn't truly evil, that he just had the bad luck to sort of fall into trouble's way.

Even when news had come of his criminal activities, she'd naively supposed he'd just pulled a gun, threatened ''your money or your life'' as the highwaymen of romance novels did, and the people had simply turned over their valuables without a shot being fired. She'd never supposed for a minute he'd actually killed anyone!

''I know a lot more that you don't, that never even made it into any of the reports you received, Mr. Griffith,'' Jack said. His voice was deep and ragged. ''I'm grateful to you for excluding what you did.''

''I didn't do it for your sake, you confounded jackass,'' Mr. Griffith growled. ''I did it for your aunt and uncle, and so that association with you wouldn't ruin your cousin's prospects for a normal life and a happy marriage with a good man.''

''I sort of figured that, too.''

For just a moment, Maude believed she detected, behind the defiant gleam in Jack's green eyes, that small hint of sadness and hurt that she'd once seen through the gleam of boyish mischief.

''Did you let them see—?''

''Of course not! Certainly not your sensitive aunt, who cries even when she opens her Christmas presents. Not even your uncle. You'd already caused them enough trouble and heartbreak. I wasn't about to go adding insult to injury. I wrote and edited those stories myself and burned the reports as soon as I was done."

"Not even Maude?" Jack asked, glancing again in her direction.

"Of course not."

"Then I'm sorry I brought this up in front of her."

"Someone Miss Randolph's age needs to be protected. But Maude . . . well, these modern girls are different. It must be the food. Or the war. Or maybe the times are just changing." Mr. Griffith shrugged his shoulders. "It's late, Jack. I think you need to be getting home."

Jack turned to her once again. He appeared to want to say something. But Maude was so exhausted, so puzzled, so unbelievably hurt and ultimately disappointed, that she was having difficulty concentrating. He could have told her anything at this moment, and she wouldn't have comprehended a word. She couldn't think of anything to say to him now. Silently she turned away from him.

Jack headed out the door.

Her father was sitting on the sofa, his elbows resting on his knees, his hands hanging limp between them. His shoulders seemed more stooped than she could remember seeing them— except when her mother had died. The worry of Georgie's running away, the turmoil of his argument with Miss Randolph, and the strain of keeping his emotions in check in his confrontation with Jack had all taken their toll on him. Her father was only forty-six—not so old when she looked at him—but when she considered that most men his age were already dead, it gave her something to worry about.

"I feel so very old tonight," he said quietly.

"It's been a long day." Maude sat on the arm of the sofa, reached out, and patted her father's shoulder. "You'll feel better after a night's sleep."

"I never did like that boy."

"I know."

"When he first came to live here, I felt sorry for him, seeing as how his family was killed and all, but—"

"Killed?" Maude's hand fell still. For just a moment, she felt as if the beating of her heart, the workings of her lungs, and even the thoughts in her mind had come to a halt, as well. After what seemed an eternity, she was able to blink and breathe, and finally to make her mouth move enough to say, "Wait a minute. Papa, do you mean Jack was telling the truth? That his parents really were killed?"

Her father lifted his head and straightened his back. She supposed, no matter what, he'd never feel too old or too tired to report any news, no matter how long ago it had happened.

"They were killed in an Indian attack on their wagon train while heading out to California through the Utah Territory. Do you mean to say, after all these years, you never knew that?"

"I knew Jack was an orphan. I was so young when he came here, and after that he was always getting into so much other trouble, no one really thought much about his past. I guess I figured his parents died because they got sick from the cholera or typhoid or whatever went through the wagon trains. I . . . never once figured Jack might be telling the truth. I guess that means those gruesome stories he used to tell about how he'd watched everybody being hacked to bits while he hid under the burning wagon pretending he was already dead, even when they jabbed him in the arm with an arrow . . . were true."

"Of course, that was Jack's version of the massacre, and everyone knew how incredibly unreliable he always had been—even from the tender age of six."

"I just figured he was making up another outlandish story, as he always did about everything else. He took great pride in showing off that scar on his arm to everyone in school who had the cent to pay him for a peek. I always suspected he'd gotten it falling out of a tree instead, and I didn't pay him one bit of attention—or money."

"Smart girl. But, yes, that's the truth of it. They were killed by a band of Indians—Thaddeus Kingston's brother, Leonard, and his wife, and the baby."

"The . . . baby?" Maude repeated very slowly.

"Little boy a couple of months old. It's a shame to say I forget his name now."

She felt a cold chill embrace her arms, holding her completely immobile, and choking her so that she could barely whisper, "Oh, my. Jack had a brother?"

Her father looked at her with surprise. "You didn't know?"

"He never mentioned his brother at all."

"The soldiers said they'd found the baby under Jack, as if he'd been trying to protect him . . . not knowing he was already dead. They said Jack put up a hell of a fight when they tried to get him away from the bodies. Figures, with Jack. I understand they buried the three of them out there at Fort Crittenden, then sent the boy back here.''

Her father shook his head. ''I swear, I should've known—when everyone else in that party was killed, and Jack somehow managed to survive and not get carried off by the Indians, but was brought back to torment us, I should've known right then and there that boy was a jinx! I've often wondered what it was he did to rile those Indians into a murderous rage. I know full well I ought to have some sympathy and charity for the boy, but I've never liked him since the time he burned my outhouse down.''

''He claimed it was an accident, Papa,'' Maude offered weakly. She knew she had to stop thinking about Jack and this new revelation of his hidden past, and revert again to the dutiful daughter she'd always been, comforting her troubled father. ''At least no one was in it at the time.''

''I never could see why some people liked him so much.''

''Me, neither.''

Well, that wasn't entirely true. From a purely earthy point of view, Maude certainly could understand what a woman of strong appetites—like Clarice—might find attractive about Jack; or what women with no intelligence or common sense—like Ruthie or Jessica—might find fascinating about him.

''I hate him now for the trouble he's caused between me and my only son. I hate him for the trouble he's caused between Adelaide and myself—just when things looked so . . . promising. Your mother's been gone so long and—''

Maude patted his shoulder a little more firmly. ''Miss Randolph's a sensible woman. I'm sure she's genuinely fond of you.''

He looked up at her with a worried expression in his eyes. ''Then you approve?''

''Of course. I'm sure you'll be able to mend things tomorrow.''

''He's even made me go against my own principles.''

''You did it to spare the Kingstons' feelings, certainly a noble self-sacrifice on your part,'' she assured him.

''There's not an aspect of my life that damn Jack hasn't

touched and ruined—except for my girls. That damn Jack just better damn-sight leave my daughters alone!''

Maude knew her father was angry. She hadn't heard him use that much profanity since Jack had knocked over and spilled all the type drawers at the newspaper office.

''I know you're a grown woman now, Maude, and handling all the responsibilities of a grown woman. But I'm still your father and I need to tell you one thing.''

''What's that, Papa?''

''Don't dance with that damned Jack so much at these parties.''

''I'll try not to, Papa. But, well, I can't hardly be rude if he asks me.''

She wanted to obey her father. She'd *always* obeyed her father, ever since she was a little girl—all right, except for leaving the house this afternoon when he'd told her not to. But she wanted to dance with Jack again. She liked dancing with him. She *liked* feeling his arms around her.

''It doesn't matter much anyway, Papa. If Jack remains true to his character, he's not even going to stay around until the next party.''

She hoped she was wrong!

The front door slammed shut.

''I'm home! Have you found Georgie yet?'' Jessica cried, bouncing into the house. Her hair had come loose again, and there was a deep layer of mud coating the hem of her skirt.

Caleb, battered felt hat in hand, cautiously followed.

Mr. Griffith slowly and steadily rose to his feet. Her father might claim to be feeling weary to his bones and aged beyond his years, but he sprang into battle like a seasoned war horse. Taking his customary place of authority in the center of the parlor, he crossed his arms over his chest and glared at Jessica.

''Do you have any idea what time it is? Where have you been?''

''I went looking for Georgie, of course.''

From the smile on her sister's face, Maude didn't think she appeared the least bit worried about her lost brother, or sorry for being tardy, or for any worry she might have caused.

''I know you told us to stay home, but . . . well, I thought I knew exactly where he was, even though I didn't, and Maude's better at staying home than I am, anyway, so I left her here and—''

"Maude didn't stay home, either," Mr. Griffith announced.

"*Maude* disobeyed you?" Jessica's blue eyes grew wide with disbelief. Then she burst out laughing.

"She also found Georgie."

"Oh, well, good then. . . . Thanks for all your help, Caleb. Good night." Jessica turned and headed for the stairs.

Wasn't she even going to ask where they'd found Georgie? Maude thought angrily.

"Just a moment there, young lady," Mr. Griffith said.

Jessica stopped.

"I think you still have some explaining to do."

Caleb grimaced. "I—I'm afraid Miss Jessica being out so late is all my fault."

"I wouldn't lay all the blame at your doorstep, Caleb."

"You see, I was just coming in from working in the fields when Miss Jessica arrived at our farm, looking for Georgie."

"I wouldn't have been so late getting there, except I went to see Miss Hawkins and the kittens first, figuring that's where Georgie probably went," Jessica interjected. "You know how Miss Hawkins is—once she gets started talking, you just can't stop her."

Maude was sure Miss Hawkins wasn't the only one to blame in this matter.

Caleb shuffled his hat around the brim. "When she arrived at our farm, I was slopping the hogs, and—''

"I wanted to help," Jessica continued. "You know, it's a shame you're a newspaper editor, Papa, instead of a farmer, because I've had so much fun helping—''

"I wonder if you'd feel that way if Caleb were the undertaker," Mr. Griffith grumbled.

"We got to discussing the piglets," Caleb continued, "and a few other things. All real harmless, I assure you. The next thing we knew, it was dark and Miss Jessica hadn't eaten, and Reuben had made ham and bean soup, so I suggested—''

"I told him I could walk home alone, but—''

"I couldn't let her go home alone in the dark and on an empty stomach. It's not healthy. It's not safe."

"He insisted on making me ride in that bouncing buckboard

of his,'' Jessica complained. She grimaced and jabbed Caleb in the ribs with her elbow.

"That shouldn't bother you," Maude remarked, sure her sarcasm went completely unnoticed by her sister.

"So here I am!" Jessica declared.

"Safe and sound, sir. I respect Miss Jessica and this whole family too much to do anything that wasn't proper."

"I'm sure you do, Caleb," Mr. Griffith answered.

"If you don't believe me, sir, I'm ... willing to do the honorable thing by Miss Jessica."

The honorable thing? Maude repeated, distractedly. Then it suddenly dawned on her. Good heavens, was he actually offering to marry her sister to make an honest woman of her? How kind, how noble—how horrible! If Caleb were forced to marry her foolish sister, what in heaven's name would *she* do?

"That won't be necessary, Caleb," Mr. Griffith assured him.

Maude was more shocked to realize that her moment of sheer panic came not so much from the idea of losing Caleb than from the problems that the rush of making hurried arrangements for a proper wedding and reception would cause. Maybe her family and friends were right. Maybe she *was* too occupied with other people's lives.

"Thank you for your kindness when the rest of the family was in quite a turmoil. It's rather comforting to see there are still some young men around here with morals and a sense of honor," Mr. Griffith continued. "Not like some other folks, who drop in here from time to time as they darn well please."

∞

PAPA CERTAINLY NEEDN'T WORRY about *her,* Maude thought as she prepared for bed that evening. *She* was the sensible sister. Hadn't so many people told her as much for as long as she could remember?

Imagine Jessica getting so involved with a litter of piglets that she'd forgotten her own brother was missing!

What a dear Caleb was to bring the heedless girl home safe! Maude thought as she walked to her window. So considerate. So honest and trustworthy. Always willing to do a good turn, always aiming to keep the peace among his neighbors. Not always stirring up trouble, like that darned Jack.

Of course, Caleb had spent his whole life so far on his farm. He'd cared for his parents until they'd died peacefully in their beds, not seen them murdered. He had four surviving brothers. What did Jack have? She felt a twinge of guilt, having under-estimated Jack's capacity for any depth of feeling. It certainly explained why he'd always thought so much of Georgie. If only she'd known! Perhaps if she'd known, that was one area in which she never would have been so hard on him.

No, her father was correct. Jack was a jinx—making Georgie run away, causing Miss Randolph and her father to argue, mak-ing her friends (and even herself) doubt her skills at quilting, making Florence question the suitability of her beau, and even causing Katy to doubt the rightness of her marriage.

Feeling restless, she watched a few clouds skitter across the growing face of the moon. She could see Jack perfectly well, leaning out his window again, waving to her with those muscular arms and calloused, sun-browned hands. He was smiling at her, his firm lips parted just enough to show a bit of those even white teeth.

No, she would *not* turn, she told herself sternly. Yes, she knew perfectly well that he knew perfectly well that she could see him. But she would *not* acknowledge him, not tonight, not even if he stood there waiting all night. No matter how much sympathy she felt for him, it just wasn't proper.

What kind of gentleman deliberately peered into a lady's bed-room window? What sort of perverted wretch was he to keep watching?

For goodness' sake, she was all the way up on the second floor. She didn't live in the middle of town like Molly Fischer used to. There was plenty of space between her house and the neighbors', and a tall, broad tree growing between. She'd never had to worry about drawing her curtains when she got ready for bed before. But that was before Jack had returned.

She reached up, seized her draperies in tightly balled fists, and yanked them closed. If she could have moved her heavy ward-robe, she'd have pushed it in front of the window, for extra protection from Jack. She didn't trust him for one second. She knew he was still watching her window. She could vividly recall his piercing gaze sweeping through her body, and his danger-ously seductive grin that seemed to draw her more tightly into his web. She found herself thinking about his green eyes—and missing him terribly.

This wasn't right! It just wasn't right.

∽

JACK LOOKED OUT HIS bedroom window. Finally Maude had closed those blasted drapes!

How could he get done the things he had to do, with her watching him? He wouldn't make the same mistake he'd made before, underestimating Maude's desire to keep track of everything that was going on; falling victim to a chance glance out of a bedroom window. He couldn't have her following him again.

He couldn't get done the things he had to do, if he was going to be watching her, either. He'd been fascinated with her when he'd first seen her again after so many years. He'd figured he'd get over it quickly enough. But he hadn't. She held a grip on him he was finding hard to account for by any other means. He couldn't let this feeling stand in his way. He still had a job to do.

He pulled on his old jacket. Criminy, he hated the smell of this thing. The first thing he'd do with his money would be to buy a new jacket and burn this one! He checked his revolver and looked out the window one last time.

Maude's lamp still burned, but her curtains were tightly drawn. This time he figured it was safe.

He slipped the sash upward, climbed out his window and down the tree, and headed into town.

∽

BENJAMIN STOOD IN HIS darkened parlor and watched out the window. It had been a long day—small wonder he couldn't sleep.

He thanked the Almighty for allowing him to retrieve his son from an uncertain life on the road. He prayed that the Almighty in his wisdom and mercy might allow him to mend his quarrel with Adelaide and enjoy, in his impending declining years, the joys and comforts her soft, feminine presence could bring to his bed and board.

He never expected to see Jack skulking across his neighbors' lawn.

He never had trusted that boy. Even if Jack was up to his ears in the creek and swearing he was wet, there was something about him that made a wise man not trust him. Benjamin always prided himself on being a wise man.

Even now, Jack kept doing things that prompted Benjamin to regard him with suspicion. What honest man would go slipping out of his house in the middle of the night? What honest man hung silently around the bank, watching who came and went, who withdrew and who made deposits, and how the clerks got into the safe?

He'd noticed this from the very first day. He couldn't help but notice it—the newspaper office was directly across the street from the bank, and Jack was so very obvious about it.

Of course, Jack probably thought he was being so clever. Benjamin figured he hadn't been a newspaperman this much time on this earth not to pick up a clever trick or two himself.

He wouldn't say anything about it—not yet. Not privately to Jack or to Sheriff Tucker. He'd always figured if a body gave Jack enough rope, the dang fool would hang himself eventually. He prayed that whatever Jack was up to, someone would stop him before he brought financial disaster to the town, heaped untold humiliation on his aunt and uncle, and ended up swinging from the end of a rope.

He just wanted to be around to watch when it all happened. That was all he asked—just to be around to watch.

Whatever happened, he figured Jack certainly had it coming to him.

16

JACK WAS—HAD ALWAYS been, now that Maude thought about it—so very different from any man she'd ever known. He'd seen his family slaughtered before his very eyes. He'd sheltered his own baby brother, and gone in search of hers. She'd seen him charm all the ladies and even be kind to shy, plain Ann Engles.

On the other hand, he'd killed a sheriff and robbed the bank. By his own admission, there were things about him so horrible someone had seen fit not to include them in the reports her father had received. What should she believe? Her respected father—or the evidence she'd seen with her own eyes?

Had Jack learned his lesson, had he paid for his crimes and decided to follow the straight and narrow path? Or would he return to his life of crime? Maude didn't know what to think about Jack anymore. The only thing she knew for certain was that she couldn't stop thinking about him.

Even though it was late and she was weary to her very bones, even though the light from the kerosene lamp wasn't very good, she felt she needed something to reassure her that, once Jack had disappeared out onto the prairie again, as he always did, her life would revert to its normal course; that she could continue with the plans she'd carefully made, as if nothing else had ever happened.

She made her way to the foot of her bed, to the painted wooden chest Grandpa Pratt, her mother's father, had sent her all the way from Baltimore as soon as the war was over, when she'd turned eighteen.

She opened the lid. She pulled out a half-finished quilt top and the unattached blocks. Beneath it lay several quilt tops she'd already finished piecing: a light and dark Log Cabin like Florence's, a multicolored Star of Bethlehem, a blue and white Delectable Mountains, a red and white Carpenter's Wheel, and a red and green Peony. She and her friends would get together and quilt them when she became officially engaged to Caleb.

She also had several sets of embroidered pillow slips with tatted or crocheted edgings, and even one with a cherished knitted lace edge Grandmother Griffith had made and given her for her birthday the year before she'd passed away. She also had several less delicate, more serviceable tea and kitchen towels and aprons.

She laid the loose blocks on her bed. Then, with a flourish, she spread out the rest of the top.

Her Baltimore bride's quilt, she thought with pride. She knew her friends would make a friendship quilt for her—one with neat but simple little squares and rectangles of calico and muslin, whose corners would meet with varying degrees of accuracy, with their names and appropriate sentiments penned with indelible ink into the large blank space in the center of each block. But she was the best seamstress of them all, and she deserved to make herself something extra special.

Lord forgive me my sin of pride, she thought, but was it wrong to be proud of something that was the truth? She was good, and she wanted to make something very special for herself. This was it.

Maude smiled as she examined each individual block, carefully appliquéd with a different design—a basket, a spray of flowers, a round wreath, even a heart-shaped wreath, in carefully arranged bits of red, green, blue, and yellow calico, and bleached muslin. She'd embroidered little details on the blocks, too—a flower stem, a bee, a butterfly.

Mama had been born and raised in Baltimore. Maude remembered her mother telling her about those days, about how she and her friends had made intricate quilts like this for each other. The ladies had had time for leisurely, intricate stitching many years before the Yankees came.

In spite of her illness, Mama had painstakingly taught her her own considerable skills and, after her death, in her honor, Maude had worked hard to perfect them.

Maude grimaced as she recalled her ever-patient mother trying to teach Jessica, too, and inevitably throwing up her hands in resignation. Jessica had no skill with a needle, Mama had declared, and even less patience to sit and learn. As Mama had grown weaker, her patience had worn thin, too.

Maude paused a little longer, looking at her special center block. No one else in town could combine the embroidery and quilting into such a special arrangement of flowers, ribbons, and initials as she could.

As she stood admiring her quilt, she felt her smile of pride turning into a little grimace, and she sighed. It still wasn't quite right. Maybe she was being too picky. No. She shook her head. It was definitely wrong. But there had to be *something* she could do to make it right!

It was late, and she had a lot of work to do tomorrow. Still, she lifted the quilt block and carried it to her seat by the window.

She sat in her rocking chair. Was Jack still leaning out his window, watching her curtains, on the chance he'd spot her through a small opening?

She mustn't think about him now. She'd work on her special block instead. She'd fix it so that her initials and Caleb's looked right, if it was the last thing she did; if she died from bleeding to death from sticking her fingers too many times; if they found her withered, emaciated corpse bent over her quilt! She'd make it right.

She pulled a needle threaded with green embroidery floss out of her sewing basket. She began stitching the stems of the lilies of the valley. The short, repetitive movements of her stitching and the rocking of the chair comforted her. The tension in her jaw lessened. She wasn't holding her arms so tightly, as if she were ready to deflect—or deal—a blow. Slowly she felt herself begin to relax. Her needlework had always been soothing to her.

There, that was better, she decided. She held the block out in front of her to examine the workmanship she knew for certain would be acceptable to her now. Yes, indeed. It looked so much better. She breathed a deep sigh of relief that, at last, she'd made it right. The roses, the lilies of the valley, and the ribbons all blended beautifully with the initials, *MG* and—*oh, no!*

How could she have done that? She dropped the quilt block as if it were poisoned. Had she fallen asleep, or into some sort of spiritualistic trance that had enabled some evil demon to possess her while she stitched and caused her to do what she'd done? How could such a beautiful design contain the initials *MG* and *JK?*

James Kingston! Who else could it stand for? She knew of no one else in town with those initials.

Angrily she picked at the green threads—ripping out some in long strands to leave holes in the muslin, breaking some to leave short strands sticking out like mown-down grass—until all traces of Jack's initials were gone. Now there was no evidence that could be used against her.

Heedless of sticking herself with the pins and needles, she scooped up the entire quilt, hauled it over to her chest, and stuffed it in. She eyed it with distaste, as if the pieces of fabric were some kind of Frankenstein monster she'd sewn together and given life to, that now threatened to break out and destroy her as the monster had tried to destroy its creator. She slammed the lid shut and sat on it. She'd never allow it to escape and ruin her life.

∞

"HAVE SOME. IT'S DELICIOUS," Jessica said, holding out a full glass to Maude.

Maude laid the block she was piecing in her lap and took the glass from her sister. Holding it up against the light of the setting sun, she examined it. "What is it?"

"Apple cider. What else?"

"With you, I'm never sure." She took a sip. She frowned, then sipped again. "This cider's turned hard."

"Nonsense."

"Jessica, it's as hard as your head," Maude insisted.

"And mighty refreshing," Jessica added with a grin.

In spite of the piquant taste, Maude finished her drink and held out her glass for more.

"I thought you said it had turned hard."

"There's still no sense in wasting it," Maude replied.

"Just like you, Maude—always so sensible." Jessica refilled Maude's glass, then left the jug on the table in front of her. "I'll be helping Miss Hawkins clean out her storeroom tonight while the store is closed."

Maude watched Jessica flit away toward town, then took up her piecing again. Papa had taken Georgie to the newspaper office this evening, getting him started working there. She had the entire evening to herself and intended to enjoy it, in the quiet and solitude of her own back porch, swinging and piecing her quilt blocks, and occasionally sipping that delicious cider.

She hadn't intended to begin a new quilt until her other one was finished. But she couldn't bear to think about working on that monstrously threatening bride's quilt lurking in her bedroom. This new one was perfectly harmless—simple muslin squares and triangles arranged with squares and triangles of a pretty blue calico. Even the name had a pleasant, homey connotation—Sister's Choice. Best of all, it had absolutely nothing to do with Jack.

"Just as I always maintained—there sits Maude, always cleaning or sewing something."

Maude looked up quickly to see Jack strolling toward her across the backyard. Too quickly. She blinked and clasped the arm of the swing. How could it spin like that when her feet were still firmly planted on the porch? She didn't recall the porch floor being slanted, either. To her knowledge, the railing had never moved before. She closed her eyes and tried to still the swirling house. When she opened them again, Jack was standing at the foot of the steps.

She couldn't believe it was possible for him to look better now than when she'd first seen him—but he did. He certainly wasn't any taller. He might have filled out just a little more because of his aunt's good cooking, as well as all the other treats unmarried ladies in town were continually dropping off at the Kingstons' for him. She'd laughed as she'd watched them from her kitchen window, parading their goodies in, hoping to convince Jack what excellent cooks they were and homemakers they'd make. She knew perfectly well their mothers had made it all.

She tried not to grin so broadly. That was hard to do, considering how pleasant the cider made her feel. She tried to make her voice not sound so breathless, like that trollop Clarice's. She didn't want Jack to think she was too glad to see him again.

"I . . . I've been wondering where you were. You're welcome to sit a spell and . . . have some cider." She poured him a glass, then refilled her own. Dutch Courage, they called it—as she downed her drink, she figured she was going to need all the courage she could get.

"Thanks." He settled beside her in the big double swing. "I have to admit I was a little afraid to come over."

"I never thought *you'd* be afraid of anything," she told him as she resumed her piecing.

"There are a few things."

"I never dreamed I'd hear you admit it."

"I didn't think you'd still be talking to me," he confessed, "now that you know all about me."

"I don't think anyone will ever know *all* about you, Jack," she replied. Then her voice grew softer in the quiet of the waning light. "But I do know a little more about you now—more than I did before. More than I ever imagined—"

"You know I killed—"

"That's not it," she interrupted quickly. That was one part of his life she definitely didn't want to hear about. "In war, it's . . . a duty. You've served time in jail to pay for your part in the robbery." She shook her head. She laid aside her piecing and, very softly, said, "My father also told me about . . . your brother."

She watched a brief flicker of pain flash across his eyes.

"Why didn't you ever say anything about him, Jack?"

"Not much to say. Johnny hadn't done much in his short life. Not many people even remember him anymore. John Adams Kingston—big name for such a little fellow."

She should have figured, no matter what, Jack would never forget. "I'm very sorry."

"It was a long time ago. Utah, the war, Dry Creek—everything seems as though it happened such a long time ago."

"I think I understand you a little better now. I like to think I know you well enough to believe you'd have a good reason for doing . . . whatever you did—even if it doesn't seem like a good reason to anybody else."

He just shrugged.

"I never did thank you properly for bringing Georgie back, either."

"Oh, he'd have probably come back on his own, when his money ran out—or it got dark," he added with a chuckle.

"You're pretty much an authority on runaways." She managed to summon enough courage to cast him a teasing smile.

"I know a restless man when I see one."

"Like when you look in the mirror each morning?"

She was only teasing, but his reply was so serious. "Yes. There are a lot of restless men in this town—in every town I've ever passed through. Look at Caleb, with four brothers, all of them trying to make a living off that farm. Someday he'll leave."

"He's been talking about going west for a long time and never done anything. I'm beginning to doubt he ever will."

"He's like a covered pot of water sitting over a blazing fire. Everything might look calm and quiet on the outside, but sooner or later he'll build up enough steam. Then he'll leave."

Maude pressed her lips tightly together. She hoped he was wrong, but knowing Jack, and knowing Caleb, she was afraid he was right.

She took up her sewing again. "Is that what you're doing, Jack?" she asked, pretending to be absorbed in her piecing. "Just waiting here to build up enough steam to leave?"

"No." His answer was abrupt, as if he really didn't want to deal with that subject at all. As if it could help him avoid answering her, he reached for his glass and sipped the cider.

"Maude, what are you drinking?" he demanded, peering into the glass. "This cider has gone hard."

"Not *that* hard."

"You're drunk, Maude."

"I am not!" she protested as ferociously as she could. "I'm as sober as a judge. See." She held up the block she'd been working on. How had she managed to sew the short ends of the triangles together, then sew seven squares across instead of only five?

"Yes, you are," he insisted.

She threw down the obstreperous block and took up her glass. "That's strange. Somehow I seem to recall my hand . . . wasn't that far away the last time I looked at it. Maybe I really am turning into an old maid and need spectacles!"

She lifted her glass to finish off the contents. The cider splashed out over her bottom lip.

"Oh, dear. I thought I clearly remembered exactly where I'd left my mouth."

Jack laughed and quickly produced a handkerchief. "I think that cider is a little more potent—and you've had a little more of it—than you realize."

He held her chin steady with one hand and, with the other, gave a little dab to her bottom lip. The soft cotton of the handkerchief teased at a nerve that undoubtedly ran from the edge of her mouth directly down her throat to divide and run to the tips of her breasts. She'd never imagined they could feel so sensitive, that they could ache to be touched.

She'd never felt this longing on the few occasions when Caleb had held her hand so politely. She liked it. She wanted to feel this way again and again. The only thing she'd change would be to lose that blasted handkerchief and feel Jack's calloused fingertips, which held her chin so steadily, brushing against her lips. She closed her eyes to the giddy sensation of the spinning porch and the thought of Jack's fingertips tracing a thin line from her lips, down her throat, to the tips of her breasts, peaked and swollen, waiting for him.

She'd have pressed her hands firmly against her bodice, forcing her breasts to be calm, and flat, and not so sensitive to the soft cotton of her chemise.

"There," he said, releasing her chin. "Now you look presentable."

She opened her eyes. "Thank you," she said, when she really wanted to say, "Hold me. Touch me!"

He slid nearer. His knee brushed against her leg. He placed his arm across the back of the swing, so that he could have touched her shoulder and the back of her neck.

She wanted him to pull her closer to his body—firm, strong, and muscular. She wanted him to wrap his arms around her. She wanted to throw down these pieces of cloth and snuggle into his arms.

"Why haven't you ever married, Maude?"

She blinked and stared at him in surprise.

"I . . . have obligations," she said. "I can't just go off and leave when Georgie still needs someone to watch out for him, and Jessica needs a perpetual keeper. Papa can't run his newspaper and take care of the household, too.'' She tried to glare at him, but the nearness of him banished all her anger. "He—even Georgie and Jessica—might have been happy with Miss Randolph until *you* caused that argument between them.''

"That wasn't an argument.''

"Really? I guess they call those things by a different name where you come from.''

"It's just a little misunderstanding caused by all the excitement of Georgie running away. They'll be back together again.''

Maude threw him a skeptical glance.

"Why don't you believe me? Haven't you done a quilt block for those two to tell you it's all going to work out fine?''

"No, I haven't. Anyway, I thought you didn't believe in all that hogwash.''

"I don't. But you do. Have you made a block for yourself, Maude?''

"I'm not about to tell *you!*''

"You said you hadn't set your cap for Matthew Conway—so, who is it, Maude?''

She didn't answer.

"If I had to put money on it, I'd say you don't have anybody special right now. Do you?''

"You can believe what you like, and I'll warn you there's nothing you can say or do that'll prod me into telling you anything.''

"So there *is* someone special.''

If she shook her head to tell him no, not only would she be giving him an answer, but she'd be lying. If she shook her head to indicate she wouldn't give him a clue, he might take it to mean there was no one special. She didn't want to allow him to think that and leave herself vulnerable to . . . To what? To a few more sly waves from a window? To a little more teasing from Jack before he finally took out across the prairie and she never saw him again—until years later when he came back for his aunt or uncle's funeral?

"I just can't figure out how a woman as sensible as you—No, I won't mince words, Maude.'' He pulled her closer to him. "We know each other too well for that. You can try to hide it as much as you want, but I can feel how you react when I touch you—all warm blood and soft skin. How can a woman like you put her faith in cold cloth and steel needles to tell you who to love? Don't you believe in love, Maude?''

"Yes, of course I do.''

"Don't you believe that love's more important than all the carefully laid plans, all the arrangements between well-meaning relatives and friends, all the supposed social suitability of a man and a woman for each other?''

"Well, yes, but I never imagined you did.''

"When a fellow sits in a prison cell, he's got a whole lot of time to think. How did you learn what love is? From the books we had to read in Miss Randolph's English class? From watching all the other people whose lives you're so wound up in that you don't have a life of your own?''

She stared at him for his audacity, and feared she'd actually have to answer him.

"Do you even know what love is, Maude?'' he challenged her.

17

"DON'T BE RIDICULOUS!" MAUDE frowned at the very idea of his outlandish assertion. "Of course I know what love is—and you do, too, so don't ask me foolish questions."

"What is it, Maude?"

"It's . . . a feeling, a very strong feeling."

"Like hot, cold, hungry?"

"You're being ridiculous again."

"No, I'm not. You read a lot. You've always been so darned smart."

"I thought that was one of the things about me that always irritated you . . . why you were always trying to get me in trouble in school."

"Maybe I admired you for it. Maybe I was just jealous."

Maude laughed. "*You* jealous of *me*? But I never did anything."

"I never was particularly good at book learning. I was never really smart—or I wouldn't have gotten myself into the scrapes I did. But I was slick—maybe a little conniving. A fellow doesn't usually come up against love when he's being clever. So I don't think I'm stepping out of bounds when I ask a lady like you to tell me—what's love?"

"It's hard to explain. But—"

"But you know it when you feel it."

"You know it when you see it in other people," she answered evasively. "My parents were in love with each other. Your parents must have been, too, even if you were too young at the time to notice it. Your aunt and uncle still are, after all these years. I've seen my friends—"

"What about yourself?" he asked softly. "Haven't you ever been in love, Maude?"

She wasn't sure anymore, so she said nothing.

"Isn't there someone you're in love with?" He almost sounded as if he were pleading to know.

Don't be silly, she scolded herself. Why should Jack care about her and her hopes for the future?

It could be so easy. All she had to do was tell him she was going to marry Caleb—whenever she got the rest of her family settled; whenever he managed to stop talking about his wild dreams and actually made up his mind to court her.

But Jack didn't know that. All she had to do was tell him she was in love with Caleb, and he'd go away and leave her alone. If nothing came of it, well, he'd only find out about it after Louise wrote to him that Maude had eventually married someone else. But who else could she bear to spend the rest of her life with? That wasn't something she had to worry about telling him right now.

All she had to do was tell him she was in love with Caleb. But she couldn't do it. She just couldn't do it.

It wasn't that she *wasn't* in love with Caleb. She liked him a lot. He was honest, intelligent, ambitious, and hard-working. She'd always imagined she could be very happy married to him; taking care of the large house filled with many fine things they'd have when he eventually made his fortune, as she'd always been sure he would.

He was handsome. She'd supposed they'd have beautiful, healthy, intelligent children. She just couldn't imagine *making* those children with Caleb. She just didn't have that "feeling" about Caleb.

She couldn't imagine wanting to feel the press of his warm lips on hers, or longing to feel his arms around her, or his naked body lying heavy atop her—not the way she wanted Jack.

She knew very well Jack couldn't read her thoughts. Still, the image of him, warm and naked beside her in bed, raised a heated flush to her cheeks. She could feel short tendrils of her hair clinging to the dampness on her forehead and at the back of her neck. Even when a welcome, cooling breeze swept over them, she still felt unaccountably warm.

Was this a part of all the other "feelings" that went to make up that one overwhelming sensation of love? The hot, the cold, the hungry. She did feel hot and cold all at the same time when she looked at Jack and he looked back at her with that certain gleam in his eyes. She felt hungry, too, when she looked at Jack but couldn't touch him. But not the kind of hunger that could be satisfied with mere food. It was the kind of hunger that ate away at her heart.

"You look flushed. I'd say you've had too much cider."

"I'm fine." She certainly couldn't tell him it was thoughts of him that were making her blush.

"You haven't laced your corset too tight, have you?"

"How dare you ask such a question!"

Worse yet, how dare he slowly move his hand across her shoulder—just an inch or two and very gently, but she could feel it anyway. Why, the next thing she knew, he'd be trailing his finger across the front of her throat, down her chest toward her breasts, unfastening her laces! Thoughts of him touching her, watching her as her bare skin was gradually exposed to his gaze, made her shiver and grow warm again, all at the same time.

She'd known the cider was hard, and she'd drunk a lot of it anyway. Now she was paying the price for her intemperance and gluttony. What other sins would she have to pay for before Jack finally went away?

All she had to do was pull away from him. His embrace didn't hold her entrapped. She could freely move away from him any time she wanted. The thing of it was, she really didn't want to.

"As hard as this might be for you to believe, all the while I was away," Jack said as he continued to toy with the lace at her throat, "all the while I stared at pillaged houses and charred woods, at bleak prairie landscapes, and at the bare, gray walls of my prison cell, waiting to be released, I always remembered everything beautiful about Apple Grove—the people, the buildings, what all the fields look like—morning, noon, and night, spring to summer and fall to winter. But I'm sorry to say, there's one thing I never realized until very recently."

He turned to her. Very slowly he reached out and placed his

hand on her arms. Cautiously he turned her to face him. His green eyes sparkled. She was glad to see the spark in his eyes. She'd gotten used to it in the past few days, and missed it when she didn't see it.

"I never realized before, Maude, how very beautiful you are."

His hold on her arm eased. Was this his way of letting her know that, if she protested, he'd let her go—let her stand and retreat into the house for protection? How could she tell him she'd never protest? How could she let him know this was a moment she'd longed for—whether she'd realized it at first or not, and no matter how much she'd fought against that realization—for many nights? All this time had her scorn for Jack just been a hidden desire for this wild, impetuous, adventurous, dangerous man?

Slowly his hand slid up her arm and across her shoulder. She didn't move—she could barely breathe. He reached up to take her chin in his hand again. She reached out and laid her hand against his face. It was almost as if lightning were striking her palm where it touched him, coursing through her body, to exit where his hand touched her—except it seemed to be traveling at an extremely slow rate of motion, pausing to send sparks into her heart, her stomach, and lower, into her quivering depths.

His rough fingers smoothed up her neck and held her chin, lifting her face to his. How could she have been so foolish to stay out here with him in the softly seductive spring evening? How could she have been so foolish to be alone with him when she knew very well she wasn't in complete control of all her faculties? She had no idea what could happen with him—and right now she really didn't care. She drew in a deep breath. She was going to need it. Jack was going to kiss her—and she was going to love it!

As she held her breath, she looked into his eyes. Jack had always seemed so arrogant, so cocksure of himself. But now his eyes held a desperate uncertainty.

She couldn't blame him. She'd pulled her curtains shut right in his face. She'd actually turned away from him without a word when he'd been so good as to find her brother. She'd blamed him for just about everything from famine and plague to her shoes not fitting right.

There was nothing she could do—short of grabbing him and kissing him—to reassure him she wouldn't reject him this time.

No matter how much she wanted him, and wanted him to want her, she couldn't bring herself to behave that way.

All she could do was wait. If he hadn't figured out by now that she wasn't going to run away from him screaming, there really wasn't much hope for the man.

Kiss me! she wanted to cry. She didn't think she could hold her breath much longer.

The corners of Jack's mouth turned up ever so slightly. But that and the gleam in his eyes were enough to let her know his doubts had disappeared.

Slowly his face moved closer to her. Slowly, cautiously, she felt herself moving closer to him, too. She drew in one more quick breath and closed her eyes. For the first time in her life, she was actually going to trust him!

His lips touched hers—a petal-soft tenderness just brushing the edges of her lips—tentative, tickling, teasing her nerves to increasingly potent sensations.

She raised her own arms to encircle his neck. This single, simple movement banished all his uncertainties. His lips pressed more earnestly, transforming his kiss from the gentle, hesitant touch to a burning brand searing her lips with his passionate desire, down to her very soul.

He gave a small, deep groan as his lips pulled away from hers for only a moment, then descended again and again in small, demanding kisses.

Maude had thought the gentle touch of his fingers to her lips had stirred the feelings in her breast, but she gasped as his kisses trailed across her cheek and down her throat, sending breathtaking tingles to the hardening tips of her breasts, and the same gentle unfurling of longing into the pit of her stomach. There was more to come—so much more. She felt it was true. She knew it had to be so. She waited with increasing longing.

A warm rush of his breath brushed across her face as she pulled away from him to catch her own breath.

"Oh, Maude, I've been wanting to do that since—"

"Don't you dare tell me you've been wanting to do that since you first laid eyes on me!" she whispered as a playful scold. Her lips brushed against his cheek. It felt so good to hold him so close, she never wanted to lose the sensation of that touch.

"I wouldn't—couldn't—lie to you like that. The first time I saw you, you were only three years old." He laughed, then grew more serious as he gazed longingly into her eyes. "I don't ever want to lie to you—to tell you tales as I have to do for everyone else. I want to kiss you again and again. If you'll let me."

She eased her arms from around his neck and held his face gently between both her hands. His cheeks were rough from the stubble of his beard, but his skin was soft and warm. Tilting her head slightly to the side, she pulled his head down and kissed him again.

His lips possessed hers with a rough tenderness that reached out to capture her soul.

She felt his fingers tracing light lines of pleasure over her neck and into the small hollow at the base of her throat. The shoulder of her bodice slipped down as she felt his calloused palm moving across her shoulder.

Barely touching her, his palm skimmed over the side of her bodice. She felt the pressure, but the thick layers kept them apart.

"Blast these things!" he mumbled against her lips. "How can I hold you? How can I get near you as I want to when these damn things—" He gave another low groan. "I want you so much, Maude!"

This time, very slowly, Jack raised his head away from her. He reached up and took hold of both of her hands and very gently pulled them away from his cheeks. Folding her hands between his, he held her there, very still, and looked into her eyes. His breath was coming in deep, ragged gasps. Gradually she could hear him forcing himself to breathe more slowly. He took in several long, slow breaths.

She tried to read the expression on his face, but once again, Jack's gaze shielded any truth she might have seen.

"I don't want to stop here, Maude, and you know it." His expression grew very serious. "You're woman enough to know exactly what I mean by that, too."

She swallowed hard. "Yes, I know. I want—"

"No." He gave a short laugh that didn't sound all that humorous to Maude. "I might not have much of a reputation, in this town or anywhere else, but I know you do. I know enough to realize you've had a little too much cider."

"I'm fine. Really I am."

"Whether you believe it or not, you're not quite up to making impartial decisions right now. I care about you, Maude. I guess I've still got a bit too much of the gentleman in me to take advantage of you when you're in this condition."

"Don't be silly. I know exactly what I'm doing—what you're doing." In a voice barely above a whisper, she added, "What *we're* doing."

"Yes, but I also know while this might not be a bad place, it sure isn't the right time." He backed up from her far enough so that she couldn't hold on to him anymore. "You still have obligations to fulfill—and so do I. But I'll never forget you or this moment, Maude—no matter what happens."

"What . . . do you mean by that?" she demanded, but she knew her head was spinning too wildly to ever understand any explanation.

His fingers slipped out of her grasp as he moved away. "I think it's time you went inside—went to bed. I . . . think it's time I took a cold swim in Miller's Pond!"

∽

SURELY THE EFFECTS OF the cider should have worn off by now, but they hadn't. Maude was grateful she hadn't fallen while she'd tottered up the stairs to bed. It was all her own fault, too. This was one of the few things she couldn't blame on Jack.

To the contrary, Jack had done nothing but make her feel incredibly wonderful. She cherished the phantom feel of his lips on hers and the dizzying joy as his arms encircled her.

She closed her bedroom door and moved to look out her window. Jack was across the way. She could barely see him now through the thickening coverage of the leaves. But there he was again, watching out his window. He waved at her and gave her that irresistibly charming grin.

He was watching her, as he had for so many nights. But tonight was different. Tonight she didn't angrily seize her drapes with tightened fists and pull them closed. Tonight she grinned back at him.

She raised her hands and unfastened the first small button at the front of her dress.

My goodness! If she continued to stand here, unfastening one small button after the other, a body might think she was just as wanton as Clarice. She'd already allowed Jack to kiss her— unheard-of behavior! She couldn't allow him to think she was some sort of loose woman.

Jack would merely think she'd simply forgotten to close her curtains, not that she was putting on this particular show solely for his benefit and enjoyment. She would *never* do something like that! Or would she? she thought with a wicked, wanton grin.

18

WITHOUT ACTUALLY LOOKING OUT the window, she glanced up from under her eyelashes. She wouldn't want him to think she was making sure he was watching her. Yes, indeed. Jack was still standing at his window, gazing out at her, fascinated, enchanted, bewitched. She held him captive, just as he'd captured her. A small shiver ran through her body as she realized she was going to enjoy this almost as much as he was.

But she couldn't just stand there, bold as brass, taking off her clothing in front of an open window. She couldn't let Jack see everything all at once, either. Not right away, she decided with a little giggle of mischief. He probably thought he was, but *she* was in control this time, and she was going to make him wait. As she slowly undid the last button at the bottom of her bodice, she turned her back to the window.

She slipped her bodice from one shoulder, then from the other. Carelessly she allowed it to fall to the floor. She didn't even bother to bend down to pick it up. She didn't think she could. That cider would bowl her over if she bent down. She just turned to her left and unfastened the hooks and eyes of her skirt, and of her cotton petticoat. With a soft, rustling sound, they, too, slid to the floor.

She'd laced her corset too tight earlier this evening, she decided as she glanced down. Her breasts, like twin mounds of soft, white snow, peeked out from the top of her chemise.

She turned around. Jack was still standing at his window, looking at her. The grin had left his face. His eyes were bright with longing.

Hook by hook, she unfastened the front of her corset. She drew in a much-needed deep breath, held out the corset at arm's length, and let it fall to the floor. The cool air seeped through her chemise, chilling her heated flesh, tightening her nipples.

Throwing her head back, she stretched her arms high over her head. One after the other, she plucked the pins from her hair until the mass cascaded down her back. Then, with a slow, languid movement, she smoothed her fingers through her hair, shaking out the curls. Her hair tickled her shoulders and her back. She could imagine Jack gently tracing his fingers across her skin. She ached to feel him actually touching her again, more and more, covering her body with his caresses—his hands, his lips, his entire strong, muscular, masculine body.

She crossed one arm over the other and ran her hands over her shoulders, then uncrossed them and slid her palms over her chemise, easing her breasts, now loosened from their tight restrictions. She'd never done such a thing before. How could any respectable woman touch herself this way? She never imagined it could feel so good. How much better it would feel if Jack touched her with his rough hands and needful passions!

There was only one thing yet to do. She reached to the center of her chest, directly over her heart. She pulled the thin pink ribbon from where it was tucked into her chemise and gave it a little tug. The tiny bow easily came undone. The gathers of her chemise opened. With a little shrug, she slipped the cotton fabric first from one shoulder and then the other. Her chemise clung to her skin, the small ribbon casing perched on the taut, pink tips of her nipples.

She reached down to the hem of her chemise and gave it the final tug that released it. It tumbled over her hips and down to the floor. The air was cool against her bare breasts, in contrast to the heat of the lamp. The knowledge that Jack stood across the way, watching her from his window, was the warmest thought of all.

Reaching forward, she extinguished her lamp.

In the dark she could still see Jack in silhouette, standing at his window, staring out at her. His hand was clutching at the sash. She wondered if he had the same urge to moan that she did. She had the strangest feeling he was gritting his teeth.

∞

"COME, COME," KATY URGED Maude, seizing her hand and pulling her into her house. "Sam Ferguson delivered it the other day, and I've just been dying to show you."

Maude felt glad to see her friend fairly glowing with excitement this afternoon. For the past several days, she'd looked decidedly peaked. She followed Katy into the parlor.

"Behold!" Katy said, proudly pointing to a dark mahogany, ornately carved, almost oriental-looking table with a white marble top. Sitting in the parlor of the Konigsbergs' modest farmhouse, the fantastic table looked almost as out of place as the Crown Jewels of England in a barnyard. "How do you like it?"

"It's very . . . interesting," Maude said. "Very . . . interesting, indeed." She wished she could think of another adjective. It might help her with the illusion of sounding more sincere if she could be more diverse with her praise. "Did you choose it yourself?"

"Mama helped me."

Maude should have figured. "Very . . . nice."

"Mr. Baumgartner had a table in his cabinetry shop that Willard and I liked better, but . . . well, Mama persuaded me to send all the way to Chicago for this out of one of those catalogues. She said it was much more stylish. I suppose she was right."

Willard, seated in his chair by the fireside, reading his *Gazette*, gave a disgruntled snort.

Katy threw him a brief, venomous glance. "Willard says we ought to patronize the people in our own hometown rather than go buying things without having actually seen them." Then she sat more erect in her chair and proclaimed, "But I told him, 'Willard, your domain is the working of this farm so that it'll be prosperous, and mine is the running of this household within my budget. Therefore, I shall decorate it as I see fit to provide for your comfort'—just as Mama told me to tell him."

Maude smiled politely and looked around. It was only a small farmhouse built on the southernmost corner of the senior Konigsbergs' farm, with a sparsely decorated parlor and an even emptier dining room in front, a large kitchen and a tiny bedroom in the rear, and an outhouse out back—a fact that caused the ambitious Mrs. Hardesty untold humiliation when her only daughter had set her cap for a mere farmer. But the house sat on one hundred and thirty acres of prime farmland and had the potential to be expanded on almost every side.

Katy had set out a pot of tea and a little plate of cakes on her new table in front of the sofa. At first Maude thought the dark cakes were spice or gingerbread, or maybe even chocolate, until she bit into one and was greeted with the acrid taste of charcoal. How had Katy managed to burn them so evenly? That in itself was quite a talent.

Maude tactfully replaced the half-eaten cake on the edge of her saucer. If she were seated closer to the fire, she'd have tried to divert Katy's attention to something across the room and given the horrible cake a toss into the flames. She took a sip of tea. It was weak, but it was better than nothing to rid her of the bitter taste in her mouth. She glanced around the parlor. Maybe if she kept talking, Katy wouldn't notice she wasn't eating.

She leaned forward and whispered to Maude, "Lord knows, · I've done my best to make him happy."

"I . . . I hope you are," Maude replied. What else could she say to such an unusual revelation?

Katy gave a very loud, very wistful sigh. "Louise still looks so very happy."

"She ought to," Willard mumbled from behind his *Gazette*. "She's only been married a week or so."

"I give her and Fred about another month before he manages to wipe that smile off her face."

Maude forced a laugh. "Goodness, Katy. Your predictions sound as gloomy as Jack's."

Katy placed her cup on the table. She folded her hands in her lap and gazed off into the distance, as if trying to appear very contemplative. "You know, Maude, Jack's a bit older than us."

"Only about three years older—and if we didn't have his aunt and uncle's word for it," Maude added with a little laugh, "I believe he'd lie about even that."

Katy looked as if she were trying to laugh at Maude's joke, but couldn't quite manage it. "Jack's seen so much more of the world than we have. So much more than we'll ever get to see. Perhaps he truly does know more about life, about human nature, about . . . things than we, who have led such sheltered lives, can possibly know.''

"I'd say being confined to prison for two years was leading a sheltered life," Maude pointed out. "I don't believe one can learn too much of the world from inside a cell, and I wouldn't want to associate with the people from whom Jack learned what he knows of human nature. I think I'd prefer to remain here where I'm happy, and see only as far as the horizon on every side, than to travel far and wide, and then spend two years staring at the inside of a jail. My goodness! I didn't mean to preach a sermon.''

"Really, they must have some sort of windows in those cells," Katy said. "Even if they don't have nice draperies and the view is marred by iron bars. They must let the prisoners out periodically for some sort of exercise. Don't they?''

"I'm sure I don't know.''

"Maybe we ought to ask Willard," Katy suggested. "He spends so much time out lately, chatting with Jack. I'm sure they've touched upon that subject at least once. Haven't you, Willard?''

Maude didn't really want to know anything about jails. She especially didn't want to hear anything about Jack's experience with them. She'd regained her senses after that horribly embarrassing incident yesterday evening. What could have possessed her to do such a thing? Undoubtedly the same demon that had caused her to embroider Jack's initials in the place of Caleb's on her special quilt block. She'd come to visit Katy today in the hopes of going someplace she could actually avoid the very mention of Jack.

"Don't they, Willard?" Katy repeated.

At last Willard lowered his newspaper. "How would I know? I'd say for a married man the walls of what is supposed to be his castle could turn into enough of a prison.''

"A prison, you say?''

Maude could see her friend's eyes narrowing with anger. Her rounded cheeks were growing flushed. Maybe it was time she went home.

"I don't suppose you could consider the meals I slave over a hot stove all day preparing for you, and then wait on you hand and foot to serve to you, dry bread and water! Do you?''

Willard ruffled the pages of the newspaper out in front of him and retreated behind it.

Katy turned to Maude. "Just because my biscuits were a little dry and hard and the chicken could've fried a little longer so it wouldn't have been so bloody when he sliced it—"

"Bloody?" Willard grumbled from behind his *Gazette*. "Why, it fairly clucked!"

"He never lets me forget what a remarkably good cook his mother is, who never served an underdone roast or an overdone biscuit in her life."

Willard mumbled something unintelligible behind his newspaper.

"I'll get no coherent conversation from him this afternoon," Katy complained.

"I can't talk because I broke all my teeth on those darned biscuits."

Katy sprang up from the sofa. "It's amazing how you can't talk, but you certainly can snore!"

"Please, Katy. We don't have to bring up all this unpleasantness while Maude is here."

"But I have to have a witness to tell the judge why I murdered you in your sleep!"

"You don't have to murder me in my sleep!" He jumped up from his chair and threw his *Gazette* to the floor. "You can just poison me!"

"If you don't like the way I cook, why don't you just go eat at your sainted mother's all the time?"

"I just might do that."

"Good. You can take your smelly socks with you!"

Katy stormed down the hallway. Maude could hear her pulling dresser drawers open, rummaging through them, and slamming them shut. She emerged with an armload of loose black socks.

"Well, that certainly looks silly," Willard said.

"Of course, *you* never did anything silly," she countered.

"The silliest thing I ever did was marry you!"

"Is that the way you feel?"

Shedding black socks as she moved, Katy stomped over to the front door and pulled it open. She tossed the entire armload out the door. Black socks dotted the front porch and red brick walk like drops of the shed blood of some horrendous monster. Black socks hung on the newly budding bushes out front like strangely morbid, poison fruit.

"I'm surprised the grass hasn't died and the bushes wilted already!" Katy declared. "Oh, look. One of the horses has collapsed in the paddock."

Willard stood in the doorway, pointing at the mess outside. "Now that has got to be the silliest thing I've ever seen."

"No, it's not!" Katy vanished into the bedroom and emerged with an armload of Willard's underclothes. "This is!" She tossed everything out onto the front lawn.

Willard's face grew as red as Mrs. Crowley's pickled beets. "Katy! Pick them up, now!"

"I will not!" She crossed her arms over her breast and stood her ground.

"You've got to pick them up." Instead of waiting to see if she'd defy him again, he rushed out and started gathering everything up himself. "What will the neighbors say?"

"We don't have any neighbors!" she called out the door. "Unless you want to count your mother, always spying on us out her back window."

"Their house is all the way over on the other side of the farm. They can't see us from here."

"That doesn't mean she's not trying."

"Katy, come out here and help me pick these things up, now."

"Pooh! Get your mother to do it. I'm sure she'll have them all washed, sorted, and darned before she gets back to the house. She does everything else so blasted perfectly."

Maude stared in amazement as Katy slammed the door on him and locked it. It suddenly occurred to her that not once this afternoon had Katy called him "Willie-poo," nor had he called her "tweetlebird." This wasn't merely some lovers' quarrel. This was very serious.

"I feel so much better now!" Katy exclaimed. Then she covered her face with her hands and began to wail.

"Katherine Ellen Hardesty Konigsberg, I am your husband!" Willard's voice boomed authoritatively as he pounded on the solid oak door. "This is my house. It is my God-given right to be in my own home. I command you, let me in!"

"No!" Apparently Katy wasn't as heartbroken as her tears would seem to indicate. "Go away!"

"But it's *my* house, tweetlebird," he whined. Maude noted he seemed to be changing his tactics. He certainly was a versatile fellow.

"The farm is yours, and the house is mine. I'll stay here, and you can go back to your mother. Or go hang around with that horrid Jack, who's put ideas in your head not fit for a happily married man."

"Rebellion isn't a becoming trait for a loving, obedient wife, Katy. It's small wonder I'm beginning to have doubts about whether I'm a happily married man or not."

"I don't care! I wish I'd never gotten married! I wish I'd never met you!"

Katy bolted for the kitchen. Maude stood in the hallway for a little longer, listening to Willard pounding on the door.

It certainly wasn't her place to keep him out, Maude figured, or, in loyalty to her friend, to let him back in again.

The pounding degenerated into knocks, and further into weak taps. At last Willard stopped knocking altogether. Perhaps he'd given up and gone back to his mother. She hoped his smelly socks hadn't actually suffocated him and they wouldn't find him lying dead on the front porch. She hoped the senior Mrs. Konigsberg was prepared to set an extra place for dinner.

Now that the house was quieter, she could hear sniffing coming from the back.

"Katy?" Maude called tentatively.

"Back here."

At least that's what Maude thought she'd said. It was kind of hard to tell, when Katy was obviously talking with her mouth full. Maude would have bet it wasn't those horrible charcoal cakes.

Cautiously Maude moved down the hallway to the bedroom at the back of the house. The big, four-poster bed dominated the room. The dresser drawers were open, and an assortment of men's clothing was scattered over the bed and the floor.

"It looks like Chalky Pike's store exploded in here." Maude glanced around in amusement and awe of the total disarray.

Katy sat in the middle of the bed. She'd propped the pillows against the tall, ornately carved wooden headboard, and was leaning against them with her feet tucked up. She cradled a large, open crock in her lap and was digging into it with a fork.

Maude sniffed. The odor of new wood and fresh paint still clung to the recently built house. The odor of Willard's socks drifted from the open drawers and from a few stray socks that had managed to escape eviction. The lavender from Katy's sachets made a valiant, if futile, attempt to do their fragrant duty. A pungent, acidic odor assailed her nostrils, too. What in the world was that?

Katy nodded to a spot beside her. "Have a seat." She scooped up a chunk of the contents of the dark brown crock. Long, translucent, dripping strings of pungent sauerkraut hung down. She lifted the fork and trickled them into her mouth. "Want some?"

"No, thank you." After the taste of charcoal from the cake, Maude didn't think her stomach could handle sauerkraut. "What are you doing?"

"Eating. Mrs. Ingram gave it to us—to *me* as a present. Someday I'll have to get her to teach me how . . . Oh, but it'll only be me, sitting here, eating sauerkraut . . . without that horrible Willard snoring in my ear, and smelling up the bedroom with his socks . . . and I'll be here all alone!"

Katy burst into loud wails, interspersed with consuming mouthfuls of sauerkraut.

"What's the matter with him? With us? What was the matter with *you*?" Katy accused her.

"Me? I'm just visiting here, remember?"

"No. First your quilt tells me we're going to be blissfully happy. Then you assure me our problems are minor. Now look at what's happened. You've got to do something."

"I can't plug up his nose or cut off his feet, Katy. Be reasonable!"

"I certainly don't know what to do. I don't want to ask Mama. She'll just tell me she'd warned me against marrying a farmer when I could have had a doctor or a lawyer or a minister. But I didn't want a doctor or a lawyer or a minister. I want my Williepoo!"

She started to wail again.

"I love him. I love the jokes he makes and the way the corners of his eyes crinkle up when he laughs at his own bad jokes. I love the way he holds me. How will I sleep without him cuddling beside me?"

Maude sat on the edge of the bed and gave her friend a hug. Katy continued to sob. She let the crock roll out of her lap and across the bed. Maude made a grab for it. As she righted it and placed the fork back inside, it made a clinking sound. She realized the crock was empty. Katy had eaten the whole thing!

"You've got to get him back for me. You owe it to me, Maude."

"How—?"

"You told me my marriage would be perfect, and it's not. It's up to you to make it right again."

"I didn't think my quilts came with any guarantees. I wasn't even the one who made up this silly superstition."

"You've *got* to get him back for me." She dabbed at her red-rimmed eyes with the edge of her handkerchief, then blew her bright pink nose. "He wouldn't listen to me now, but he'd listen to you."

"I'm not so sure about that." She disengaged herself from Katy's pathetic, clinging embrace and rose from the side of the bed. "But I'll try."

Willard shouldn't be too hard to find, Maude figured. She'd managed to find Georgie. Well, actually Jack had found him. If worse came to worst, she could try to talk Jack into finding Willard for her, too. After last night, he might just be willing to do almost anything for her. And he did owe it to her, and to Katy and Willard. It wasn't her mis-stitching of the famous quilt block that was to blame for this. It was Jack's dire predictions of the incorrectness of her quilt that had caused doubts in Katy's mind in the first place. Yes, indeed. Jack owed them all.

19

"MR. KONIGSBERG. OH, MR. Konigsberg! Willard!" Maude called to him. She clutched at her flapping shawl with one hand and, with the other, tried to clamp her bonnet down onto her head.

She must look like some kind of insane blackbird, but she was on a mission of mercy to preserve a sacred institution that was essential to maintaining the cherished American way of life. She couldn't be bothered with an unimportant little thing like mere personal appearance now.

Willard was hurrying away from her just as quickly as she was trying to catch up to him on the sidewalk without breaking into a dead run. She could tell he was trying very hard to pretend he hadn't heard a word she said as he strode past Mr. Kingston's hardware store, past the feed and grain store, past the tobacco shop, past the barbershop—all such manly places of business, carrying masculine commodities—heading for the other end of town.

Maude *never* went to the other side of town unless she absolutely needed something from the blacksmith and couldn't find Georgie to fetch it for her. It would take something as important as this to make her follow Willard there. He was heading for the place right next door to the blacksmith's—to the Pink Garters Saloon.

She'd been past the place a few times and she'd never been inside. But she knew the place's reputation very well. It was the first public place Jack had gotten thrown out of for fighting with Hiram, and the last place anyone could recall seeing him visit before he'd run away to the war.

Maude just hoped she could catch up to Willard before he went in there. Her promise to Katy notwithstanding, she wasn't about to go inside the Pink Garters Saloon!

"Willard, please stop. I don't think I can run anymore," she pleaded.

He kept on walking.

"I really don't think it looks too proper to have an unmarried woman running down the street, yelling after a married man, heading for the saloon."

Willard stopped directly in front of the swinging doors of the Pink Garters Saloon. "What do you want?" he asked wearily.

"*I* don't want anything, except for my friends to be happy. Katy wants you to come back home."

He frowned at her. It was pretty clear his anger wasn't directed at Katy, but at Maude. "You wouldn't let me back in my own house earlier. What business is it of yours now?"

Maude looked about, searching for some sort of answer that would convince him she had every right to order him around.

"Because Katy's my friend," Maude answered weakly.

"I thought you were my friend, too."

Maude shrugged. "I am, but—"

"Do friendships between girls outweigh friendships between any other two people?" Jack asked.

She turned quickly to see him leaning against one of the swinging doors of the saloon. He was grinning at her. The lamps in the darkened interior of the saloon glowed red, like the fires of hell. Cigar smoke billowed out from behind him. He looked liked an imp, or an incubus—one of those demons who visited women in the middle of the night to tempt them to all sorts of lewd, lascivious, luscious acts of sin! He didn't even have to come into her room. All he had to do was look at her.

He ought to still be grinning, after the show she'd put on for him last night! She only hoped he'd be able to keep his mouth shut about this as well as he was able to keep silent about his mysterious activities during and since the war. The only trouble with that was, even mysteries had a way of being found out, even years later.

The worse part of it for her was, if she had it to do all over again, she would! Nothing else in her life could ever equal the wonderful sensation of Jack's searing gaze and crushing embrace.

There he stood now, in front of her, with the same memories. But what else was he thinking? she wondered. Was he wanting her as much as she longed to touch him? Or was he just laughing to himself that he'd made staid, sensible Maude Griffith do something so wildly, wickedly wanton?

Maude cringed and blushed. Jack's gaze swept lightly over her body. His grin widened. She pulled her shawl more tightly about her shoulders. He wanted her again, all right. Of that, there could be no doubt.

"Is there some kind of secret agreement you ladies all come to while sitting around making your quilts, kind of like the fellows in the gloves and aprons do over at the Masonic Lodge?" Jack continued with that same wicked, teasing grin. "Do you make solemn vows over your quilting needles, scissors, and rulers like they do with their squares, swords, and compasses? Do you march in special file around your quilt frame like they parade around in that room of theirs upstairs?"

"This is serious, so will you kindly stop making light of it?" she scolded him. "If you don't mind, Jack, this is a private message from Katy to Willard."

"If this is just between Willard and Katy, why are you here?"

Why was she here? What she really wanted to do was forget all about Katy and Willard and their silly socks and sauerkraut argument. She wanted to run to Jack and embrace him. She wanted him to seize her with all the passion she knew was stored inside of him, carry her to one of the forbidden upstairs rooms of the Pink Garters Saloon, and finish what he'd hinted at last night on the back porch. She wanted to surrender to him what she'd promised at her window last night.

But she'd made a promise. She cast Jack a pleading look. If their kisses, caresses, and everything else last night had meant nothing else, at least he ought to help her to help her friends.

"Please, Willard. I need to talk to you, for Katy's sake."

"You're here because you're Katy's friend?" Willard demanded. "Well, Jack's my friend. Anything Katy told you to say to me, you can tell me in front of him."

"I don't think you realize what you're getting yourself into," she warned him.

"Nonsense. Of course I do."

"Very well. But remember, I warned you." Maude drew in a deep breath. " 'Tweetlebird still loves her Willie-poo,' " she quoted. As an aside, quickly casting Jack a worried glance, she added, "Mind you, this is all quoting verbatim. I . . . wouldn't really come up with this sort of . . . drivel myself."

Jack chuckled. "I sort of figured as much."

She cast him an icy glare, but he obviously chose to ignore her. She had to admit it was pretty ridiculous. As silly as the pet names had sounded when spoken by interested parties, they sounded even sillier when she had to repeat them as dispassionately as she could. Well, she had a job to do and, come what may, she was going to do it.

" 'Tweetlebird misses her Willie-poo and wants him back, no matter what. Tweetlebird doesn't care if Willie-poo wants to visit his precious, perfect mama seven days a week as long as he comes home at night to their own little nest. Tweetlebird—' "

"Excuse me," Jack interrupted, "but before we have to resort to killing the messenger, do you think we could just agree to accept 'she' or 'Katy' as reasonable substitutes, and dispense with the word 'tweetlebird' in the future?"

"You sound like a lawyer," she accused.

"Please continue."

" 'Twee—excuse me, *she* would like to have you back, smelly feet and all, considering there's probably no other way.' "

"Thank you very much, Maude, for delivering the message and for your efforts on her behalf. But I'm not going back to the house until Katy *personally* asks me back," Willard declared. "She's the one who threw me out and she's the one who must invite me back. No—not invite!" His voice grew louder. "I want her to tell me she was wrong to treat me the way she did. I want her to beg, to plead, to *grovel*!"

"You've got a snowflake's chance in hell for that, friend," Jack told him, laughing. "Why don't you just magnanimously settle for a simple apology?"

Maude would rather bite her tongue than say so, but she had to admit Jack was probably right. Except for that part about the apology. Katy was the wronged party here, surely.

"Evening, Maude." Willard touched the brim of his hat to her and turned away. "Come on, Jack. After all that's happened, I have a powerful hankering to wet my whistle." He moved to enter the saloon, but Jack still hadn't moved out of his way and didn't show any sign of doing so.

"You know, there's something else you can do," Jack said.

Willard looked at him, clearly puzzled. Maude was slightly puzzled herself, but she had a bad feeling she knew exactly where Jack was heading. She hoped he wasn't. She hoped he had learned better than to make trouble for the folks in Apple Grove.

"You know, Willard, you don't have to go back to her at all."

"Stay out of this, Jack," Maude warned.

"*You* didn't stay out of this," he countered. "If you're going to tell him he has to go home, I may as well let him know what else is out there if he doesn't."

Maude glared at him. "Loneliness? Hunger? Prison?" She tried her best to make everything sound as gloomy as possible.

Jack grinned smugly, then lifted his eyebrows and uttered the magic word. "Gold."

Maude could feel her shoulders slump in defeat. Since the beginning of time, the lure of gold had always made grown men fight and kill, lie and steal, and generally act worse than any dangerously spoiled child or wild animal ever could. No word she could utter would ever exert such a powerful influence over Willard or any other man.

"Now you sound like Caleb," she scolded Jack. She never thought she'd be holding up Caleb as a *bad* example. Wasn't Caleb the man she wanted to marry?

"You know, that fellow doesn't have such a bad idea," Willard said with more enthusiasm than Maude had heard from him since his wedding.

"You're not going to leave Katy, are you?" Maude demanded. "She's your wife. She loves you."

"She has a funny way of showing it," Willard defended himself.

"Go back to her," Maude urged.

"She can waste my money decorating it any way she—or that meddling mother of hers—damn well pleases," Willard responded. Then he turned back to Jack, and said enthusiastically, "I could go out West with Caleb."

"Yeah, I understand he's real eager to be heading that way."

"You know, we could pool our resources, form some kind of company. Mr. Lester would *have* to lend us the money if it wasn't just some harebrained scheme of a single person, but if we really had an actual mining company."

"Sure. That's a great idea. Say, I've been out there. I know all about it." Jack jerked his head back into the saloon. "Why don't you come on inside and we'll talk—*man to man*? I'll tell you all about it."

"No, Willard!" Maude cautioned.

But it was too late. Jack backed away from the saloon doors to let Willard enter.

"Jack, don't do this," she pleaded.

She watched Jack's back as he disappeared with Willard into the dark, smoky depths of the saloon. She wanted to scream. She wanted to rush up and slap some sense into Willard—Jack, too. But, knowing Jack, he'd probably grab hold of her and drag her into the saloon. It was bad enough she'd privately ruined her self-respect in front of Jack. She didn't need his help to completely ruin her reputation once and for all in front of the entire town.

The man wasn't a tempting incubus. Her father had been right. He was a demon from hell, sent here to ruin them all.

As she stood alone on the sidewalk in the gathering dusk, staring into the forbidden depths of the saloon, she sighed. She'd thought Jack had changed. She'd thought she could trust him. But there he was—actually encouraging Willard to desert the woman he'd sworn before God and all of Apple Grove to love and to cherish until death did them part.

How was she going to go back to Katy and tell her she'd failed to return her husband to her? How wrong she'd been about Jack! How completely evil could that man be?

☙

"I'M REALLY GLAD I didn't hang around this boring town after the war. I'm glad I took off for the gold fields."

"Is that where you went?"

Might as well let him think that's where he'd gone.

"It was an experience I wouldn't have missed," Jack declared.

Grover Wilson, the barkeeper, had brought them a bottle of whiskey. Jack pushed it across the ring-stained wooden table toward Willard, who poured himself a generous glassful.

"I'll buy a couple of pans from Ingrams'," Willard said.

"Pans? No. All the placer deposits are plumb worked out, unless you feel like traipsing into the backwoods up in the high country with the bears."

"Bears?"

"They've always been cantankerous, but nowhere near as mean as the mountain lions."

"Lions?"

"And the Indians. For some strange reason, the more folks go out West, the angrier those Indians get." Jack frowned. "How good a shot are you?"

"Fair . . . fair to middling."

Doubt number one planted, Jack mentally kept score. Willard was a farmer, not a hunter. Probably the only thing he'd ever shot was a fox in his henhouse, and even then, he'd probably destroyed more of his chickens with his own ineptitude than the fox could eat in a week.

He urged another whiskey onto Willard. "Yeah, gone are the days when a fellow could just relax in the shade beside a little creek, swirling water through his pan, and coming up with a chunk of gold the size of your fist. No, the good days are over. It's all tunneling now. I guess you and Caleb will get to be real good at digging—unless, of course, you can convince Mr. Lester to lend you enough money to buy some of that big, heavy excavation equipment."

"Well, not yet. I guess at first we'll have to do it on our own."

"You could try hiring some Irish—or some of them Chinese. Do you speak Chinese, Willard?"

"No. I never thought—"

Doubt number two. Time to change the subject.

"Most of the fellows take jerky with them," Jack advised. "After a while, you don't even notice how much it tastes like shoe leather. On the other hand, in its favor I'd just like to point out how it wears considerably better."

"But there's lots of fresh game, isn't there?"

Jack laughed. "You'll be so busy collecting gold, you won't have time for hunting. You'll be digging all the time—or watching out, making sure some lowdown sidewinder doesn't jump your claim."

He leaned forward and slowly tapped his finger on the ring-marked table.

"Say, Willard, I don't mean to insult Caleb by saying this, but . . ." He leaned forward even closer and glanced from side to side, as if making absolutely sure no one else could hear him. He lowered his voice to a whisper. "Exactly how friendly are you with Caleb?"

"Why, he's an absolutely swell fellow!"

"But how well do you know him?" Jack persisted, deepening his voice ominously.

"What do you mean? We went to school together. We go to the same church."

"Yes?" Jack let the word linger in the air, as if there were a whole lot more he could say, but wouldn't. There was, but he wouldn't.

"I know him well enough, I suppose."

Doubt number three. Jack leaned back and gave Willard a wide smile, as if all his worries had been banished. Then he stopped, as if he'd just suddenly remembered something else. "You do have a gun, don't you?"

"A shotgun."

"No, I mean a real gun, one you can wear without attracting too much notice—from anyone; one that's always handy." He slipped the front of his jacket back just far enough for Willard to see his own revolver.

Willard's eyes grew wide.

Jack covered his gun and leaned back comfortably in his chair. "Have you figured out how many mules you'll need? Or will you be using oxen?"

"I . . . kind of thought we'd use horses, since I'm, well, we're both used to them."

Jack shook his head. "Then I reckon you better head for some-place that has lots of water."

"You think so?"

Jack shot back another drink and mentally shook his head at Willard's monumental stupidity. He didn't have any more idea of what he was getting himself into out West than Caleb did. Those two were going to make great partners—straight into bankruptcy. If ever there was a contest to send the two biggest idiots out in search of gold, those two would surely win.

"Well, you needn't worry about the particulars now. You'll be having the time of your life. It was the best damn time I ever had with my clothes on. Of course, nothing quite beats having fun with your clothes *off.*" As if he were revealing an extremely important afterthought, he said, "Say, I didn't tell you about all the women out there, did I?"

"Women?"

"Sure, pretty little black-eyed, bronze-skinned squaws who'll do your every bidding better than any hardheaded white woman ever would." Jack laughed. "Of course, they have been known upon occasion to serve a man his dog for dinner."

Willard choked back his whiskey.

"Or those quiet, tiny little Chinese women, if you ever make it to San Francisco to spend all the gold you're bound to find. Of course, you can't understand a damn word they're saying, and they always sound like they're trying to talk through their nose. Damn shame the way they wrap up their feet so they can't walk."

"No feet?" Willard shot back another drink.

"Then there's them saucy French women. Ooo-la-la! Oh, yes. Red curls, black lace drawers, and big blue eyes. Say, you don't mind taking a small dose of mercury every now and then, do you?"

"Mercury?"

"Keeps the pox from doing too much damage to your brain and eyes and—"

"The pox?"

"You know—the French fever. Anyway, I hear tell the mercury keeps your you-know-what from falling off." Jack pointed deliberately at Willard's lap.

"Falling off?" Willard repeated with alarm and glanced fearfully at his lap.

Jack was surprised the dang fool didn't just jump up and grab his crotch, just to make sure all the working parts were still hanging there.

"Sure. You're pretty much a man of the world, Willard. You don't suppose for one second that you're going to be the first man to be with one of those charming little soiled doves, do you?"

"I guess not, but . . ." Willard apparently found more satisfaction in finishing off the bottle of whiskey than in finishing his sentence.

"No offense, but you know, for all their beauty, most of them aren't too particular about who they entertain. Yes, indeed. It's a hell of a lot more exciting, dangerous, scintillating with those daughters of Venus than with some pretty little gal who's smart and clean, who actually has both eyes and all her natural teeth, who actually cares about you instead of just what you can pay her—or what she can steal from you."

Jack called to Grover for another bottle. He deserved a little relaxation. After all, he'd worked pretty hard, done a lot of talking, and he was satisfied in the knowledge that he'd pretty much sown all the seeds of doubt he needed to.

20

THE SOUNDS OF THE creaking leather and jingling brass of the harness, the neighing, and the clopping of the huge hooves of the dappled gray Percherons resounded through the night air as Mr. Olson pulled his large wagon to a halt in front of his front porch, brightly illuminated with several large lanterns swinging from the eaves.

"Come along!" Florence cried excitedly as she dashed toward the wagon.

She motioned her friends forward with a frantic wave of her hand. She ran up to Edgar, who was waiting for her by the wagon. He held her about the waist and lifted her into the back of the wagon, then climbed up after her. She headed for the coziness of the front of the wagon, but Edgar plopped himself down in the middle so that she had no choice but to sit beside him on one of the blankets laid out over the straw.

"The evening of a full moon is the best time of all to look at the apple blossoms," Edgar said. "During the day, there are too many bees."

"But I need the little honeybees if I want to have apples this fall," Mr. Olson declared from his seat at the front of the wagon. "So do you, if you want to eat pie made with honey, and drink apple cider."

Maude cringed at the very mention of the dangerous brew. Out of the corner of her eye, she glanced over at the edge of the group, where Jack was standing, talking with Caleb and Peter. She looked around for Willard, but couldn't spot him.

Suddenly Maude noticed Katy approaching. Horrors! She was here by herself. Had Willard gone to his parents' house? Or had he left Katy forever? What had Jack said to him? She certainly wasn't about to ask Jack. He'd made a big point of excluding her from that discussion.

"Katy, you look horrible!" Wilma exclaimed, rushing up to her.

"I *feel* horrible," Katy answered. "Thank you for reminding me."

Maude stared speechlessly at her friend as she drew closer. Katy did indeed look horrible. Her usually clear skin was pallid, but there were dark purple crescents dotted with red under her eyes and uneven blotches of pink on her cheeks. Her lips looked slightly dry and cracked. As Maude looked a little closer at her friend in the waning light, she noticed how bloodshot Katy's eyes were.

In spite of all her crying, she hadn't looked that terrible when Maude had left her last night, even after she'd been given the heartbreaking news that Willard had refused to leave the company of Jack in the Pink Garters Saloon.

"What's wrong with you?" Louise asked. In a whisper, she added, "The monthly complaint's never made you this sick."

Katy shook her head.

"You poor dear, what's wrong, then?"

"I was very sick this morning, and it's sort of stuck with me through the day," Katy explained.

"How sick?"

"I threw up."

"You don't have a fever, do you?"

"No."

"Oh, I hope it's not something contagious!" Wilma said, stepping back a few paces.

"Have you called Doc Ketcham in to look at you?" Louise asked.

Katy only moved her head from right to left and back again once, as if even that little bit of movement was too much for her to bear in her condition.

"Have you taken some tonic?"

"No."

"Have you talked to your mother?"

"No."

"Well, why not?"

"I only ate some sauerkraut," Katy whined.

"How much?"

"Just one crock."

"One of Mrs. Ingram's big ones?"

Katy nodded.

"Merciful heavens, Katy!" Jessica exclaimed. "You deserve to throw up if you insist on making a hog of yourself like that."

"Thank you so much for your sympathy."

"What in the world prompted you to eat a whole crock of sauerkraut?" Wilma demanded, screwing her face up into a grimace. "An entire pie I could understand, especially if it's peaches. But sauerkraut?"

"It's all Maude's fault," Katy pronounced.

"My fault?" Maude echoed. She realized now how Jack must feel. Katy had blamed her for everything from bad quilting to her dining indiscretions. "How do you figure it's my fault?"

"You let me eat all that sauerkraut."

"As I recall, there wasn't much discussion about it. By the time I figured into it, you'd already downed half the crock. I don't exactly recall standing over you, shoveling it into your mouth, either."

"By the way, where's Willard?" Clarice asked.

Leave it to Clarice to ask that monstrous question! Maude perked up and waited for the answer. What kind of answer could Katy possibly give?

Katy shrugged. "He . . . had something else he'd rather do."

Maude figured that was as good an answer as any. Nobody could ever claim Katy had lied to them.

"I can't believe Willard would be such a fool as to let you venture out of the house all alone when you're not feeling well," Louise said angrily.

Katy lifted her chin. "I don't care if he's decided he has better things to do. I've never missed one of Mr. Olson's apple blossom rides, and I don't intend to miss this one."

"All right, ladies!" Jack called to them. "Enough chatting.

Time for a ride.'' He waved enthusiastically for them to join the others who were already in the wagon.

Clarice, Ruthie, and Jessica quickly abandoned Katy and any feelings of sympathy they may have had for her and rushed over to the wagon. Jack was going to be helping them into the wagon, and those three weren't about to miss it for the world! At least Wilma showed just a little more finesse as she lined up a bit more slowly. She took great pains to avoid the slowly walking Katy, probably because she was still afraid of catching something.

Louise, of course, had her beloved Fred to help lift her into the wagon. The two of them found a cozy place leaning against one of the sides and cuddled against the spring chill in one of the blankets. Wilma was looking around for Peter, but he'd already climbed into the wagon alone.

Clarice squealed loudly as Jack seized her around the waist and hoisted her into the wagon, to be caught by Caleb. The rest of the girls were laughing, giggling, and squealing in anticipation of the wonderful moment when the notorious Suicide Jack would grab them and handsome, ambitious Caleb would catch them. Eligible Matthew and Peter had ranged themselves in the center along the length of the wagon and were helping to steady the ladies as everyone found comfortable seats in the hay.

Maude saw no reason at all to hurry. She lingered at the back of the group until only she needed to be lifted into the wagon.

Jack had been laughing with the fun of lifting the girls, but when Maude stood in front of him, the smile left his face.

He's as angry with me as I am with him, Maude thought regretfully.

After her argument with Jack over Willard and Katy, would he still remember their kisses with the same stirring feelings she did? Or was he as determined as she to put the incident behind them? But was she really determined to forget about him? she asked herself. Could she ever forget about Jack?

She suddenly called a halt to those erroneous thoughts. Why should he be angry with her? *She* had only been delivering an extremely important message entrusted to her by a desperate friend. *He,* on the other hand, had undoubtedly been encouraging unreliable, irresponsible behavior on the part of his friend.

But Jack's eyes gleamed with the same longing that had always shone there when he looked at her. If anything, her own actions had stoked the fires so that his eyes burned with more desire for her.

Couldn't he tell she was angry with him? The man was as dense as a Christmas fruitcake!

Jack seized her about the waist and pulled her close to him, so he could lift her better. She really didn't recall him holding any of the other girls this close—not even the ones who were heavier than she; not even Clarice, no matter how much she'd tried to get near him.

"Why don't we just stand here like this and let the wagon pull off without us?" he whispered invitingly in her ear.

She wanted to. Couldn't he tell by the way she kept both feet firmly planted on solid ground instead of lifting herself? It didn't matter that Caleb was still in the wagon. He seemed so completely remote at the moment. But how could she stay here, happy with Jack, when Katy was huddled alone at the side of the wagon—and Jack's bad advice was the reason for it?

Why did she always have to be so darned selfless? she lamented. Why did she have to see her father, her sister, her friends all settled, before she'd ever give a thought to her own happiness? Why could Jack—when no one else ever had—make her want to?

"Get in," Mr. Olson called back over his shoulder.

"Don't you mean 'All aboard'?" Albert asked, laughing.

"Can't say that until they finally decide to run a railroad through here someday," Mr. Olson replied.

Before Maude could blink, Jack had lifted her in his strong arms and tossed her into the back of the wagon. She scrambled through the hay to right herself. She'd been expecting Caleb to catch her. After all, he'd been standing there, leaning down to catch all the other ladies whom Jack had tossed up to him. Where was he now? How could she ever forget Jack and convince Caleb he should marry her when Jack finally went away, if Caleb was never around?

Mr. Olson slapped the reins on his horses' backs. The wagon took off with a lurch, sending Maude tumbling through the hay again. She could hear all the ladies behind her squealing with mock horror. She could just imagine them all doing their best to hold on to whichever gentleman was closest. If she could have reached Caleb, she'd have held on to him. But he was all the way at the front, with Ruthie and Jessica laughing and squealing on either side.

Maude looked down. Jack wasn't in the wagon. He was jogging along behind, trying to catch up. Let him run, she figured. But she wanted him on board, beside her. She wanted Jack to wrap his arms around her again. She wanted to be holding on to him the way Louise was holding Fred; the way Katy should be holding Willard.

She found herself holding out her hand to him. "Come on, Jack," she encouraged.

"Wait! Wait for Jack!" Clarice cried.

Maude grimaced. She'd kick Clarice out of this wagon before she'd let her get her hands on him. Heavens, what was she thinking?

"Wait for the wagon, wait for the wagon." Matthew began to sing the chorus in his loud, clear tenor. The rest of the crowd in the wagon joined him in finishing the chorus, then continued with the verses—all three, long ones.

Obviously spurred on by their encouraging tune, Jack sped up, made a mad leap, pushed himself up with his hands, and landed in the back of the wagon as it lumbered over the ruts between the long rows of apple trees. He plopped down squarely beside Maude. The wagon jolted along through the orchard.

The full moon shone down brightly on every blossom. Without the yellow glare of the lanterns, everything had transformed to a snowy white. A gentle breeze plucked the fragrant petals one by one from the trees, showering them down on the party.

"There's music in the ai-ir," Matthew sang. "When the infant morn is nigh . . ."

The rest of the folks joined in, too. It didn't seem to matter if they were all singing in the same key or if they got the words right or not, so long as they were all merrily singing together as they rode through the sweet-smelling apple orchard.

Maude bobbed her head from side to side in time to the music. She'd never considered herself much of a singer, but she enjoyed music as much as the next person. Every once in a while, everyone's voice jolted an octave when Mr. Olson's wagon hit another bump, but somehow they all managed to pick up again on the same beat they'd left off at, more or less on the same note.

"Mr. Olson must know where every rut and ridge is in this orchard," Jack told her.

"He's making sure he hits every one of them, too," she replied.

They hit an exceptionally big jolt. Maude tried to hang on, but no one had put the backboard across the end of the wagon, and she was too far from either sideboard to cling to one of them. There were also plenty of other people already leaning against the side for support, so there wasn't room for her. She tried to dig her hands into the bottom, but there wasn't going to be anything to hold on to at the flat bottom of the wagon.

"Talk about clutching at straws," Jack said with a laugh. He nodded down to her fingers, scrabbling through the hay. "You know, if you really want to hold on to something, there's always me."

Maude held her breath as he slowly placed his arm behind her, very nonchalantly, very unobtrusively. Why, a body'd hardly notice he'd placed his arm just so she could—if she really wanted to—lean back against him.

She started to lean against him. It would feel so good to cradle in his arms. She wanted to feel his strong arms and warm body close against her. But she couldn't—not yet.

"Who's Katy going to hold on to?" she asked, pulling slightly away.

"Well, let's see," Jack said, twisting around to look behind him at the rest of the people sitting in the bed of the wagon. "There's Matthew, sitting beside her. Peter or Phineas. Sam's sitting right across from her. I don't think any of those good fellows would let her go tumbling out of the wagon."

She glared at him in the darkness. "You can't possibly be so stupid that you don't know the difference between having a mere acquaintance help a lady or having her dear husband around to keep her safe—"

"He's still around," Jack said quietly, looking left and right, as if Willard's continued presence in town was a big secret that no one but they should know about.

She felt a mixture of disbelief—how could anyone trust anything that traitorous Jack had to say?—and relief for Katy's sake. Her frown eased somewhat. If Willard was still in town, there was a chance for him and Katy to be reconciled.

"If he's in town, why isn't he here tonight?"

"I don't know. I'm not my brother's keeper."

"No, of course not," she replied angrily. "You're the one who tried to talk him into leaving."

"Excuse me. As I seem to recall, he was thrown out."

"Where is he, then? You didn't leave him at the saloon, did you?"

"Hey! Hush back there!" Peter scolded. "We're trying to sing up here. You're making so much noise, you're throwing us off the beat."

Maude ducked her head down guiltily. Maybe if she was very quiet and tiny, they wouldn't notice her in the dark, and they'd think all the noise was coming from Jack alone, sitting in the rear of the wagon. Once again, if she could only convince everyone that everything was Jack's fault.

"I'm—we're sorry," Jack called back.

It figured he'd have to say "we" and include her as a wrong-doer.

"If you want to make noise, come on up here and sing with us," Peter invited very pleasantly this time, probably so he wouldn't be considered a complete grouch by the rest of the group.

Matthew started them all off again. "I gave my love a cherry that has no stone . . ."

Jack quietly continued, "He's staying with his parents."

Now she had to look at him in complete surprise. "How do you know?"

"Because I took him there when he was too drunk to make his way home by himself. Who knows where he would have landed if I hadn't. He might have ended up floating facedown in Miller's Pond."

"Why did you have to get him drunk in the first place?"

"I didn't. It was his idea. Anyway, it made it easier for me to get him to listen—and think what I wanted him to think."

"What are you talking about? Why on earth did you take him *there*? Why on earth didn't you take him back to his own house?"

"Because he swore he'd never set foot in that house again until Katy begged him to come home."

"He was drunk. You ought to know better than to listen to a drunk."

"He was sober at the time."

"Of course, you had to encourage him in his rash decision."

"I did not," Jack firmly defended himself. "He might have been drunk, but he wasn't unconscious, and I could hardly knock him out, throw him over my shoulder, and haul him on home."

"You could have tried to talk to him, convince him—"

"Just between you, me, and the apple blossoms, I don't think it would take much begging on Katy's part."

It would have been bad enough if he'd just leaned a bit closer to her in the moonlight in order to impart this bit of secrecy to her. But he had to scoot his entire body closer to her. Every bump of the wagon jolted her against his side. He leaned toward her so close that his chin brushed against her shoulder.

"I think he'd go back to her in a minute if she'd just say please."

"So you think she's the one who ought to apologize," Maude accused. She didn't mean for her voice to be so loud, but even in a crowd of people, Jack's nearness, and the memory of his embrace and kisses, still disturbed her. "How *dare* you assume she's in the wrong!"

"Hey!" Peter called again. "If you two want to argue, we're going to have to kick you out of here."

"Sorry." Jack turned his back to them. He let his legs hang over the back of the wagon. "She did throw him out."

"Did it ever occur to you that she might have a very good reason for throwing him out?"

"No."

"You've only heard Willard's side of the argument. *I* heard them both. *I* was there."

"I don't think you qualify as an impartial observer."

"I don't think you do, either."

"You must admit, you women seem to look at everything with an extremely emotional—"

She gave him an angry little push. "Now you sound like my father. Honestly, you'd think a man with all his intelligence and education would have a little more sense when it came to dealing with women. Of course, I'd expect as much from an idiot like you!"

"I know," Jack said with a deep, forced sigh. "A man has to be so careful what he says—those emotional creatures fly off the handle so easily."

She gave him a little harder push. "It's because you men drive us to distraction!"

"See, you can't discuss anything logically, dispassionately—"

"If Miss Randolph wouldn't take any hogwash like that from my father, I'm sure not going to take any from you!" She gave him the hardest push she could manage.

Just before he tumbled off the wagon, he wrapped both arms around her. There was no way she could pull herself clear.

All Maude saw was a dizzying swirl of stars, apple blossoms, and dark ground, all rapidly tumbling at her. They hit the ground with a thud.

She groaned and drew in a deep breath. Why was the ground moaning? She hadn't hit it that hard. She'd always thought the earth was a little tougher than that.

She tried to rise on her elbow.

"Ouch!"

She looked down. Jack was sprawled out under her. His arms were still wrapped tightly around her. He blinked a few times, then grinned at her.

"What have you done?"

"Cushioned your fall," he replied with another groan. "I'm glad Mr. Olson doesn't usually leave pitchforks lying around his orchard."

"You ought to be glad I don't carry one."

His embrace eased just a bit as he smoothed his hand up her arm. "No, you're as soft as pillow down, as smooth as cream."

"I've got to get up," she protested. She didn't mean a word she said. She could feel his strong chest, moving up and down with each breath he took. She could feel his firm stomach muscles, taut from supporting her on the ground. She could feel his long legs stretched out beneath her, and other important bumps and ridges pressing against her leg.

She pushed her hands against his chest—not very hard, just enough to make the effort in case anyone on the wagon was still watching them. She had to move. "I really have to get up."

"No, you don't. But I would appreciate you taking your elbow out of my liver."

She quickly shifted, but he still held her close to him. His hands brushed her arms with the gentlest hold, but she still felt bound to him, not by any bands or bars, but by her own will. She wanted to stay there with him, lying atop him on the soft-scented, newly sprouting grass and damp, rich earth, with pink and white blossoms and moonlight covering them.

In the shades of gray of the spring night, his eyes no longer appeared so green. But his gaze still held the fire of longing she'd seen there before.

"I . . . we have to get up," she protested. "They'll be stopping. They'll be coming back to look for us, to pick us up."

She managed to pull herself away from his embrace and raise herself to sitting on the grass beside him. All she saw of the wagon were a few glints of white off someone's bonnet. She could barely hear them singing anymore.

"I don't think they miss us one bit." Jack raised himself up on one elbow. His long legs stretched out in front of her. "As a matter of fact, I think they might be glad to be rid of us so they can sing without interruption."

She couldn't hear them singing anymore. They were too far away. "I'm afraid you're right."

Once again, she felt Jack's hand caress her arm. "Did you get hurt when you fell out of the wagon?"

She turned and glared at him. "A lot you care! You pulled me out with you."

"You *pushed* me out!"

"You deserved to fall. I didn't."

Jack stared ahead of them at the wagon lumbering away into the darkness. "Maybe, but we both still have a long walk home ahead of us."

She glared at him. "Actually, you deserve to have the wagon run over you."

"Are you still blaming me for everything?"

"Not everything. I've narrowed it down to Willard and Katy separating and the Spanish Inquisition."

"They're *not* separating," he insisted. He pulled himself up to sit beside her. "He'll come back to her as soon as she apologizes."

"Unless he leaves with Caleb on that harebrained search for gold first."

"He won't be leaving." He rose to stand above her.

She looked up at him. He was a dark silhouette against the bright moonlit sky. "How can you be so sure? Did you tie him to the sofa at his parents' house or lock him in the jail?"

"No. I just had a little . . . chat with him."

"I know that. But I wouldn't know anything else," she snapped. "You didn't see fit to include me."

He held his hand down to help her up, and she took it. He pulled her to stand so close to him that their hands touched each other's chest. He closed his other hand over hers, holding her close to him.

"You don't have to be included in it," he told her bluntly. "You can relax sometimes, Maude. You don't have to be in charge of everything in everybody's life. It was the kind of talk men have when ladies aren't around. If I'd have told him everything I had to say in front of you, he'd have thought we were working together."

"How did you manage to convince him to stay when I couldn't?" She wouldn't admit she was more than a little jealous. She'd always considered herself rather intelligent, so why hadn't she been able to think of something to say to convince Willard when clever Jack had?

Jack tucked her arm into the crook of his elbow. "It's going to be a long walk home in the dark. Why don't we get started, and I'll tell you."

She began to walk with him over the rutted ground. "So, what's your secret for getting him to stay?"

"I didn't tell him to stay."

"I know that. That was the one part I heard very clearly."

"I figured Willard Konigsberg's about as hardheaded a Dutchman as they make. If I had told him he had to stay, it only would have made him more determined to leave."

"So you encouraged him to leave? That's got to be the worst—"

"Not exactly. I just sort of . . . enlightened him about all the wonderful things he was going to see and do when he went to the mining camps out West."

"Such as?"

"Such as eating ungodly things—"

"He already eats Katy's cooking."

"Well, then, it's no wonder he didn't seem too swayed by that part of my argument."

Was it the cool, calming air and the pleasant scent of the apple orchard in the moonlight, or was it the presence of Jack, holding her close to him, that was making her begin to believe that everything might actually be all right?

Even with the light of the full moon, it was difficult to see every rut and hillock in the ground. As they left the orchard and the extra light reflected by the white petals, and began walking down the road back into town, their surroundings grew darker. She clung to him for support, and he held her tightly. With each step, he drew her closer to him until she was tucked so close beneath his arm that she had to hold his waist. She shouldn't do it—but she did. And she enjoyed it!

It was so comfortable to walk side by side with Jack, almost as if she'd been doing it all her life—and needed to do so for the rest of her life. At the same time, there was an excitement to holding him so close that she knew she would never grow so familiar with that she could ever take it for granted; an excitement she never wanted to stop feeling.

If the road just continued on without end, and she was doomed to walk it until the end of time with Jack's arm about her, leaning against his warm body, at this moment she could think of no better fate.

Far in the distance, she could see the silhouette of her own home rising against the star-flecked sky. The gleam of a single lamp in the window might have shed a helpful light to guide them home, but every window was now completely dark. Apparently everyone had gone to bed. Had no one noticed she was missing? Did no one care? Everyone had made a big enough fuss when Georgie went missing. She was merely the one who did all the cooking, cleaning, shopping, sewing. Didn't anyone care about her?

"I warned Willard about how much expensive equipment he was going to need."

"That shouldn't bother him too much if he thinks he can get the money from Mr. Lester."

"I also sort of mentioned how cantankerous the bears and mountain lions can be. I get the feeling Willard's not real handy with a gun."

"Ol' Man Grunder with the palsy shoots better than Willard."

"Then I warned him how a fellow has to watch out for claim jumpers, and . . . well, I sort of cast aspersion on Caleb's honesty and integrity."

"Caleb dishonest? How could you say that? He doesn't even cheat when he's playing Blindman's Bluff!"

He looked down at her in the darkness. "Well, you certainly

spring to his defense with amazing quickness. Is *he* the one you've set your cap for?''

Maude felt her face grow cold at his blunt question. Of all the outlandish things Jack had asked her, this was undoubtedly the worst! Of all the answers she'd ever had to come up with—even in Miss Randolph's most difficult examinations—this one was going to have to be the best.

''No, he's not,'' she replied, and was amazed at how steady her voice sounded. The strangest part was, she was absolutely sure deep down inside that this time she really was telling the truth.

Jack drew her closer to him.

''Goodness, Jack, you'd be able to sell dancing shoes to a one-legged man if you could convince anybody Caleb could be dishonest.''

''Mind you, none of this is going to get Willard and Katy back together again,'' he warned. ''That's something the two of them have to work out together—without any interference from anyone, especially not their mothers. But I think I managed to keep him in town so those two could get to talking to each other again.''

''How are we going to do that?''

''I have a feeling Mother Nature will sort of take care of that.''

''What do you mean?''

''Well, Maude, a man has certain . . . needs.''

''I think I've heard that excuse before.''

''Well, it's true. So I sort of pointed out to Willard how . . . risky and basically . . . unsatisfying taking care of some of those needs could be with some of the . . . soiled prairie partridges.''

''You didn't!''

She could feel him pull his shoulders up with pride. ''I most certainly did. So you see, I'm not a complete, unregenerate reprobate, even though at times I may talk like one. But it was done for a good purpose, and that's all I'll say on the matter for fear of offending your delicate sensibilities.''

''There you go again,'' she said testily, ''talking about my delicate sensibilities.''

''Don't be angry with me, Maude.'' He stopped in the center of the road, turned, and pulled her to him. ''I couldn't bear it if you were always angry with me.''

''Do you think a lady with delicate sensibilities could've acted the way I did the other night?'' Goodness! It must be the moonlight, or the heady perfume of the blossoms, or the presence of Jack. What was wrong with her to bring up that particularly sensitive subject?

"Oh, yes!" His breath was warm across her face. His embrace was insistent. "You are delicate, Maude, my darling."

He crushed her against him and kissed her fiercely.

Had the Olsons grown locoweed in their fields along with the apples, that she would respond this way? Maude recalled the way she'd felt when she'd had a little too much hard cider. Then she realized she didn't need anything to make her feel the way she did about Jack. It was right and true and natural. Then she thought of nothing else.

She lifted her arms to curl them about Jack's neck. All she knew was that she returned his kisses with total and complete joy and enthusiasm.

"I want you, Maude," he whispered against her ear. "I want every beautiful, delicate part of you. I won't rest until I've made every bit of you all mine."

21

"I NEED YOU, MAUDE," Jack whispered in her ear.

He nibbled small kisses against her earlobe and across her cheek. She curled up against him with the tiny shuddering sensations his kisses burned into her flesh. Her bonnet knocked to the side, all askew—like her emotions.

"I need to make you mine."

"I need you, too, Jack, but—"

His lips descended on hers, silencing her budding protest.

"I've needed you since I saw you sitting there, all grown up, working on Louise's quilt. I don't know why I never realized it before. I guess I was just a kid—too wrapped up in myself, too eager to go out and see the world beyond Apple Grove—too stupid to see what happiness there could be for me right next door."

"Jack, you don't know—"

"You need me, too. You know you do. We can't fight it. Your family's happy. Your friends are happy." He kissed her between each word and sentence—again and again. "I'll kiss you, one time for each friend . . . each brother . . . sister . . . cousin . . . great-uncle . . . old maid aunt you have—not to mention all their pets . . . friends . . . and neighbors. I'll kiss you until you're convinced they're happy—and until we're just as happy as anyone else in the entire world could ever be.''

"No, no," she protested. Her protests sounded weak in her own ears. She knew she couldn't refuse Jack—even if she wanted to. The power of his passion wouldn't let her. "What happens when I run out of relatives?''

"We'll start our own line of descendants," he murmured huskily.

"I never realized how much I wanted you, too," she admitted. "Until . . . you touched me through Louise's quilt."

"Until then, you hated me."

"No. I didn't like you very much," she reluctantly admitted. "But that was before I knew you—"

"You've always known me."

"I mean really knew you and seen how you'd— No, not changed."

"Then what?"

"Seen how you'd let what was always good inside you come through."

"I've always been able to do that."

She gave him her most skeptical glare.

"It was just you who could finally see it."

He kissed her again.

"Just think, I owe all this to my coming over to see what you were doing to my cousin's quilt. I'll always consider quilts good luck for me. I found you under one."

With a great laugh, he swept her up into his arms.

"Hush, they'll hear us," she whispered, glancing nervously up to her darkened house.

"No, they won't. They're all asleep. We won't disturb them."

He carried her into her darkened barn, redolent with hay and leather. He found an empty stall piled high with clean, fragrant hay. He pulled a clean, red blanket from where it hung over the side of the stall and, with a flourish, spread it out over the mound of hay. A cloud of pale dust rose as Jack placed Maude in the center of the blanket and reclined beside her. They sank into the scratchy softness, making their own little hollow.

"Come to me, Maude," he invited, holding his arms wide for her. "Come to me freely. Let me know you want me, too. Let me hold you. Be mine and let me be yours."

"I want you, Jack. I love you." She rolled to her side, into his embrace.

She tentatively reached up and stroked his cheek. His skin was smooth and soft, and felt more so under the short stubble of beard. She ran her finger back and forth over the edge of his chin, and skittered along his strong jawline.

She smelled the pungent, pleasant aroma of the hay, hoarding last summer's leftover sunshine. From time to time, the fragrance of a few of the Kingstons' late-blooming lilacs drifted through the barn on the night air.

She heard the barn owl hoot once as he settled onto his perch in the highest rafters of the barn. The passenger pigeons cooed and fluttered their wings in protest as the owl disturbed them, then settled down again into a peaceful sleep. She could believe all the world was silent, except for the drumming of her own heart.

Jack reached up beneath her chin and untied the brown gros-grain ribbon that held her bonnet on her head.

"You're not going to be needing this," he told her. "It's warm in here. No one's going to think it's scandalous if you don't have on your bonnet." He gave her bonnet a toss into the hay at their feet.

"I feel scandalous."

He smoothed his hand up and down her cheek. "No, you feel wonderful." He laughed again. "Is it warm in here or is it me? Or is it you, Maude?"

"Me?"

"You—who makes my blood overheat to the point where I'm afraid I'll explode." He pulled himself to sit, and removed his jacket. He tossed it into the pile at his feet.

She gasped.

"No, it didn't land on your bonnet," he assured her. "I may be a fool in love with you, Maude, but I'm not such a fool I'd ruin a lady's bonnet."

She giggled. "It might be a little difficult to explain."

"Tell them when you fell out of the wagon you landed on your head."

"I must have," she agreed with him. "How else could I find myself in the barn with the notorious Suicide Jack, holding him, kissing him, loving him?"

"Am I that dangerous to be around?"

"Yes. Why else would I be enjoying every moment of it?"

He laughed again. She reached out her hand and ran her fingers up and down the blue and buff stripes of his woolen vest. She could feel his muscles and his ribs.

"You need to eat more. Being in jail has made you too thin."

"No, I'm not." He flinched.

"Are you ticklish?"

"No."

She laughed and grabbed for his side again.

"No!" He flinched again, and Maude realized it was more from pain than from pleasure.

She pulled her hand back as if she'd been burnt, almost as if she could feel his pain. "Oh, my goodness. I'm so sorry, Jack. I forgot."

"That's all right. I'd like to forget it, too," he told her as he unbuttoned his vest.

"You made such a brief mention of it in Ingrams'. I wasn't sure whether you were telling the truth or just spinning another tale, or just trying to silence Mr. Potter."

"It's real all right and, by golly, I guess it *is* on the left side." He gave a small, mirthless chuckle.

Maude tried to laugh at his joke, but she knew there wasn't anything funny about his pain.

"I thought it was an old wound . . . that it wouldn't hurt."

"It is old, but it . . . well, it was pretty deep. They tell me it'll probably always bother me. But at least if I live long enough, I'll be able to predict thunderstorms, like Ol' Man Grunder can with his 'ru-ma-tiz.' "

She tentatively reached out again, this time holding her hand palm out. Being careful not to actually touch his side, she placed the flat of her palm on his back. Slowly she slid her hand beneath his vest. His flesh was warm through his cotton shirt. Very gently she stroked his side. The scar felt puckered beneath her touch.

"I'm so sorry. I never want to hurt you."

"The surgeon who stitched me up told me afterward, half an inch deeper and I'd have been done for; or if I'd have lost one more drop of blood, I'd have been gone."

She winced at the very thought. "How did it happen?"

"Bayonet."

"Where?" she asked. As much as she loved him, there were still some aspects of Jack that were so hidden, so mysterious.

She couldn't help but be curious. What he called the battle might give her a hint as to which side he'd favored.

"In the ribs."

She'd give it one more chance with a more direct question. "Yankee or Rebel?"

"Mine."

"Who stabbed at you?"

He laughed. "No matter where I go, *everybody* wants to kill me."

It had been at least five years ago, when they were all very young and vulnerable. Five years could be a long time. Was she going to be like Mr. Potter, who couldn't forgive and forget? Or was she just going to love Jack for who he was now? It really *didn't* matter anymore.

"I don't, Jack. Not anymore."

"That's the best news I've had in a long time."

He leaned toward her, bending his body over hers. Supporting himself over her with both hands, he kissed her lips. She reached up and wrapped her arms around his neck, holding him close to her. He slipped out of her embrace to slide his kisses across her cheek and down her neck.

Her chin was soft. He hoped his calloused fingers and rough, sun-burned skin wouldn't scratch her delicate flesh.

She threw her head back and raised her arms above her head.

He rolled to his side, all the while trying to kiss her throat. With one hand, he began to tug at the small buttons ranging down the front of her bodice.

"You might be very good at quilting," he told her, "but I'm going to have to talk to you about making your buttonholes too tight."

She laughed, reached down, and slowly began to unfasten her own buttons. Was she moving so slowly out of modesty, or because she was trying to drive him crazier still with desire for her?

Jack carefully, gently lifted each layer of clothing, as he might turn over each leaf of a book of fantastic secrets that she would reveal only to him, only on the final page. Her taut breasts stood out against her soft chemise. He loosened the ribbon that held her chemise closed. As the gathers extended, he slipped the garment over her head.

Her breasts shone like twin pale moons in the darkness. Jack held his breath and gazed at her.

He'd never been able to find again the love and affection he'd known when he was very small—the love of a family that had been brutally torn from him. He knew his aunt and uncle cared for him; that was their duty. But there was always a price to pay. If he wasn't a good boy, they all swore they or somebody else would kill him someday. He'd pushed and pushed, to see how far they'd let him go before he'd get killed, to see how much they really loved him. But they'd never lived up to their word, and he'd been strangely disappointed. He guessed they hadn't even cared enough about him to kill him, either.

As he grew older, the ladies all seemed to like him, but there was always a price to pay there, too. Money, war secrets they sought to discover, demands for promises to marry them—always something in exchange.

But here was this exquisite woman—beautiful, intelligent, good—ready to give herself to him for no other reason than that she loved him. No money. He'd never mentioned marriage. Hell, he didn't even think he'd told her he loved her—not yet, even though he did; not the way he really wanted to tell her. But she loved him and was willing to show him exactly how much.

How else could he cherish this woman? If things didn't work out, if he was shot dead in the street tomorrow, if they threw him in jail forever and tossed away the key, he could carry the memory of this moment with him until he rotted there and died.

There was only one secret left to reveal. A single tug at a thin ribbon undid the bow that held her secrets from him. He tugged at the white ribbon that tied her pantaloons. With a quiet moan, he slipped the soft pantaloons from her hips, down her legs, off her. He couldn't just toss them away onto the pile with everything else. This was the last of the veils that held her precious secrets. He slowly placed her pantaloons beside him.

He gazed down at her, completely naked before him, gleaming white like a goddess made of moonbeams and starlight. A small dark triangle and two rosy spots marked the boundaries of the temple where he'd come to worship.

"I want you so much." His voice sounded rough.

"You know I want you, too."

She lay there, watching him as he removed his shirt. Could she feel his fingers trembling with desire and anticipation? Could she hear his heart pounding as he could hear it in his own ears? Did she know every muscle in his body was taut and tense, and ready to love her? She would soon. What would she think of him? Slowly he removed his trousers.

She looked at him and smiled. "Take me, Jack. I want to be yours tonight."

"I'll be gentle, Maude," he promised, and hoped he wouldn't turn into a wretched liar again. He wanted her so badly. It was going to be so damned hard to hold back.

She was soft and warm to his lips as he kissed her mouth, then trailed kisses down to her pale breasts. She held his head close, running her fingers through his hair as he savored the tenderness of each ruby nipple. He flicked his tongue across each contracting bud until she moaned.

"I want you," she whispered.

"I'm still a gentleman, Maude. I always will be for you. I'll give you a chance to refuse me. I'll leave. I'll go dunk myself in Miller's ice-cold pond until I shrivel up and can act like a normal man again."

"Shut up and make love to me," she commanded hoarsely.

"I will, my love. I will."

His lips descended to hers. His body fell atop her, seeking, searching. She moved her legs apart to allow him to enter.

Slowly, gradually, he felt as if his own insides were being twisted and torn apart with his yearning to plunge into her and satisfy his own intense longing for her. He found his entry and pressed.

She groaned and pulled back a bit.

"I'll . . . I'll stop—"

"Liar. If you ever were a liar in your life, Jack Kingston," she whispered, "be a liar to me about this."

"I do love you, Maude. That's the truth."

She lifted her hips to meet him. He sank into the moist warmth of her. He surged with the turning of the earth, the eternal movement of the stars, the spinning into the brightness and darkness of infinity. She rocked beneath him, soft and steady, sacred and beautiful, receiving his love.

She released a small, high-pitched moan of surprise and another, slightly lower, of contentment. She seemed to purr as he rested inside her, reluctant to leave.

Slowly he slid to her side. He reached over and pulled the

blanket over both of them. He cradled her head in the crook of his arm.

"I love you, Jack," Maude murmured as she placed her arm across his stomach. The small, curling hairs tickled her arm. "I can't believe it took me this long to realize it."

"I'll love you for as long as I live," he told her. He only wished he could reckon a little better about how much longer that might be.

∞

"MY GOD! WHAT HAVE I done?" Maude whispered to herself.

When she finally awoke in the pale gray light just before dawn, she couldn't believe her utterly stupid wantonness! Why, she'd turned as flighty as Jessica, as stupid as Ruthie, as cheap and easy as Clarice. And she'd never felt such pleasure, such sheer, wild abandonment as she had in Jack's treasured embrace!

What had she done?

She lifted her arm from his waist and rolled onto her back. She stared at the bleak rafters above and listened to Jack's slow, even breathing. With nervous fingers, she clutched at the edge of the rough blanket he'd thrown over the two of them when they'd lain there, drowsy and spent with making love, but never tired of being in love.

She turned to watch him in his sleep. In the half light of dawn, he was as handsome as when she'd held him to her by starlight. His dark hair was tousled and dotted with short strands of straw and chaff. His naked throat was strong and sinewy. His chin was still squared, even in the relaxation of sleep.

Short curls of dark hair twined across the muscles of his chest as they moved up and down with his rhythmic breathing. She longed to place her hands on his chest again, to feel his warmth and strength as he breathed.

His long, dark lashes shaded his closed eyes. It wasn't fair! Some women would kill for eyelashes like those.

Her father'd kill him if he found them here like this. Most likely he'd kill her, too.

How could she have been so foolish as to make love to Suicide Jack, who came and went like the wind? Suppose she'd got in a family way, like Sylvia Weber, who didn't know who the father was and didn't care? Would she end up like her, keeping a boardinghouse somewhere up in Wisconsin? Suppose she'd got in a family way, like poor little Betsy Nash, whose fiancé had been killed at Vicksburg before he'd had the chance to come home and marry her and make everything right? Would her family throw her out of the house as Mr. Nash had? Nobody knew where poor Betsy had ended up.

Maybe an enlightened man like Papa would spare her life. Maybe he wouldn't throw her out, either. After all, if he did he'd have to put up with Jessica's cooking or his own. She felt sure he'd spare her—but what kind of life would she have without Jack?

She had a bad feeling she was going to find out anyway. How long would it be before he left again? He had to leave, she knew it.

What kind of life could she have with him? she worried. He had no job that she knew of, or prospects for one in the near future. Of course, Jack never had been real talkative about his past or his plans.

He had no place to live. As much as she loved him, she was supposed to be smart, sensible, logical. The cold light of day was a lot more logical than the romance of apple blossoms and moonlight with Jack. She had to start using her brain again!

Maybe she *hadn't* gotten in a family way, she desperately hoped. After all, they'd only done it once. It had been her very first time. She tried to recall as many old wives' tales as she could, trying to reassure herself it couldn't possibly happen to her.

Maybe no one but she and Jack would ever know this night had happened. Maybe when Jack left—as she'd always known he'd have to—she'd still marry Caleb. But her life would never, ever be the same again.

Perhaps Caleb would never figure out what really happened between her and Jack; perhaps after their marriage he'd be magnanimous and overlook it; perhaps he'd believe she'd lost her virginity horseback riding—yes, that was it! There was only one catch. She'd have to start doing a lot more horseback riding.

She'd always sort of imagined she'd give herself, a virgin bride, to Caleb on their wedding night in an elegantly decorated boudoir in their magnificent mansion after he'd made his fortune.

Somehow all those images disintegrated in the memory of Jack's warm embrace in the barn.

Well, it was too late now. No sense crying over spilled milk. No sense locking the barn door after the horse was stolen. No sense, no sense. She'd had no blasted sense when she'd made love to him—and she still thought it was the best, the most wonderful thing she'd ever done. She released a long, deep sigh with the pleasure of her memories. There wasn't one wonderful thing about last night that she'd change. Not one blessed thing.

She stood and began to dress quickly. She had to get back into the house, wash, and change into a different dress, brush her hair, and start breakfast before anyone realized she hadn't even spent the night in the house.

She hoped no one noticed her sneaking out of the barn so early in the morning, in the same clothing she'd worn to the party last night. She hoped, if anyone saw her, they'd remember she was the *sensible* Griffith sister, and assume she had a very logical reason for being in the barn—although for the life of her, right now she couldn't think of one.

This morning the barn seemed cold as she left Jack lying there sleeping alone, as cold as she'd be sleeping without him for the rest of her life.

∞

WHAT HAD HE DONE?

Jack sat upright on the blanket in the lonely barn and shook his head. He thought, in his dreams just before waking, that he'd felt her stirring beside him. But when he woke up, she was already gone.

Last night he'd made love to the most beautiful, wonderful woman in his entire, miserable, misspent life. He'd ruined her completely. Now what was he going to do? What kind of prospects did he have? What could he offer her?

He could probably take the job with his uncle in the hardware store—put on sleeve garters and an apron and dole out hammers and nails to the farmers around here. He might eventually even become a partner, and probably stood to inherit the place when Uncle Tad passed away. Some of the people in town might eventually forget his unsavory reputation. Why, he might even become a veritable pillar of the community, he thought with a bitter laugh. Not an exciting life, but a fairly safe one.

He'd marry Maude in a heartbeat if he could. They'd build a little house on the outskirts of town where she could sit and quilt to her heart's content, and every night he'd come home to her and their healthy, happy, noisy brood of children. They'd have lots of children.

If they let him live long enough.

He still had this job to do—just this one job left to do—and then he'd quit, for Maude's sake. If they let him.

He had a duty, an obligation. He'd never let them down yet. He wasn't about to now. At first he'd chafed to get it done and get out of town. Every day he stayed here, he became increasingly involved, never realizing until it was too late how hard it was going to be to leave when he had to.

How was he going to leave Maude now? He'd sooner cut out his still-beating heart and leave it here than abandon her.

He sat there naked on the blanket in the barn, his elbows propped on his knees, his head hanging in his hands. What in God's name was he going to do now?

∞

BENJAMIN SIPPED HIS COFFEE and looked out his bedroom window, studying the shades of grayness of the world just before dawn. First the sky would lighten a little. Then a slight breeze would pick up over the silent landscape. The breeze brought the birdsongs.

It happened in the same order all the time; it was only the hour that brought the dawn and the birds' songs that changed. In the winter all he heard was the twitter of the snowbirds. In spring and fall, he could hear the geese honking as they flew high overhead and, closer to earth, the little pipits' tinkling call. Summer brought meadowlarks, dickcissels, bobolinks, and so many others. He didn't need to go to a big city and sit in some uncomfortable plush seat in some big, gilded opera hall in order to listen to some fancy orchestra made up of beaten metal, dead wood, and strung-out cats' guts. He had a real live symphony right in front of him all the time, and the best seat in the house.

Yes, indeed, he thought as he took another sip of his coffee, in spite of the petty problems humans could cause, the world was a mighty beautiful place, and he was glad to be in it. Of course, he would be even happier if Adelaide were here with him now, watching the sunrise. He'd have to do something about her— soon.

Suddenly he noticed the dark shadow making its way out of his barn. He frowned. Who the dickens was sneaking around his barn?

Thunderation! It was Maude.

What in the world was Maude doing out at this time of the morning? She might have an unusual reason for going to the outhouse in the middle of the night instead of using her chamber pot, but what reason did she have to go into the barn? He heard the kitchen door squeak open and close. He listened as his daughter's footsteps caused the back stairs to creak as she made her way up to her bed.

What a poor excuse for a father he was, he thought bitterly. No wonder Georgie had tried to run away. No wonder his younger daughter flittered all over town instead of settling down. He hadn't even noticed his older daughter hadn't been at home all night.

He'd expect this sort of behavior from Jessica. Not Maude.

Benjamin watched and waited. Just as he'd feared—and hoped wouldn't happen—a second, larger shadow emerged from the barn. It wasn't exactly the sort of behavior he'd expect from Maude, but, well, he'd always been told women were human, too—probably. As long as the fellow intended to make an honest woman of her eventually, he guessed there wouldn't be too much harm done. There wasn't too much he could do after the fact, was there?

Was it Caleb? he wondered as he squinted to try to see better in the half light at this distance. She'd seemed sort of interested in him. Could it be Matthew? he debated. She was always talking about him to Jessica and did seem mighty interested in his bookstore.

He almost choked on his coffee.

It was that damned Jack Kingston! He'd been in the barn all night with Maude, and it was a certainty they hadn't been counting bales of hay.

Very slowly he put his cup down on the top of the dresser. He knew if he continued to hold it, in his anger he'd crush the fragile china cup.

He'd kill him! He'd grab his loaded shotgun from over the

mantel, take aim right from his bedroom window, and blow the treacherous, lascivious blackguard back to hell where he came from.

No. He wouldn't pick him off from a distance. He wanted Jack to see exactly who was killing him, and he wanted him to know exactly why.

He couldn't ambush him, either. Then everyone would wonder what had happened to poor, unfortunate Jack—waylaid by roving marauders and shot down in the prime of his life when he was only paying a pleasant visit to his family for the happy occasion of his cousin's wedding. He couldn't do that. He refused to be a party to engendering any sympathy for the miserable scoundrel.

He'd wait; he'd get dressed, Benjamin decided. He'd go out, at high noon, right in the middle of town, and denounce him for the vile despoiler of fair womanhood that he was! That would certainly keep everyone from feeling too sorry for him—except for some of the more witless women in town, who would wish he'd been their ruination!

But Jack always carried a gun. He made his living with it, and—getting caught robbing a bank notwithstanding—he was probably very good with it. The only thing Benjamin would accomplish by calling Jack out would be his own violent, painful death, as well as making himself look like a dang fool for calling the boy out in the first place when he should have known better. If anyone in town should know how dangerous Jack could be, it was him.

He, at least, was a civilized man, Benjamin thought proudly. Jack might be the sort of scum who would shoot it out in the middle of the street at high noon with an enemy, but Benjamin hadn't worked, read, and studied all his life to resort to such desperate measures. He hadn't reported about criminals and their activities not to know a little bit about how to outfox them.

Jack might be good with a gun, but Benjamin had a brain, and he knew how to use it. He'd outthink the treacherous scum.

He'd wait, Benjamin decided, like the *smart, educated* gentleman he was. He'd bide his time. *He'd* decide when he'd get even with Jack for ruining his daughter. When he finally got his revenge, Jack would never forget it.

22

WHY WAS EVERYONE ACTING as if they were walking on eggshells today? Maude wondered as she sat at her quilt frame, trying to think of pleasant questions that wouldn't antagonize anyone. Had the complaints and confessions of last week's quilting meeting put everyone on edge, and made everyone cautious of what they said? She hated to think that could be so. They'd all had so much fun getting together and quilting. They had so many other quilts to finish for everyone's hope chests.

"It seems so odd, not doing anything," Maude observed. She placed her hands on the empty bar of her quilting frame. "We look sort of silly, just sitting here in our chairs, the frame all set up, thimbles all ready, needles all threaded—"

"Even a pie," Katy said, grinning widely and looking longingly at the golden-crusted confection on the table by the bookcase.

"With no top to quilt."

"Where *is* Florence?" Louise demanded. "She's never late."

"Especially not since we've been working on *her* quilts," Wilma said.

Maude glanced over to the clock sitting on the mantel. "Why don't we wait ten more minutes?"

"Good morning, ladies," Jack declared as he strode through

the front door. He nodded, especially to her. "Maude."

She'd sworn to herself to be calm and sensible the next time she saw him. But when she looked at him sauntering into the parlor on those strong, muscular legs, she felt her heart beat faster in spite of her stout resolutions. He gave her a wide grin and a wink.

She shook her head and sighed. "Honestly, Jack. Sometimes I wonder if you'll ever learn to knock," she scolded him playfully.

He had to be able to tell she couldn't take her eyes off him. She just hoped no one else noticed. Every other girl in town had made such a fool of herself gawking at Jack. She was smarter than them all. She had to be able to keep her feelings for him a secret until—

Until what? Until he decided to ride off into the sunset? He'd done that before. How could wanting a man hurt so much? How could loving him hurt even more?

She wished Florence would get here with her quilt top, so they could put it into the frame and start quilting it. That would give her something besides Jack to occupy her thoughts. That would provide her itchy fingers with some constructive activity, when all she really longed to do was hold Jack and run her fingers over his body—and feel his hands caressing her.

"When I woke up this morning, I thought I smelled a pie baking, and I knew I had to come over here and claim it for my very own," he said.

They might have thought he was making a joke for all of them to laugh at, Maude thought as she watched her friends watching Jack. But she knew, from the way he was looking at her and her alone, that he wanted—no, he already had—claimed something in this house as his very own. Whatever happened from this day onward, Jack had laid claim to her, body and soul—and he knew it, too. He'd already accepted her body and heart, but would he be willing to take the entire life that she offered him?

"Oh, yes, Jack," Clarice said enthusiastically, all thoughts of waiting for Florence obviously completely forgotten. "You must have a piece of pie."

She sprang from her seat before anyone else could move, rushed to the small table by the bookcase, and began slicing the pie.

"I want you to know how much I appreciate your feeding a

poor, wayfaring stranger," Jack said with a grin as he took the proffered plate of pie from Clarice.

Maude cringed inwardly at the words. He'd leave again, she'd always known that. But she didn't want to be reminded.

"I'll kill him!" Florence declared as she stormed through the front door. She dropped a pile of quilt tops on the floor, then reached down and began tossing them, one by one, to her friends. "Take them! Take them all! I won't need them anymore. Maybe you'll all have better luck with them than I did."

"Florence, what are you talking about?" Louise asked.

Florence spun around and confronted Maude. Maude drew back and watched her with wide eyes and raised eyebrows. "As for that blasted special quilt block you're making for me—well, you can just burn the damned thing!"

"Florence!"

She raised her hand. "As God is my witness, if I ever lay eyes on that man again, I'll kill him! I'll stab him, I'll shoot him, I'll batter him with my rolling pin, I'll strangle him with my bare hands!" Florence stood there, her knuckles white from clutching at the last quilt top she held in her hands. Any minute now, Maude fully expected to hear her growl and see her start foaming at the mouth and chewing on her quilt.

Maude looked around at her friends. They were still staring at Florence, eyes wide with shock and mouths gaping open, looking as emptyheaded as extinguished All Hallow's Eve jack-o'-lanterns. Jack had taken his plate and tactfully retreated to the doorway to the kitchen. The man was undoubtedly very good at making quick, emergency escapes through back doors. If she could have climbed over the bony quilt frame, she would have joined him. On the other hand, she had a bad feeling Florence was going to be in desperate need of help, and she had to be there for her friend.

"Who will you kill, Florence?" Maude at last managed to ask. She tried to keep her voice soft and low, so as not to agitate her friend any further. If she couldn't find the man she wanted to kill, would she turn her anger on them all and hack them to death with her sewing scissors?

"Edgar—curse him!"

"Goodness, Florence!" Katy exclaimed. "What happened?"

"He's gone. Away. Forever. Without me!" With a loud wail, Florence slumped into a limp pile of tears and cloth on the floor.

She reached into her bodice and pulled out a damp, crumpled note. "No warning. No hints he was unhappy with me, with our engagement, with my mother."

"I thought you said he hated your mother," Clarice said. "As a matter of fact, I seem to recall you mentioning the fact that you weren't so sure you wanted to marry him. Something about you hating how he reads the newspaper."

"I'm allowed to have my doubts," Florence asserted. "I'm supposed to be the blushing bride. He was the one who asked me to marry him. He was the one who was supposed to be certain of what he wanted. He wasn't supposed to change his blasted mind!" She crumpled the note between her fingers. "If I ever see him again, I'll blow his brains out so bad he won't be able to find enough of his mind to change!"

She shook the note out in front of her. She uncrumpled it. Then she unfolded it, tearing it as she did so along its already worn creases. She smoothed it out in her lap and held it up to read.

" 'Dear Florence, I have taken my carpentry tools, bid my parents farewell, and set out westward to make my fortune. I understand there is always a place for a skilled craftsman such as myself to make a good living. I wish you well. Best regards, Edgar.' "

She gave a scream, crumpled the note in her clenched fingers, and drummed her feet on the floor.

"That's it! After months of keeping company, after months of being betrothed, after all the plans and expenditures—that's it. A lousy one-paragraph note! 'Best regards'—my aunt Sally's bloomers! I thought he said he *loved* me! I'll kill him! My mother's going to kill him. My father's going to kill him. Making them spend all that money for nothing. The rotten coward couldn't even talk to me like a man—face-to-face. I suppose now I'll have to send back all the wedding presents, even the dishes! Well, I'll tell you, I'm keeping this engagement ring—puny though it may be." She tucked her left hand close to her side, as if defying anyone to try to take it from her.

Katy gave a disdainful sniff. "Then I'm glad I bought my table from the catalogue and not the one in his horrible old store!"

"When I got the note, I went directly to Edgar's parents' house, hoping to catch him, but he'd already left," Florence managed to explain with a little more control, perhaps taking comfort from knowing she had friends on her side. "His mother told me he'd taken everything he could fit in one bag, withdrawn his savings from the bank, packed his tools, and headed out early this morning. Why didn't he say good-bye to me?" She started wailing all over again.

Maude's heart ached for her friend. How could Edgar do such a terrible thing to her without a word—not even a hint? At least she *knew* Jack would be leaving her someday soon—even though the knowledge really didn't hurt any less.

"How could the dirty, low-down, miserable coward do such a despicable thing?" Clarice muttered. "You *should* shoot him!"

"I should've listened to you, Maude," Florence said, casting a tear-stained glance up to her.

"Me? What did I say?"

"You tried to warn me. Your quilt tried to warn me."

"My quilt?"

"Don't you recall how every time I asked you how my special quilt block was progressing, you'd hem and haw and never give me a definite answer?"

Maude knew she'd been having trouble with that particular block, but she couldn't recall mentioning it to Florence or anyone else. But she wasn't about to argue with her about that now.

"I should've realized then you were only trying to spare my feelings from the horrible truth. You're a true friend to me. When I'm a miserable, feeble old maid, living alone with only my cats for company, I shall always cherish your dear friendship."

"I'm glad to hear that, Florence, but don't you think you might—"

"I shall never forgive *you* for this!" Florence declared, pointing an accusing finger at Jack in the doorway.

Jack glanced up cautiously from his last bite of pie. "Me?" He swallowed hard.

"He's only following your bad example. You left without even saying good-bye to your aunt and uncle. You were too much of a coward to face them for the tearful farewell, and he was too much of a coward to face me."

"Florence, I haven't done a whole lot of talking to Edgar since I came to town."

He set his plate on the table. Maude wondered if he was getting ready to flee or to fend off Florence's angry attack.

"I don't know why you all seem to think just because I ride into town from out West that I'm going to be talking all your menfolks into running off there. If you'll all stop to think about it, I really didn't have too much fun out there. Why would I try to talk somebody else into going there? Why would they be stupid enough to believe me? If Edgar's been talking to anybody who could convince him to go out West, it's been Caleb, not me."

"Caleb?"

"Don't sound so surprised," Jack told her. "I've only been here a few weeks. Caleb's been here every day for months and years, probably always talking about the same darned thing."

Florence sat there, silent for a moment. From the deep frown on her face, Maude could only suppose she was thinking. She hoped she was thinking sensibly, for Jack's sake—and for her own. She'd have to calm down and learn to cope with this terrible blow.

"No." Florence adamantly shook her head. "It's your fault, Jack. You know how you can mix all the flour, sugar, and salt into a pan, and it'll just sit there, doing nothing, for years and years. But you add just a little yeast, and everything starts moving. That's you, Jack. You're the yeast. You're the one who comes in, stirs things up, and forces things to happen around here—and not always good things."

She stumbled to her feet, untangling herself from her wrinkled skirts.

"We were all happy, just fine and dandy around here—until you came back. Now everything has turned out horrible, and it's all your fault."

Florence spun on her heels and burst out the door.

"I don't suppose we'll be doing any quilting today, will we?" Katy asked.

"I don't know what we'll do."

Wilma lifted the quilt top Florence had thrown at her. "You know, I'll have to thank Florence for this when she calms down. It really is nice of her to—"

"You'll do nothing of the sort!" Louise scolded, snatching the quilt top from Wilma's hand. She folded it neatly and placed it on the edge of the sofa. Then she gathered up all the other ones and folded them. "We'll give these right back to her. She *will* need them, whether that faithless, worthless Edgar comes back to her again or not. Florence is sweet and smart, and her father is wealthy. She'll find a beau again—just like that!" Louise snapped her fingers.

"But what'll we do today?" Ruthie asked.

"I guess we'll just have to eat our pie and go home," Katy suggested.

"Don't you have any tops ready to quilt, Maude?" Louise suggested.

"No, not really." Of all the ladies here today, Maude considered herself the least likely to be needing her quilts any time in the future.

"Of course you must," Louise insisted.

"Sure, Maude," Jack said, casting her a wide grin. "You're always sewing something."

"I've been so busy lately, I don't have anything ready. Really, I don't."

Maude had no intention of bringing out her threatening monster quilt—the one that she'd mistakenly embroidered Jack's and her initials on—that had looked so perfect. It was especially disconcerting, in light of Florence's new development, to think how right it had looked.

She used to find such comfort in sewing together her carefully cut patches into neat, orderly blocks, resting secure in the certainty that she'd eventually use them in her beautiful home when she married Caleb. But Jack had taken her life and wildly torn it up, like badly shaped, mismatched patches. He'd disarranged everything she'd thought she believed in, or hoped for, in the life she thought she'd laid out in such an orderly fashion, like a carefully planned quilt.

Worst of all, she knew she could never sleep with Caleb under one of those quilts. She'd never feel about Caleb the way she felt about Jack. Florence had been right about one thing. Jack did indeed cause things to happen. He ignited passions in her she never dreamed existed. She felt longings for him she'd always heard no decent woman should feel—and she was glad, proud of it! It was more than just physical passion she felt for Jack. She knew she loved him with all her heart, too.

But would he ever stay around long enough? Sure, Caleb talked a lot about leaving, but he never did, and Maude had a sneaking suspicion he never would. But Jack was the kind of man who could never be happy unless he was on the move. No woman—no matter how much she loved him or how much he might claim to love her—would ever be able to still his restless spirit. Not even with love.

∞

"I'VE DONE IT!" JESSICA announced as she bounced into the parlor that evening. "Yes, yes! How wonderful for me!"

Her hair was more disheveled than usual. Her blue eyes were shining, and her cheeks and lips looked as if they'd been buffed a bright pink. Maude had seen her sister excited before, but she'd never seen her in this state.

Mr. Griffith immediately silenced his reading aloud of Washington Irving's *Tales of the Alhambra*. Maude looked up from her piecing.

"Well, *we've* done it," Jessica corrected herself.

"What have you done?" Maude managed to ask. She hoped her voice didn't sound as fearful as she truly was. Jessica could be up to anything, and it sounded as if she'd dragged someone else into her mischief as well.

"I'm getting married," Jessica announced.

Maude squealed with delight, tossed her piecing into the air, and sprang to her feet. She ran over and, for the first time in a long while, actually embraced her sister with joy. "Jessica, I'm so happy for you!"

"My goodness, Maude." Jessica gasped for air. "I've never seen you this excited."

Mr. Griffith was a little slower at rising, but his embrace of his daughter was no less joyful.

"We'll start making plans," Maude said. "We'll talk to Miss Hawkins about what she can sew for you."

"No, you don't understand, Maude. We don't have that much time."

"Oh . . . oh, Jessica." Suddenly the joyous smile plummeted from Maude's face. She seized her sister by the arm and pulled her slightly away from their father. She leaned closer to Jessica and whispered, "You're not in a condition like poor Betsy Nash, are you?"

"What?" she squealed. "Gracious, no! Maude, how could you even think such a thing about me?"

"I'm sorry. But I don't see the need for such a rush to marry if you're not. After all, I don't think Matthew's about to go moving his store—"

"Matthew?" Jessica demanded. Some of the bounce had gone out of her, and she was frowning. "Matthew *Conway*?"

"Yes," Maude replied a little hesitantly. If Jessica had to ask, something was wrong. "The only other Matthew in town is Polly Foster's son, and he's only seven years old."

"No, not Matthew," Jessica said with a scornful laugh. "I'm going to marry Caleb!"

Maude opened her mouth to repeat the name, just to make sure she'd heard her sister right, but the sound caught in her throat, choking her. At last she gave a cough to unstick her throat and get her heart beating again.

"Caleb *Johnson*?"

"Yes. There *aren't* any other people by that name in town, not of any age."

"You're . . . marrying Caleb Johnson. He . . . actually asked you."

"Yes. It's a little hard to have a wedding without the groom knowing about it." Jessica turned to her father. "He'll be stopping by later this evening to talk to you about it, Papa, and get your permission."

When Mr. Griffith finally stopped laughing, he managed to say, "You've never asked my permission to do anything you really wanted to do."

"Well, that's true," Jessica admitted with a little giggle. "But we'd like to get your approval—and your blessing."

Mr. Griffith reached out and patted Jessica's hand. "Of course, my dear. Of course."

Jessica turned to Maude and began to explain. "We don't have time for a lot of fancy preparations. Just enough time to get together the basic necessities. We'll be getting married April twenty-eighth so we can be in Cedar Rapids before May the first."

"Why are you going to Cedar Rapids?" Mr. Griffith demanded.

"May the first is the day the last wagon trains leave for Oregon in order to make it across the prairie and over the mountains before winter sets in."

"Oregon?" Mr. Griffith repeated.

"Caleb's actually—*we're* actually going to do it. He's saved up a bit of money, got his brothers to add in some. Somehow he managed to talk Mr. Lester into lending him some money. There are plenty of opportunities to make his fortune out there. You've always said how ambitious and hard-working he is. He's been telling me all about his plans. They're so exciting. I just know he's going to succeed. He's going to be so busy, working so hard to make a success of his—*our*—mine. He's going to need someone to take good care of him—someone who loves him very much.''

"I . . . thought you liked . . . Matthew,'' Maude muttered. She'd heard and understood everything her father and sister had been saying to each other and to her, but she was still working on understanding exactly what had prompted her sister to do such a crazy thing. "He's so sensible, so right for you. You helped him in his bookstore.''

"I help Miss Hawkins in her store, too, but that doesn't mean I'm going to marry her, silly.''

Maude couldn't say anything more. Her knees wouldn't support her. She made her way to her chair and sat down again. Jessica flounced her skirts around her as she plopped down on the floor beside Maude's chair.

"I'd like to go see Miss Hawkins tomorrow. When we were cleaning out her storeroom, I found a piece I might be able to use as a veil. I figured we—I mean you—could take in Mama's wedding gown in time for me to wear that. You could wear the gown you wore for Louise's wedding. That would save us a lot of time.'' Jessica babbled on and on until Maude thought her head would burst, and her stomach, already churning with surprise, would finally upturn everything she'd had for dinner.

"Do you think the lilies of the valley will be blooming enough in time for me to have a little nosegay?'' Jessica asked. "I'd love to have them. They smell so good.''

"Probably.'' Maude just couldn't seem to generate much enthusiasm to answer more than that.

"Do you think I should have Cousin Prunella as a bridesmaid?''

"Probably.''

She frowned. "Even though she could stand to lose about fifty pounds.''

"Probably.''

"She could probably get away with wearing her wedding

gown again—as long as the pink goes with your gown—if she can still fit into it.''

"Probably."

"And, of course, I want you for my maid of honor."

"Probably."

"Maude!" Jessica exclaimed, slapping at her hand to get her attention. "Have you been listening to a word I've been saying?"

"What? Yes, Jessica," she replied wearily. "I've heard every single word you've said."

"And, well, I . . . know this is really going to be asking a lot, but . . . do you think you and your friends might possibly be able to get together, real quick, to make me a bride's quilt? Nothing fancy, just—"

"What?" Maude sprang to her feet. She began pacing back and forth across the parlor floor. She'd never meant to start ranting and raving, but all the many years of tolerating and excusing Jessica's irresponsible behavior had finally added up to one too many, and she had to let it out.

"Oh, no! That's the limit. That's where I draw the line. *This* is the feather that breaks the horse's back! You never did a thing to help yourself if it looked like it was going to be too much work, and now you expect me to do that, too! Sewing a few patches together isn't that hard to do. Mama tried to teach you, but, oh no, you wouldn't learn—not you, not when you could get somebody else to do it for you. I'd have even helped you. But all the while I cooked and cleaned and mended, looked after Papa and Georgie, and still found time to make all the things I'd need for my hope chest, you were running around the town, chatting and being sociable, and wasting your time. You could've stayed home once in a while. We'd have been happy to have you join our quilting circle on Wednesdays. But now, at the last darned minute, you have to have a bride's quilt. Well, *I* have other things to do. There is no way in hell I'm making anything for *you*!''

23

"THANK YOU SO MUCH, Mrs. Kingston," Jessica said. "I don't have one of these."

She took the cast-iron skillet from her and placed it on the little table in front of the bookcase, beside the five matching glasses Mrs. Hardesty had given her earlier today, explaining that there once had been six matching glasses.

"I know it's been pretty well used," Mrs. Kingston said apologetically. "But it's so big, and now that I'm just cooking for Mr. Kingston and myself, I really don't need one that size, and Louise received a large one from Mrs. Ingram's sister in St. Louis, so she doesn't need this one, either."

Maude could tell Mrs. Kingston was rambling because she was embarrassed to be giving Jessica one of her castoffs as a wedding present. Maude would be, too, and she felt rather sorry for her next-door neighbor. She'd be embarrassed to be receiving second-hand items as wedding presents, too. Jessica, on the other hand, was pretty hard to embarrass. She seemed absolutely delighted with the patched and worn things.

"If I'd have had time, you certainly know I'd have bought you something very special, something beautiful or lacy," Mrs. Kingston continued. "Something fancy ordered from a catalogue. Or if I'd have had time to make you something—"

"I know you would, Mrs. Kingston," Jessica said, giving the lady's hand an affectionate pat.

"Jack told me I ought to get something useful for you instead of just pretty," Mrs. Kingston said. "I'm glad I had something on hand."

"I'll get a lot of use out of this." Jessica turned to Maude. "Isn't this a nice frying pan?"

Maude wanted to tell her silly sister that when you've seen one frying pan, big or small, you've just about seen them all. She wanted to snatch the darn thing out of her sister's hand and whack her in the head with it. But they'd never let her get away with it.

Instead, she said, "How very nice. Do you know what it's for?"

Jessica glared at her through narrowed eyelids, but smiled nevertheless. "Of course I do, silly."

It didn't matter who gave what to her sister; Jessica didn't have the slightest idea how to cook or sew or run a household. How in the world was she going to manage out there on her own?

"I hope you can use this, too, Jessica," Louise said, handing her another decorated box. "Jack said you would."

Maude was happy to see Jessica at least had the good manners to admire the colored paper and ribbons that Louise had gone to the trouble to tie around the box before she actually opened it. Of course, knowing Jessica, she didn't waste too much time admiring the wrapping. Quickly she pulled off the ribbon and paper and lifted the lid.

"Kitchen towels!" Jessica exclaimed with as much enthusiasm as if Louise had given her a large silver platter. "How did you know I don't have any kitchen towels?"

"Because Maude said you didn't have any."

Maude decided Louise was a true and loyal friend; she'd wisely refrained from finishing what Maude had actually told her—that Jessica didn't have anything, not even a brain.

"Maude, look at these towels Louise was kind enough to give me."

"How very nice. Do you know they'll be useful for drying things?"

Peeking out the front window, Maude noticed Clarice and Mrs. Dalton coming up the walk. She gritted her teeth. At this moment, she was in no mood to have to deal with Clarice.

When Clarice spied Jessica, threw open her arms, and cried, "There's the lucky bride! How I envy you!" She glanced around to the other ladies in the parlor, pausing pointedly at Maude. "Don't all of us unmarried ladies just envy her so?"

Mrs. Dalton handed Jessica a large box.

"What could it be?" Jessica lifted the lid. "A blanket. How very thoughtful of you."

"When I heard you'd be going out West, I figured I ought to ask someone who'd been there exactly what would be a good gift for you." Clarice cast a smug glance in Maude's direction. "So, I went—personally—and asked Jack what you might be needing the most. Jack was so sweet, so helpful to me."

"It's only got one little hole in it, which I embroidered this little daisy over so it's covered," Mrs. Dalton explained.

"How sweet," Maude remarked, not bothering to keep the sarcasm from her voice. Mrs. Dalton was very likely to embroider a daisy, while she figured Clarice would be more suited to a vulture. At this moment, she herself felt rather like a wasp.

"Every time I see this, Mrs. Dalton, even though I'm miles away, I'll be reminded of the daisies growing in your front yard," Jessica told her.

"At least you'll have something to sleep under now. It's such a pity Maude and her friends couldn't make a special quilt for you and Caleb," Mrs. Dalton said.

"I don't have time," Maude replied through tightened lips. "Maybe if I'd had a bit more notice. Or if Jessica herself had been a bit more prepared—"

"Maude's so busy with everything else, she just doesn't have time," Jessica repeated.

"Still," Clarice offered, "you'd think she could manage for *you.*"

It was bad enough Jack was advising Jessica on what to take and what not to—even though, if anyone ought to know, he would, Maude thought glumly. It was bad enough Jack was also advising their friends and neighbors on their choice of gifts for the ill-prepared bride and groom. At least he wasn't hanging around, watching Jessica make an absolute ninny of herself, accepting other people's trash.

"I hope our gift won't be redundant, then," Mrs. Lester said, raising her hand to her cheek in a gesture of dismay. "I did ask

Jack about it first. He did say it was a good idea.''

Jessica opened the Lesters' gift. "Another blanket. Oh, yes, how wonderful. I understand it gets very cold in the mountains. I'm sure two blankets will be doubly useful.''

"It's fairly new," Mrs. Lester said. "Granny Saunders only used it about six months before she passed away.''

A dead woman's blankets! How mortifying, Maude thought with distaste. She'd rather freeze!

"At first we thought Florence might be passing a quilt along to you, but . . . well, it seems . . .''

Florence straightened her spine and smiled out at the group of ladies, but she never said a word. Maude supposed that was what mothers were for.

"We really can't stay here too late this afternoon, Maude," Mrs. Lester said. "We have guests coming for dinner.''

"The Fitzroys," Florence announced.

"How very nice," Maude said. She cast a worried look in Wilma's direction. On top of everything else, how could this be happening now?

"Mr. and Mrs. Fitzroy are very nice, and Peter is so . . . entertaining.''

He doesn't waste much time, either, Maude silently observed. Aloud, she said, "I hope you have a nice dinner.''

"I hope you choke," Wilma stated flatly. She rose and headed out the door.

"My goodness, Wilma," Florence said. "Don't make such a fuss of it. It's only a . . . visit.''

"I'm sure. A much more suitable visit than they ever would have made to me and my family." By the side of Maude's chair, Wilma stopped. "This is all your fault, you know.''

"Mine?''

"If you hadn't continually put it off, if you'd made my quilt block when you should have, it would be all set, and none of this ever would have happened.''

Maude stared at her. "I really think you're carrying this quilt block superstition much too far.''

"I'll never speak to you again as long as I live," Wilma pronounced and headed out the door.

"Oh, my. Did I say the wrong thing?" Mrs. Lester asked.

"Probably," Maude muttered.

"I mean, Peter Fitzroy, what with the hotel and the descent

from a king and all, is so much more appropriate a beau for my Florence, what with her father being the president of the Apple Grove Farmers and Merchants Savings and Loan Association, you know, than a mere cabinetmaker.''

''The Baumgartners are both very good cabinetmakers,'' Maude mumbled. The whole world was turning upside down.

''And she for him, if you take my meaning,'' Mrs. Lester continued, intent on her own conversation.

''Probably.''

''Talk about some people putting on airs. I never could understand what she thought the son of the owner of the hotel would see in a baker's daughter.''

''I don't suppose so.''

With each gift Jessica opened, Maude felt herself growing increasingly agitated. Mrs. Lester's thoughtlessness had surprised her, and Wilma's reaction had hurt her to the quick. If Jessica and all the others didn't shut up about these worn-out gifts and get out of her house immediately, she was going to explode!

Georgie was working afternoons at the newspaper office and already eagerly making plans to go away to the University of Iowa when he turned sixteen. Wilma swore she'd never speak to her again, and Katy wasn't too friendly toward her, either. Her sister was leaving with Caleb. Caleb was marrying Jessica—not her! Maude felt as if everyone important to her was abandoning her.

When would Jack leave? When would he decide he'd gotten what he'd wanted from her and was prepared to discard her? She thought she'd crumble with the ache in her heart at the very thought of it. He'd said he had obligations, just as she had. She might understand that but, for the life of her, she wished she knew what they were. She wished she knew why they kept them apart. She wished she knew what she was going to do when Caleb and Jack were gone. For the first time in her life since Mama had died, Maude had absolutely no idea what she was going to be doing from one rotten day to the next.

∞

''WELL, I MUST SAY, there are some pretty nice things here,'' Jessica remarked after their guests had all left at last. She stood, legs astride, hands on hips, proudly surveying the things they'd brought her like a pirate inspecting his booty.

Maude, for her part, surveyed the dirty dishes and glasses piled on the dining room table and in the kitchen. She looked around at the crumpled paper, unraveled ribbons, and empty boxes strewn across the parlor. Jessica would be playing with all her pretty new presents, and Maude would do the dishes—as usual.

"There are some nice things here, not counting some of the things I've managed to dig up that we haven't used in ages. All in all—"

"Are you out of your mind?" Maude demanded. She'd been trying so hard to contain herself all afternoon, but now she'd had all she could bear. She flung her hand disdainfully across the heap. "This is junk! This is trash! Instead of tossing it out into the garbage, they wrapped it up in a fancy box and handed it off to you."

"Goodness, what's stuck in your craw?"

"How can you be so grateful for other people's trash?"

"Be sensible, Maude."

"You're telling me to be sensible? That's rich!"

"You're usually so sensible. Why can't you be now?"

"Because I see my sister drooling like an idiot over trash. Have you no sense? No pride? No dignity? Mama would be absolutely mortified to see you taking on so over a few old cast-offs. Your telling me to be sensible would be so laughable, so highly ironic, if it weren't so horribly disturbing. You've never been sensible in your life."

"I never had to be. I always had you to do it for me. But soon I won't, so now I'll just have to be sensible."

"What's so sensible about this?"

"I can't take beautiful new things across the prairie to a rough mining camp where they'll no doubt be ruined in a matter of months, *if* they survive the trek across the prairie in the first place. I'll just be happy with other people's secondhand things until Caleb strikes it rich and I can buy nice new things of my own."

"You'll take anything, then," Maude accused.

"Anything I can use."

"Anything! Just anything! You'll take a dead woman's blankets, used pots, and chipped cups. You'll even take the man *I* wanted to marry!"

For a moment, Jessica stood there staring at her as if she had no idea that Maude was even speaking English. It wasn't the staring that was so unusual. Not even the pale white cast to Jessica's features was startling. It wasn't that Jessica wasn't comprehending what Maude was saying to her. What really let Maude know her sister was truly puzzled, and was listening to her for some kind of clear explanation, was the fact that Jessica finally—probably for the first time in her life—was standing absolutely still.

"What do you mean, Maude? Are you telling me you wanted to marry Caleb?"

"Yes!"

"But you never said anything."

"I know I never came right out and said anything to you. I didn't think I had to. Nobody else had her cap set for Caleb that I knew of. I liked him. He was always pleasant to me. I . . . I thought I had time. I had to make sure you were all taken care of before I could go looking to marry him. But, well, yes. I thought Caleb would make a good husband for me."

"Just like you thought Matthew would make a good husband for me?"

"Yes."

Jessica laughed. Maude had all she could do not to reach out and choke her.

"How silly can you be? You'd be a terrible wife for Caleb. You have to have everything just perfect. I can't imagine you living out of a wagon or living in a tent or a soddy. You'd drive each other crazy in no time."

"Do you think you'd be a good wife? You're always losing or breaking things."

"Then I'll just have to learn to make do with what I have. Isn't that what I'm doing now?"

"Yes, that's exactly what you're doing. You're taking something I wanted."

"How was I to know? I thought you wanted to marry Matthew! You were always talking about how smart he was, how frugal, how responsible, how nice he was. I thought you were in love with him."

"No. I . . ."

She couldn't bring herself to say she was in love with Caleb. She'd once thought she was, but she knew now what true love really felt like, and she knew for certain she'd never been in love with Caleb. But she'd never thought her sister was, either.

"Never mind," she said, feeling more weary than she'd ever felt in her life. "It doesn't matter now, anyway. It just doesn't matter. Do what you please. I know you will. You always have, regardless of what anyone else has ever said or done. Regardless of anyone else's feelings, all you've ever cared about was what you wanted. Well, now you get it all—the wedding, the attention, the gifts, the man. I wish you well."

She turned her back on Jessica and headed up the stairs. Then she stopped and turned.

"For a start, you can clean up your own damned mess."

∞

HE'D REPORTED THE WAR with Mexico. He'd packed up his young wife and family, left Baltimore, and moved out to Apple Grove, Iowa. He'd run his own newspaper, raised three children, and buried his dear wife. He wasn't a cowardly man. But this was one of the toughest things Benjamin Franklin Griffith had ever had to do.

Hat in hand, he knocked on the frame of the open schoolhouse door.

Adelaide looked up from the papers spread out over her desk. She laid her pen down and pushed her spectacles up her nose. Her big blue eyes blinked at him in surprise.

"Mr. Griffith, I'm surprised to see you here. Georgie has been so well behaved since we came to our agreement."

"I didn't come here to discuss Georgie."

"Oh." She blinked again. Then, as if finally coming to her senses, she gestured toward the bench in front of her desk. "I'm forgetting my manners. Please, won't you have a seat?"

Benjamin glanced down at the low bench. "I don't think I'd fit. Anyway, I didn't come here to take up a lot of your time."

"Oh." Adelaide looked definitely disappointed.

They'd had so much fun discussing things before. Dare he hope she'd forgive his foolish blustering when he'd clearly been understandably agitated?

"I've come here today to request your assistance in a particular matter."

"What can I do for you, Mr. Griffith?"

He wanted to shout, "You can stop calling me Mr. Griffith.

Call me Benjamin, the way you used to before that meddling troublemaker Jack poked his nose in my business and ruined my life!''

But he was an adult. He was an educated gentleman. Adelaide was a cultured, educated lady. He couldn't do anything so rude. So he just stood there in front of her and fidgeted with the band on his hat.

"It's my daughters this time."

"What's wrong with Maude and Jessica? I hardly think they'd have run away like Georgie."

"Jessica might as well have. I suppose you've heard the news that she's getting married."

"Yes, and I must stop by and offer her my heartiest best wishes. I have a little something to give her that I think she might find useful. My, your house must be in quite a turmoil."

"That, in a nutshell, is the whole problem."

"I didn't realize," she said. Lifting her fingertips to her mouth, she frowned. "Please, do elaborate. I shall listen and do my best to offer whatever insights I might have."

"They fight," he stated.

"Jessica and Caleb? Then why are they getting married?"

"No. Jessica and Maude. They fight worse than any cats and dogs. We'll be sitting at the dining room table, trying to eat dinner in the most morbid silence, and the next thing I know, they've blown up. They stand up, shouting in each other's faces until I could believe they were on the verge of throwing things at each other. Then, the next thing I know, they won't even talk to—won't even look at—each other for hours. I tell you, Adelaide, I'm about at my wits' end with those two."

"Why would they be fighting? One would suppose that this monumental event in a woman's life would actually draw the two of them together into a closer bond."

"I don't know. I just don't know." Benjamin shook his head. "Maybe if I were a woman, I could figure these things out. But I can't. I've tried my best to raise the girls, but it appears as if I've failed—rather miserably, too."

"Don't blame yourself."

"I'd be grateful if you'd talk to them."

"Me?"

Her eyes were growing wider again. He really liked her big blue eyes. He wished she'd manage to smile a little more. There was a point when she'd smiled at him a lot, before that damned Jack came along and made them argue. He'd fix it. He'd fix Jack, and he'd make Adelaide smile at him again. He swore he would!

"What makes you think I can do anything with them if their own father can't?"

"Because you've been their teacher, and I like to believe they've learned many things from you, and could probably still stand to learn a few more."

"I haven't been their teacher for many years, Mr. Griffith."

"Because they still respect you and your opinions, I thought perhaps you could act as a sort of impartial referee between the two of them."

"I'm not sure they would welcome my interference."

"Because . . . because, damn it, Adelaide, you're a woman!"

"One of those silly, emotional women who can't think logically?"

"Yes, darn it! No, damn it! You're not, and you are." All this fighting in his house had made him very upset lately.

"Now who is being too emotional to think rationally?" she asked him with a mischievous grin.

"You're both, and I like you that way. I . . . I'm inordinately fond of you. I need your help. I can't continue on my own anymore, not with my children and not in my private life. Adelaide, I need you. So please stop calling me Mr. Griffith."

∞

JESSICA PICKED UP A dish in one hand and one of the kitchen towels Louise had given her in the other and passed it to Miss Randolph, who was standing by the large barrel that would get placed in the bottom of the wagon.

"Maude, could you please fold these dishes in that tablecloth?" Jessica asked.

Maude looked scornfully at the mended lace tablecloth Mrs. Hardesty had given them. "No, I can't. I have other things to do." She began peeling potatoes for dinner.

"Miss Randolph, Jack suggested we use the towel to cushion the breakables," Jessica said.

"Then put the cast-iron pots on top," Maude quipped.

Jessica cast Maude an acid glare, then returned to her packing. "Jack says if we wrap the good dishes—"

"You mean the ones with only the little chips out of the edges that Mrs. Hoffmann gave you from the missionary basket," Maude interrupted bitterly. "Not the ones with the big cracks in the center that Mrs. Olson didn't want anymore."

"Yes," Jessica replied steadily. "Please try to keep the two with the little blue flowers around the edges together. They're the only two that aren't chipped, so I'm trying to save them for Caleb's Sunday dinner."

"Is that the special day you'll be serving charred prairie dog instead of just bread and water?"

Jessica gave her mouth a wry twist and gave Maude a dead stare. "Yes."

"Of course, that's on the supposition that Caleb will be able to take time away from panning all that gold he's going to find in order to provide you with something to eat besides weevils and hardtack."

"Yes," Jessica replied even more tightly.

Maude stared straight back at her. "Then, when you go, do be sure and take with you a jar of the crab apple jelly that *I* put up last fall without any help at all from *you*. It goes so well with prairie dog."

"Of course, you'd know a lot about being a crab apple," Jessica snapped. She threw down the towel and headed in her sister's direction.

Maude threw the potato into the pot, splashing water over the kitchen table. She turned to confront Jessica. "More than you know about a lot of things. More than you know—or even care—about how other people feel—"

"Girls, girls, you're both being very silly," Miss Randolph scolded. They both turned to stare at her. "You know very well mint jelly is the only appropriate garnish for prairie dog."

Jessica laughed and backed away.

Maude grimly returned to the pot of potatoes. She didn't want to laugh. She had nothing to laugh about. She didn't even want to smile.

Much more seriously, Miss Randolph continued, "You're also both being very foolish wasting this time with each other."

"I *never* waste time," Maude told her haughtily and turned to peeling her potatoes with a vengeance.

"You might not think you do, hustling and bustling all about the house, making sure everyone in your family—and all your friends, too—have everything all set up for them just the way you think they ought to. But there are more ways to waste time than you've thought of.''

Maude stared at her former teacher with surprise. She'd supposedly come here today to help Jessica pack. Instead, there she stood, scolding Maude as if she were still in the first grade and had just wet her pants. She liked Miss Randolph, but at this point she didn't appreciate her interference one bit. She didn't appreciate her father siccing her on them, either.

Jessica chuckled. "I guess she told you."

"Don't you be so smug, either." Miss Randolph turned to Jessica and scolded, "I've had my eye on you from the first day you entered my schoolhouse. You've elevated wasting time into an art."

For the first time in days, Maude was able to laugh. But she knew it sounded bitter and humorless.

"Is this why Papa asked you here today, Miss Randolph?" Maude asked her bluntly. "To scold us the way he can't quite summon up the courage to?"

"Don't you dare talk that way about your father." Miss Randolph leveled a finger at her. "He's a good man and deserves to live in the home he's worked hard for all his life in a little peace and quiet, not with two daughters who bicker like cranky old hens who are good for nothing but the stew pot. He didn't send me here to scold you. He asked if I'd come talk to you as friends and equals, as women together."

Maude decided now would be a good time to remain silent. She glanced over at Jessica. For once, the girl seemed to have chosen wisely and remained silent as well.

"One would suppose that two sisters would get along better."

"We've never really had too much in common," Maude admitted quietly. If Miss Randolph was going to try to accentuate the rational side of this conversation, Maude was certainly prepared to beat her at her own game.

"You're sisters. That's enough in common."

"But—" Jessica began.

"You've had the same parents and siblings. You've lived together in this house with the same neighbors, the same school friends. You've shared births and deaths and Christmases."

"But—"

"You're going away," Miss Randolph told Jessica. "It'll take you months to get there—if you get there at all. You'll be traveling through harsh country, filled with dangers, not just from humans, but from wild animals, diseases, and Mother Nature herself. There are deserts, alkaline pools, snowstorms, sheer drops from cliffs. You'll be living in primitive conditions with no doctor or medicine—and sometimes no food or water—around for hundreds of miles.''

She glanced from Maude to Jessica and back. "Don't you two realize that, from the moment Jessica boards that wagon, you two may never see each other again?" Miss Randolph paused and waited.

Maude had to admit the schoolteacher was good—very good. Too good, she acknowledged as an unpleasant chill ran through her. She'd really made her point.

"But there you both are, wasting time."

"I'll try to work harder," Jessica promised.

Miss Randolph shook her head. Maude had to silently agree with her. Jessica had always needed to have everything spelled out very clearly for her.

"You still don't quite get the point, do you, Jessica dear?" Very gently, Miss Randolph continued to explain. "The work will get done. Somehow it always seems to get done eventually. But you two have so very little precious time left together, and you're both wasting it. Instead of yelling and arguing with each other, instead of not even talking to each other, you should be trying to remember as many of the happy times together as you can. Those are the things you can't pack, but they're the things you never want to forget. Those are the things that can't get lost or broken or stolen somewhere along the trail. Those are the real treasures you should take with you."

Miss Randolph quietly folded the towel around the chipped dish and placed it in the barrel.

∞

MAUDE LOCKED HER BEDROOM door and drew her curtains very tightly together. After all the shock of Jessica's completely unexpected announcement, and all the excitement of the past few days' preparations, she really felt she needed a little time alone. She might have gone for a walk in the fields, but she was bound to encounter someone there. She thought it would have been nice to go into the quiet, empty church, with its warm, comforting smells of wood and candlewax, and its close, calming atmosphere, but she was sure to encounter the Reverend or Mrs. Hoffmann there, and they'd want to know what she was doing there, and then she'd have to explain it all. She didn't want to have to explain. She just wanted to think.

So she'd come to her room, the best place she could find.

She'd try not to think of Jack, so close on the other side of the tree—and so far away from her, with the imminent threat of his leaving hanging over her head.

Her mother was gone. Georgie would be going to the university. Her father seemed happy with Miss Randolph again, and she was glad. Jessica would marry Caleb.

She'd fulfilled all the obligations she'd taken on herself when her mother had died. What was there now for her to do? Nobody else needed her anymore. What had she done wrong? Now what would she do—all alone—for the rest of her life?

She'd always been able to derive some comfort from piecing and quilting. With all the excitement, she hadn't had much time to work on her own things lately. Maybe that would make her feel better.

She opened her hope chest and almost slammed it shut again immediately. There it crouched, ready to spring, staring up at her like the Frankenstein monster it was—her bride's quilt! She'd thought she'd relegated it to its tomb, where it couldn't hurt her anymore. But here it lurked, still alive and dangerous, waiting to be reanimated, just like the monster—a horrible reminder of her shattered dreams.

No sense in trying to finish it now, she decided. As if afraid it would bite her, she cautiously reached down and pulled the loose blocks from the chest. She tossed them carelessly from hand to hand. Beautiful, useless creatures. Some of the joined blocks twisted around her arms like poisonous snakes. Some of the separate blocks fell to the floor, where she left them. There was nothing else to do with them now but toss it all into the fire.

Her dreams of a life with Caleb were gone—as if they'd ever actually existed in the first place, she had to acknowledge with a bitter shake of her head. She'd only been deluding herself. Caleb had never cared about her, and she'd never really loved Caleb. She realized that now.

She loved Jack with all her heart. Jack—a completely irresponsible man who came and went as he pleased and who, most likely, it would please to be leaving any time now.

"Well, this thing is completely useless," she said as she gave a last look at her quilt blocks. "If nothing else, the darned thing can keep me warm tonight."

She gathered them up, intent on tossing them one by one into the flames. She spied the specially embroidered block—the one that was supposed to go in the center; the one that was supposed to prove she and Caleb were a match made in heaven.

"Botheration! This one was the biggest waste of time of all. The biggest mistake I ever made." She strode intently over to the fireplace. She dangled it over the hungry, flickering orange and yellow flames. "Well, in you go."

Then she saw exactly what she needed to do to make it right.

24

MAUDE SNATCHED THE BEAUTIFUL block back from the flames. She held it up to the light. Thank goodness it hadn't been singed. She clasped it to her bosom. It didn't even smell smoky. So far, luck was with her.

"Yes, indeed!" she exclaimed with more interest than she'd felt for anything in the past several days. She held up the block to examine it more closely and muttered frantically to herself. "That's exactly where I went wrong. Why didn't I see that before? For Caleb and myself, there was always something not quite right about this block. All I have to do is rip out the *M* and replace it with *J* for Jessica. For Jessica and Caleb, it's absolutely perfect!"

She didn't think she could invent any more superlatives to describe the new idea she had for the design for this block. *This one* was going to be her best one yet.

She scooped up all the loose blocks that had fallen to the floor, carried them to her chair by the window, and dumped them on the floor there. She started arranging them in rows, with the special block in the center.

"I'll finish it," she decided enthusiastically. "I'll give it to her as a wedding gift. I hope it makes up for how horrible I've been to her. With all those other worn-out, secondhand things, she ought to have at least one special, brand-new thing to take to Oregon with her. Something to remember her family and friends by. This should be it. She even asked for a quilt, and I''—she heaved a deep, regretful sigh—''in my shortsighted self-ishness, told her no. This should come as a mighty big surprise to her.''

But there were only two more days until the wedding.

"How will I ever finish it in time!"

Should she call in some of her friends? she wondered. They could have it done in no time at all. But it would be pretty hard to finish it in secret with half a dozen chattering friends in her house. Even if they all went to someone else's house to finish it, Jessica would notice her absence, and sooner or later one of her friends was bound to let the cat out of the bag. If Maude wanted to keep this quilt truly a secret, she was the only one who could know about it.

"I'll do it myself."

She'd have to sit there, all by herself, finish the embroidery, piece the top together, then quilt the entire quilt and bind it—in two days. It couldn't be anything as simple as tying, either. It had to look just as beautiful as all the other quilts she'd taken such care and time with.

She'd do it! She was determined. If she had to lock herself in her room and not do anything else; if she didn't sleep or bathe or stop to eat a bite; if they found her exhausted, emaciated, smelly dead body slumped over the finished quilt—she'd have it ready for the day of the wedding.

This was the craziest thing she'd ever done in her life—probably the only crazy thing she'd done. Except for loving Jack.

Well, she'd spent her entire young life being sensible. Georgie could do silly things. Jessica certainly was in her heyday doing irresponsible things. It was high time she did something crazy, too!

She flipped open the lid of her sewing box and, heedless of sticking her fingers on loose needles and pins, began digging around, tossing things out onto the table in search of her green embroidery floss. Several spools of thread went rolling to the floor, where she decided to leave them. She had too much to think about now to waste time on them.

Then Maude noticed the little holes where she'd made one last, futile effort to stitch in Caleb's initials with hers, but had ended up inadvertently stitching in Jack's instead, and had pee-vishly ripped them out. Suddenly she was seized with a deep regret about finishing this block. Changing the bride's initials from hers to her sister's and keeping the groom's as Caleb's would mean it really was true. Her sister was marrying Caleb. She'd never marry him, never live in a big house and be incredibly wealthy. For her sister's sake, she hoped her predictions were still true. Caleb wealthy and successful—just with a different wife.

As each tiny green stitch of Caleb's initials covered the small holes remaining from Jack's, Maude had the horrible feeling her time with Jack was also ending. Each stitch she ripped from her own initials felt like a thousand pinpricks straight into her heart. But Jessica's and Caleb's initials looked so completely right in the design—how could she fight against it?

She couldn't remember who'd first concocted the silly tale of the superstition of her quilt block. Considering all the evidence—Louise and Fred so happy, Florence and Edgar done for, Wilma and Peter a complete failure—all she could figure was that the blocks were right. Perhaps there really was something to the superstition. Perhaps they really were made for each other. Then again, she paused, what about Katy and Willard?

She recalled the ripped-out initials she was replacing in this block. That would mean her initials and Jack's *did* belong together. Were she and Jack really made for each other, too?

She couldn't convince him of it. Look how wrong she'd been about Caleb. What was she going to do about Jack?

"BUT, MAUDE, I'VE GOT these problems in mathematics I just can't do!" Georgie whined through the locked door.

"I'm sorry, Georgie," she called back sweetly. If she died of exhaustion or starvation while finishing this quilt, at least her bereaved family would be left with fond memories of her. "I'm very busy right now. Why don't you see if you can get Jessica to help you with it?"

"Ha, ha, Maude. That's very funny. You know Jessica can't do math."

"Ask Miss Randolph."

"I did. She explained it all to me again, but she said she wouldn't do the problems for me."

"Neither will I. Ask Papa."

"He and Caleb are busy trying to fix up that old bed in the barn for them to take with them."

"You'll just have to find someone else, won't you?"

Georgie muttered something unintelligible on the other side of the door. No, she was determined not to give in. At last, more loudly, he said, "I suppose I could go over and see if Rusty's figured it out. He's at my grade, and he's pretty good with math."

"That's a great idea." She'd been trying for years to get him to associate more with his schoolmates. Had she actually managed to accomplish more by her absence than by her smothering attentions? As happy as she felt for Georgie, it wasn't actually a very comforting thought to know she was more useful when she wasn't around.

The sun went down. Maude lit the kerosene lamp and continued to appliqué the unfinished blocks.

"Maude," Jessica called through her rapping on the door.

Maude kept stitching. "What is it?"

"I need your help with this rice."

"What are you doing with rice?"

"I'm trying to cook it for dinner."

"Good luck."

"No, really. I need your help."

"I'm sorry, I can't come out now. Why don't you go next door and ask Mrs. Kingston?"

"Because Mrs. Kingston'll want to know why you're not doing it, and I don't want to tell her you can't do it because you've locked yourself in your room because then I'd have to explain why you've locked yourself in your room, and I can't explain why you've locked yourself in your room because I don't know why!" Jessica's voice trailed off to a pathetic wail.

Maude kept stitching.

"Maude? You haven't gone insane or anything like that, have you?"

"Of course not."

"Maude?" Jessica's plaintive voice came through the door. "Are you still angry with me?"

"No, of course not!" Even though she couldn't see her sister through the door, or hug her, or let her see her own sincere expression, Maude hoped she conveyed it all to her in the tone of her voice.

"Then why have you locked yourself in your room?"

"I can't tell you."

"I'm worried about you, Maude."

"It's about time you learned to worry about someone besides yourself."

"You're going to starve up here. I'll never forgive you if we have to turn my wedding into your funeral."

"I have food and water up here. I won't starve."

"Aren't you even going to come down for dinner?"

"Not if you're cooking."

"I'm getting better at it."

"No, you're not. I smelled the corn burning last night."

"Oh. Do you think I could get Miss Randolph to help me with the rice?"

"I don't know. You could ask her."

"All right. She's been very helpful with getting my veil at Miss Hawkins, and helping me take Mama's wedding dress in. Are you sure you won't come down and help me with dinner?"

"Just look on this as something you have to learn to do anyway. After all, I'm not going out to Oregon with you, all the other women in the wagon train are going to be too busy taking care of their own families to coddle you, and I don't think you're going to be wealthy enough to hire servants for some time."

"Oh." Jessica sounded so disappointed.

Maude hoped her sister wasn't finding her first experience with reality too distasteful.

∞

MAUDE FELT HER HEAD nodding. She couldn't fall asleep now! She was almost done sewing all the blocks together. It had taken longer to appliqué the designs and then sew them together than she'd expected. She prayed she'd be able to finish quilting it in time, but she was beginning to have serious doubts.

The rapping at the window made Maude jerk her head up. At first she thought she was dreaming, but there it went again.

Was it a bird, trying to get in the window? Horrors! That was an omen of death. Did that mean she really would die trying to finish this quilt?

There it was again—tap, tap, tap at the window. It couldn't be a bird, she thought with a little relief. Birds don't usually have knuckles.

Knuckles! What in heaven's name was trying to get into her window? Who in their right mind would try to get up this high? Right mind—that should have been her first clue.

She put down her needle and thimble, and rose. She had a strange feeling she already knew what she was going to find on the other side of that window. She pulled aside the curtain.

Yes, indeed. There he was, sitting right on the narrow ledge outside her window, grinning at her. She threw up the sash.

"What are you doing out there?"

"I'm on a mission of mercy."

"You're going to fall and end up in Doc Ketcham's surgery— or one of Mr. Volz's coffins. Personally, for climbing up here, I think they ought to lock you away in an insane asylum!"

"You know, it's not easy clinging to the side of your house with one hand."

"One hand?"

"Could we settle for me coming inside your room for now and I'll explain?"

Maude grimaced. "Get in here before you fall."

She quickly moved the lamp to the floor, then pushed her small table away from the window so he could enter.

He held out a coffee cup to her. "Do you think you could give me a hand with this?"

"What is it?" She took the cup and peered down into it. Only about half of the light brown liquid was left.

He clung to the window sash and swung his long legs into the room. He laughed. "You're looking at it as if you've never seen a coffee cup before."

"Not like that, I haven't," she said, plucking a floating leaf from inside. "What did you do?"

"Well, it was supposed to be a whole cup of coffee, with cream and sugar, but this is all that made it across."

"Across?" she repeated, setting the cup on the table. She stuck her head out the window and looked down. "How'd you get here, anyway? Someone's going to notice a ladder, and then you'll be in big trouble. *I'll* be in big trouble."

"I already thought of that. I climbed across the tree."

"The tree! Is there any particular reason for your playing ape this time of night?"

"I have the feeling your father would shoot me as soon as look at me if he saw me coming across your lawn."

Maude shook her head in dismissal of the idea. "He's always felt that way about you. What are you doing here, anyway?"

"I was worried about you. I have every reason to be." Now that he was safely settled on solid flooring, he glanced around. "What happened to your room? It looks like a tornado tore through here."

"I've been too busy quilting to clean up."

"I thought so." He took a step closer to her and held her hands in his. He turned her hands palm upward. "Just look at what you've done to yourself."

Her fingertips were pricked and red. Even with the protection of her thimble, she'd managed to stick herself, or just plain wear off a layer or two of skin. With one finger, he began tracing the marks on her fingers, then running his finger into her palm, tracing the lines there. He might as well be running his hands over her body, Maude thought as she trembled, waiting and hoping for him to seize her in his embrace.

He bent his head to kiss her fingertips. She ached to feel his kisses again, to make love to him one more time before he decided to leave without a moment's notice.

"I . . . I can't." She shook herself awake from his spell and pulled away. "I have so much to do."

"Is that why I haven't seen you outside in a while? I've been watching your light come on at night and go off at dawn, so I figured you must still be alive. I've been worried about you. There've been all kinds of rumors about where you are, you know."

"Really?" Maude walked over to her frame and began setting her quilt layers into it.

"Some say Wilma's so angry with you, she finally poisoned you."

Maude nodded. "Understandable."

"Some who've heard you and Jessica arguing—and you two can be really loud, did you know?—maintain that she's done you in, although there's speculation about whether she poisoned you or stabbed you."

"Charming." She nodded toward the Dalton house. "I bet I know who started that one."

"Some say you were so shocked by your younger sister getting married before you, and in such haste, that you went into a decline and died, but your family's hiding the body until afterward because they don't want to have to postpone the wedding for your funeral."

"No one came up with the idea that I ran off to join a circus?"

"Not yet." He gestured toward the coffee cup. "You know, you ought to drink that before it gets any colder, especially after all the trouble I took to bring it to you."

"Yes, thank you." She took a sip. It was already cold, but she was too hungry to care.

"I also brought you this." He reached into his breast pocket and pulled out a large white napkin. Pulling apart the flaps, he revealed a slightly squashed piece of cake. "It's a piece of Aunt Nell's rose geranium cake. It's fresh and still fairly edible."

Maude felt her eyes widening with delight. She reached out for it eagerly. "All I've had is water, crackers, and apples. It's a little hard to keep food up here."

He settled onto her bed while she ate. "Why are you up here, Maude? I know I teased you once about him, and you said no, but . . . Are you really that heartbroken that Caleb's marrying Jessica?"

She almost choked on her cake. His eyes looked so worried. What did he have to worry about? *She* wasn't going anywhere.

"No," she answered. There was no sense in being anything less than honest, especially not now, after she'd made love to him. Maybe it would inspire Jack to be honest with her. "Not anymore."

"So you did think of marrying him?" he asked very quietly.

"Once. Not anymore."

"What changed your mind?" As she bent her head over her quilting, he ran his fingers along the back of her neck.

What would happen if she told him "You did"? She'd fall into his arms, they'd make love, and he'd leave anyway. And she still wouldn't have Jessica's quilt finished. There was such a thing as carrying honesty too far.

"I have to finish this quilt for Jessica," she told him. Her voice was raspy with unrelieved passion. She hoped he'd think it was because she was tired from staying up all night instead.

"Well, then," he said as he settled down on the edge of her bed, "why don't I stay and keep you company?"

"You don't have to do that." It was unnerving enough to have him sitting on her very own bed where, in the dark seclusion of her lonely nights, she lay dreaming of him. It was almost impossible to continue quilting with him here.

"I don't have much else to do."

"If you don't leave, I'll throw you out," she threatened weakly.

"Then how will you explain to your father how I got here in the first place?"

"Never mind," she muttered and continued quilting. "I don't have time to do any explaining."

"I think you'll find I can be very useful, Maude. Very useful indeed."

He scooted across her bed and fluffed up her pillows against the headboard. He folded his long arms up behind his head and stretched his long legs out in front of him—all on her bed! She could think of some very useful things for him to do. She longed to stretch out beside him and forget the rest of the world. Then she'd never get this blasted quilt finished!

"I'll help you stay awake while you work. I can bring you food—"

"You can't go down to the kitchen and bring things up to me without being noticed."

He chuckled. "You'd be surprised how many places I've slipped into and out of without being noticed."

"Not in this house, what with Papa storming through here on a regular basis, Jessica bouncing off the walls, and Miss Randolph, Mrs. Dietrich, and your aunt cooking up a storm in the kitchen."

"Why are you working so hard to finish this quilt?"

"Jessica ought to have a bride's quilt. Everybody else does. If it kills me, she will, too. I owe it to her." She looked up from her work to glare at him as threateningly as she could manage. "By the way, this is a secret—a *big* secret—so if you tell her, my father won't be the only one wanting to see your head on a stake."

He laughed and held up his hand in a solemn vow. "I'll never tell. But why do you do it, Maude? Why have you always tried to take care of everybody else first?"

"Because, as the older daughter, I always felt it was sort of my duty. Anyway, nobody else wanted the job."

"You've done a good job."

"Oh, yes. That's why the house is in such turmoil now."

"No, seriously. Your mother would be proud of you."

"I hope so." She sighed. "But sometimes the responsibilities just get to be too much."

"Like now?"

"Like now."

"Why do you deprive yourself of sleep and food, and stitch your fingers raw and bloody for someone else?"

"Why did you risk your neck climbing across that tree to bring me half a cup of lukewarm coffee and a squashed piece of cake?"

He laughed. "I live for danger."

"Is that why you've always run away?"

"I wanted to fight for my country. They wouldn't let me. So I lied and did it anyway." He gave a conspiratorial chuckle. "By the way, as long as we're sharing secrets—and I think if anyone can keep a secret, you can—if Mr. Potter would have his important friends check the 5th Infantry for a John Adams, he just might find me."

Maude stuck herself and dropped her thimble. She twisted around in her chair to face him. "You used your brother's name."

"He'd have wanted to fight, too."

"You *did* fight for the Union."

"No, I didn't."

"But you just said—"

"I never fought."

"How—?"

"I've always been right good at getting myself into and out of a lot of sticky situations, even in the Army. When the officers discovered my considerable talent—and exactly how old I really was—instead of sending me back home, they decided I'd draw less attention than other soldiers. I started slipping through the lines . . . finding out things they'd talk about around a poor, lost little farm boy that they'd never discuss with a grown man. Of course, not even Mr. Potter or his friends would be able to find *this* information in any records."

"The war's been over for five years. Why can't you tell people . . . ?"

"Don't you understand? There's no real record of me as James Kingston. No proof. Technically, as far as the Army goes, I never existed."

"Couldn't you even set your uncle's mind to rest?"

"Not yet. I still have . . . things I have to do."

She swallowed hard and decided, since they were being fairly honest with each other, she might as well ask him this question, too. "Does it have anything to do with why you were in prison?"

"Yes."

"Why were you in prison, Jack?"

"You know why. I shot the sheriff and robbed the bank."

"I think by now you and I both know better than to settle for that story."

"I didn't shoot the sheriff. Another . . . agent did."

"Agent?"

He ignored her question. "The sheriff was actually part of the gang, and we had to get him out of the way. Another agent shot him, but I took the blame so he wouldn't ruin his disguise. I took the sheriff's job and worked my way into the gang. I thought I knew what they were up to, but they robbed the bank a day ahead of what was planned. I had to go along with them, notify the other agents as best I could. . . ."

"Is this some of the information that *wasn't* included in the reports sent to the newspapers?"

"Some of it." Jack's shrug told her there was a lot more he'd never be able to tell anyone, and maybe a lot he'd rather forget. "There was a shoot-out. Some of the gang got killed, the rest went to jail. I had to go to jail, too, or I'd have ruined my cover and wouldn't be effective on future assignments."

"You're a Federal agent."

"Pinkerton now."

"Why don't you tell anybody else? At least tell your aunt and uncle to set their minds at ease."

"Tell Aunt Nell? Ha! Then everyone will know. The two fastest means of communication—telegraph and tell Aunt Nell."

"Why do you take the blame for so many horrible lies?"

"Because it's my job," he answered with deadly seriousness. "I'm very good at what I do."

She asked the question that had been nagging her. "Is that

where you get your money, without seeming to have a real job?''

"Yes."

"Is that where you got those horrible clothes?''

He laughed. She was glad to see him able to laugh again after such a serious turn to their conversation. "Yes, heaven help me. I hate that awful jacket. It stinks of whiskey, but sometimes it's part of a disguise.''

Then she asked the question she didn't really want to. But she had to know the answer, no matter how heartbreaking it might be. "You . . . you always claimed you were leaving town right after Louise's wedding. Are you staying in town . . . so long . . . as part of your job?''

He didn't answer her for a while. She held her breath, waiting, until she thought she'd go insane not knowing, all the while figuring the longer it took him to answer, the more likely the answer was to be the one she didn't want to hear.

At last he replied, "I came here to do a job. We're tracking some of the bank robbers who escaped. They're very dangerous men. We've got to stop them. We figured if they knew I was here, and still wanting to be part of their gang, they'd send me word. I'm supposed to send word to other agents waiting nearby.''

"Oh." She turned away from him and went back to her quilting. "Am I just something to keep you occupied?''

He sat bolt upright. "Don't *ever* think that! You can doubt my other motives but, my darling Maude, don't ever doubt how very much I love you.''

She cast him an apologetic smile.

"If I didn't know how very intent you were upon finishing that quilt, I'd come right over there and show you exactly how much I love you.''

Very softly she asked, "Why are you finally telling me all this about yourself now, Jack?''

"Because I trust you as I trust no one else, and I feel as if I have to tell somebody I trust the real truth about me before—''

She held her breath. Was he going to tell her he was leaving now?

"I have to tell you so you'll know the truth about me before I die.''

"What?'' Her hands were shaking again as she tried to continue her quilting. She tried to laugh. He was teasing her again, as he always did, wasn't he? "If you keep climbing back and forth across that tree, you'll get yourself killed."

"No, not like that." He was still very serious. "That's something I can control. It's just that . . . I get these feelings—like when you were following me, like which way Georgie went. Your father's been watching me, too."

"He wouldn't—!"

"No, not him. But I've got a bad feeling now about . . . things. So I need to tell you now, and I ask that afterward you set my aunt's and uncle's minds to rest on the matter."

"Good Lord, Jack, don't say such things!" She didn't know what else to say to a man who was certain he was going to die— soon. "I don't want you to die!"

"Well, my goodness!" he declared, springing up from the bed and heading for the window, as if his furious action would dispel the gloom. "I think it's high time you had another piece of cake and some better coffee. You keep quilting, and don't fall asleep while I'm gone."

∽

"MAUDE," JACK WHISPERED. "MAUDE."

She jerked her head up. Jack was climbing back in through the window for what seemed like the hundredth time. She wondered what goodies he'd brought her this time, and why Mrs. Kingston wasn't starting to notice her food was missing.

"What time is it?" she asked him.

"About midnight. I've brought you some more coffee. I even managed to fry up an egg and stick it between two slices of bread. Did you finish the quilt?"

"Almost."

"Good for you." He laid his hand on her shoulder encouragingly. "I knew you could do it."

"I just need to put the binding on."

"Let's see it."

She stood unsteadily on her stiff legs. Her shoulders ached, her buttocks ached, and her spine felt as if it were locked in a permanent curve. She'd been sitting hunched in one position far too long. She flipped the quilt out wide, covering the floor with it.

"You did a beautiful job, Maude. Let's see if I can find

them." He bent over the center block. "I must admit, you've hidden them well. But there they are. I see them."

His fingers traced through the intricate arrangement of stems and leaves to find Jessica and Caleb's initials and the date of their wedding—tomorrow morning.

"What's this?"

Maude hoped he couldn't see them—the little holes left in the muslin after she'd picked his initials out. But he was pointing to the small green stitches at the bottom of the bouquet.

"My initials," she said proudly. "A good artist always signs her work."

"I see. Well, a good artist needs to eat, too. It'll help you stay awake. When was the last time you slept?"

"I don't remember." All she could remember about her meals, for that matter, had been that on a regular basis Jack had been pressing something edible upon her, and she'd trustingly stuck it in her mouth and chewed.

"Have you slept at all?"

"Of course. I just don't remember exactly when."

He was scowling at her.

"Don't turn into such an old granny," she scolded right back at him. "I'm fine. I'll get plenty of sleep after the wedding."

She tottered as she stood there.

"Get some sleep!" he commanded.

"I can't. I'm almost done."

"Then sew the damned binding on and go to sleep."

"Yes, that's what I'll do." She stumbled over to her chair, picked up her needle, and bent over her stitching. She frowned. She'd always thought the closer it got to dawn, the lighter it got. Why was everything going so dark?

25

MAUDE OPENED HER EYES to the gray light of dawn seeping in her window and smiled. Today was Jessica and Caleb's wedding day. Today was the day she'd give her sister the special quilt—

"Oh, no!" What was she doing in bed?

She sat up with a cry and threw off the covers. Except for her shoes, she was completely dressed. Jack was sitting in the chair by the window, completely dressed—shoes and all. His eyes were closed, and his squared chin drooped on his chest.

"How could you let me fall asleep!" she cried as she bounded out of bed.

She started rummaging around the messy room, searching for her shoes, which were tucked neatly under her bed, toes in, the way she liked them, ready to be put on. She tried to smooth her hair into some kind of order.

"You were supposed to be here keeping me awake so I could finish that darn quilt, and here you are sleeping, too! Wake up!"

She gave his arm a little push as she sped by him, rushing about the room. Slowly Jack pulled his eyes open.

"Get up! How could you let me fall asleep? I'll never finish sewing on that binding now. I guess I could give it to her this way, but it just makes it look so shoddy, when it's supposed to be so special."

He drew in a deep, leisurely breath and stretched his arms and legs out in all directions, flexing his muscles stiffened from sleep. For just a moment, she was so tempted to crawl back into her bed and invite him in. Even when she was rushed beyond comprehension, and angry with him for being so careless, she had to admit he still held an unbelievably powerful attraction for her. Even in her frantic rush, she couldn't resist walking over to him again.

"My goodness, you certainly take a lot of room to wake up," she said. She reached out her hand to touch his shoulder more gently this time, to slide her hand down his arm, to pull him into her still-warm bed—

But she couldn't! She didn't have time!

"Wake up! Get up! Get out of here." She grabbed his arm and began pulling him out of the chair. "You've got to get out of here before the sun comes up and people see you leaving my bedroom. Papa will turn Jessica's wedding into your funeral for sure. And I still have to finish the quilt."

"It's finished."

"No, it's not. You big, stupid oaf, you let me fall asleep before I could—"

"No, really. It's finished."

"Yes, that's very amusing, Jack. I don't have time for your teasing now."

"Really. I finished it."

She paused for just a moment, speechless. If he was telling the truth, she couldn't bear to think what her beautiful quilt must look like now.

"Where is it?" she asked very slowly, as if asking where they'd laid the body of a murder victim dear to her.

Jack nodded toward the box on the floor by the door.

"Oh, dear." She felt as if she were approaching the coffin of a loved one snatched away by tragedy before his time. Slowly she bent down, knelt beside it, and lifted the lid.

All the fabric was tucked neatly into the box. The quilt had been folded so that the special center block was facing out. It looked neat enough, she decided. Maybe Jessica would be too excited to take it out of the box, and no one would notice the shoddily applied binding until Jessica was all the way out in Wyoming or someplace.

No, better not take chances, she decided. Jack was full of surprises, and she wanted to be prepared for every one of them. Carefully she reached in and pulled out the quilt. Cringing at the thought of what she'd see, Maude looked at the edges. She felt her eyes growing wide with surprise, trying to take it all in.

"It's . . . it's beautiful."

Jack wasn't stupid. He *had* to hear the surprise in her voice.

"It's really very well done. How . . . ?" She rose and frowned at him accusingly. "Did you convince Miss Randolph or Miss Hawkins or your aunt to come up here while I was sleeping to finish this?"

"No. I did it," he declared proudly.

"How?"

He gave her a playfully smug grin. "I'm afraid modesty prevents me from admitting to you that I am, indeed, a man of many talents."

"Yes, you are."

"A man with no wife to take care of him has to do a few things for himself. I learned to do some stitching—nothing fancy, mind you. I mean, I never could do that quilting like you do it, but I know enough to mend my own socks and sew on a button or a binding."

"Thank you, Jack," she said, slowly and steadily walking toward him. "Thank you so much for making my quilt for Jessica look so beautiful."

She bent down and kissed him. He pulled her onto his lap, surrounding her with his strong arms. She cuddled into his embrace, enjoying the warmth of him, enjoying the way his hands clutched at her arms and at her back. She loved the hardness of his chest against her hands and the firmness of his thighs against her legs. She could feel his manhood as well, and blushed and shuddered with longing at the same time. His unshaved beard was rougher against her cheeks than she'd ever felt it, and she was thankful for all his masculinity.

"How will I ever be able to thank you?" she whispered into his ear. She kissed his earlobe, then flicked her tongue across his neck.

"I'm easy to please," he murmured. "Do you have anything in particular in mind?"

"Yes."

He'd be leaving her again soon. Knowing what she now knew of his job and the kind of work he did, knowing how important it was to him and to their country, she could hardly selfishly beg him to stay. All she could do was love him for as long as he stayed with her and cherish the times they were together. Just as Miss Randolph had advised Jessica and her, when he was gone, she could only treasure her memories.

"Make love to me again, Jack," she asked him, her voice deep and husky with longing. "Make love to me now."

"Criminy, woman!" he growled huskily in her ear. "Why do I get stuck with all the thankless tasks?"

Before she could respond, he lifted her in his arms and stood up. She stifled a little squeal as he joyously swirled her round and round. She couldn't have everybody rushing in to see what was wrong. Would her father kill Jack or just insist on a double wedding? Would the latter be so bad?

Before she had time to think, Jack had crossed her room in a few long strides. He laid her on her bed.

Standing tall above her, he stripped off his jacket and vest. He slipped off his boots and slid into bed beside her.

"Why did you leave my clothes on me when you put me to bed last night?" she asked. She ran her fingertip around the button at the neck of his shirt, then moved down to the next one, and the next one.

"Because I knew if I started to take anything off," he replied, doing the same to the small, rounded buttons that ran down her bodice, "I'd never stop, and then neither one of us would ever get that darned quilt finished." He kissed her again. "That and, as much as I desire you, I wouldn't take advantage of you while you were sleeping."

"I'm glad. I want to be wide awake to enjoy every wonderful moment of being with you." *For as long as it lasts,* she silently—and sadly—added. She reached over and unfastened the top button. "On the other hand, I wouldn't mind being taken advantage of—by you."

"I've taken advantage of a lot of people in my day—mostly witless fools who deserved to lose their money, or boots, or horse, gambling. I couldn't take advantage of you, Maude. I love you too much. I guess this sounds pretty silly coming from the likes of me, but I respect you."

She held the front of his shirt and roughly pulled the two edges wide, exposing the muscles of his chest. She reached inside and slowly moved her hand up his chest, through the tendrils of dark hair, to his strong throat. She stroked his chin, his jaw, his cheek.

She slipped his shirt from his shoulders.

"Where's that famous arrow scar?"

"That you were too stingy to pay a cent to see?" Jack tilted his right arm toward her. It wasn't a big scar. It had all but faded away in twenty years.

"That's it?" Maude demanded.

"It was a big deal when I was six."

"You had the nerve to charge gullible kids to see this?"

"Yes, I did. But"—he held his finger before her face—"I *never* charged Runt."

"That's mighty generous of you."

"It means a lot to me, Maude."

More seriously, she replied, "Yes, I guess it does."

"You get to see it for free, too, you lucky woman."

She laughed. She lifted herself up on one elbow to lean forward and place a kiss on what was left of his scar. Slowly she left a little trail of kisses up his shoulder, across his chest, and up his neck again.

He gave a deep, gravelly moan. He leaned forward to kiss her. His lips were warm with passion. She could feel her own face and throat growing warm with desire for him. If he didn't take some of her clothes off soon, she feared she'd burst into flames.

He slowly removed her bodice and skirt, then her underpinnings. He pulled up the quilt from the bottom of the bed to cover them against the chill of the early-morning spring air. She inched down between the soft coziness of the mattress and the quilt and curled tightly against his warm, hard body.

Her body tingled with a thousand sensations of heat and chill, as his hands roved over her body, making feather-light demands, while his lips sought hers. His mouth demanded more, covering her neck, her breasts, her belly with passionate licks and nibbles.

"I need you," she murmured against his chest. "I need to feel you inside me, Jack, again and again."

His hands slid down her sides, causing exquisite twinges of desire to course through her. Gently he moved her legs apart and covered her. He was warm with passion and hard with desire. She felt as if she were melting against him.

Holding her breath, she closed her eyes as the tip of him met her. She quivered, waiting for the exquisite moment when they became one in body as well as heart. She drew in a deep gasp of pleasure as he entered her.

The bed creaked. The feather pillows crackled. The fabric of the quilt rustled against the sheets as they moved in time to their love.

She arched against him with magical pleasures and sweet release from her longing. Even as he rested against her, warm and damp, she knew her desire for him could never be completely sated. She would always love him, no matter what, for as long as she lived.

She felt the morning breeze picking up as the sky lightened. The larks began to sing.

"I love you, Maude."

She'd always remember the sound of his voice, the look in his eyes, when he'd told her. "I love you, too, Jack."

"It's going to be so difficult trying to behave at Jessica's wedding, when all I really want to do is sweep you up in my arms and run off with you where no one would ever find us and force us to return to our duties."

He shook his head with what they both knew was the futility of wishing. Then he rose from their bed and began to dress again.

"You'd better get up. You have a present to wrap, and you have to get dressed, too. You're going to look even more beautiful than the bride."

She smiled, still glowing inwardly from his love.

"I'll never stop needing you, Maude." Then he climbed out the window.

Holding her breath, she watched him skitter across the tree limbs as nimble as any squirrel and disappear into his own bedroom. No matter how wonderful their lovemaking, she knew as surely as she knew the sun was rising that he'd leave her someday, disappearing just as he'd gone from sight through his bedroom window.

"I'll never stop needing you, either, Jack," she murmured.

∽

MR. GRIFFITH WAS DETERMINED not to show any sign of miserliness at his daughter's wedding, including beverages, even at such short notice. Apparently he'd kept to his word, Maude thought as she watched Mr. Hardesty, glass in hand, weaving his way through the guests on the lawn.

"Great party, Benjamin!" Mr. Hardesty exclaimed, sloshing the contents of his drink over his hand and onto his shoe. "Glad you're not one of those temperance people."

"Temperance is just fine," Mr. Griffith replied, "when done in moderation."

Mr. Hardesty guffawed and spilled more of his drink. "Imagine them wanting to take our liquor from us. Never happen."

Mr. Griffith grimaced. "Never say never, Gerald," he cautioned.

"Do you want me to get you a glass of whatever Mr. Hardesty's drinking?" Jack offered Maude.

"Thank you, no," she answered. "I think henceforth I'll avoid all strong drink—even hard cider."

"Did you feel too bad the next day?"

"No, but I remember what happened under the influence. Who knows what might happen now?"

Jack grinned at her. "I'd certainly like to find out."

"Hush! Miss Randolph looks very comfortable presiding over the refreshment table," Maude observed, taking great care to change the subject completely. "I think she and my father will be very happy together."

"Florence and Peter look pretty happy, too."

"They don't stand a chance if their mothers have decided they belong together."

"Mrs. Lester and Mrs. Fitzroy talked all through the wedding service," he told her with a grimace. "I know. I had the misfortune to sit right in front of them. But, you know, I don't think I've ever seen any other couple dance as well as Florence and Edgar."

"I guess other things get in the way sometimes, and nothing— not even a special quilt—can keep a couple together."

She tried to keep from sighing. Florence seemed happy now, but Maude would never forget her friend's heartbreak. She couldn't forget Wilma's great disappointment, either, at Peter's sudden change of mind and heart. She didn't think Florence and Wilma would ever be friends again. Maude wondered if Wilma would ever talk to her again.

She couldn't help but fear that, no matter how much she and

Jack might love each other, no matter how wonderful their love-making was for both of them—other things, beyond their control, would come between them, too.

Don't think about that now, she cautioned herself. *Love Jack while you have him.*

Maude winced and almost hid behind Jack for protection when she noticed Wilma dancing in her direction. She turned away, trying to find something else in the barn that needed her immediate attention.

"I'm a coward," she whispered to Jack. "Is she still heading in my direction?"

"Yes. But she's smiling."

Maude turned around. "Goodness, she's dancing with Matthew! Why didn't you tell me?"

Wilma paused for only a moment in front of her. "I just may forgive you someday," she whispered. "But only because I still want you to make me a special quilt block."

"If the block turns out right this time, will you forgive me completely?" Maude asked.

Wilma just laughed as Matthew swung her away from them. Maude breathed a sigh of relief. "Do you think something might come of this?"

"Even if it doesn't, at least she has hope again."

Maude wasn't surprised to find Katy at the refreshment table. She had hoped, after she'd emerged from her self-imposed quilting hibernation, to find Katy and Willard reconciled, but it just wasn't so.

Jack brought her a glass of lemonade. She decided a piece of Mrs. Kingston's rose geranium cake or anything Miss Randolph had made would be safe.

Maude heard Katy give a little cough to clear her throat. If it looked as if Willard wasn't coming back to her, Maude wondered with dismay, was Katy rehearsing to take over the schoolteacher's job?

"I've talked to my mother," Katy announced.

"How nice," Clarice commented. "Especially since you don't have anyone else there at that house to talk to."

Maude cringed. It didn't take long for news—especially bad news—to circulate through town.

"I've also talked to Doc Ketcham," Katy added.

"Oh, dear. I was afraid it was contagious," Ruthie lamented.

"Yes, indeed, it is," Katy replied with a giggle. Her pale cheeks were turning a bright pink. "A lady gets it from her husband."

"What? Goodness, is that why Willard hasn't been at home much?" Ruthie asked.

Clarice glared at her. "You *are* dense!"

Katy's giggle turned into bright laughter. "I'm going to have a baby!"

The ladies all dumped their refreshments onto empty spaces around the table and rushed up to Katy. They hugged her and, if they couldn't get close enough, patted her shoulders in an effort to extend to her their sincerest best wishes and congratulations.

"How wonderful! A wedding and a new baby!" Mrs. Dietrich exclaimed. "And in two different families."

"I suppose this and not the sauerkraut is responsible for your feeling so sick," Maude said.

"I hope so. I'd hate to think I'd have to give up eating it." Sheepishly she admitted, "I suppose that accounts for my grouchy temper, too."

"You shouldn't be standing at this refreshment table. You ought to sit down and prop your feet up," Louise counselled. "I'll bring you a lemonade."

"Thank you. I wouldn't mind some more of that kugel, too," Katy remarked.

"Have you told Willard yet?" Maude asked.

Katy looked at her as if she'd just asked her if she could take off from the roof of the Griffiths' barn, flap her arms, and fly to Chicago.

"Of course not. Thank you for asking," Katy replied sharply. "How can I? I never see him." She began to sniffle.

"You must tell him," Maude urged. "This is just the news to bring him back."

Katy lifted her chin and proudly declared, "If he's only staying for the baby and not for me, I don't really think I want him."

"You won't know that until you tell him."

"Will you—?"

"No, I will not! It didn't work before when I served as your messenger."

Katy thought for just a moment. "I suppose this is something I have to do myself."

"It certainly is."

"Does anyone know where he is?"

"Over there," Clarice told her, pointing eagerly to the far side of the barn.

Trust Clarice to know the precise location of any man in the room, Maude thought wryly.

"Wish me luck," Katy said as she marched across the barn.

"I can't watch!" Louise wailed and covered her face with her fingers. "Tell me what happens."

Well, Willard didn't run away when he saw Katy approaching him, Maude gratefully observed. They were still talking. Still talking. She held her breath and waited.

Suddenly Willard grabbed Katy in his arms, spun her around, and let out a loud whoop. Hand in hand, they headed toward the door.

"I think Willard's going home," Jack said.

∞

"JESSICA, OPEN YOUR SPECIAL present from Maude!" Louise cried.

"It's so big," Jessica said, laughing as she examined the large box set before her on the table. "What can it be? Is it what I think it is?"

Maude stood there, grinning. She wasn't about to say a word and give away the surprise. None of her friends knew, although by now they certainly should have guessed. Jack, too, had kept her secret.

"Oh, and you told me you wouldn't make me anything. I can't wait to see it," Jessica said. She reached out to lift the lid.

"Mr. Lester! Mr. Lester!" Ronald Mulgrew suddenly burst into the barn, shouting.

"I need to see Mr. Lester right away!" Ronald exclaimed.

"What's wrong, Ronald?" Mr. Lester asked his chief teller.

"Someone robbed the bank!"

Jessica dropped the lid without even looking at her quilt.

26

EVERYONE TURNED WITH DESPERATE cries. "My savings!" "The mortgage!" "The rent!" "My business!" "My payroll!" "We're ruined!"

Guests left the refreshment table and stopped dancing to gather around a breathless Ronald. His blond hair stood out in wild, sweaty spikes. He bent over, resting his hands on his knees, gasping for breath. He looked as if he'd run all the way from town.

Mr. Lester handed him a drink, which he gulped down. "What are you talking about?"

"Somebody robbed the bank!" he repeated.

"Don't be silly," Sheriff Tucker said scornfully. "We'd have heard an explosion, gunshots, something—"

"No. It's been robbed already, probably sometime last night," Ronald replied. "Everything looked normal when I opened the front door, but when I went over to the safe to open it and count the money, there it stood, gaping wide open, empty as Ruthie's head."

"How—?"

"The back window bars were still in place, but there was a little hole drilled through a bare piece of wood in the back door, almost as if whoever did it knew exactly where the metal plating wasn't. Looked like somebody slipped a hook through there, slipped the bolt, and then picked the lock on the safe—near as I can figure.''

Maude heard Jack, standing beside her, give a low groan. She stood very still, as if the lack of motion from her body might also stop the swirl of jumbled thoughts in her head.

Was he groaning because he'd failed at his job? The last thing he'd told her was he was waiting for the gang to send him word. Apparently they'd decided to rob the bank without him. Did that mean they didn't want him? Was his cover destroyed? Would they try to kill him for betraying them in Dry Creek?

On the other hand, was he groaning because the people of Apple Grove had found him out? No. It couldn't be! she insisted to herself. Jack couldn't have robbed the bank. He'd been with her last night. He'd put her to bed. He'd been sleeping in the chair by the window when she'd awakened. He'd been with her all night. Or had he?

Could she be sure? In spite of her firm resolutions, she'd fallen asleep. Could he have slipped out then, done what he needed to do, and slipped back in again? He'd said he was good at what he did. Was he so good that he might even have had time to rob the bank and then actually sew the binding on, too? Had he really been asleep in the chair when she woke him—or only pretending to sleep?

No! Jack couldn't do such a thing! How could she even think it? Yet, it was the first thought that had sprung into her mind.

"The gang that did it knew exactly what day there'd be the most money in the safe," Ronald continued. "They knew where the safe was kept—although any dummy could figure that out. But they also were pretty slick, knowing how to get into the bank from the back door, where nobody on Main Street would see them; knowing how to break into that safe."

Maude felt her insides go cold and numb. Hadn't she seen Jack, with her own eyes, going around to the back of the bank?

Mr. Potter's voice oozed like pitch on a hot day as he sidled through the agitated crowd. "The only people who'd know the day before Mr. Lester sends the deposits into Des Moines, and how to get into the safe, and what the locks on the back door of the bank look like are the people who work there—"

"I didn't!" Ronald exclaimed. "Lord knows I wouldn't—"

"I'd vouch for Mr. Mulgrew's honesty and integrity any day,"

Mr. Lester said, boldly coming to stand beside the distraught teller and confronting the accusing Mr. Potter. "I'd do the same for Abner Kellerman, my other teller, too."

"I sort of figured you would," Mr. Potter replied.

He had a sly glint in his eye that Maude didn't like at all. It seemed Mr. Potter was leading the crowd's thoughts where he wanted them to go, and she didn't like the direction she suspected, either.

"But it wasn't a gang that did this. A gang would be noticed," Mr. Potter continued, his voice growing louder, less oily, more sharp. "You only need one man to drill a door, pick a lock. A gang would make a lot of noise, just hanging around. They'd be pretty noticeable. You wouldn't need a gang to rob that bank, when only one man would do."

"Yeah," Walt piped up. "Mr. Potter's right."

Maude grimaced. Walt would agree with anything Mr. Potter said if he thought it'd start an argument.

"Makes sense to me," Hiram agreed.

"But there's one other person who'd likely know those facts, too, who's been hanging around the bank, looking sort of suspicious, if you ask me, ever since he got here."

Maude cringed. That was just where he was heading, she thought. She looked out over the sea of faces, some a little more befuddled than others, with her father's liberally flowing supply of alcohol. She didn't like the looks of this at all. What could she possibly do?

"Who's that?" Hiram asked. He was circulating through the crowd, nudging folks, whispering innuendos, casting doubts.

"Jack Kingston. Who else?"

"Yeah, Jack Kingston," Walt declared from the other side of the crowd. He was circulating, too, spreading the same lies Hiram was on this side.

"I didn't do it," Jack stated firmly, adamantly.

"If Jack did it, why is he still here in town?" Mr. Kingston demanded on Jack's behalf. "Why wouldn't he have taken off again with all that money?"

"Yeah! Why not?" Albert demanded.

Maude was glad to see at least one more person in this room was on Jack's side.

"It was his partner who took it, and Jack stayed in town to

put us off guard. Later, he'll meet up with his partner and split the money.''

"Partner? What partner? You're crazy. You've got no proof of any of that," Mr. Kingston insisted.

"Yes, I do. Jack's still here, isn't he? And the money's gone!"

"But—''

Maude hated to see Mr. Kingston's protests weakening. Just because Mr. Potter could talk longer and louder, it still didn't make him right.

"Oh, Jack may look like he's being a jolly fellow, charming all the ladies, and entertaining us all with amusing tales at the general store," Mr. Potter said. "But when he wasn't there, where was he? Hanging around at the bank, wasn't he? I ask you—where is that general store?" He only paused a second before answering his own question. "Right across from the bank, isn't it?"

"No!" Georgie cried.

Maude was relieved to hear someone trying to inject some reason and sanity into this conversation, but did it have to be her brother putting himself on the line? What could a mere boy do?

Georgie struggled to push his way through to where Mr. Potter stood. "No, it's not."

She watched Walt and Hiram both begin to head for her brother like wolves cutting a weakling calf from the herd. She stuck out her foot. Hiram went sprawling against Mrs. Kingston, who smacked him in the face with her fan.

"The sheriff's office and the newspaper are directly across from the bank," Georgie corrected.

"What's right next door to the newspaper office?"

"Ingrams' store," he answered reluctantly.

"I rest my case."

"Since when did this turn into a trial, Gordon?" Mr. Kingston asked grimly.

Mr. Potter twisted his lips around his cigar, then continued. "It's not a trial yet, but there will be one. We got us a bank robber right here." He swung around and pointed an accusing finger. "Jack Kingston!"

"No!" Maude cried. Georgie, Louise, and Mrs. Kingston joined her protest.

"You've got to admit, he's done it before," Mr. Potter pointed out. "Hasn't he, Sheriff?"

"Well, yes, but . . . don't you think a fellow could sort of see the light and reform?"

"A leopard can't change his spots," Mr. Potter said.

"No, he can't," Hiram was urging the crowd to repeat.

"Jack's not a leopard!" Georgie protested. In spite of Walt trying to get in his way, he now stood nose to nose with Mr. Potter. "You don't know what you're talking about, you big, blustering old fool."

Mr. Potter looked around. "Benjamin, do something with this boy of yours, will you?"

"Come on, son," Mr. Griffith said. "Don't go making a scene at your sister's wedding."

"I didn't start this," Georgie protested. "Mr. Potter started this because he's hated Jack for as long as I can remember. You can't let him accuse somebody without evidence, without proof. You've got no proof!"

"I've got enough evidence."

"That's not the same as proof."

"He's been lurking around the bank, hasn't he? We've all seen him."

"I have," Walt said. He nudged Sam Ferguson.

"Yeah, I . . . I've seen him," Sam said.

"Who else has seen him?" Mr. Potter called, holding out his arms, looking out over the crowd, waiting for more people.

"I have," Hiram called.

"You, Miss Hawkins?" Mr. Potter said.

"Yes, once or twice."

"You, Mr. Fitzroy?"

"Yes, I've seen him sneaking around the bank. My hotel, too."

"You, Mr. Griffith?"

Maude held her breath. What would her father say? Would this be his chance to get even with Jack? Jack had said he'd seen her father watching him. Would her father spare the Kingstons' feelings again, or, if pressed, would he tell the truth?

"Yes, I've seen him," Mr. Griffith replied very quietly.

Maude winced. She heard Jack, still beside her, groan.

"Knowing Jack's unsavory past, I've sort of been keeping a watchful eye on him." Mr. Griffith leveled a steady, narrow gaze at Jack.

Maude waited, listening to her own heart pounding nervously

in her ears. Now was her father's chance not just to hold the
coat of the man who was about to beat Jack up, but to land a
few devastating blows himself. How she wished he could just
forget!

"I've seen him watching the bank when we all think he's just
sitting over at Ingrams' keeping us all amused," Mr. Griffith
continued. "I've seen him lurking around outside the bank, too,
and sitting inside, just watching the people come and go. Worst
of all, I've seen him sneaking out of his uncle's house in the
middle of the night and heading into town—"

"No, Pa! No!" Georgie cried. "It's Jack! He couldn't have
done it. You can't go telling them he did. You can't do this to
Jack!"

"Will somebody get this kid out of here when men have work
to do?" Mr. Potter grumbled.

"I don't want to do a man's work if it means accusing an
innocent man!" Georgie declared.

"Come on, Jack," Sheriff Tucker said, taking him by the arm.
"I don't have much choice in the matter right now. Looks like
I'll be taking you to jail."

"No!" Maude cried. What else could she say that wouldn't
damn her, too? She knew Jack didn't do it. All their suspicions
aside, no one in town, not even Mr. Potter, could prove Jack had
robbed the bank. But could she prove he hadn't?

There'd be a trial, but they'd find him innocent. They had to!

"It'll be all right, Georgie," Maude said, trying to calm him.

Miss Randolph came up and took Georgie, still yelling his
protests, by the hand.

"Come on, Georgie," she said quietly, leading him toward
the doorway. "This isn't the way to get proof of Jack's innocence. We'll find some other way. We'll find it," she insisted,
"and we'll prove he didn't do it."

∽

JACK LOOKED AROUND HIM at the three bleak, red-brick
walls and the single wall of vertical iron bars. It all looked so
familiar. He stared at the floor.

He'd never let anyone—man or woman, armed or unarmed—
interfere with him doing his duty. When he'd been watching for

someone, he'd never let his guard down until he'd found them and stopped them. But this time he'd failed.

How could he have been so stupid? He should have known all along making love to Maude was a mistake. He should have felt it in his bones, the way he did other things.

But he hadn't felt wrong about her. Loving Maude was the best thing he'd ever done in his whole, misbegotten life.

He'd get out of this, just as he did everything else—even if he had been having that awful premonition he was going to die. All he had to do was claim Maude as his alibi and he'd get out of this bleak, crumbling, small-town jail—and completely ruin Maude's fine reputation.

He loved her. He couldn't do that to her—no matter what it meant to him. He'd just rely on his good luck. He always had. It hadn't failed him yet.

"Jack! Jack!"

Jack looked up to see Georgie peering at him through the bars of his cell.

"Runt! How'd you get in here?"

"Sheriff Tucker let me in. He's just doing his job, Jack. He's not such a bad sort."

"I guess not."

"I know you didn't rob the bank, Jack. I got to prove to them you didn't. I just don't know how."

"I'm not sure, either, Runt. I guess I'll just sort of trust my luck, as I always have, but—"

Was his luck ready to run out on him? he wondered. Not yet.

"Say, Runt. Maybe *you're* my luck."

"Me?"

"I need you to send a telegram."

"Me? To who? Where? What should I say? How will I pay for it? Is this my chance for a real adventure, like yours?"

"Sort of, except you're on the right side of the bars. See, they took all my money, my guns, everything. You'll have to lend me some of that money you've been saving up to run away with."

"Yeah, sure."

"You've got to send it to the Pinkerton office."

"Do you think they'll really come out here?"

"They've been waiting to hear from me."

"Don't tell me you're a Pinkerton!"

"Yes, but you can't tell anyone else, okay?"

"Swell! Yeah, sure, anything, Jack."

"Tell them, 'No word. Birds flown. Arrowhead down.' "

"That's it?" He sounded disappointed. Jack could hardly blame him. On the surface, it didn't sound like much of a message.

"That's my code name—Arrowhead. But you can't tell anybody. That's the way they'll know for certain the message is from me."

"Oh, I get it," he said with a laugh.

"Yeah, real funny. They'll know what I mean. Just send it, now, as fast as you can." He looked at Georgie as seriously as he could. "My life depends on this."

∞

"I NEVER DID TRUST that boy," Benjamin said, shaking his head as he poured himself another glass of whiskey.

He supposed Adelaide, Jessica, and Maude were in the house, making the final preparations for Jessica to leave first thing tomorrow morning. The rest of the women were cleaning up the wedding chaos in the barn while the men sat around the refreshment table, still drinking. Some of them were starting to lean a little lower on the table.

"It's a shame that damn Jack had to ruin Jessica's wedding by going and getting himself arrested," Benjamin said.

Damn shame the rotten degenerate had to go and completely ruin his other daughter, he thought angrily. At least he was in jail tonight, and in a couple more days they'd probably haul him back to prison, where he couldn't get to Maude anymore. He pushed the bottle toward Mr. Hardesty.

Mr. Hardesty poured himself another drink, sloshing a good deal of the whiskey over his hand before he actually hit the glass. "Me neither, damn him."

"I've never liked that boy since he persuaded that cute little Irish girl we had working as a maid at the hotel to let him help her, then the brat went and short-sheeted all the beds. I tell you, my guests were furious. Damn that Jack Kingston." Mr. Fitzroy helped himself to the bourbon. "I don't know how I'm going to meet my payroll this month if that money isn't recovered."

"I thought you were rich," Albert said. "I thought you had lots of money layin' 'round."

"That's why I'm rich, because I don't leave it just laying around where I can spend it on any fool contraption that takes my fancy."

"Oh."

"Let that be a free lesson in financial success to you."

"Thanks. I think. Say, pass me that bottle, will you?" Albert asked.

"If you can't pay me, Mr. Fitzroy, I don't know if the Ingrams'll let me put any more on my tab," Bob Townsend said. "Then what's my wife and kids gonna eat? Grass? Damn Jack."

"It's all his fault, you know," Mr. Potter said angrily.

"It sure is!" Hiram declared.

"We shouldn't let him ruin the whole town like this." Mr. Fitzroy's voice was growing louder and angrier. He slammed his fist down on the table, rattling the glasses and making the half-empty bottles teeter.

"He's been running roughshod all over this town since he was a kid," Mr. Potter complained. "His aunt and uncle never did a damn thing to discipline the boy."

"Time in the Army didn't seem to straighten him out," Mr. Dalton said. His voice was growing angrier, too.

"We still don't know as he actually served, much less which side he was on," Mr. Potter reminded them. "For my money, he was a damned Reb spy."

"Even time in jail didn't seem to teach him a lesson," Mr. Foster said.

"We're not going to be able to depend on the law to teach him anything," Mr. Potter continued. "You can see Sheriff Tucker's going easy on him, not even putting him in leg irons or manacles to haul his ass off to jail."

"He's not tough, like old Sheriff Fischer used to be."

"Nope, sure ain't," Hiram agreed.

Benjamin watched him shoot back some of his expensive whiskey, not the rotgut folks usually found the sloppy sot drinking at the Pink Garters Saloon.

"Sheriff Fischer would've had him jailed, tried, convicted, and hung by now!" Walt exclaimed. He grabbed the bottle of the expensive whiskey away from Hiram.

"That was when the men in this country knew how to defend themselves!"

"Yeah!"

"We were tough back then, forging through this country when it was nothing but a wilderness—no Army forts or fancy hotels to stop your wagon train at on your way out West."

"Didn't mess around with no jails then, neither. If a man stole your things, hell! You just shot him. No questions asked."

"Or hung him, if you could find a good enough tree."

"We used to have that big cottonwood over at the Johnson place. That's all gone now. We ain't had a good hangin' 'round here since then."

"I sure do miss the good old days."

"That's what we need!" Mr. Potter declared. "Good, old-fashioned justice!"

"Yeah!" Hiram and Walt agreed.

"That railing along the top of the porch of the Regal Hotel ought to be strong enough to hoist him up on."

"Yeah!" Walt shouted.

"Let's go get him," Mr. Potter pronounced.

All the men seated around his table, except Benjamin himself, sprang to their feet. They snatched the fullest whiskey bottles from the table and headed out the barn door. He'd been so busy with his problems and thoughts, he hadn't even noticed who was coming and going.

Where in the world had all these people come from? It seemed as if the whole town had gathered in his barn again. Benjamin couldn't even remember inviting most of these people to the wedding. He had a bad feeling this was going to turn into a different kind of party—not a pretty one.

"Wait! Stop! Where are you going?" he called with alarm.

"To show this town what *real* justice is!" Mr. Potter declared. "We're not waiting for any useless trial. We know the bastard's guilty."

"No! No, you don't!" Benjamin declared, rapidly sitting upright in his seat. "You're all drunk. Stop and think about what you're doing."

"We done thunk about it," Walt said.

"We're done thinkin'," Hiram told him.

"You haven't been thinking since you sat down with a whiskey bottle in your hand," Benjamin said. "Gerald, Thaddeus, you're sensible men. Gordon, you can't do this.''

If he'd known it was going to come to this, he'd have locked his liquor away and sent them all home. He never would have denounced Jack if he'd known they were going to get this riled.

A couple of the men grabbed some of the lanterns hanging along the walls. They started marching into town.

"Stop! Stop!" Benjamin might as well have tried to tell that tornado not to uproot that cottonwood.

∞

"I SENT THE TELEGRAM, like you asked, Jack," Georgie told him.

"Thanks, Runt. Now all I can do is sit and wait." He sat there a moment. "Do you think your sister's mad at me?"

"Shucks, no. Jessica's too busy getting everything ready to leave tomorrow."

"I mean Maude."

"Oh, well, yeah. She's pretty riled."

Jack grimaced. He'd thought he'd heard her telling everybody no. He'd really hoped she'd believe in him enough to know he wasn't here to rob the bank. He'd known Mr. Griffith didn't like him, but he'd never thought he'd denounce him.

Boy, that was two people he'd misread. It was definitely time for him to quit the business if he was getting this bad. The trouble was, this time it looked as though he was going to have a hard time just staying alive.

"What's that noise?"

Jack turned to the pounding on the door of the jail. "I don't think it's some of the ladies bringing me cookies."

The wooden door cracked on its hinges as it slammed open against the wall.

"That's it, Kingston!" Mr. Potter shouted as he burst through the door. "Get the keys," he ordered Hiram.

Hiram snatched the keys off the ring by the window, fumbled through the clinking keys, and unlocked the door to Jack's cell.

"Stop!" Georgie cried. "What are you doing?"

Mr. Potter pushed him away so hard he fell backward over the sheriff's chair. He shook his head and jumped to his feet again.

"Don't fight them, Runt," Jack yelled as they pulled him from his cell. "They'll hurt you, too. Think, Runt. Think!"

The doorway was blocked by a mob of smelly, tottering, livid men. Georgie knew that by the time he'd finally managed to get through the last of the crowd at the doorway, the first ones out could have Jack strung up and dead already. How could he stop them?

He knew he was big—the biggest kid in school, and the strongest, too. He knew Sheriff Tucker hadn't kept the jail repaired. He knew what he *could* do, but was he crazy enough to try it? Was he strong enough to do it? Well, he figured, a man's crazy adventures had to start somewhere.

With a mad leap, he slammed into the window. The glass shattered. The iron bars grated against the cement. He tried again. The old bricks crumbled, and the bars fell to the ground as he slammed through.

"Damn!" He pulled a piece of glass from his arm and took off at a run to find his father.

He met them marching up the street toward him. Sheriff Tucker carried his rifle. Pa even had his shotgun! Maude was marching between them. It seemed like every lady in town was behind him. He thought he saw Mrs. Dietrich with her rolling pin and Mrs. Ingram with her broom. Maude just had her mouth—that was her worst weapon.

"They've got Jack!" he yelled. "They're taking him over to lynch him!"

"Yes, I know! I saw them leave," Mr. Griffith answered. "We've got to stop them!"

"I thought you hated Jack."

"That doesn't mean I'll stand by to see him lynched."

"Georgie, you're bleeding!" Maude exclaimed. "What happened? If they hurt you, I'll—"

"It's just a little cut. I swear. I'll be all right. You've got to help them save Jack."

"Come with me, Georgie," Miss Randolph said, holding out her arms to him. She turned to Maude. "I'll take care of him. You've got to stop them before they lynch Jack."

Even from a distance, Maude could see someone toss a rope up and over the rail around the top of the hotel porch. As they drew closer, she saw a definite smile of satisfaction on Mr. Potter's face as he placed the noose around Jack's neck. She winced. Her own throat felt so tight with fear, she could barely breathe.

"I'm not even going to ask you if you have any last words," Mr. Potter said, "because I know they'd just be more of your lies."

Maude stared, appalled at how the crowd could turn against Jack just because a little liquor befuddled their thoughts, and Mr. Potter made such convincing, and ultimately wrong, arguments against him.

Sheriff Tucker fired a shot into the air. "Stop this now."

"Or what?" Mr. Potter demanded. "You'll shoot us all? There's too many of us, Sheriff. Even if you got one or two of us, I'd still be able to kick this box out from under Jack before you can stop me."

"Don't press me, Gordon." Sheriff Tucker slid back the bolt of his rifle. "Jack would be dead, but so would you."

"We don't need any shooting! Isn't this the kind of thing we're trying to stop?" Mr. Griffith demanded. "You all said back in my barn that this was the kind of justice you had in the old days, but I'm asking you, isn't this the kind of justice some of you, some of your ancestors, came here to get away from in the first place?"

"What the hell are you talking about?" Mr. Potter demanded.

"I'm talking about you, Angus McGregor." Mr. Griffith pointed straight at him.

"My family's been in this country a long time."

"Since about 1740? Didn't you tell me once your family came here because that English lord kicked them off his property for no reason?"

"Yeah, so?"

"How about you, Abner Kellerman? Didn't your family come here to be able to worship the way you wanted?"

"Yes."

"Mr. Rossoff, didn't your father die in prison in—"

"Yes. Don't bring that up, Benjamin!"

"And you, Hans Dietrich? Aren't you supposed to be in prison in Germany?"

"No. Yes. *Scheisse!* Why do you ask us these questions?"

"Because you all came here to live with freedom and justice. I'm a newspaperman. I don't believe just in freedom of speech and the press. I believe in the whole system. It's got to work, or we're no better than the old ways we left. Now, I'm not saying Jack's innocent."

Maude gave a loud gasp.

"I'm not saying he's guilty, either. I'm just saying in this country a man's innocent until a court—not a mob—proves he's guilty. You came here to be treated that way. It's your duty to see that Jack—and everybody—is treated the same way."

"Pretty speech, Griffith," Mr. Potter said, reaching for the rope. "I don't give a damn."

"Don't do it, Gordon," Mr. Griffith warned. "I'll find the best damn lawyer I can to bring murder charges against you. My newspaper will have this story all over the state—all over the whole country. Then where will your governorship be?"

"I'll buy any judge—I can afford the best."

"But you can't afford them all—and there are some who can't be bought."

"Stop!" Maude pushed against their backs, toppling over men too drunk to stand upright anymore. She jabbed men in the ribs with her elbow or her fist until they had to move or risk stopping breathing. She slammed against Mr. Potter, toppling him off balance in his drunkenness. His hand grasped for the rope out of his reach.

"Jack's innocent!" Maude declared. She gave Mr. Potter one last shove, sending him completely to the ground, away from Jack.

"They've all said that," he growled from the dirt. "It doesn't mean anything."

"But I can *prove* it."

"How?"

"When the bank was robbed last night—" She paused to draw in one deep breath. After she said what she had to say, it might save Jack's life, but it would certainly ruin her reputation once and for all. "Jack was sleeping with me."

27

"OH, MAUDE!" SHE HEARD her father moan.

"Oh, no! It can't be," Louise protested.

"You don't have to do this, Maude," Jack said. His voice sounded so sad, so pleading.

But it was too late. She had to do this for him.

"All the while I was finishing my sister's quilt, Jack was with me. He watched me stitch it together. He watched me quilt every line. When I was done, he stayed with me the entire night."

Mr. Griffith closed his eyes and turned away.

"Not *Maude!*" Jessica exclaimed. "There's no way on earth I'll believe my sensible, prudent, *prudish* sister did anything like that."

"Shut up, Jessica," Maude warned.

"No! Too sensible you are such foolish things to do," Mrs. Ingram declared.

"I won't believe Maude would do anything so . . . so immoral," Mrs. Hoffmann maintained.

"Impossible! Highly unlikely at best," the Reverend Hoffmann insisted.

"I have proof," Maude said. "The proof is in Jessica's quilt."

"I'd like to see this so-called proof," Mr. Potter demanded as he struggled to his feet and brushed his hands on the seat of his trousers.

"I think we all need to see this proof and put an end to this lunacy once and for all," Sheriff Tucker said. "Where's the quilt?"

Maude nodded for Jessica to give it to her.

"I couldn't imagine why you wanted me to bring this," Jessica said. "Why didn't you just tell me?"

"It takes too long to explain things to you."

Maude reached into the box and pulled out the whole quilt. The box went tumbling to the ground. She gave the quilt a hard shake, sending it billowing out like waves on the ocean.

"It's there, in the middle block," she declared, pointing to it. "You know how I always hide the bride and groom's initials, the date of the wedding, and my own initials in the stems and leaves of the flowers, so that nobody can find them. Jack knows where these are."

"Well, now, little lady," Mr. Potter said with all the pomposity he was capable of—which was considerable, "I'm not real familiar with all that female-type stuff. It's going to take a lot to convince me you ladies can put anything that can save a man's life into your little quilts."

Maude pursed her lips and glared at him.

"Shut up, Gordon. She's right," Mrs. Potter called from the crowd below. "You haven't seen her quilts."

"She did it for my Katy's quilt," Mrs. Hardesty agreed.

"She did it for mine," Louise said.

"And mine," Prunella called.

"And mine," Annabelle Smith added.

"Jack knows where they are in Jessica's quilt," Maude said. "He watched me put them there. Didn't you, Jack?"

Maude hauled the heavy quilt over to him.

"Sure, they're right there," Jack said. He was trying to point out everything to them with his hands tied together. "See, Sheriff. You can vouch for me telling the truth."

Maude watched him with growing relief as he traced a sure, steady finger along the lines of green floss.

"Everybody knows about that! Anybody could've told him!" Hiram called.

"What's that?" Jessica asked, screwing up her face as if that could help her see better. She pointed to a small cluster of leaves at the very left-hand base of the flower arrangement.

"I have no idea," Maude murmured.

After all her efforts to save Jack, after all the men's stupid, stubborn refusal to believe her or the evidence of her quilting and of their very own eyes, she hated to admit she didn't know what was in her own handwork. "I didn't put it there."

"What is it?" Jessica asked again.

"Danged if I can tell," Sheriff Tucker said. He stuck his finger in his mouth, pulled out a wad of spit, and tried to rub the mark off the quilt.

"Good heavens!" Jessica pulled her quilt back before he could ruin it further. The marks were still there.

"It's not dirt. Looks like it's stitched into the quilt," Sheriff Tucker said.

"Let me see that!" Mr. Potter demanded. "I'm not about to let you two go trying to pull a fast one on me." He pulled the quilt block closer to his face.

Maude held her breath, waiting for a tumbling ash from his smelly cigar to ignite the quilt, sending her final bit of evidence, her final attempt to save Jack's life, up in smoke.

"Danged if I can see what it is."

"That's not like you, Maude," Louise said. "You always have a specific reason for putting everything into those blocks, right down to the very last detail."

"Yes, she does," Mrs. Kingston agreed.

"Indeed!" Annabelle added.

"But *I* didn't do it," Maude insisted.

"*I* did," Jack said.

"You?"

"That's it!" Jessica cried. "It's Jack's initials!"

"What?" Sheriff Tucker snatched the quilt away from Mr. Potter and pulled it closer to his face.

"See, see!" Jessica pointed frantically at the stitching. "*JMK*. James Madison Kingston—although I don't know why he didn't just put *SJ* there instead, for Suicide Jack."

"Let me see, please," Maude pleaded. She hadn't even noticed it when she'd peeked at the finished quilt in the box. She'd been too busy getting ready for the wedding, too preoccupied with loving Jack. She couldn't believe her sister, who was usually so obtuse about everything else, would actually be the first one to decipher the cryptic lines of stitching. Sure enough, there they were. Jack's initials.

"I don't believe this!" Mr. Potter declared. "They're sisters. They worked this out between the two of them."

"*I'll* look at it," Miss Hawkins said. "If anyone can figure it out, it's me."

"Yes, if anyone knows about sewing, it's Miss Hawkins," Mrs. Hardesty said. Several of the other women called out their agreement. "We'd believe her!"

Miss Hawkins slid her spectacles down her nose and carefully regarded the work for a long time.

"Well, it's not the same quality of stitching as the rest of the block, so I'd figure Maude didn't do it. Someone else did, and if it wasn't Jack, I don't know who it could be. But that sure is what it says. *JMK.*"

"You know," said Florence as she, too, examined the quilt, "it really looks like it belongs there. I guess that's why we didn't all notice it at first. I mean, if it didn't belong there, wouldn't it sort of stick out like a sore thumb—like my block with Mr. You-Know-Who that never would look right. Right, Maude?"

"Yes, you're right, Florence," Wilma agreed. "If it's not meant to be, there's not much a body can do about it. This was clearly meant to be part of the design."

"Yes, indeed. It can be none other than Jack's!" Louise stuck her fists on her hips and glared out at the crowd. "Why, it's as plain as the noses on your faces. What in the world's wrong with all you stupid menfolks that you can't see this? You're all too drunk, that's what. You all need to go home and sleep it off, and put these silly notions of lynching a man out of your empty heads!"

Maude was surprised to hear Florence and Wilma mentioning the ill-fated quilt block, and even more surprised to hear Wilma acknowledge hers had been a wrong choice. She was surprised those two were talking to each other again. Most of all, she was surprised to hear shy Louise scolding the entire town.

"Well, I worked on the darned quilt," Jack maintained. "I think I ought to be able to take a little bit of the credit for it. After all, a good artist always signs his work."

"I guess you're right, Jack," Sheriff Tucker said. He slipped the noose from around Jack's neck and untied his hands. "You really were . . . with Maude . . . when all that fuss was going on at the bank.''

Maude watched the crowd. They were all staring blankly at each other. Maybe having to think about what was actually in the quilt block wore out their alcohol-pickled brains so they couldn't be angry. Maybe the effects of the liquor and the lateness of the hour was making them sleepy and they were thinking more about a good night's sleep than with hanging a man. Maybe they were starting to feel ashamed and guilty for their outright stupidity. Whatever their reasons, they all started to wander away.

''Say, Fitzroy, who're you thinking about for mayor next election?'' Mr. Hardesty asked as the two of them leaned on each other for support walking down the street.

''Don't know. Sure as hell ain't Potter. What a low-down weasel!''

''Jack! Jack!'' Miss Randolph came running up to him. ''Eustace Purdy just delivered a telegram. They've caught the real bank robbers.''

''Runt. How is he?''

Maude should have figured Jack would be more concerned with Georgie than anything else.

''It's not such a big cut, but he got quite a few bruises,'' Miss Randolph reported. ''He's going to be a little sore for a while, but he'll be fine. I think he'll need to stay out of school for a few days.''

''I'm glad to hear he's all right. He's a brave fellow.''

''The telegram said the Pinkerton detectives caught the robbers with the money still in the sacks that said Apple Grove Savings and Loan. They also had a private message for you. They said it was a job well done.''

Jack just nodded.

''I should've figured you'd go into that line of work,'' Miss Randolph told him with a grin. ''You always were sneaking around, getting into trouble—your own or somebody else's.''

Mr. Griffith slowly approached Jack. ''I guess I owe you an apology—a big apology. I suppose a man *can* change for the better. This isn't easy to say, but when I look at everything, I guess I can say I am proud of the way you turned out. Maybe you're not so worthless after all.''

He gave Jack a grin and extended his hand. Jack took it.

"However," Mr. Griffith added, "there's still the matter of your compromising situation with my daughter. We haven't settled that yet."

Maude held her breath. What would Jack tell her father? What was her father about to say next to Jack? After trying to save his neck from the noose, would he still try to put a bullet through his head for other offenses?

"Well, we sort of got carried away," Jack admitted.

"I'd say so." His face was still grim.

"But I love Maude. She loves me. I want to marry her, if she'll have me. I'll support her. I'll cherish her."

"I don't have any doubt but that she'll see you do. You could just be getting into the biggest trouble of your life," Mr. Griffith warned him. With a smug grin on his face, he stuck one hand in his trouser pocket, shouldered his shotgun, fell into step with Miss Randolph, and started strolling home.

Jack stood in the middle of the street, watching Maude.

"You saved my life," he said quietly. "Your quilt saved my life."

"Our quilt."

"Didn't I say I'd always consider quilts my good luck from now on?"

"Mine, too."

"You had the courage to come forward with the truth. When one person tells the truth, the rest of them usually fall in line behind them. I love you, Maude."

"You're free, Jack," she told him with a sigh. "You've fulfilled all your obligations. They've caught the bank robbers. The money will be returned. You're free to leave town any time you like."

"No, I'm not. I'm not free at all. You've captured me, Maude. You've bound me to your heart with bands as silken and velvety as your soft warm skin. How could I ever leave you when I love you so much?"

She stopped in the middle of the road and stared at him.

"Did I ever actually tell you how much I love you?"

"I think so."

"I love you, Maude," he said, catching her up in his embrace. "I won't leave you—ever. I'm sending the Pinkertons my resignation."

"No! You love your job."

"Expecting to get killed every time I turn the corner? They actually made me sit in that damned jail in Dry Creek! I *hate* this job!"

"But you said you have a duty, a responsibility."

"Yes, I guess I did," he said, running his fingers through his hair. "But I think I'm ready for a different kind of responsibility now. One that involves a regular job with regular hours in one specific place, that involves bringing home my pay to a loving wife. I'm going to talk to Uncle Tad about the hardware store."

"I think you'll look good in an apron and sleeve garters," she said with a little laugh.

"I look even better without them—or my shirt or my trousers. And you look absolutely terrific without any clothes on, either, under a big, warm quilt. Marry me, Maude."

"Are you really asking me?"

"Marry me tomorrow!"

"I can't do that," she answered with a nervous laugh of disbelief.

"Don't you love me?"

"Of course I do. You know I do, but—"

"Marry me tomorrow," he repeated insistently. "Before Jessica and Caleb leave for Cedar Rapids. Your father'll be happy we can use the leftover food from today."

"You're silly!"

"Say you'll marry me, Maude. Tell me yes right now."

"Yes! But I still need time, Jack," she stammered in her excitement. "There's so much to do. I have to talk to Miss Hawkins about a veil. I'll have to see if I can alter Mama's wedding gown to fit me or make a new one. I have to get my friends together to quilt all my tops. My goodness, I'll have to make myself another Baltimore bride's quilt all over again—and you know how long that can take."

"I can't wait that long!" he declared as he swept her up in his embrace. He swirled her around in the middle of Main Street. "Marry me now—and make baby quilts instead!"

A Quilting Romance

Patterns of Love
by Christine Holden

When Lord Grayling Dunston appears on Baines Marshall's doorstep asking for her only quilt, she sends him on his way. But Baines discovers that Mary's Fortune is no ordinary quilt—its pattern reveals the map to a treasure Gray desperately needs to pay off his debts. When the quilt suddenly disappears from her home the two embark on a journey that deepens their attraction and changes their lives...

❏ 0-515-12481-8/$5.99

JONATHAN KAUFMAN is a reporter for *The Boston Globe*, and a co-winner of a Pulitzer Prize for articles on racism and job discrimination in that city.